THEY STAY

THEY STAY

CLAIRE FRAISE

Sabertooth
Press

PRAISE FOR THEY STAY

"This story held me in its ghostly grip from start to finish, and the twists left me reeling."—*Kat Ellis, author of Harrow Lake and Burden Falls*

"An intriguing paranormal mystery with unforgettable characters."—*Emma Berquist, author of Missing, Presumed Dead*

"A tense thrill-ride of a read. I couldn't flip the pages fast enough, partly because I was so engrossed and partly because I knew I had to finish it before nightfall or I'd never sleep a wink."—*E.E. Holmes, bestselling author of Spirit Legacy*

THEY STAY.

Book 1 of the They Stay Series.

Published in the United States by Sabertooth Press. McLeod, Montana. Visit us online at *www.sabertoothpress.com*.

Library of Congress Control Number: 2021912119

ISBN: 978-1-7372253-0-0 (paperback)

Cover design by Books Covered.

For Tristan,
and everyone out there who has a little brother.

Monsters are real, and ghosts are real too.
They live inside us, and sometimes, they win.

— STEPHEN KING

1

SHILOH

If Max doesn't put his shirt on right now, I'm going to kill him.

He does this every week. The second I fish his red T-shirt out of his drawer and tell him it's time to get dressed for tee-ball, he throws a fit. But I don't have the energy for this fight today.

"Come on, buddy." I do my best to fit my six-year-old brother's arms through the sleeves of his T-shirt. "Please."

Max wriggles away from me. "I'm not going."

"You have to."

Dad won't let Max quit tee-ball, but he should. He's not the one who has to pull Max off the floor, wrestle him into his uniform every Saturday morning, and promise to buy him ice cream after practice if he'd just put on his shirt already.

Dad signed Max up for tee-ball because Max is a shy kid, and Dad wants to break him out of his shell. What Dad doesn't realize is that Max isn't shy. He just shuts down around Dad. But Dad will never admit this, so it's all "baseball is the great American pastime" this, and "tee-ball will get you used to the game" that. I wish he'd let it go. Just because Dad wants Max to play shouldn't mean Max has to, but I know damn well Dad won't listen if I say anything, so I keep my mouth shut.

Max sniffs a booger back up his nose. "I hate tee-ball."

"I know," I say.

"I'm bad at it."

"You just need to practice."

"I don't want to." He wrinkles his nose. "This is a goddamn nightmare."

The side of my mouth tugs up. Mom uses that phrase all the time, like when she gets lost while driving or drops a box of dry pasta onto the floor. "A goddamn nightmare," I echo.

Max had a real nightmare last night. He came into my room around two and poked the soft part of my cheek.

I shot upright. Seeing it was only Max, relief washed over me. "What is it?"

"There's a green monster in my room." His eyes were wide with panic. "It stood on its hind legs and had blood all over its teeth."

Most of Max's nightmares are about monsters in our house. Usually, they sneak in when he's asleep, and he wakes up to find them standing over his bed.

A yawn pulled at my lips. I'd only just fallen asleep, but Max needed me, so with a groan, I scooted over, and Max climbed under my sheets. I made up a story about tall, leaf-eating dinosaurs to help him go back to sleep because he likes those and doesn't think they're scary. When I drifted off again, I dreamed of a long-necked dinosaur looming over my bed. Hot saliva dripped from its jaws and burned holes through my shirt and skin. It got closer to my face until it was an inch from my nose. I stayed still as it opened its mouth to display rows of razor-sharp teeth embedded in its gums. With a venomous roar, it bit me in half.

The dream sounds dumb now, but it scared me. I told Max about it this morning.

"Don't be silly," he told me. "The big guys with the long

necks are harmless. It's the angry ones with short arms you got to be scared of."

Back in the present, Max rubs his nose. "Can I get an extra scoop of ice cream today?"

A laugh rises from my chest, the kind only Max can get out of me. He blinks up at me with his sad, brown eyes, and it's like a fist curls around my heart. Those eyes, man. They get me every time. Mine are the same—according to my mom, anyway. She says that even when Max and I are happy, our eyes are still a teeny bit sad.

"Mom is picking you up from practice." I tug on his shirt. "So you'll have to ask her."

He ignores me. "Can I get three scoops?"

"That's a lot of scoops."

"Please, can you ask Mom?"

Ice cream. The best bargaining tool. "Sure, I'll ask her."

I pull on my work vest before hoisting Max onto my back and walking to the kitchen like I did when we came out for breakfast this morning. Mom will have finished cleaning up the broken glass by now, but I still want to carry Max in case she'd missed any tiny shards.

Gospel music floats through the hallway, reaching my ears before I enter the kitchen. Mom is at the sink scraping egg off a frying pan. Dad is in the living room. He has his legs propped up on his La-Z-Boy recliner and is half-watching some cooking show while skimming the paper. He looks so comfortable. Calm, even. As if nothing happened last night. As if making breakfast could make me forget the anger burning behind his eyes or how hard he'd shoved Mom's face into the couch. I'd covered Max's eyes before he could see, ushering him into his room. I'd heard Dad break that glass from there. I can still smell it. The scotch. Simmering under the smell of bacon, like his anger simmers beneath him now.

Mom looks over at us and smiles through closed lips. "Are you leaving for the park?"

I give her a swift nod. At the sound of Mom's voice, Dad lowers his paper and crosses the room to pull Max off my back.

"There's my big, strong man," Dad says, holding Max by the crook of his arms. Dad isn't that tall—average height, nothing special—but his shoulders are broad. His arms curve and bulge underneath his zip-up sweatshirt, and his biceps are almost the size of my head. He doesn't let me forget it. "You know what practice makes?"

This is one of Dad's go-to sayings. Max has heard this before, so he offers a small "Champions."

Dad grins. "Champions. Yeah." He nestles Max onto his hip. I can see in Max's eyes how badly he wants Dad to let him go, but he's too scared to say anything. Dad's sober now. He won't do anything to hurt Max, but I want him to put Max down just the same. "Champions are made at practice."

He puts Max on the floor. I take Max's hand to pull him closer to me. "We have to go."

"Have you eaten enough?" Mom dries her frail hands on her apron as she walks over to us.

"Are you kidding?" Dad asks. "They ate like kings this morning. Especially this one over here." Dad pokes me in the stomach. I flinch, and he laughs. "I'm joking. No, Heidi, they're fine."

"Please, just take a snack." Mom hurries back to the kitchen to grab small bags of Goldfish for us. I can't tell how bad last night was for her just by looking. Sometimes I can, if I glimpse a mark beneath the sleeve of her pajama shirt, or if the light hits her neck the right way and I notice the concealer blending into her skin. There's none of that today, but I can tell by the exhausted shadows weighing down the skin beneath her eyes and the way her fingers tremble on the crinkled Goldfish bags that something's wrong.

I used to hate her. Especially when things with Dad first got bad. Part of me thought she deserved what happened to her because she didn't do anything to stop it, but I know it's more complicated than that. She loves him. He wasn't always like this.

There are good parts of Dad, but some things in life are just uncomplicated. People do unforgivable things, and when they do, it doesn't matter how good they are. That one thing cancels out the rest.

Because of this, I don't see it as my responsibility to protect Mom. I have to focus on Max.

I keep my eyes trained on Mom as I ask, "Are you sure you can pick Max up today?"

I'm usually the one who picks Max up from tee-ball on Saturday mornings, but one of my coworkers asked me to pick up her shift today. Mom said it was fine. If I wanted to take an extra shift, she'd pick Max up from practice herself. Not a problem. Still, it feels wrong.

"I am," Mom assures me. "One fifteen, right?"

"Yes. And three scoops of ice cream after." I grip Max's hand tighter. I know Mom can pick Max up from practice, but I can't shake the feeling in my stomach that something bad is going to happen. I like being in control of Max's schedule. So I know he's safe.

"Three scoops," Dad says to Max. "Lucky man."

Mom wrings her hands. "I will be there."

"Okay." I jerk my chin toward the door. "We're going."

"Play hard," Dad says, wandering back over to the La-Z-Boy and sinking down into the leather. "Be good, kids."

Max puts on his sneakers. I grab his hand and we walk out the door.

It's sunny today and warm for September. The sun beats down on my face and warms the blue fibers of my employee vest. I tie my hair up in a ponytail and keep a strong hand on Max's as we walk. There are cars out. I don't want him to run into the road.

I fill my lungs with balmy air. A lot of the time, our house feels like it's closing in around us, but when I'm outside with Max and there's just the two of us, it's like I can breathe again.

"What did the sauropod in your dream look like?" Max asks.

It takes me a second to remember sauropod is the word for a long-necked dinosaur. "I just remember the long neck."

"What else?"

Jeez, I don't know. I try to remember. I know a little about dinosaurs because I've read Max so many books about them, but the one in my dream wasn't exactly biologically accurate. None of the long-necked dinosaurs I know have teeth like that. "Maybe it had a bump on its head?"

"It could be a brachiosaurus." He pauses. "You know, the largest sauropods were 160 feet long, and could be up to 130 feet tall."

"Awesome."

"I know, right?"

We turn off our road. Bethany is a small town. Only a couple thousand people live here, which is actually pretty big by Ohio standards. Most of the houses look the same. One-story homes with shutters on their windows. Inside them live women in aprons and old men in overalls or suede suit jackets. If a couple is young, they're about to start pumping out kids. If they're old, they already have. The boys at my high school wear camouflage and like to hunt and fish. The girls wear dark eye makeup. I know this town is a good place to live. It has hayrides in the fall and big community events and the kind of neighbors who bring over random baked goods for no reason except they were thinking about us. Everyone I know seems happy to live here, but I'm not. I feel like a prisoner in my own house, which makes everyone around me an unwitting guard.

I pass Duncan's Restaurant and Pub—the gross bar where Dad drinks. I go past the gun store, the florist, and a bakery called Simply Sweet, which makes some killer sugar cookies. A hiking trail stretches across Route 13 and runs along the river to the pond where Mom and Dad used to take me swimming before Max was born.

As we're crossing the street by the tire place, I notice one of my classmates walking toward us and I grip Max's hand a little tighter. Francesca Russo's wild, black hair frizzes up in every direction. She has an oval face with acne-covered skin and lips so chapped they flake. A dress clings to her round shoulders, which looks like it was made from an old painter's shirt.

I try not to stare at her as we pass. Usually when you hear rumors about people, they're lies, but I know for a fact the rumors about Francesca are true. My parents were at the funeral where she burned that corpse. Literally doused a dead guy's body in kerosene and set him on fire while his widow begged for her to stop.

Someone put the fire out. Nobody got hurt or anything, but still. Francesca's creepy. She tells everyone she burned the man because his ghost asked her to, but I think it's some kind of mental thing. One of those disorders that makes you hear voices.

I feel sorry for her. I heard another rumor a month or so ago that she lives in a trailer with her older brother, Richie, who's a prick. He's dumped the contents of my backpack into the hall tons of times. I glance over my shoulder and watch Francesca wander away from us. I'm pretty sure her mom is dead and her dad remarried or something. I don't know. It must be lonely. If the only people I had to talk to were imaginary, I'd feel pretty alone, too.

Standing up for her in school would put a target on my back. Even though it might make me a bad person, I don't have enough energy to deal with that on top of everything at home.

Max and I reach the park. Some of the other boys have already arrived and are standing around kicking the grass or fixing small plastic helmets onto their small heads.

Max stops. I glance down to see him shaking his head.

I drop in front of him and hold his arms. "You have to, buddy."

"Can I please stay with you?"

"I have work." I flatten his blond cowlick, but it springs back up again. The sun is really beating down today. I hope Max doesn't get sunburned. I forgot to put sunscreen on him. "Mom is going to be here at one fifteen, and when I get home, I'll play dinosaurs with you until dinner."

7

This seems to get to him. "All the way until dinner?"

"You heard me."

Before I can say anything else, Max flings his arms around my neck. I hug him back, resting my chin on his bony shoulder. For a couple of seconds, everything is right in the world. It's just Max and me, soaking in the last of the sun outside on a Saturday. Then he worms free. I'm jarred back to reality to see him walking over to where Coach Boeshart is taking attendance.

"I love you," I call after Max.

He turns around and smiles at me without his front teeth. "Bye, Shiloh."

———

I pass a plastic bag over the counter to a girl in a band T-shirt. "Have a good one."

The girl turns in a swirl of long purple hair to leave the store. There's nobody else in line, so I glance up at the wall clock under the Rite Aid logo. It's just after one fifteen. Max should be done with tee-ball by now.

A shaky breath leaves my lips. This isn't right. I should be there, picking him up.

I run my palms down my face. Dad thinks I have this job to save for college, but that's a lie. I'm not saving for college. I'm saving up to run away as soon as I turn eighteen. I have to get a good, safe place to live and prove I'm able to hold a steady job if the court is going to take me seriously when I apply for custody of Max. I need to show them that I'm not messing around, and I need to prove what Dad has done to us.

Hidden in an app on my iPod are pictures of my bruises and welts, along with photos I've managed to sneak of the house after he's done ripping through it. If Mom doesn't clean up after Dad breaks plates and glasses, I take photos after they've gone to bed. I started doing this two years ago, so I don't have many photos, but I'll keep going for the next two years until my birthday. I just hope it's enough.

8

Max is only six. I don't want him to grow up in that house if I can do anything to stop it.

I wonder if Mom is going to remember to take Max for ice cream. I'm sure Max will remind her if she forgets.

An old man in a tattered bucket hat slides his basket across the counter. I scan a packet of gum and a pint of vanilla ice cream. Something twinges in the pit of my stomach. I wonder which flavor of ice cream Max chose today. He usually opts for chocolate and gets the brown syrup all over his lips, but in the last two weeks, he's chosen chocolate chip.

I'll call Mom during my break to ask which flavor he got. Maybe Brian will let me borrow his phone.

"Have a nice day," I call after the old guy before leaning into the counter and hanging my head. He half-raises a liver-spotted hand, and the door bleeps as he leaves.

———

During my break, I find my coworker Brian in the back room with his vest unbuttoned. He unwraps a cheese stick and peels off a fat chunk.

I sit at the round table across from him and lean my forearms against the metal. "Can I borrow your phone?"

Brian doesn't look up. His fingers punch the screen. I can see the reflection of messages in his rectangular glasses. "I'm texting right now, so no."

He does this every time I ask him, but it only takes a little persistence and buttering up to persuade him. I lean my cheek into my palm and stick my bottom lip out. Just a tad. "What are you texting about?"

A piece of cheese falls out of his open mouth as he chews. It lands in his unbuttoned vest, and he picks it up and pops it back in his mouth. "I've recently discovered evidence to suggest that the girl who was kidnapped last month was actually abducted."

I only know about the girl who went missing last month because I've seen her posters on telephone poles around town.

It's super sad. She was twelve, I think, and never made it home from school. She wasn't from our town. She lived in Mount Keenan, which is a twenty-minute drive and eight times as big as our town. Bethany is small and nothing ever happens here, but there's actual crime in Mount Keenan.

When that girl first went missing, Dad told Max and me not to stay out after dark, but I could tell he wasn't that worried. This is Bethany we're talking about. People in Bethany don't kidnap each other's kids. "Abducted?"

"By aliens," Brian says.

A small sound of disbelief slips from my lips. I regret it as soon as it happens because Brian looks offended.

"Oh, so you think aliens aren't real, huh? Well, I'd take a hard look at yourself if I were you, because our universe is so big that if you think you're the only life force out there, then your ego needs to shrink."

"Can I please use your phone?" I plaster on a big smile. I wish Dad would just let me have one already. It would save me from conversations like these. "I just need to make one call."

Brian's lip twitches. He finishes what he's typing and slides his phone across the table. I run my thumb through the residue of sweat on the screen before entering Mom's number and holding the phone up to my ear.

Voicemail. That's weird. I dial again. Voicemail. Mom's usually good about picking up her phone.

As much as I don't want to, I know I should try Dad. My fingers curl around the phone.

Dad picks up on the fifth ring. "You've got Ernest Oleson."

"Dad?" I swivel around in my chair, away from Brian. Dad doesn't like it when I call him unless it's important. I hope he doesn't get mad. "Have Mom and Max come home yet?"

He doesn't respond. I can hear voices in the background, and the clinking of glasses. He screams something indecipherable. The sound explodes from the phone, and I jump at the outburst. He clears his throat before saying, "Sorry, Scooter Girl. I'm watching the game at Duncan's. What did you say?"

I take in a sharp breath. I wonder how much he's had. "Is Mom home from picking up Max?"

"Mom's not feeling well." Dad shouts something again. "I'm picking him up."

No. No. No. "You should have picked him up forty-five minutes ago."

"He's done at two fifteen."

"One fifteen."

"Your mother said two fifteen, and you know she's never wrong about these things."

I clamp my teeth around my knuckles. Fighting to keep my words steady, I ask, "Can you please go pick him up now?"

"I'd be early."

"I promise you, Dad. It's one fifteen. He's been waiting for forty-five minutes already." I glance at the door. Merwin Park is on the other side of town, and I don't have a car. It would take me twenty minutes to get there, even if I ran all the way. "Can you please go now?"

"Jesus, Shiloh, you're a pain in the ass. I'll go, but if I'm early …"

Before I can ask him to call me when he has Max, Dad hangs up the phone. I stare at the screen.

Brian sticks out his palm and wriggles his fingers. "Do you mind?"

I protect Max whenever I can, but I can't be with him all the time. Mom looked okay this morning, but usually "Mom isn't feeling well" is code for Dad's done something to hurt her.

Dad wasn't always like this. He used to actually listen to Mom. Sure, he'd raise his voice at us every once in a while, but he never got violent or anything. That started happening after Uncle Jim died. Max was only two. One night, Dad came home to find Max using a permanent marker to draw squiggles all over the living room wall. Dad didn't say a word. He just walked right over and smashed Max's forehead into the wall. The agony I feel when Max is in pain pierced my chest. I pulled him into my arms, picked him up, and ran into his bedroom, locking the door and leaning my back against it. Dad didn't follow us. He apologized the next morning after he'd sobered up, but that day, I swore Dad was never going to hurt Max again. Not if I had anything to do with it.

Take a deep breath, I assure myself. Everything will be fine. Coach Boeshart will wait with Max, just like he did when I was ten minutes late picking him up a few weeks ago. Boeshart is a good man. Deep down, anyway. He's a bit of a brick, but he wouldn't abandon Max.

I hand Brian his phone with a soft, "Thank you." I imagine Max waiting beside Coach Boeshart after all the other boys have been picked up, wondering why nobody has come for him yet. Picturing the disappointed look on his face turns my stomach. I hate Dad for forgetting Max. I hate him for lashing out at Mom. I hate that instead of having two parents who love and protect him, Max only has me. I try my best to keep him happy, but it's not the same. I know Mom and Dad love him, but Dad is bad when he's drunk, and Mom is tired all the time. I should have been there to pick him up today.

As soon as my shift ends, I run home. Rite Aid's about a ten-minute walk from our house, but if I run, I can make it in five.

I'm going to play dinosaurs with Max so enthusiastically today. To make it up to him.

I enter through the garage and kick my shoes off onto the rack. I open the door and call through the opening, "Max, go get Trish Triceratops and tell her we're ready to play."

No response. Mom and Dad are in the living room. Mom is crumpled on the couch, clutching a quilt to her mouth in her frail hands. Dad's standing over her in uniform.

I wrinkle my brow. "Is everything okay?"

A squeak escapes Mom's throat. Dad's eyes are sober, sad, and serious. Lamplight glints off the sheriff's badge pinned to his chest. "Shiloh, come over here and take a seat."

Oh no. Something's wrong. He never has that look on his face unless he's done something bad. "What's happened?"

"Max wasn't at the park when I arrived to pick him up."

Above his head, the ceiling fan whirs, gently tossing his hair and flattening the shoulders of his collared shirt.

I don't understand. "So where was he?"

"Rob Boeshart didn't see Max at the end of practice. He went up to bat, then sat back down. Next minute, he was gone."

The blades of the fan seem to spin faster, slicing through the air and wobbling the rod securing it to the ceiling.

"So," I say, "what you're saying is—"

"He's missing," Dad cuts me off. "Something happened, and we don't know where he is."

Once, when I was twelve or thirteen, Dad pushed me down the basement stairs. I tumbled down head over heels and landed on the concrete floor. All the breath flew from my lungs. I gasped for air, trying to remember how to breathe as he stood at the top of the stairs staring down at me.

That's how I feel now. I'm at the bottom of the stairs and Dad is staring at me as I force air in and out of my lungs.

I grab the counter to steady myself. Somewhere far away, Dad speaks. He's still speaking when I run across the room and pound my fists into his chest. "What did you do to him?"

Dad grabs my wrist. Hard. "Calm down, Shiloh."

I try to pull my wrist free, but his grip is strong. "Where is he?"

"I told you, I don't know." Dad pushes me off. A sour smell rides his breath. I guess I was wrong. He was drinking at Duncan's after all, when he should have been picking up Max. "None of the parents saw anything, but I have my people combing through the area. I'm about to go join them."

I bend over my hands and knees. My face breaks open and I sob in gasps.

"I promise," Dad says over my head. I dig my fingernails into my thighs. "I swear on my life I'm going to bring him home."

13

York County Police searching for missing 6-year-old boy
September 7, 2019

BETHANY, Ohio: Bethany Police need your help in locating a missing 6-year-old boy.

According to investigators, Maxwell Oleson was last seen on Saturday afternoon at around 12:45 p.m. in the area of 9 Long Street near Merwin Park. He was wearing a red shirt, white pants, and gray sneakers. He was at tee-ball practice at the time.

If you know of Maxwell's whereabouts, or have any information pertaining to his disappearance, contact Sheriff Ernest Oleson immediately at (740) 244-5555.

2

FRANCESCA

In the whole of my sophomore class at Bethany High School, there is not a girl who is more odd than me.

I can see it in their eyes when they look at me. The other children at school. The boy with the kind face doing the bags at the grocery store. Even my teachers peer at me strangely when I walk into the classroom and sit at a desk in the back in the hope it will stop everyone from looking at me. I have gotten used to the attention, but I do not particularly enjoy it.

Do you see that creepy girl? they whisper. *That's Francesca Russo. Francesca Firestarter. Eight years ago, she burned a guy. Lit his dead body on fire at his own funeral. Hey, Francesca, he was dead anyway. What was the point?*

While their words are mean, it is true. I did exactly what they said I did. But what is also true, but what nobody cares to believe, is that I did not burn him because I am crazy.

I burned him because he asked me to.

I was eight years old on the day of George R. Haggarty's funeral. The service was rather dull. George Haggarty died not long after my mother died, and I was not pleased to be back in the pews, sandwiched between my father and brother, smelling of wood polish and sanctity and listening to sad strangers give speeches and trying hard not to cry. Next to me, a woman was sobbing soundlessly. I watched her chest heave, saw her tears flow, and had to stop myself from reaching out and holding her hand. I have never been afraid of death because when people die, they are never actually gone.

When somebody dies, their soul exits their body and morphs into a version of themselves made of mist and moonlight. I cannot touch souls. As far as I know, I am the only person who can see them. They linger in our world for a certain amount of time and then fade away. I am not sure where they go, but I can no longer see or hear them. My friend Mrs. Lewis had been in the cemetery for nearly five years, but when my mother died, she faded away before I got a chance to see her.

I missed her. I wished I could still see her. Nothing about her death was fair.

The service ended. My father knew the Haggartys quite well, so he wanted to stay for the reception. I stood beside him and trained my eyes on an old photograph displaying the two owners of the Eugene J. Haggarty Funeral Home. I was fairly certain George was one of Eugene's sons. It must have been awfully hard, having to put makeup on the body of your own son. Embalmers put makeup on bodies for their funerals to make them look more like people and less like bodies. At least, that is what Mrs. Lewis told me, because she was not fond of the way they painted her face for hers.

I glanced around the room. Heavy-shouldered guests passed around hors d'oeuvres and condolences.

A deep moan sounded as if from far away. It was a horrible, hideous groaning, like somebody was in so much pain that the sound had to force its way out of them.

I wandered over to my older brother Richie, who was stuffing pigs-in-a-blanket into his pockets.

I tugged on the back of his puckered dress shirt. "Do you hear that sound?"

Richie spun around. I had pulled his tie against his throat from behind as he was trying to swallow, and now he was making choking sounds of his own, almost in harmony with the groans. It was rather amusing. I let out a shrill laugh, and heads turned.

"Quit it, Frankie. For Christ's sake." Richie's cheeks bulged from the pigs-in-a-blanket, and he sprayed me with half-chewed bits.

"I did not mean to hurt you. Do you hear that strange sound?"

"What sound?"

"The crying."

"Ain't no crying."

I gestured to his pockets. "Does Father know you are taking those?"

"You tell him, and I'll kill you." He jabbed his fat finger into my face, and I giggled. "I mean it. I'll smother you in your sleep."

Richie walked away to go talk to his friends. I began to follow him when the moan sounded again. Louder this time.

I was definitely not imagining it. The sound was not coming from the reception. It was coming from farther down the hallway, from the parlor where we had all sat for Mr. Haggarty's service.

I wove through the black pants and tights stretching up around me like cauterized trees. My shiny shoes made small taps on the floor like drops of rain on an upside-down bucket. I pressed my hand against the door. I had to be brave. So I opened the door.

The parlor was silent. Had I imagined the groaning? It sounded again, and a shiver of terror shot up my spine.

The noise was coming from Mr. Haggarty's casket.

Why was Mr. Haggarty crying? George was a lovely fellow. One time, a couple of days after Halloween, he gave me a

Hershey's Kiss that melted over my tongue. It was the most delicious chocolate I had ever tasted.

My mother used to always tell me to love my neighbor as I loved myself. Because of that, I needed to help George.

Careful not to draw attention to myself, I closed the door behind me, walked down the aisle, and pried open the casket. Sound exploded from it. I dropped the lid.

Slowly, I reopened the top half of the lid and stood on my tiptoes to peer inside. A gasp caught in my throat.

George Haggarty's corpse lay in the silk-lined, padded interior. Wrinkles cut into its skin. Deep burns peeled the skin back across George's throat. He looked healthy, nearly unnaturally so, but then I noticed his makeup. Perhaps he was upset because he did not like his makeup, just like Mrs. Lewis had not liked hers.

"Your makeup looks very nice," I said to him.

Inside George's corpse was a shimmering silhouette. His soul was fighting to lift itself out of his body, spitting and sputtering like hot oil jumping up out of a pan.

George's eyes split open. "Is that little Francesca Russo?"

"Yes, sir."

George threw his head back and screeched. I jumped at the unexpected sound, and my hands shot up to cover my ears.

"You need to help me," he said. Slowly, I lowered my hands. "This world, it never ends. I'm not supposed to be here."

I did not understand what he meant. "You look upset, Mr. Haggarty. Is everything all right?"

"Do I look all right?"

"The embalmers did a lovely job."

This did not seem to cheer him up. "You need to kill me again," he said. "You need to get rid of me." To nobody in particular, he asked, "How can you get rid of me?"

"I am not sure."

Suddenly, he gazed at me like I was the brightest, most all-consuming light he could see. "Burn me."

"Excuse me?"

"You have to burn me. I'm stuck in my body. If you burn my body, it will burn me."

This sounded like an outrageous idea. I stepped back. "Mr. Haggarty, I am not too sure about this."

George Haggarty screamed again. The amount of misery wrapped in the sound froze me in place.

"Please," he sobbed. "Francesca Russo. You've got to help me. You're my only hope."

Love your neighbor. My mother's voice bounced around inside my head. Part of love is helping others when needed. Even though it made me scared, I knew I had to help George Haggarty.

"There is a shed outside with a box of matches in it," George said. "There's a can of kerosene in there, too. I'm sure of it. It should be somewhere on the floor, near the lawnmower."

As I walked toward the door, George cried: "And for the love of God, please hurry."

I kept my head down as I hurried through the reception and turned the golden doorknob to go outside. The shed was old, made of wood, and filled with dust and spider webs. I am rather fond of spiders. They are misunderstood creatures, and remarkable artists. I hid the matches in the pocket of my blue dress and wiped the grime off the kerosene container before wrapping it in my cardigan. The can was heavy. The beady eyes of a stuffed boar followed me as I closed the shed door and tiptoed back inside the building.

I wished my mother were here. She had believed me when I told her about the souls I could see.

"You're not the only person in the world who has this gift," my mother told me. "But it's rare, and you must treasure it. Remember, there's a lot the dead can teach you about the living."

I got back to the parlor through the reception, praying nobody would notice the bundle in my arms. Nobody did.

"Did you find it?" George asked.

I pulled the matches out of my pocket.

"Where's the kerosene?" he asked.

I removed the plastic can from inside my cardigan.

George Haggarty's voice was squeaky as he instructed, "Unscrew the cap and pour it on me."

With shaking fingers, I removed the cap. A sharp, sweet smell filled my lungs. I glanced at George for permission.

"Pour it on me," he said.

Careful not to spill any of the kerosene, I climbed on top of the casket. It was closed over his legs but open over his chest. I straddled the closed part like I was riding an overweight donkey and looked down at George with the opening poised above him.

"Go ahead, pour it," he urged, with wide and hopeful eyes.

I poured the kerosene onto George's face. Colorless liquid bounced off his suit jacket. The gas ran straight through George, whose eyes were shut in gleeful anticipation. "Is that enough?" I asked.

"More."

"I can't reach your legs."

"Cover my chest. It'll be enough."

I poured until the container was empty, and I jumped off the casket.

"Get the matches."

"My father does not allow me to play with matches."

"Put your finger up against the end and press down."

"The red part?"

He nodded. "Hurry!"

I pressed my finger up against the red-dipped end. I scratched the match against the striker strip, and a flame engulfed the tip.

"Drop it! For God's sake, drop it now."

I lifted the match above his body. The door burst open and Deborah Haggarty stepped into the parlor. Her eyes locked onto mine, and her mouth dropped open into an *O*.

She screamed.

"*Drop it!*" George barked. "Please, Francesca—"

The match tumbled from my fingers and collided with the

brown corduroy of George's suit. It bounced once and fell flat. I ran away. George's torso erupted in flames.

Deborah Haggarty screamed again, louder this time. An unfamiliar man wearing a suit broke the glass to free the fire extinguisher against the wall. Deborah hobbled down the aisle on her tall heels with her arms out, ready to catch me. Her eyes were pinned on me. My heart slammed against my ribs as I ran into the pews.

"*What did you do!?*" She swiped at me with her sharp nails. I ducked, sending her off-balance.

"George instructed me to do it," I exclaimed. "He asked me to."

Deborah was gaining on me like a clumsy giraffe. The fire had engulfed George's exposed torso, shooting up from him. The smoke formed a cloud against the ceiling. An alarm blared from over my head. I covered my ears. It was too loud. I wanted to bury myself under the pews and hide.

But Deborah would catch me. I had to reach the door. I dropped my hands and forced myself to run. A loud hissing sound cut through the commotion. I whipped my head around in time to see powder shoot out of the fire extinguisher and cover the casket. The fire dimmed. George's screams pierced my ears again. The sound was the worst one of all. He was in so much pain, and I could not take it anymore. I clapped my hands over my ears.

Deborah caught up to me and grabbed me by the wrists. "Where is your father?"

My father ran toward us, folding his cell phone into his back pocket. Deborah yanked my arm up higher and said, "Your daughter is a *psychopath*."

"George Haggarty asked me to burn him." My lip quivered. "He was crying."

My father frowned at Deborah. "Goodness, Deborah. I am so sorry for all this."

"Get her the hell out of here," Deborah said. "I don't ever want to see her face again, you hear me?"

"Mom would have understood," I cried to my father on the drive home, but he was stony-faced. Richie stayed silent. He looked at me as if he were scared, as if somebody had taken his sister away and put a monster there in her place, in her clothes, in her body.

"Your mother is dead," my father said. The words drew more tears from my eyes.

The next morning, my father had me apologize to the Haggarty family. I was not sorry for what I had done. They didn't understand. George gave me the instructions. I was trying to help him.

Because I was so young, Deborah did not press charges. My father never again spoke of what happened. He took me to see a nice woman in an office who did not believe a word out of my mouth.

I did not know what to expect in school, but the moment I arrived on Monday, it became clear my life had changed. My classmates looked at me like I was dangerous, as if they were afraid I would hurt them like I hurt that man at the funeral home. I told them I would not, but nobody believed me. My father found anonymous notes in our mailbox threatening to come and kill me in my sleep. I walked home from school every day wondering what I had done wrong, and why everyone disliked me when I had just been trying to help poor George.

Six years later, my father married another woman and moved to Columbus, leaving me with Richie in a trailer because I had turned our family into a spectacle, and he could not handle all the threats.

"Cranky Frankie," the kids at my school still call me. "Don't make eye contact. She'll burn you alive!"

Richie does not believe me either. He hates me for driving our father away. He has a special name for me. Psycho Sis. *Get out of my face, Psycho Sis. What's for dinner, Psycho Sis?*

Perhaps I am disturbed. I do not wish to complain. I am lucky to have the ghosts as my friends. But at night, when I lie awake on the couch and listen to Richie snore from the only bed in our trailer, I dream that somewhere out there is somebody like me, someone else who is treated like they are crazy but does not feel crazy. In my dreams, that person assures me that my mother was right, that there is nothing wrong with me, and that I did a good thing by helping George. I hope I find that person soon.

3

FRANCESCA

"Did Psycho Russo just come in here?"

My hand pauses on the toilet flush. I do not have time to cover myself before Ashley Christensen's mousy ponytail smacks against the tiles as she peeps under the stall door.

She smacks her red lips together. "Here, Tara. I got her."

Ashley enters the stall beside mine. I zip up my pants and try to open the door, but it does not budge. I can see Tara's hands gripping the top of the door. She must be pulling on it to stop me from getting out.

I am aware of what they are about to do. I slap my palms against the door. "Please, Tara. Will you please let me out?"

"Tara, you know something that amazes me?" Ashley says. Plastic crinkles. "Cranky Frankie was able to drive both of her parents to leave her. Not just one. Isn't that crazy?"

Tara snickers. "They must have really hated her."

"Her mom was so embarrassed by her that a tumor grew in her head," Ashley says.

"And her dad was so ashamed he left her all alone," Tara replies.

My hands ball into fists, but I stretch them flat. I should not judge those who are mean. They could be having a harder day than I am having.

Ashley is in a relationship with Richie. I do not understand why. He has quite a big personality. I imagine he makes her days hard.

Richie tells Ashley more about my life than I am comfortable with. She found out about the trailer when they started seeing each other six months ago. Instead of keeping it to herself, she spread it through school. Every rumor she has started has morphed into a more imaginative version of itself. Richie and Francesca do not have a home. Richie and Francesca live in the woods behind the school. Richie and Francesca turn into wolves when the moon is full and lick the insides of each other's mouths. There are more, but I cannot remember them all at the moment. The rumors spread so far that a school administrator called my father to inquire into our housing situation, but Richie is over eighteen now. He is allowed to live alone, and I am simply living with him.

"I quite like the trailer." My voice is softer than I would like it to be. "My father pays a visit every couple of weeks."

"Sure," Ashley says. "At the end of a freaking gun."

"Are you feeling all right today, Ashley?" I ask. "You sound upset about something."

Ashley slams her hand against the stall. "You know what upsets me, Psycho? Your ugly face. Richie is scared of you, you know. He thinks you'll burn him too one night when he's asleep."

Paper rustles in the stall beside me. Before I can prepare myself, a barrage of used tampons, pads, and feminine wipes falls onto my head. A banana peel lands with a splat between my shoes.

"Are there any dead people in the trash today?" Ashley shakes out the rest of the trash barrel. "Do you see any?"

Ashley and Tara leave the bathroom, overcome with laughter. I sink onto the toilet and wrap my arms around my stomach. I should be used to this by now. Ashley has been mean to me since elementary school. Why do her words still hook into my heart like small barbs?

Perhaps Ashley would not be as mean if I looked more like her. Not only is the story of George Haggarty's funeral following me like a wayward soul, but I am also heavier than Ashley and her friends. I have a big nose and crooked teeth and wear Richie's hand-me-downs a lot of the time because my father rarely sends enough money for new clothes. I used my grandmother's thread to embroider flowers and bees into my jackets. It does not matter. I feel silly for even worrying about this. I would not care so much about my appearance if everyone around me did not care so much about theirs.

I pick up every piece of trash and put it back into the barrel before leaving for the cemetery. I try to steady my breathing. Once I get there, Mrs. Lewis will tell me everything is going to be all right in a voice as soft as a blanket. She will warm me up.

Behind the houses to the left of me there is a long field of corn. Green, leafy stalks peek through the trees and stretch all the way into the distance. I adore cornfields. I have lived in Bethany my entire life, so I am used to being surrounded by corn, but they never stop taking my breath away.

In the fall, my mother used to bring me to corn mazes, entwining her fingers with mine as we strolled among the stalks. She told me once that the corn has secrets.

"These fields have seen more than you ever have, and more than you ever will." My mother held a finger to her lips. "If you're really quiet, you might be able to hear them whisper."

I stopped eating my pretzel and listened very hard, but I did not hear anything. After my mother passed away, I used to sneak into the cornfields at night and listen for her voice. I never heard anything except the wind in the stalks.

I stop at the crosswalk. A buggy, pulled by a spectacular chestnut horse with a white stripe down the front of its nose, stops. I scurry across the road before I can inconvenience the driver.

I unlatch the wrought-iron gate leading into the cemetery and look around. Usually, when I visit the cemetery, every soul is milling about. Not today. They are all gathered under the oak tree. Well, everybody except for Jeremy Noonan, that is, for he is sitting on a gravestone watching a squirrel collect acorns.

Jeremy is in his twenties and has a long face like a camel's, except he is emaciated and drained of blood and life. Homemade tattoos cover his bare arms and shoulders, and thin facial hair pokes out right above his upper lip and on the point of his chin. Jeremy died of a heroin overdose two years ago. I do not enjoy speaking to him because he says things that make me uncomfortable.

Jeremy abandons the squirrel and weaves over to me. "Hey, Kika. Has anyone ever told you how smoking hot you'd be if you didn't wear such nasty-looking clothes?"

I let out a long sigh. Jeremy is the only person in the world who calls me Kika. I believe it was the name of a female dancer he once knew. "How are you doing today, Jeremy?"

Jeremy shrugs. His eyelids droop as if he were high. He told me once that he misses cannabis more than any other drug. I used to wonder if souls go through withdrawal when they die, but I do not think that is the case. If they did experience symptoms, Jeremy would have complained about it.

"Why is everybody standing under the oak tree?" I ask.

"They're in a meeting."

"How mysterious." I tuck my hair behind my ears, but it springs free. "Why?"

"Some guy came here last night." Jeremy scratches his head as if his hair could itch. I have always found it intriguing how the dead hang on to their mannerisms from life. Fixing their hair. Licking their lips. "Dude was chatting with Gus or Charlie. People are saying he's evil or something."

Did I hear that right? "A man saw Gus with his eyes?"

Jeremy glares at me. "No, Kika, he saw him through his ass."

"Somebody else can see the dead?"

"Guess you aren't alone after all," Jeremy says. Oh, how I

want to believe him, but his grasp on reality can falter some days, so I leave him with the squirrel and hurry over to the group.

I weave through gravestones, memorial plaques, and tombs. There is a rock wall around the cemetery with lichen and moss growing out of the gaps in the stones. I step over a row of unmarked, crumbling graves. Because Bethany is small, death doesn't happen here often. Most of the souls in the cemetery come from people's grandparents, victims of farming accidents, or people who have overdosed on opioids, like Jeremy. There are a few children in the cemetery, too, but children do not usually stay for long.

I glance around for Mrs. Lewis and find her standing beside her husband, Mr. Lewis, near the edge of the group. Mrs. Lewis has shoulder-length white hair and wears a cardigan with roses on it. Every time I've ever seen her, she has been wearing the same cardigan.

Mrs. Lewis smiles at me. "Good morning, Francesca."

"It's the afternoon," Mr. Lewis grumbles. He is wearing overalls and has straw in his hair.

I smile. "How are you today, Mrs. Lewis?"

"A bit bewildered, to be honest." She lowers her voice. "A man visited us last night."

"Jeremy said he could see the twins. Is that true?"

Mrs. Lewis does not respond. Instead, she touches my face, her translucent fingers passing through my skin with a slight tingle. "What's this on your face?"

Oh. Something must have gotten on my face from the trash bin earlier. "I am not sure."

Mrs. Lewis frowns. "Is this your blood?"

"Somebody else's." I rub the back of my neck. "Ashley Christensen was having a bad day."

"Oh, honey." Mrs. Lewis's mouth presses into a line. "I don't know how you put up with that girl."

She is looking at me like she is pitying me. I drop my gaze to my feet. I have told Mrs. Lewis about the girls at school before, but the bullying has been going on for so long that the story is old. I am happy in the cemetery. I do not want to think about Ashley and Tara here.

"Hating those who hate you creates rot where there could be sugar," I say. Mrs. Lewis blinks at me like she does not understand, so I add, "It is something my mother used to say."

"Girls can be so mean," Mrs. Lewis says, "but you are one tough cookie, sweetheart. You'll be okay."

I smile without showing my teeth and turn my head to watch Reverend Guessford standing under the tree.

"Did he say anything else?" Reverend Guessford asks the identical ivory-haired twins, Charlie and Gus. Reverend Guessford is a short, heavyset man dressed in robes with a round face that gets so flushed when he feels any sort of emotion that it looks like his whole head is in danger of popping off like a cork. Reverend Guessford has been in the cemetery for twenty years. He is the oldest dead person I know. He told me once that he believes there is a final judgment after you fade away, where God decides whether you belong in Heaven or Hell. I wonder what he did for his final judgment to take so long.

"He grabbed my face like this," says Gus, pinching Charlie's cheeks to demonstrate. Esther, their mother, winces. The three of them, along with Esther's seven-day-old baby, died in a house fire, along with Esther's husband, who faded away a couple of months ago. "Then he said, 'not you,' and walked away."

"He had terrible breath," says Charlie.

"Just awful," Gus affirms.

"Did anybody else speak to the man?" Reverend Guessford asks.

Eleven-year-old Natalie Dorado steps forward. "I saw the little bitch talking to Henry."

Natalie died from leukemia one year ago. Her eyes narrowed into perpetual slits like she had already seen all this world had to offer and found it boring.

"Bitch" is Natalie's favorite word. She calls everyone a bitch because her parents are not around to stop her.

Reverend Guessford gasps. "What did he say?"

Natalie crosses her arms. "I don't know. I couldn't hear."

"You didn't hear anything?" he asks.

"That's what I said, bitch."

Reverend Guessford ignores her. Everyone knows by now that Natalie doesn't mean any harm. I actually find her rather amusing.

"Who else did the man speak to?" the Reverend asks.

"He grabbed Henry's face, too," Natalie says. "He grabbed it like he did Gus's."

Hang on a minute. Could this man touch souls, too?

"I am sorry to interrupt, Reverend Guessford," I say, waving hello. "How are you doing today?"

The wrinkles disappear from between his eyebrows. "I'm all right, Francesca. Thank you for asking."

I turn to Natalie. "You said he was able to grab them?"

"What, are you dumb?" Natalie pushes her hair out of her face. When she first arrived at the cemetery, her head was as smooth as an egg, but now, her hair has sprung back. It is usually those with the most horrendous ends who hold on to their appearance from death the longest. Eventually, most souls take on the appearance they had before their death, before the marks of trauma took charge of their faces. "I literally just said that."

"Nobody can touch ghosts."

"Well, this one did."

"What does he look like?"

Natalie shrugs. "He was wearing a long green coat."

Henry stands behind Natalie like he is made of marble. He cannot be older than twelve, and he has a crop of deep gray hair, which I imagine was red when he was alive. I do not remember how he died. I do not know Henry well. He does not speak very much.

Reverend Guessford leans over to meet Henry's eyes. "Did he grab you, Henry?"

Everyone leans forward to watch Henry pull up the sleeve of his jacket to reveal a dark bruise on his arm.

I gasp. Everyone explodes into concerned chatter.

"Did the man do that?"

"How is that possible?

"The dead can't bruise."

"Is Henry hurt?"

"It doesn't make sense," says a middle-aged woman with yellowing teeth and a tight braid, whose name I cannot remember. "We don't know who he is, why he came, or whether he's going to come again. Do you think he's going to come back?" Nobody answers her. Without any warning, she wails, "He's going to kill us all!"

"Yeah, bitch," Natalie mutters. "We're going to die twice."

"Everyone," Reverend Guessford calls. "Please, compose yourselves."

The voices grow louder. A cold wind slips between the gravestones and I shiver, but I do not feel cold. In fact, my chest is warm. If what everybody is saying is true, there is somebody else out there like me. I need to find this man. He may be able to tell me why I can see ghosts when no one else can. If there is one other person like me, perhaps there are more.

When I look over at Mrs. Lewis, a chill runs down my spine.

"Something isn't right about this," she says, and her eyes are so intense that they appear brighter than the rest of her body. "I can feel it, honey, and I swear it on my life—something evil is coming here."

31

4

SHILOH

Foggy wisps of air slip through my lips. My hands curl around the flashlight as I trudge through the woods.

"Max!" I scream. "Max, where are you?"

A damp, musty smell wafts up from the wet leaves on the ground as I scan the shadows for something red. A splash of color. Something. Anything that stands out against the blanket of brown.

The search party has grown over the last six hours. It seems like half of Bethany has shown up in sweaters, overcoats, and scarves, holding out lamps to light up the trees and the dark ground.

"Max?" my boyfriend, Miles, calls into the shadows. His voice is too quiet. Max won't hear it.

Voices murmur behind me. Two women. Their attempts to keep their voices low only make them louder.

"This is so sad," one whispers.

"I know," the other hisses.

"It's just like what happened to that little girl."

"The one in Mount Keenan?"

"Gone without a trace."

"I'm praying this little guy just wandered off."

"Kids do that, don't they? Maybe he went on an adventure and couldn't find his way home."

Max didn't just go on an adventure. He knows he's not supposed to go off on his own. I taught him better than that.

I remember Dad last night, grabbing hold of Mom's turtleneck sweater and pressing her face into the couch. I didn't hear what he got mad about. I was watching funny videos with Max on the living room desktop when I heard Mom tell Dad to let her go, and I scooped Max into my arms and covered his eyes with my hand. I stood by the chair, frozen, as Dad's knuckles dug into Mom's skin. She tapped his forearm with her thin wrist like a wrestler submitting, as if begging him to let go. I wanted to do something. Say something. Mom needed my help, and all I could do was watch. But I couldn't risk Dad paying any attention to me and turning whatever he was feeling onto Max, so instead I ushered Max back to his room and pressed my back against the door to catch my breath.

Max had rubbed his eyes. "Why did we stop watching videos?"

Good. I didn't think he had seen anything. "Because I'm tired, and I want to keep reading that book."

Max's face had opened up in excitement. "The one with Agent Gorilla?"

"That's the one." I got Max ready for bed, and I read him the book I'd gotten from the library about a gorilla and his friends who had to work together to find a missing dog. Occasionally, as I was reading, I'd hear Mom and Dad fighting through the walls. Dad would yell something. Mom's voice would rise. When Dad smashed that glass, my stomach lodged itself in my throat. I glanced down to see if Max noticed, but he didn't react. He was looking up at me as if to ask, "Why did you stop reading?"

Logically, I know it's possible that Max could have run away, but I just don't think he would. It doesn't make sense that he'd do it today. Dad didn't hurt him, or me. And Max and I spend every day together. If he was going to run away, wouldn't he say goodbye?

Something happened to him. I know it did.

A hand drops onto my shoulder. I glance up to see one of Max's teachers, Mrs. Rosenfarb, frowning at me.

"Bob's getting tired, so we're going to head out." Light from Miles's headlamp glints off Mrs. Rosenfarb's glasses. "I'm so sorry, honey."

I tense, but keep my mouth shut. Everyone in the search party keeps trying to talk to me. They're trying to comfort me, I get it, but I wish they'd leave me alone.

Once Mrs. Rosenfarb realizes I'm not going to say anything, she and her husband walk up to Mom and Dad leading the group. Dad is still in his uniform. It makes his shoulders look broad enough to fit both Mom and me inside his rib cage.

Dad's the sheriff of York County. Everyone in town loves him because they think of him as the town's protector. I know why. The image of him in everybody's heads is the photo he slapped on his campaign ads, the one showing off his flinty eyes, the confident set of his jaw, and that sense of All-American youthfulness he had when he graduated from Ohio State, where he had played football, joined a fraternity, and driven home every weekend to visit his chemically blond high school sweetheart, who soon became his wife. In those ads, he looked like the before photo of a soldier heading off to war—all swagger and buzz cut, without any of the grief lines he'd gotten after his brother Jim died, lines carved into his face as if with a chisel. People still see him as the "before" photo.

Dad comes from a long line of farmers right here in Bethany. He cares about this town. It's our community, he tells us. And according to Madeline Carter, who works at the bakery on Main Street, he has "a smile that can melt butter." Melt her too, judging by how giggly she gets when Dad goes in there to buy Max and me apology cookies.

In the town's eyes, Ernest Oleson is close to God. It's a load of crap.

Next to me, Miles clears his throat. "Is there, uh, anything I can do for you, Shiloh?"

He could stop trying to talk to me. That would be helpful. Instead of replying, I scream out into the shadows.

"Max!"

I told Max not to talk to strangers. I told him never to go with anyone who wasn't Mom or me. We practiced this. I told him this.

I had one job. To keep Max safe. And I couldn't even do that.

I grip the flashlight so tight my knuckles ache. Dad's strides are long and confident. As if Max isn't missing. As if he hadn't been late.

I wish something had happened to Dad instead of Max. It would serve him right.

Dad glances over his shoulder and slows his pace to fall into stride with me. "It's time to go home."

I struggle to wrap my mind around his words. "We can't go home. We have to keep looking."

"Your mother is getting tired." Dad jerks his chin at Mom, who's wrapping a shawl tightly over her thin, trembling shoulders. "It's getting late."

I gape at him. "We can't stop."

Dad gestures at two other police officers, walking a few paces behind me. "Brendan and Scott will keep looking with me. We can take it from here." Dad touches my back and I squirm away from him. "You can't do anything for him now, Scooter. You and your mother need to rest so you can help with the search in the morning."

I bristle. He looks sad and exhausted, but he doesn't look at all guilty. It's like he doesn't believe this was his fault. If he'd been on time to pick Max up, this wouldn't have happened.

"I can help now," I snap. "What if Max is out here?"

"If he's out there, we'll find him," Dad assures me. When my eyes drop to my shoes, Dad reaches over her to shake Miles's hand. I almost forgot he was there. "Good night, son, and thanks."

Miles nods at him. "Good night, sir."

Dad tugs his hat low and gestures for me to follow him. "Come on, now. I'm walking you home."

Putting up a fight will get me nowhere. I trudge after Dad as Miles calls out goodnight. I don't have the energy to say it back.

My feet drag as I follow my parents back to our house. Dad wraps his arm around Mom and pulls her along as she cries. Wiping my gummy nose, I wonder why I'm not crying. My entire body is numb. If someone were to drop a coin into my chest cavity, it would fall straight down to my diaphragm and land flat.

Dad opens the mudroom door and Mom hangs her shawl on the hook. On my way inside, I throw my shoes onto the rack. There is a clatter as they tumble off and fall onto the wood.

Dad glares at the sneakers. "Shiloh, put your shoes away."

Keeping my eyes on him, I pick up my sneakers and line them up on the shelf. Dad nods. He goes to the kitchen, takes a glass out of the cabinet, and pours himself a drink.

I watch him lower himself onto the La-Z-Boy. Is he serious right now? He's drinking? I usually stay quiet around Dad, but this is absurd.

"You said you were going back out there," I say, wiping my sweaty palms against my pants.

I brace myself for his response, but he only takes off his hat and places it on the side table, stretching his feet out in front of him. "I'm stressed right now. I'm going to sit for five minutes." He holds his index finger up. "One drink."

I should just shut up. Mom's upset. I don't want to make things worse for her. But he can't force us to come home and then sit here doing nothing. He has to go back out there.

"You're acting like you don't care about him."

Mom takes my hand. "Please, Shiloh."

"Watch your tone," Dad warns.

Cold sets into my bones. Dad had been drinking before going to pick up Max.

"Did you do something to him?" I ask, my voice trembling. "Did you hurt him?"

Dad smashes his glass onto the floor. Shards fly across the wood and onto the carpet. I jump backward to avoid them, glad he didn't throw it at my head. A fluttering sigh escapes Mom.

Dad points at me. "I would never do anything to hurt him. He is my son."

That hasn't stopped him before. I don't move. I can see Dad trying to restrain himself. His chest moves up and down with effort, as if there's an invisible sandbag weighing him down.

"You don't understand," he says finally. "There are no leads. Nobody saw where he went."

"There has to be something."

Without warning, Dad steps over the glass to where I'm standing and wraps his arms around Mom. She flinches at the touch. Her arms stay by her sides.

"I'm sorry, honey," he says, his voice muffled through Mom's thin hair. He cups his hand around her head. Her mouth tenses. "I'm sorry I was late to pick him up. There are no leads. I'm trying."

"You're doing everything you can," Mom says, and I want to gag.

"Yeah." Dad pulls backward and cups Mom's face. The gesture is so intimate I have to look away. "I promise I'm going to bring him home. I just need a plan."

Dad walks back into the living room. Mom goes to get the dustpan out of the closet. Dad splashes more Scotch into a new glass before turning on the radio and sinking into his recliner with a creak, leaning his head back into the leather and closing his eyes.

I stand there watching Mom clean. After tipping the pieces of broken glass into the trash can, she kisses me on the head.

"Be kind to your father," she says. "He may not show it, but he's having a hard time, too."

I don't care if Dad is hurting. He should be hurting. Mom retreats to her bedroom. A dull ache reverberates through my chest as I watch her go. Be kind to your father. Is she serious? I spend a lot of time trying to figure out why she stays with him, and I think a lot of it comes down to that. She still sees him as someone worth loving. Someone she needs to take care of. I bet part of it also goes back to the town. Given the choice, would the town choose to be on her side, or would it be on his, their protector, their great Ernest Oleson? Dad will make up lies to cover his ass, and where would that leave Mom? She would be a liar. Someone trying to ruin Dad's life. So will Max and I. Staying with him means not going through that.

I go to the kitchen and lean across the cold granite countertop, stretching my arms out in front of me and pulling on the blue rubber bracelet on my wrist. Max gave it to me last year. It was part of a goody bag he got from some kid's superhero-themed birthday party. He asked me not to take it off. I promised I never would.

Dad groans from the La-Z-Boy. It takes me a moment to realize he's fallen asleep.

I pause. Should I wake him up? He's supposed to go back out there and search, but I can't bring myself to move.

The song on the radio changes. My eyes shoot over to the recliner.

In our living room, there's a portable silver radio with two bulging speakers sitting above the fireplace. Every day after work, Dad turns the radio on and falls asleep in his La-Z-Boy recliner with an empty beer can on the table beside him. He's played the same country music station ever since I was little. It has the same host, too—Rodney Jackson, on WCKO. Whenever I hear Rodney in the living room, it means Dad's home, so my stomach gets a heavy feeling. It doesn't matter how friendly Rodney sounds. I'm never happy to hear his voice.

Dad is snoring over Waylon Jennings. His bald spot is just visible over the top of the leather chair. It rises and falls out of time with the song. He always sets the volume high enough that I can hear it from every corner of our one-story home, but neither Mom nor I can lower it. Even five points would wake him.

Every part of me wants to walk over to the mantle, pick up the radio, and smash it into Dad's head so hard that it splits his skin.

I need to leave before the temptation grows. I'm standing up from the stool when I get an idea.

I glance over at the basement door.

Dad converted the basement into his office four years ago. Max and I aren't allowed to go down there. Max has never tried. He's afraid of the dark. I tried once, soon after Dad made the rule, because Max was missing his old plastic dump truck and I had a feeling I'd left it in the basement while I was bringing his toys upstairs. I thought Dad was out. When I made it to the top of the stairs with the dump truck, Dad saw me and got so angry he pushed me backward, making me fall hard on the concrete. After I'd regained my breath, I remember thinking it'd been a pretty dumb way of keeping me out of the basement.

Dad spends hours down there on weekends. His computer has remote access to his office—and all police records.

There's no way Max disappeared without a trace. There are always parents milling around tee-ball practice. Parents with cellphones. Somebody had to have seen something.

I don't think Dad hurt Max. Even though he's violent and has a quick temper, he's not evil.

But what if something did happen? What if Dad knows something he isn't telling me?

I cross the living room. I open the basement door with a click.

Dad stays asleep. Relief blooming in my chest, I slip around the door and close it behind me.

I keep my hand on the rough wall as I walk down the stairs, aware of every creak under my feet. The wood is splintered from years of use. The stairs are steep. As I step onto the concrete, my feet land in a coating of dirt. A musty smell hits my nose. Damp air clogs my lungs and makes me cough. I feel around for the light switch. In the dark, every jar and box takes on a different meaning. Something scary. Something out to get me.

I'm being stupid. Monsters aren't real. Not monsters like that, anyway.

I glance over my shoulder at the closed basement door and hope Dad doesn't wake up. My hand finds the switch. The naked lightbulb flickers to life.

The basement looks different from how I remember it. Its shelves used to hold food, laundry detergent, and other household items, but all the shelves are gone now. A bookcase and a tall refrigerator sandwich Dad's desk. There are two photos taped to the fridge—one is our Christmas card from last year, and the other is a picture of Dad and his brother Jim holding a trout when they couldn't have been older than twenty. Jim hung himself when I was twelve. I don't know the whole story because Dad never talks about it, but I know from Mom that Dad blames himself for it.

On the desk is a stack of manila folders and an old computer plugged into the wall. Dad doesn't let me have a phone, and I can't have my own laptop either. The only computers in the house are the family desktop in the living room, which I use to do my homework, and this one.

I wiggle the mouse. The monitor asks me for a password. I don't know what his password could be, and I'm scared of getting it wrong in case it locks the computer long enough for Dad to figure out somebody was down here. Max hasn't been missing long enough for Dad to have a paper file down here. I don't think he's been in the basement since this afternoon.

Since I'm already here, I still want to have a look around. I reach over a cluster of empty beer cans to pick up a manilla folder. It's an arrest report for a man charged with a DUI six months ago. Another folder catches my eye. Careful not to knock anything over, I pick it up. It's dated to a month ago. Printed above the date is the name Poppy Rooney.

Poppy Rooney. That's the name of the missing girl.

I open the folder. At the top, there's a summary of what

happened to her. She got off the school bus at approximately 3:15 p.m. but never made it home. A witness saw her get off the bus. Edward Metty. I lower myself onto Dad's chair. Lieutenant Vaughn disregarded Metty's testimony because of his contradicting descriptions of what he'd seen.

I hold the file up to the light and start to read.

Edward METTY saw Poppy get off the bus and wait in front of 9 BAKER RD for approximately 10 minutes before a young man picked her up in his car. METTY stated she went willingly. METTY's daughter was with him at the time and saw nothing.

Poppy's school photo is clipped to the inside of the folder. I trace my finger over the girl's smiling face. Blond braids frame a face full of freckles. She's grinning through braces that are trying to hold back too many top teeth. Something warms in my chest. Her smile looks as if she has gathered up all the beautiful things in this world and is sending them back out to whoever would stop to look at her.

A floorboard creaks over my head. I drop the folder. Rodney Jackson's voice cuts off mid-sentence, and I throw myself across the room to shut off the light. Darkness falls over me.

I listen for Dad's footsteps. Everything is still. I cup my hands over my nose and mouth to keep myself from breathing too loudly.

The basement door opens.

I drop behind a cardboard box under the stairs. My knees crash into the dirty concrete, and I clamp my teeth onto my lip to prevent myself from crying out. Each stair bends under Dad's weight. He turns on the light. I lower myself closer to the ground. A spider twitches, upside down under my nose. I must have crushed it with my knee. Out of mercy, I flatten it with my thumb.

I can't breathe. I can't move. I imagine Dad's nostrils flaring as he stalks through the office. Pausing. Sniffing the air.

Something snaps under Dad's boot. He's close to me now. I press my forehead into the ground and pray he doesn't see me.

Dad turns off the light and climbs the stairs, slamming the

door behind him. I listen to him stomp across the wood in his heavy boots, grab his keys, and close the front door. A sigh slips through my lips. I fall onto my side and hug my knees. He left to rejoin the search. He's not going to find me.

Once my breathing slows, I grab Poppy Rooney's case file, run upstairs to my room, and sob into my pillow.

Detective-Lieutenant Scott Finnegan: Can you tell me about Ernest Oleson's relationship with his children?

Sandra O'Leary: My cat got out once. Scampered up a tree and refused to come down. I called the police. I didn't know what to do, but Ernest answered the call. He had Max along with him that day. The boy sat in the grass as Ernest climbed the tree to get my Missy back.

Jaqueline Orr: It's a tragedy, and I still pray that Max gets home safe. I have nothing more to say on the matter.

Mrs. Rosenfarb: I can't say I'd seen them interact more than my other second graders. Max was a quiet kid. I'm sorry—*is* a quiet kid. I mean, you know how kids are. I knew he was getting picked on. I had a conversation with Ernest and Heidi about it. Quite frankly, Ernest seemed more worried than she did, which isn't usually the case. It's usually the mothers.

Robert Boeshart: He's a good guy and a decent parent. Yeah, he was late to pick the kid up that day, but he never did nothing to raise any eyebrows.

Nicole Yoo: I've never seen a man be more loving with his children. I remember one time, when they were small, my husband and I were at their house for the Fourth of July. Fourth of July at the Olesons' was a blast. We go every year. One year, Ernest did this Johnny Cash impression that wasn't half-bad, and oh how it made the children laugh. *Burning ring of fire.* He was singing right there at the barbecue. He held the grilling tongs in his teeth and did the do-si-do. He was laughing. Heck, we were all laughing. He was so proud of his kids. Especially Max. He showed my husband photos at all our dinners.

Mark Yoo: Johnny Cash impression? Yeah, I remember him doing that.

Fred Riddle: This has nothing to do with the Olesons. Pedophiles are taking the children. There was a girl in Grafton. Body turned up in a ditch three days after she disappeared, and you know what? She'd been raped. The DNA was all over. There ain't nothing some guys won't do.

Adonica Kordelski: Oh, you can't possibly believe Ernest could have anything to do with this. I've worked for the man for twenty years. Ernest wouldn't hurt a fly.

Detective-Sergeant Kyle Babin: Ernest Oleson has an alibi, Scott. Kershner has him at Duncan's. Why are we still talking about this?

5

SHILOH

I tap my bare foot against the living room carpet as Mom walks back in with a mug in each hand. She hands one to Detective Babin.

He takes it with a smile. "Thank you, Heidi."

Mom gives the other to Detective Finnegan. Both men are sitting in the armchairs to the side of the fireplace. Finnegan adjusts himself on the La-Z-Boy, springs creaking under his weight. Dad never lets anyone sit in that chair, but he hasn't said a word to Finnegan. Given the circumstances, Dad will let Finnegan do pretty much whatever he wants.

In these cases, statistically, it's someone close to the child who's involved. That's what Dad told us this morning. Babin and Finnegan are going to ask us a few questions, but that doesn't mean we're in trouble. They know none of us would hurt Max.

I remember Dad smashing Max's head into the wall. The memory rises in my throat like sour bile.

Mom sits beside me, resting her frail palms over her knees. She looks sadder. Even since yesterday. I didn't sleep at all last night. As soon as there was even a sliver of light, I pulled myself out of bed to find Mom and Dad both awake. We drove to Merwin Park and walked down every side street, through the woods, along the winding road beside the Monroe's farm, weeding through the brush to try to find a scrap of clothing, a shoe—anything. When we returned to the house, Babin and Finnegan were already parked outside. I wondered if they had bad news, and it was like all the life drained from my body.

But they just needed to talk to us. I know they need to talk to the family, but I didn't expect it would make me feel so dirty. Like they think I could have done something.

"We just want to have a conversation," Detective Babin says, "to understand the timeline we're working with, here."

Finnegan glares at me through beady eyes. I cross my arms over my chest to try to push down how uncomfortable I feel.

Dad tells them his timeline. Just after noon, he arrived at Duncan's to watch the Buckeyes. He sat there, ordered a drink, you know how it goes, until I called him around two to remind him Max needed to be picked up. He drove straight to the park. By the time Dad arrived at ten-past, Boeshart was standing in the parking lot waiting for him to tell him that Max was gone.

Finnegan and Babin scribble it all down. They ask Dad whether the Buckeyes played a good game. I keep my jaw clamped shut, but inside I want to scream.

They don't ask why Dad was forty-five minutes late. They don't comment on how irresponsible that was.

"You left earlier than you expected," Babin says. "I take it you were clear, you know, to get behind the wheel?"

Dad raises his brow. I guess he's their boss, so this line of questioning is a little weird.

"Absolutely," he lies through his teeth. I smelled the booze on his breath. "You know me, Kyle. I love my kids. I'd never do anything to put them in danger."

Babin nods and falls quiet. Is that it? That's all they're going to ask him? I'm not saying I think Dad did anything, but they don't know that. I hope they go harder on the others they interview.

They turn their attention to Mom. What was she doing this whole time?

"I was asleep," she mumbles.

"We had a bit of a late night, the night before," Dad adds, which is true. Mom stayed up late cleaning up the Legos Dad dumped onto the floor in a fit of anger that the house was never clean. "The two of us … we got into a bit of a disagreement. Stayed awake to talk about it."

They ask where I was. Dad tells them I was at work until five o'clock, and that they can contact my manager to confirm. Before Babin and Finnegan arrived, Dad told me not to talk. I asked him why. It's not like I have anything to hide, but it's dawning on me that the reason he wants me to keep my mouth shut is so that I don't say anything about him. I wouldn't do that. If I'd wanted people to know what he's done to me, I would've already told someone. No. I don't want anyone to know because I'm scared that if they do take Max and me away, they'll separate us. In foster care, I wouldn't know where he was. I can't protect him if I'm not with him.

I don't want Babin and Finnegan finding out about any of that, but judging by the easy questions those brick heads have asked Dad so far, they won't find anything.

On their way out, Babin shakes Dad's hand. "We're talking to every parent who was there at pickup, to figure whether someone saw something. If they'll let us, we're going to talk to the kids."

"One parent saw a man they didn't recognize," Finnegan says.

"They didn't remember any distinguishing features, only that his sweater was black," Babin says. "One of those North Face types. Kind of odd because it was a warm day." He claps Dad on the shoulder. "I'll give you more this afternoon."

With that, they leave. I spot a news van parked across the

street. Seeing movement, the reporter gets out of the car, but Dad shuts the door before she can make it to our lawn.

He lets out a sharp sigh. "Nobody respects people's goddamn privacy anymore."

Mom lays a hand on my back. I push her arm away and walk back to my room, where I slam the door behind me and crawl under my sheets.

Someone saw a suspicious man at the park. Most of the parents know each other. If there was someone there whom they didn't recognize, he probably wasn't one of the parents.

I glance over at my closet, where I stashed the folder with the information about Poppy Rooney last night. I need to put it back soon. Dad might want to check for coincidences or links himself, and I don't want him to know it's missing. I sat in the closet last night poring over every word, balancing the folder on my knees with a flashlight propped up on my shoulder. The police already talked to the bus driver, Poppy's mother, her classmates, teachers, and friends. Someone working at the crop genetics plant by their house saw her walking to the bus that morning during his smoke break. There's a photograph of Poppy's stepfather, but under it someone had written that the photo had been taken by a security camera at a gas station in Utica, which means that he couldn't have been anywhere close when Poppy got off her bus. Someone had also written: "Sexual motive— pedophile?" on a separate page, but it didn't seem to connect to her stepfather.

It was clear they were trying to narrow down a list of people who could have done it, but they didn't have much to go on. The only person who offered any sort of clear picture of what happened to Poppy after getting off the bus was Edward Metty.

In one report, he said Poppy got into a truck. In another report, he said she got into a car. He said a man was driving, then he said a woman was driving. In every report, Poppy gets into some kind of vehicle.

I know this doesn't say much, but if Poppy did get into a car with someone, she must have known them, or at least trusted them enough to get into their car—unless they were a cop, I guess, but cop cars are unique and Edward Metty might have at least mentioned that once.

Poppy only disappeared a month ago. In one of Edward Metty's reports, a man drove Poppy away. She and Max both disappeared in the middle of the afternoon, in towns right next to each other.

Could the suspicious man at tee-ball practice have taken Poppy too?

I go get the folder. The word pedophile swims in front of my eyes. I rub them to dispel it.

I need to tell Dad about this. I don't think Babin and Finnegan are considering it, but there's no way to explain how I know about Edward Metty without admitting that I snuck down to his office. I clench and unclench my fist. He's going to be so mad, but if the same guy who took Poppy also took Max, Dad can use parts of what Edward Metty said to figure out what this guy looks like and ask the parents at practice if it was the same guy they saw.

It's stupid. Is it stupid? Dad's going to think I'm stupid.

I picture Max somewhere dark, where dirt and shadows mix with the tears running down his cheeks. I can't sit here doing nothing while he's out there somewhere in pain. I'm his big sister, and I'm going to find him.

I need to rehearse what I'm going to say. In fits of anger, Dad has shoved report cards into my hands and told me I'm not smart enough to amount to anything. Mom told me he didn't mean it, but I remember the look in his eyes and know she was wrong. Dad might have been drunk, but he believed it.

I know Dad has his own issues, but I also know that deep down, he's right. I do get bad grades. But I have Max, and if all I do right is keep him safe, then I'd say my life is well spent.

I have to find him.

After I've practiced what I'm going to say a few times in the mirror, I walk out into the kitchen. "Dad?"

Mom is on the couch and cranes her neck back to look at me. "Your father isn't here."

Oh. "Did he go to work?"

Mom gives a swift nod and returns her attention to the reporter on television.

Crap. I wanted to talk to him now, before we go back out to search. "When is he getting home?"

"After dinner," Mom says. "Or later, maybe."

I can't wait that long. I need to talk to him now. Going back into my room and grabbing my bag, I tell Mom I'm going to see Miles.

"Your boyfriend Miles?" she asks. I nod, although I don't know what other Miles she could be referring to. "All right, just be back by two. For the search party."

"I will," I tell her.

"Promise?"

Of course I'm going to come home to search for Max. I don't know why I have to promise—except that Mom has pills the doctor prescribes to her, and she doesn't take them often, but when she does, it's like she's on another planet. She's probably on some now, given the circumstances.

"I promise," I say, and walk out the door.

Because Bethany is so small, the Sheriff's Office is in Mount Keenan, which is a twenty-minute bus ride away.

I pull out my iPod and listen to the opening from Les Misérables sputter to life through my headphones. I close my eyes as the bus heads out on Route 13. I've never actually seen Les Misérables, but the story is told in song form, so listening to the soundtrack all the way through is almost as good. I don't know why I love this album so much. Maybe it's because all the characters in Les Misérables, from the prostitutes to the revolutionary boys, find hope in their suffering. Cosette dreams of castles while sweeping the floors. Even when Enjolras didn't know if the city would rise to join him in his fight, he and the schoolboys built the barricade anyway. I don't know if I could sacrifice my life for such an uncertain cause. Sometimes, I worry that I'm not brave enough.

Jean Valjean found his redemption in God. I could never do that because going to church reminds me too much of Dad. He used to pray with me before bed. Every night, he'd clasp my hands inside his, and I waited to hear what he would say so that I could repeat it. I wanted to be like him so badly back then. A big person. A brave person. Someone who protects people.

With a hiss of its brakes, the bus stops. I walk down the steps and am immediately greeted by a cold wind. It blows my hair into my face, so I pull the hood of my jacket over my head.

Cars speed down the main road. I turn up the volume in my headphones and walk over the moss, band-aids, and crinkled cigarette butts on the sidewalk. Strangers pass me on the road, glaring at me from under the brims of their hats.

I stop in front of the Sheriff's Department and stare up at the ugly building. It looks like it was made of shoeboxes. Some stacked on top of each other and some lying flat. The outside wall is made of worn red bricks, and the windows are small. In the glare of the sun, I can't see through them, but I know my dad's in there somewhere. Black-and-gold squad cars are parked in the driveway. They look like polished pill bugs with sun glinting off their exoskeletons.

Pulling my headphones down around my neck, I push open the door and walk up to the front desk where Adonica, the bleary-eyed secretary, sits behind a pane of glass.

I rub the snot dripping from my nose with the back of my hand. "I'm here to see my dad."

Adonica raises her head. She peers at me with delayed recognition.

"Oh, you're one of Ernest's little ones! Gee, hon, I'm so sorry to hear about your brother," she says.

I try not to scowl. I come to Dad's office once a year in December for the holiday party that Dad always drags us to. I hate it. At least I did when Max was a baby because I always ended up standing by myself holding him as Mom took long sips of whatever alcoholic beverage Adonica had contributed to the potluck. The drink is different every year, but Mom's enthusiasm for it stays the same, just like the tense car rides home and Dad's building frustration with the way Mom conducted herself at the party. The ultimate expression of that frustration usually leads to me keeping Max in my room all night, sitting on the floor and letting him grab my toy horses with his sticky hands and bang them on the floor because it's the only way to make him stop crying.

When Max got older, the two of us stuffed our cheeks with Christmas cookies and snuck into the office supply closet to make chains of paper clips and superhero capes out of printer paper.

Adonica points a pink nail at the candy bowl on the counter. "Care for a butterscotch?"

"No."

"They have healing properties, you know. I shipped them here from Peru. The website said they soothe your throat." She touches her throat as if I don't know what a throat is.

"I'm good."

"Please, take a butterscotch."

The longer I stare at her, the more I start to realize she might not let me see Dad if I don't take a butterscotch, so with careful fingers I pick one out of the bowl. I peel off the crinkled plastic and pop the yellow disc into my mouth.

Adonica smiles. "Aren't they divine? I'll call your daddy and have him come get you."

I turn the butterscotch over my tongue as I sit down in a chair to wait. In a couple of minutes, Dad opens the door.

"Hey, kid," he says, walking over and pulling me into a hug. I hug him back stiffly. Over his shoulder, two women wearing matching jackets the color of blue pen ink walk by Adonica's desk. One of them meets my eyes. Her stare is piercing. Only when they walk out do I notice the letters on their backs.

FBI.

I didn't know the FBI was here. Thank God Babin and Finnegan aren't the only ones looking for Max.

Dad lets go of me. "I didn't know you were coming in today."

"I need to talk to you," I say.

"'Kay." He squeezes my shoulder and snatches a butterscotch from the bowl. I follow him into the bullpen.

Because York County is small and barely any crime happens outside of Mount Keenan, there are only fifteen officers on the force. I've known most of them pretty much all my life. There's the famous Babin, who was at the house earlier and looks like the second knuckle of someone's thumb. If country fried steak were a person, it would be Finnegan. He looks like he's made mostly of gristle. Even his face. Brandon, the youngest, goes by his first name, and is not all that interesting. I have yet to have a conversation with him that isn't about Buffalo Wild Wings. Each man is huge. Each man is dull. Each man could snap my neck with a quick squeeze of his hand.

Then there's Connie. Cornelia Vaughn is York County's only female detective, and her desk appears to glow like a moth lamp among the others. I spot her wild red ringlets, wrestled into a bun at the base of her neck. Connie doesn't have kids of her own, but she always talks to Max and me at holiday parties.

She's cool. I like her. I don't know her all that well, but she's one of those people you feel like you've known for a long time when you haven't. She's just friendly and confident.

She sees me. Her mouth falls open, and she stands up from her desk so fast that a red ringlet falls out of her bun.

"Oh, honey." Connie barrels up to me and hugs me, trapping my arms on both sides of my body. I'm not expecting the touch, so I stiffen but relax just as quickly. It's Connie. She's one of the good guys.

She lets me go and smacks Dad on the arm. "Ernest, you rat. Why didn't you tell me Shiloh was coming in today?"

Dad smiles. "I didn't know it myself."

I look over at Connie's desk. Steam billows out of a raccoon mug resting beside a framed photograph of Connie pressing her cheek against a woman who could be her clone. They have the same crazy hair.

"I was going to stop by and see you today," Connie tells me. "I couldn't believe it when I heard. I didn't stop crying all of last night. How are you holding up?"

I search for a word to describe how I'm feeling, but I can't find one. I don't want to overshare, so I settle on, "Fine."

Connie shoots me a look that says yeah, right. "I'm here for you if you need to talk about anything. Your dad can give you my number."

"That I can," Dad says.

A smile stretches over Connie's wide mouth. I spot a piece of lettuce jammed into her gums. "Call me anytime."

I don't know her well enough to call her, but I thank her anyway and follow Dad into his office.

Dad sits down in his tall chair. He stretches his arms out before bracing them behind his head. Beside his keyboard sits an empty lowball glass. Drops of condensation cling to the outside, running down and wetting the cork coaster.

"What do you want, Shiloh?" he says, in a much deeper voice now that we're alone.

I twist the rubber bracelet Max gave me around my wrist. "I think you should go interview Edward Metty again." I'm honestly surprised at how easily that came out.

Dad quirks up an eyebrow. "How the hell do you know about Edward Metty?" With slow fingers, I pull Poppy's case file out of my backpack. Dad's face darkens. "Where did you get that?" His eyes widen. "The basement. Jesus, Shiloh, how many times have I told you not to go down there?"

"I know he's a little confused—"

"Guy has Alzheimer's."

"Alzheimer's, yes. But he gets some things right." I turn to the page with the summary of Edward Metty's interview, and I show Dad. "There, you see? Every time Edward says someone picks up Poppy, he says she gets into the car willingly."

"Metty doesn't know a truck from a station wagon."

"I know he mixes up some details," I say, "but the part about her going willingly never changes. Poppy trusted the person who kidnapped her. That could give us some clue as to who took Max."

"We don't know that."

"Poppy's disappearance happened seven miles away from Max's. They could be connected."

"You're quite the detective, aren't you?" Dad says. It's not a compliment. "Edward Metty doesn't know squat."

"But—"

"Even if they are connected, Metty won't lead us to Poppy. He's got no good information."

"He saw Poppy get into the car."

"Shiloh," Dad warns.

"I could talk to him for you." My voice is getting louder. "You wouldn't have to do anything—"

Dad swipes his arm across his desk. The lowball glass and his stack of paper files clatter onto the floor. I freeze. Dad stares at the scattered papers for a couple of seconds before sinking back into his chair, hanging his head, and pinching the bridge of his nose.

"Do me a favor, Shiloh, yeah? Shut up. Just shut up."

I wipe the sweat beading on my forehead. "But I can help."

Dad raises his head. His eyes are beady, and I can feel my chest deflate like a balloon someone released before they had finished blowing it up. "You can't do anything. Just focus on helping your mother and let me do my goddamn job."

Curled over his desk like that, Dad looks helpless. He might be acting all confident, but he has no idea what he's doing.

He slams both hands palms down on the table. "Go home, Shiloh. Get the hell out of my office."

Swallowing hard, I shove the case file into my backpack and storm out of his office. Dad's voice bounces around my head as I push through the front doors and into the parking lot.

Shut up. Just shut up.

You can't do anything.

I walk faster from the ugly shoebox monstrosity Dad works in. I walk faster from his ugly shoebox mind. I'm used to him saying I'm stupid, but I thought … I don't know. I thought that maybe this time it would be different.

Of course it isn't different. Dad only cares about himself and his control.

But this is bigger than him. This is about Max. All that matters is finding Max, and none of it is about this power stuff Dad is so obsessed with. I didn't ask for much. Only to talk to one guy. I didn't question his authority or say that he was dumb. I just made a suggestion. Who cares if I'm wrong? Going to talk to Edward Metty has to be worth trying.

When I reach the bus stop, I realize something and pull my backpack straps tighter over my shoulders.

Dad is not the only person who can talk to Edward Metty. I could go.

Going to talk to an old man alone isn't dangerous. What's he going to do? Spit on me?

Heart pounding, I run into the closest Panera. Soft background music plays as I sink into an aluminum chair and pull out the case file. I touch the top of the page. There. There's Edward Metty's address. I take my iPod out of my bag and connect to Panera's Wi-Fi before looking up the address in Maps. I zoom in. He doesn't live that far from here. A forty-five-minute walk. Tops.

I can't go now. I promised Mom I'd be home for the search party, and if I didn't come home, she'd panic and tell Dad. I need to be careful. Besides, I don't know anything about Edward Metty, apart from where he lives. I don't even know what I'm going to say to him.

I need to make a plan.

———

Dad joins the search party after a few hours because he had some things to finish up at the office. When he arrives, he walks right up to me and puts his arm around my shoulders.

"I'm sorry for what I said to you," he says, softly enough that I doubt the man behind us can hear. "It was out of line."

Of all the things he's said to me over the years, what he said today wasn't that bad. "It's fine."

He stops walking and spins me around to look at him. Other members of the search party brush past us. I'll bet they're thinking I'm having some sort of meltdown, and Dad's comforting me.

"I just want to protect you, Scooter Girl," Dad says. "We don't know who took Max, but it could be someone dangerous. If you got involved and something happened to you, I could not live with myself."

I'm just going to talk with an old guy. It's not that big a deal. Actually, now that I'm thinking about it, it is a big deal. If I get something out of Edward Metty, I'm going to follow up with it. I'm not going to stop looking. Not until Max is home.

Dad is standing so close to me that I'm uncomfortable, but I don't want to anger him by moving.

"I need you to promise me something," he says.

"Okay."

"Promise me you'll focus on helping your mother," he says. "If we're dealing with a dangerous criminal, I don't want you anywhere near him. You're going to leave that up to me, you understand?"

I swallow, even though my throat is dry. The part of me that's still twelve years old wants to tell him that I do understand. That I trust him enough to handle this. That I'll stay out of his way if it stops him from pouring himself a Scotch in the early afternoon or from hurling the glass past my head and leaving me wondering whether he meant for it to hit me. If I was twelve, all I'd want is for him to love me, but you don't throw glasses at the people you love, or tell them they aren't capable of anything.

What you do for the people you love is find them when they're missing. Even if it means lying to people who scare you.

"Please, Shiloh," Dad says. "Let me handle this."

"Okay," I lie.

"Good." He squeezes my shoulder. "I'm going to fix this. I'm going to find Max and bring him home if it's the last thing I do."

As we run to catch up to the search party, I think, *Me too.*

6

FRANCESCA

I am determined to find this man. Although I am not entirely sure how to do so, I am determined to try.

He is the first person I have ever heard of who has the ability to see the dead. He cannot be from Bethany, as everybody in town is aware of my lighting Mr. Haggarty on fire. I would hope that if there were somebody else like me who had heard the story, they would have approached me by now.

This man must be either new to town or simply passing through. However, he seemed to have come to the cemetery searching for somebody, and as he did not find them, I highly doubt he has left yet.

Nearly everybody in the cemetery provides a different description of the man. Esther says he had ears the size of dinner plates, which I explain to her is not possible, as it would make his head too heavy. Mrs. Lewis mentions she saw satin gloves that extended to his elbows. As far as I can tell, the children had the closest look at him, so I pay closer attention to their descriptions. Gus claims he had teeth that were sharpened into points. Charlie says Gus is lying, but Gus swears it's true. Henry does not speak to me, which does not come as a surprise. Natalie tells me the bitch drove a pickup truck and provides the most peculiar detail of all—he was wearing a long trench coat the color of clover that reached all the way down to his ankles.

"It was kind of hard to tell, you know, because it was night and everything, but yeah," Natalie says. "It was ugly."

I have never seen a man wearing a coat so brightly colored. I would have surely noticed that if I had seen him walking around town, especially if he was wearing satin gloves. However, if his gloves reached all the way up to his elbows like Mrs. Lewis said, he would have had to be wearing them outside his coat sleeves, which would have looked quite odd. I cannot simply wait around, hoping he will happen to wander by. I must actively search for him.

If he is a traveler, a gas station would be a good place to start.

There is only one gas station in Bethany and, luckily, it is close to the cemetery. I tell Mrs. Lewis I am going to inquire about the man. Natalie eavesdrops and invites herself along.

"I'm telling you, Francesca," Natalie says. "This dude's a crazy bitch."

"You do not know that." In fact, nothing this man did would suggest he is malevolent.

"He bruised Henry's arm."

Oh. I had forgotten about that.

It could have been an accident. If he had purposefully smashed poor Henry's face against a tree, that would be a different story. I get bruises on my arms from even the slightest bumps. The human body is quite mysterious.

Natalie winds around a telephone pole and slips between my legs as I walk. I can pass through her, but I feel as though she might trip me.

"Please be careful," I say.

"I can't wait for you to find this bitch," she replies. "So we can kill him."

I gape at her. I do not understand where her comment came

from. I never mentioned killing the man. In fact, that is not my intention at all. "I simply plan to speak with him."

"Yeah, then we kill him." A wide, toothy grin stretches across Natalie's mouth. "I'm going to distract him, and you're going to come up behind him and say, 'This one's for Henry!' and snap his freaking neck."

Natalie twists her arms around. I look away. I do not want to imagine harming the man. I do not know anything about him, and he might be my first friend in this town who is actually alive.

"You can kick him like this." Natalie kicks the air in front of her, somewhere around stomach height. "And punch him like this." She carries on until we reach the gas station, where I have to start pretending she is not there.

The gas station is small. There is a woman filling up her car. One hand is resting on her hip and the other curls around the gas dispenser as she fills up a shapeless SUV. I do not know who the woman is, but her eyes follow me from underneath her cloth visor as Natalie and I enter the building.

A tiny silver bell tinkles as the door closes slowly behind us. It is much colder in here than it was outside, and I wrap my arms around my stomach for warmth. It appears that Natalie and I are alone in here, with the exception of a young man with patchy facial hair sitting on a stool behind the checkout counter, engrossed in his cell phone. Orange curls spring out from under his camouflage cap.

I offer a wave. "Hello. How are you today?"

The young man glances up. "Oh, hi. I'm good. Can I help you?"

I move closer to read his nametag. It reads 'Eric.' "Yes, Eric," I say. "I am here to inquire if you remember seeing a mysterious man traveling through here sometime in the last several days."

In my periphery, Natalie leans down to inspect the rows of candy bars. It occurs to me that she does not get away from the cemetery often. Seeing this ordinary reminder of the time she was alive must be exciting for her, or perhaps frustrating as she cannot physically eat any of the candy in front of her.

Natalie tries to fit her mouth over a Hershey's bar and bites straight through it. She snorts in amusement.

I glance back up at Eric. He looks me up and down as if he is trying to figure out where he knows me from.

"Quite a few people come through here," he eventually says. "I don't remember."

"This man has a particular look to him," I say. "He may have been wearing a long, green trench coat."

"Sorry." Eric shakes his head and turns his mouth down at the corners. "Can't help you."

"Hey, Francesca!" Natalie calls from behind me. I know I should not look, but I cannot stop myself. I glance over my shoulder to see Natalie inside one of the refrigerators, pressed between the bottles of vitamin water and the door. Her face squishes against the glass. "I can fit in here now, see?"

I would like Eric to help me, so I do not want him to think I am strange. I force myself to ignore her and refocus my attention on Eric.

"Please. It is extremely important that you try to remember."

Natalie is beside me again. "Ask if he remembers a guy driving a truck."

That is not a bad idea. "Do you recall seeing a man driving a truck?"

"Everybody 'round here drives a truck."

"You should ask Eric how he thinks we should kill the bitch." Natalie leaps over the counter and whirls around Eric's hair, as if she's trying to make it blow. "Ask if he likes my neck snapping idea."

I pinch my temples. Natalie is jumbling my thoughts. "Please, be quiet," I tell her.

Eric scratches the corner of his mouth. "I didn't say nothing."

"I'm sorry." Focus, Francesca. Please do not make a fool of yourself. "The man I am looking for was wearing a green trench coat. I believe he might have stopped by sometime this week to fill his truck with gasoline."

Natalie pokes her head through Eric's torso and sticks out her tongue. I yelp in surprise.

"I like my neck snapping idea." Natalie grins as if she does not understand how distracting she is being. "You aren't that strong, so you'll have to kill the bitch real quick."

"Stop it." I try to keep my voice steady. "Please, Eric, it is really important that you help me."

Eric's expression changes. He gestures to me with his pointer finger.

"Hang on," he says. "You're Richie Russo's sister. Frankie the Firestarter."

Uh oh. Eric stands up from the stool, immediately becoming taller than me. He is lean and bony, peering down at me like an ostrich, tilting his head to the side and drawing it back as if he is going to peck me with his beak. I struggle to find the words to respond. He seems to take my lack of response as a response of sorts, causing a laugh to burst out of him.

"I'm right, aren't I? That's who you are." Eric twists around. "Carl, get out of the can. Cranky Frankie wants to know if we've seen a ghost come through here."

"He is not a ghost. He is alive," I say, but Eric is laughing too hard to listen.

A larger man joins Eric, buttoning up his pants. I feel exposed under their eyes, like they can see through my clothes.

"We haven't seen a man come here. Want to know why?" Eric slaps his knee. "Because ghosts don't exist."

I usher Natalie to my side. She rushes over, hiding behind me.

"Thank you for your time," I say, and hurry outside.

I can still hear them laughing after the door closes. I fill my lungs with the outdoor air and hold my breath for a second or two. Eric's reaction should not come as a surprise. I should have known better than to ask for help when everyone only sees me as whatever nickname they prefer and always will. Pressure pushes against the backs of my eyeballs. I wish this feeling would go away.

I wonder how Eric knows Richie. I have yet to encounter any friend of Richie who is kind.

As I weave between the gas station kiosks, Natalie winds around my legs. A chill runs up my spine.

"I'm sorry." Natalie blinks up at me. "I know I was annoying. I was just excited to be somewhere else."

She had been a tiny bit annoying, but I say, "You did nothing wrong."

I am back where I started. If I cannot locate the man by asking for help, I will need to coax him out of hiding on my own.

7

SHILOH

I sit up in bed, grasping the blanket with sweaty palms.

Nothing's there. I flip on the light and rub my eyes as they adjust to how bright it is. I'm in my room. There's no one here. No one is trying to kill me.

No Max.

I saw him in my dream, huddling on the dirt-caked floor in the back seat of a car. I smashed my hands on the closed window. His hair was drenched with sweat. His face was streaked with blood.

It wasn't real. But I don't know that.

I swing my legs off the bed. The soles of my feet stick to the wood as I cross the hallway into Max's room. Everything is exactly where it was that morning. His dirty clothes are on the floor. His plastic triceratops is on his nightstand, where he likes it. I can almost smell how empty it feels.

His stuffed teddy bear sits by his pillow, over the crinkled comforter I pulled half-tight and didn't tuck in because we were in a rush. Teddy's head is cocked to one side. I crawl over the footboard and hug Teddy to my chest, curling up around him and burying my nose into his fur. The smell of Max hits me immediately, like I'm holding him to me with my face in his hair.

"I'm going to find you," I say, even though he can't hear me. "I promise, I'm going to bring you home."

I hope Edward Metty tells me something useful. The fear of returning empty-handed keeps me awake until the first hint of sunlight comes in through the shutters.

I need to focus today. I need to be sharp and methodical if I'm going to get anything useful out of Edward, and to do that, I'm going to have to get rid of all this fog clogging my brain.

As soon as I walk into school, everyone stops talking. Elbows are nudged. Smiles wane. I side-eye Brittany Krazinski, who has replaced her usual judgmental eyebrow tilt with a pitying frown as I open my locker. I hate how much it bothers me. Brittany doesn't even know me. I think we talked once in sixth grade and that's it.

But it's not just her. It's everyone, peering at me, whispering about me. For once, I'm glad when class starts, and Mr. Clarke's optimistic, please-engage-with-me tone drowns it out.

In study hall, I research Alzheimer's disease using the school computers. The first article I read just talks about the disease, but I find another post on a forum written by someone whose mother had Alzheimer's. The mother used to have a cat named Boots, that she adored, and no matter how much else she'd forget, seeing Boots would always make her happy. Even when Boots died and they got another cat, the mother still called it Boots.

I guess I could make Edward comfortable by talking about the things he likes. I run a search on him. By the looks of it, he's had a pretty boring life. All I can find on him is a xeroxed Bethany Citizen article from 1977 about a state fair where he won two blue ribbons for his rabbits. There's a picture of him smiling, holding one of the rabbits. Rolls of fat bulge off the rabbit's face and neck. Or maybe rolls of fur. It's hard to tell.

Maybe I should buy a rabbit for him, like the girl in the forum post bought a cat for her mom. The side of my mouth quirks up. No. That girl getting a cat for her mom was sweet. Getting a rabbit for a stranger would be weird.

As soon as the final bell rings, I head to the newsroom to find Miles.

The door closes behind me. My eyes dart around the computer lab. Miles always comes here after his last period because he's the editor of our school paper. Every day, he stays after school for hours because he needs to oversee every word, photo, and illustration that goes into every story. I don't understand why he likes it so much, but he gets really excited talking about it, so to each their own, I guess. I spot him putting his messenger bag down and I weave around a couple of desks to reach him. He doesn't notice me at first, so I pull one of his headphones out of his ears.

He jumps. "S-Shiloh, you s-scared me." Sometimes he stutters when he gets nervous, like his mind is working too quickly for his mouth to keep up with. It's pretty cute.

"I need your help."

Miles is a tall, gangly boy with light brown skin and too many elbows and knees. His curls are gelled neatly out of his face and his curious eyes are magnified through the lenses of his thin, wire-framed glasses.

He kisses me on the cheek. "What can I do for you?"

I've been dating Miles for around three weeks now, ever since he asked me to be his girlfriend after we finished watching The Empire Strikes Back. We ate Twizzlers and he talked through the entire movie. When he kissed me good night, his lips tasted like strawberries. I had never felt so comfortable and safe in my entire life.

I don't know how he's going to respond to this, but I ask anyway. "Do you want to come to Mount Keenan with me?"

Miles looks confused. "Why?"

"Remember Poppy Rooney, the girl who went missing last month?" I ask, and he nods. "I did some digging, and I think whoever took Poppy also took Max, so I want to talk to the person who last saw her in Mount Keenan."

Miles's smile disappears. His eyebrows knit and he falls into a chair, which rolls back into a desk. "Excuse me, what?"

"I'm going to Mount Keenan because—"

"No, no, no. I got that part. It's a bad idea."

Oh. "Why?"

"B-because it's dangerous. You d-don't know who took Max. It could be someone really bad. Someone who could hurt you."

"I'm just going to talk to an old dude with Alzheimer's. How dangerous could that be?"

"I'm just saying you shouldn't go after a criminal yourself because what if they skin you alive or something?"

I try not to picture it, but a sick feeling lodges in the pit of my stomach. "Are you saying Max is going to be skinned alive?"

Miles's eyes shoot open. "What? No. Of course not. I'm just …" His voice trails off as reaches out to take my hand. I pull it away. "I d-don't w-want you to get hurt."

"I can handle myself."

"Isn't this, like, literally your dad's job?"

Miles doesn't know about the drinking or the abuse or the fact that Dad doesn't have a single clue about what happened to Max. If the police find Max, it won't be because of Dad. And they're completely ignoring Metty. "My dad has no idea what he's doing."

"Have the police already talked to this guy?"

"Technically, yes, but they scared him."

"Shiloh—"

Before he can complete his thought, I pull out a stapled copy of the 1977 article on rabbits.

Miles stares at it. "Have you taken a sudden interest in rabbits?"

I roll my eyes. "Edward Metty's rabbits won first place at the Ohio State Fair ten years in a row. Can you believe that? For ten years, he had the best rabbits in the entire state."

Miles's expression is blank. I wait for his brain to catch up, but it doesn't, so I keep talking.

"The detectives who talked to him were rough with him. No

wonder he got flustered. If I talk to him about rabbits, then maybe he'll be more comfortable around me, and I can get better information out of him."

Miles frowns. His top lip is thin. Its wide cupid's bow looks like the top of a heart that somebody sat on. "Shiloh, I know you don't want to talk about Max, but I'm getting kind of worried about you."

"Don't worry about me."

"Shiloh …"

"Stop it." I notice a William Wordsworth quote on the cover of his composition notebook. The quote reads "To begin, begin." I gesture to it. "See? I'm doing a good thing. I'm beginning my search."

Miles throws his hands in the air. "This is c-completely insane."

"It's just one conversation."

"What if you get hurt?"

"You can protect me."

He shoots his gangly arms out to the sides of his body. "With what?"

I smile. "With your big muscles."

"Do you think this is funny?" His face is getting flushed with the effort of keeping his voice down. He's told me before that even the thought of a reprimand from the newspaper advisor would make him break out in hives. "You're going after a literal criminal. An actual bad guy."

I stand up. Miles knits his brow. I can see the cogs in his brain spinning as he rolls the seam of his sweater around in his fingers, looking like an animatronic robot malfunctioning.

"I'm going to go talk to an old man," I say. "It would be awesome it if you came with me, but I know you have some stuff to finish here, so I'll wait for you at the Upside-Down Tree for one hour."

Miles opens his mouth but doesn't say anything. Instead of waiting for him to respond, I walk out of the computer lab and go straight to the weeping willow just outside the school gate.

Everyone calls it the Upside-Down Tree because in the summer when it has leaves on it, it looks kind of like the end of a giant mop, and in the winter, the skeletal branches look like roots reaching into the sky. During the long summers when school's out, the branches reach the ground in every direction, giving people the perfect cover to smoke or hook up or whatever because no one can see in from the outside. No one's in there today. I'm alone.

I pull myself onto a low-hanging branch and lean my back against the trunk. I'm pretty sure Miles is going to show. We've only been dating for three weeks so I'm not completely sure, but I don't think he's going to let me go alone.

Still, it's a relief when he pushes through the branches exactly forty-five minutes later with his thumbs hooked into the straps of his backpack. I let out a deep breath and hop down from the tree. I didn't know how badly I wanted him to come with me until he showed. "You came."

Miles shrugs. "I wasn't about to make you go alone."

"Thank you."

"I still think you're insane."

I put my arms around him and lean up to give him a quick kiss. I'm tall, so I don't have to lean up far. "Noted."

On our way to the bus stop, he holds my hand. I'm still not used to the gesture, or to someone just reaching out and touching me so comfortably, but I think I like it. It's a beautiful day out, and sunny. Hay bales have been stacked near the bandstand to welcome fall.

As we walk, we pass Ethel, who owns a bakery near the bookstore, and Carl, who was childhood friends with my dad. I can see it in their eyes: There's Shiloh. Poor Shiloh. Still no word on where her brother's gone? Oh, that poor family.

I grip Miles's hand tighter.

"Did you see Ethel has rolled out some new dinosaur cookies?" Miles asks, swinging my hand between us. "She started making triceratopses."

I smile. Max loves those dinosaur cookies. Up until now,

Ethel only made the long-necked dinosaurs and the occasional T-Rex. "She did?"

"If those cookies taste as good as they look, I'll bet no other cookies can tricera-top them."

I glare at him. "That was horrible."

"Sorry, you're right. It was ptero-ble."

I laugh. Ethel and Carl are still watching us, like the town's conscience. Do you see Shiloh Oleson with that boy, holding hands and laughing like she didn't have a care in the world? Her poor brother hasn't even been gone two days.

"I Dino what to tell you." Miles laughs at his own pun. "Do you think Ethel would give me free cookies if I told her some of my puns?"

"I wouldn't."

"Well, you have no sense of humor, so that's not saying much."

On the bus, Miles shows me a poem he wrote for the next edition of the paper. I'm not that into poetry, but he writes a lot of it and everything he's shown me so far of what he's written is actually pretty good. This poem describes watching the sun rise through his bedroom window, seeing the nighttime gray lift from his neighbors' rooftops as steam billows up from his tea. I'm pretty sure transcendentalism is the thing he likes. He writes a lot about nature. I know how powerful words can be, but sometimes when he talks about the mechanics of poetry, I stop paying attention and just listen to him talk like he's singing a song in another language. He's always giving me poems written by old dead dudes, but I prefer his poems. They feel like gifts. Presents from his brain to mine.

Climbing off the bus, he takes my hand again. Edward Metty lives near the edge of Mount Keenan in a small, red and white house with rusted roof tiles and splintering columns supporting its wraparound porch. Miles and I stand on the sidewalk, staring at it. I drop his hand.

"Do we knock?" Miles asks.

Obviously we're going to knock. It's what you do when you go to a stranger's house.

Swallowing my nerves, I unlatch the front gate and climb the steps until my sneakers are on the welcome mat.

Here goes nothing.

I knock three times and step backward so as not to crowd whoever comes to the door. I don't hear any footsteps. Is anyone home? I lean closer and try to listen for some movement. Maybe a voice. I glance back at Miles as if asking him what I should do.

He jerks his chin at the door. "Knock again."

Before I can, the door swings open. A woman wearing an orange cable-knit sweater stands there.

"Can I help you?" she asks. She's young. Well, not exactly young, but younger than Edward Metty looked in that photo of him with the rabbit. There are two holes in her orange sweater. Big ones. Big enough for me to fit two fingers through.

"Hi," I say. "Is Edward Metty home?"

The woman's fingertips are white where she's gripping the edge of the door. "Who's asking?"

"My name is Shiloh." I reach out my hand for her to shake. "My brother went missing two days ago. I was wondering if I might be able to talk to Mr. Metty, just ask him a few questions about the day Poppy Rooney disappeared."

She glances down at my hand. "I'm sorry about your brother, but my father's already spoken to the police."

"I'd really like the opportunity to talk to him again. Is he here?" I smile and raise my eyebrows just a little, because Mom said it makes me look less intense. "Please. It will only take a few minutes."

The woman's mouth twists to the side. She looks almost like she pities me, which might work out in my favor.

"I'll go see if he's awake," she says before closing the door.

I wipe my sweaty palms against my pants. Miles nudges me with his elbow. "You sounded good. Confident and professional."

72

I start to say thanks when the door opens again, and I whip around to see the woman standing there with a smile.

"Come on in." She shakes our hands as we enter the house. "I'm JoJo. Take off your shoes, if you don't mind."

I wrestle my sneakers off and follow JoJo into the living room. Sitting on the end of a couch in front of the television is the oldest and most wrinkled man I have ever seen in my life. His skin looks like the surface of a white party balloon that touched a light bulb and burst. Dressed in sweatpants and a buttoned pajama shirt made of checkered fleece, Edward Metty stares at a cartoon on the television. Bugs Bunny is leaning against a tree smoking a carrot while Elmer Fudd looks in the wrong direction. JoJo takes the remote and turns the sound down to a whisper. Next to Mr. Metty's right arm is an IV pole. Clear solution drips into his arm. He doesn't look up when we walk into the room. He keeps watching Bugs and Elmer.

"Dad." JoJo picks up an empty mug from the coffee table by his legs. "These are ..." JoJo glances at us.

"Shiloh," I say. "And this is Miles."

"Shiloh's brother went missing two days ago," JoJo says. Hearing someone else say the words tugs at my heart like a confirmation of bad news I was hoping I was only imagining. "She wants to know what else you remember about that missing girl, the one you saw on the street corner."

Edward's attention is glued to the television. I glance at the cartoon. From where I'm standing, the blobs of color look like hippos.

On the wall hangs a portrait of a fat rabbit, kind of like the one on the news. I wonder if it's the same one. "Is that one of your rabbits?"

"He doesn't have them anymore," JoJo says, clenching her hands around the mug she's holding.

Edward's eyes move over to me. They are sunken, and his irises are colorless.

A broad smile stretches over Edward's face. He glances over at the frame and says, "That's Pip."

"Pip." I tuck my hands beneath me and sit beside him, crushing the faded pink quilt hanging over the back of the couch. A sour smell clings to my nose. I can't figure out what it is. "Pip's a good-looking rabbit."

Edward doesn't say anything. Hm. Maybe if I talk about Pip some more, Edward will feel comfortable enough to talk about Poppy. I narrow my eyes at the massive ball of fur, feeling my head tilt to the side. I can't ask if Pip won a blue ribbon because, if I do, JoJo will know that I stalked Edward online and nobody likes an internet stalker. "What kind of rabbit is Pip?"

"A French Lop."

"His ears are super long." I try to think of something else to add. "They're so ... floppy."

No response from Edward. He honestly looks like he'd rather be watching his cartoon than having this conversation. JoJo shifts from foot to foot. I should just get to the point. I don't want to overstay my welcome.

"Mr. Metty," I say. "I read that you saw Poppy Rooney get into a car at the end of the street. Do you remember what kind of car it was?"

"JoJo?" Edward's voice is so unsteady that it rattles, like he doesn't have enough breath to power his words. "What's this girl talking about?"

I glance back at JoJo, who says, "The girl who went missing, Dad. Remember?"

Edward's mouth twitches. "What happened to that little girl?"

"She's still missing," JoJo says.

"Missing?"

"He has good days," JoJo says, almost like she's embarrassed. The ceiling fan flattens her flyaway hairs to her skull. "Some things he remembers better than others."

I hope he's having a good day today. "Do you remember anything about the car she got into?"

A bubble of saliva pops from his mouth. An indecipherable

groan escapes his lips. He looks far away, like his mind is floating up and out through the top of his skull like a balloon.

"Was it a black car?" I ask.

He returns his attention to the television. A gentle hand falls onto my shoulder. I glance up to see Miles standing over me with a wrinkle in his brow, as if he's telling me it's time to go. It can't be time to go yet. We just got here. Maybe if I can phrase my questions the right way, Edward will remember.

I try something new. "In one of your interviews, you said that Poppy got into a truck, and next time you said she got into a car. Could you tell me whether it was a truck or a car?"

The answer he gives could be a tie-breaker and push one answer over the other. I wait for him to say "blue car" or "black truck." At least then I'll know what type of vehicle to look for.

He still doesn't answer. I wish I could reach into his brain and pull it out of him. I want to beg him to tell me, to drop on my knees and clasp my hands and cry until the disease eating his mind takes pity on me and gives up the information.

I need him to give me something. I can't go home with nothing. "Was the driver a man or a woman?"

"Shiloh," Miles says. "I think we should go."

"No."

Miles tugs on my hand, the sweat in his palms slick against my skin. "Shiloh."

"No." I wrench out of his grip and fall back onto the couch. My arm collides with something soft. Edward shrieks. I glance over. Oh my God. I landed half on top of him. I jump to my feet.

Edward rubs his arm. JoJo rushes over to him.

"I'm so sorry," I say. "I didn't mean to hurt you. I just wanted to …"

"Get out," JoJo snaps. I flinch. "Get out. I'm serious. I don't want you in my house."

There's a moment of complete silence, broken by the television, which says What's up, Doc? in a tinny voice.

I didn't mean to hurt Edward. I can't believe I did that. I shouldn't have pushed so hard.

"I'm really sorry," I say. "Thank you so much for your time."

I drop Miles's hand, grab my sneakers, and hurry out onto the porch. The door closes behind me. Miles balances on one foot as he pulls on his shoe. I try to steady my breathing.

Looks like Dad was right. Edward didn't remember anything. Even if he did see Poppy get into a car, nothing he could tell me would help me find the car. Or the driver.

I'm right back where I started, and I've basically assaulted an old guy. I hope I didn't hurt him. I'm such an idiot.

"I should go back in there and apologize," I say, my words thick in my throat.

"You already apologized," Miles says. "You didn't fall onto him very hard. I think you just spooked the guy."

I really thought I was onto something. I don't know where to go from here.

Miles arches his brow in concern. "Are you okay?"

"I'm just trying to figure out how to go forward."

"Put on your shoes," he says, straightening his shoulders. "I want to show you something."

8

SHILOH

"Where are we going?"

Miles won't tell me. We ride the bus back to Bethany, but instead of walking back to my house, he brings me to Dairy Queen. The air conditioning roars with such force that I feel like I've jumped into a cold pool.

"This is what you had to show me?" I ask.

"We're stopping at Dairy Queen because I'm hungry, not because it's our final destination," Miles says, grinning as we get in line. He loves Dairy Queen, even though he's lactose intolerant and most menu items give him a stomachache. He gets a lot of stomachaches. Mostly when he's nervous about something. "I have an actual cool thing that I want to show you, and it's not a place we come to eat all the time."

I don't come here to eat all the time, but I get his point. I order fries even though I'm not all that hungry. Miles orders chicken strips, and we eat our food from greasy paper bags as we walk toward the community park.

Miles doesn't talk much on the walk, which is weird because he usually talks all the time. He'll comment on how beautiful the black-eyed Susans are or how much he wishes he had a mailbox shaped like a birdhouse like that house over there does. He asks me whether I think a decent song could be made of sounds from ordinary life, like lawnmowers and sprinklers and sinks and car alarms. I tell him no. I'm kind of jealous of his brain. He has so many creative thoughts that I'd never have. I bet it makes life more interesting to see things in the way he does. I wish I could climb into his brain for a day just to see what it's like.

By the time we pass the police department, I'm sweating. We cross a tall bridge suspended over the river. On the other side of it, we turn onto a hiking trail.

"Are you going to murder me?" I ask.

"What?"

"You could, you know. I barely know you. For all I know, you could be a closeted psycho killer."

"I'm not going to murder you."

"It would be pretty messed up of you to murder me right now, with everything else that's going on."

"I'm not going to murder you." A smile dances across his lips. "Would you please stop talking about it?"

I try to think of all the places he could be taking me. As far as I can tell, surprises aren't Miles's thing. Part of his charm is that he's predictable. He always says "Hi" to people. He sets an alarm for five thirty every morning to watch the sun rise before school—at least, that's what he told me. Being able to predict his behavior makes me want to be around him more. He's never raised his voice about anything, so I don't think anything I could do would set him off.

The trail has gotten narrow. Before I can ask where we're going again, we step into a meadow of long prairie grass. I stop and shield my eyes from the sun with my hand.

An old telephone pole stands in the center of the field. Oh geez. I know exactly where we are.

"Is this the labyrinth?" I ask, even though I already know the answer.

Miles's eyes sparkle with a hint of worry. "Yes?"

I sigh. I should have guessed this was where he would bring me. Miles has not shut up about this stupid labyrinth since I met him. He came here in June at the recommendation of his AP English teacher, who believes the labyrinth has spiritual properties.

I don't know if I believe that, but I have to admit—the labyrinth sure is beautiful. Even though the sun is setting, everything is buzzing. Bugs and bees whir among the grasses. Birds cling to the tree branches over our heads. I can hear the gurgling of the river, and the sky is deep blue and cloudless.

A slow wind pushes through the long grass, flipping Miles's gelled-back hair into his face.

"Ready to go through it?" he asks, beaming at the meadow.

I notice the walking path and sign indicating where to enter. "Do we have to?"

"The Oren's Field Labyrinth was created by Abraham Oren, who owns the farm past those trees." He nods to some trees. "He believed the ground contained some kind of old energy."

"Is it a maze?"

He looks excited that I asked. "Nope. Labyrinths are unicursal, meaning there's only one path, so it's impossible to get lost."

"Then what's the point of this thing?"

"It's about the journey." Miles presses his finger onto my chest. "The closer you move to its center, the closer you move to your own spiritual center." Miles drags his finger to my heart. I push it away, a small laugh slipping out of me. "I'm kidding. It's not magic or anything. I like to come here because it's a good place to think, and it's supposed to help you realize something."

"What kind of something?"

"Something spiritual. It makes you have an epiphany about yourself, or your life."

"Super."

"Want to start?"

I stare at the pole in the center of the labyrinth. Miles looks at me expectantly. I really don't feel like going on a spiritual journey right now, but I can't say no to him when he's looking at me like that.

"Fine."

With a smile, Miles goes to the entrance. I follow him. We pass a sign that reads No talking, please. The labyrinth must be traveled in silence.

Dry leaves crunch under my sneakers as I walk along the path. It's only wide enough for one person to walk at a time, which is annoying because I have to follow Miles like a toddler in trouble. This whole thing is weird. We're going in circles. Every time we get close to the center, the path takes us back to the edge. I want to check the time because it feels like we've been walking forever, but I'm worried Miles will get mad if he catches me, so I just accept the fact that this will never end and that I'll be trapped in here forever, walking in circles until I drop dead.

When the path finally ends, I collapse on the ground and lie sprawled out on my back, staring up at the sky. Miles sits and leans against the pole.

"How was that for you?" he asks.

I prop myself up on my elbow. To be honest, I felt nothing special, but how can I tell him I didn't feel have an awakening when he's looking at me with such wide and hopeful eyes?

He's being nice to me. I don't want to disappoint him, but I also don't want to lie to him, so I tug on his jacket sleeve.

"What are you doing?" he asks.

"Trying to hug you."

"Oh."

He opens his arms. I crawl inside of them, resting my head on the inside of his shoulder. The angle is awkward. Miles's elbow digs into my side. He's so bony. A bird calls above us. I glance up to see it on the very top of the pole, shaking out its ebony feathers. I pull Miles's arm closer to me and try to focus on the way he feels holding me, but all I can think about is how Edward Metty looked into the emptiness in front of him, as if trying to find something that wasn't there.

"Did you have a spiritual awakening?" Miles asks.

"No." I pause. "Did you?"

"I did." He pulls me closer. "That's a bummer. I really thought that was going to work for you."

"Spiritual stuff like that doesn't exist."

"I know. I don't believe in any of that stuff, either. It's more of a placebo effect type deal."

"Huh?"

"The field doesn't have any magical powers. But if you believe it does, then you can bring yourself to have a realization. It tricks your brain."

"What did you learn about yourself?"

"Telling you would defeat the point of the entire thing."

I pull away from him. This has been fun, but it doesn't stop the fact that I royally messed up back there with Edward Metty. My ribcage is tight. I grasp my shirt.

Miles seems to notice the change on my face. "Shiloh? What's wrong?"

"I don't know what to do."

"What do you mean?"

"I mean, I don't know where to go from here." I rub my eyes. "I didn't learn anything from Edward. All I know is there was a guy in a North Face vest hanging out at tee-ball, but what am I supposed to do with that?"

"You could join the search parties."

I scoff. Mom and her friends can search just as well as I can. I need to look for Max purposefully, not aimlessly.

"Maybe make posters?" he suggests.

I curl my fist into the grass. "That won't help."

"I don't know what you're going to do next, but whatever it is, you'll figure something out."

"How are you sure?"

"Because you love Max," Miles says. "So you aren't going to give up on him."

I don't want to keep talking about this. I curl back inside Miles's arm and release a shaky sigh.

"Sometimes," Miles says, "when I'm writing an article and

trying to make a specific point that the evidence just doesn't seem to be pointing toward, it helps me to take a step back. Figure out what the piece is really about."

I try to wrap my brain around what he's saying. "This is about finding Max."

"Right. But figuring out whether the person who kidnapped Poppy Rooney was driving a car or a truck might not be the most important thing, here. You might be able to talk to other people. Approach things from a different angle."

A different angle. "What if I can't think of anything else?"

"Just give it time. Something will come to you."

"Do you really think I can do it? Keep going with this, I mean, and find him?"

"I do." He's looking at me like he means it. I sit up a little taller. A smile grows across Miles's face as he makes his voice deeper. *"The everlasting universe of things flows through your mind."*

It takes me a minute to realize where that quote is from. "You mean the Force?"

"The Force is strong with you, young Padawan." He touches my forehead with two fingers. Everything in my brain feels like it's twisted into a coiled knot, but the longer Miles looks at me, and the longer he holds his fingers there, the looser the knot gets. "You're going to find Max and punch the bad guy in the mouth, just like—" He demonstrates with the sound effect from the movies that's made when the good guy punches the bad guy in the jaw, and I laugh a little through my nose. "Just like that."

It's getting dark. The moon looks like a fingernail in a royal blue sky, reflecting in Miles's glasses. Something flutters in my stomach. I reach up to push a strand of soft hair out of his face. He wraps a hand around the back of my head, leans down, and kisses me.

His lips are warm and soft. They make me feel warm in the evening cold. Many of the poets in the poems Miles reads to me describe kissing as fire, but this doesn't feel like fire. It feels like a hot water bottle, the kind of heat that makes you want to press into it more.

I shift closer to him, my hand shooting out for balance. As my palm comes in contact with the grass, there's a loud crunch. Pain shoots up my arm. I break away from him.

"What's wrong?" he asks.

I quickly confirm there's no blood on my hand and look down to see a bird's foot in the grass. Decomposing skin peels from the bone. The talons curl in on one another like the claw in an arcade game.

Miles pulls a face. "What is that?"

"A bird foot." I smile at him. "I double-dog dare you to touch it."

He says no. I pick up the foot and drop it on his lap. He jumps to his feet and exclaims, "Shiloh!"

I'm laughing. Belly laughs fill my entire chest. He starts laughing, too, and kicks the foot at me. When I dodge it, he barrels up to me and pulls me into his arms, and the two of us stand there laughing until Miles tells me it's time to go home.

York County Scanner Updates

September 12 at 6:02 AM

Bethany Police and Fire, 179 Cleveland Rd, at 7 AM. Meet with officers regarding missing 6-year-old to set up a search party.

Kathleen Stefanski: Please let me know if we can help in the search. Praying he is found safe and quick.

Nicole Mayfield: Hoping they find this child very soon … how scary!

Julianne Toth: Do you need more volunteers to search?

Mark Begunich: I know people willing to join the search. Haven't heard an amber alert yet.

(1 Reply)

Barbara Jerels: They only issue an alert if a child has been kidnapped and there is a description of the person or vehicle.

9

SHILOH

I'm getting my geometry book out of my locker the next day when I hear a loud thud from down the hall. Shrugging it off, I close my locker to reveal Jonah Weatherby standing with his arms crossed over his chest.

"You stay away from Miles," he says.

I roll my eyes. I'm having a rough day, and the last thing I want to do is deal with Jonah right now. "Go away."

"No."

Jonah has been trouble for as long as I've known him. But for some reason, he's been Miles's best friend since middle school, ever since Jonah dropped a pencil and Miles picked it up for him or some random cliché like that. Jonah's an ass. He's notorious for sniping inappropriate comments at teachers, spending most Saturdays in detention, and picking up girls by offering to read their palms. I'm pretty sure he stole Melissa Mulvey's underwear after they had sex in the boy's bathroom last year. Rumor has it he keeps a collection. I've heard accounts of missing underwear from a few girls in our grade.

He's on probation for something. It could be for something to do with drugs. I'm pretty sure he's a supplier.

What makes it worse is that, all things considered, he's not bad looking. He's six feet tall with pale skin and dark, shaggy hair that never seems to be combed. He's dressed head-to-toe in black. Only his eyes break the color pattern. They're blue. Bright blue, the color of slushies you get at the movie theater.

Jonah runs his hands through his greasy hair. "Miles said you're looking for that missing girl. I'm sorry for what happened to your brother, but you've got to leave Miles out of it."

I pull my headphones down to my neck. I can still hear the overture from Les Misérables playing faintly, like background music. "This has nothing to do with you."

"Miles is my best friend."

"He's my boyfriend."

"Of three weeks."

"What's that supposed to mean?"

"That you barely know the guy."

"So?"

"Listen." Jonah frowns at me. "Miles is the best person I know, and you're putting him in danger."

"We talked to one old guy."

"Back the hell off," he says. "He doesn't owe you shit, and he doesn't deserve to be pulled into your crap."

"I'm sorry, but if Miles doesn't want to help me look, he doesn't have to. He can tell me this himself."

"Miles is too nice." I can smell the smoke clinging to the fibers of his T-shirt. Probably interwoven with the spots of ketchup, or whatever else made those stains. "He won't say no to you, but I'm not going to let him get hurt hunting a serial killer just because some girl asked him to."

The words serial killer hit me square in the chest. "You don't know it's a serial killer."

"Well, it sure as hell isn't a saint."

Who does Jonah think he is, telling me what I can and can't say to Miles? I get that he cares, but being that protective of your buddy is weird.

I hug my geometry book to my stomach and stand taller. "Let me be extremely clear. My brother is missing. Miles agreed to help me look for him. None of this has anything to do with you, so if you don't mind—" I look at Jonah as if to say, Get out of my way. "Don't talk to me about Max again."

When Jonah doesn't move, I raise my eyebrows. What doesn't he get about moving out of the way? Behind me, a girl giggles. "Hi, Jonah," she says, and I roll my eyes. Jonah's smile at the girl doesn't meet his eyes.

I don't have time to prepare myself before he grabs my shoulders and leads me around the corner to the hallway in front of the bathrooms.

I shove him off. "Don't touch me."

"You're looking for the wrong guy," he says.

It takes his words a second to hit me. "What did you just say?"

"The guy who picked up Poppy in his car, the guy your old guy saw," he says. "He didn't take her."

I can't believe what I'm hearing. I narrow my eyes at him. "You're telling me you know who picked up Poppy, and you didn't say anything?" He averts his eyes, which gives me all the confirmation I need. "Why didn't you go to the police?"

"I can't."

"Why not?"

"My friend made me swear not to tell anyone, but I'll say again. He didn't do it."

I want to push him against the wall and bash his stupid wannabe emo face in for knowing this entire time and not saying anything.

Holy crap. Jonah knows.

"You have to take me to him."

Jonah steps back out into the hallway and raises his hands like I'm pointing a gun at him. "I don't have to do anything."

"Please." I follow him, dodging an oncoming kid with his nose buried in his cell phone. "Please tell me who it is. I promise I won't tell the police."

"Your dad's literally a cop."

"He doesn't even know I went to talk to Edward Metty."

"Get off my case."

Jonah continues walking. I grab his arm and pull back. Hard. "Please?"

Jonah yanks his arm away. "Just call off this dumb Scooby-Doo act and let your dad do his job."

Jonah walks down the hall. I stand there, my legs frozen in place. How is Jonah so sure his friend didn't know anything? Even if his friend didn't hurt Poppy, he could have seen something, or know something, that could lead us to her.

I need to persuade him to talk. Begging him didn't exactly work, so I need someone to beg him for me. Someone he'd actually listen to.

As soon as class is over, I race to the AP English classroom and intersect Miles as he walks out the door with some redhead in glasses.

"Can I talk to you for a second?" I ask. "It's about Jonah."

Miles says sorry to the redhead before following me down the hall. I try to keep my voice down. I don't want anyone to hear us. You never know who knows who in this town.

"Is everything okay?" Miles asks. "Did Jonah do something to offend you?"

"One of these days, Jonah will do something that doesn't offend me, and when that happens, we'll ring the town bell." I offer him an unnecessary dramatic pause. He doesn't look even close to laughing. "Jonah said he knows who picked up Poppy Rooney, but he won't tell me who it is."

A crease appears in Miles's eyebrows. "He knows?"

"I asked if he could take me to him, and he said no because his friend didn't do it and he doesn't want to go to the cops."

"If Jonah says his friend didn't do it, he didn't do it. He would have a good reason for avoiding the police."

I don't know if I believe that. "I wouldn't normally ask you to talk to him, but it's for Max."

"I understand."

"I promise I won't go to the cops."

"I mean, I understand where Jonah is coming from. Your dad is the sheriff. It doesn't get any more going-to-the-cops than that. But I'll talk to him." Miles kisses me on the cheek and leaves to walk down the hall.

Jittery excitement makes my stomach uneasy all afternoon. Even if Jonah's friend didn't kidnap Poppy, which I'm still not convinced of, he might have been the last one to see her. Maybe something in what he says can shed a new light on what happened to her.

After the bell rings, I'm on my way to the Upside-Down Tree to wait for Miles when Jonah slams into me out of nowhere and pushes me against the brick wall.

My body goes limp. The bricks are hard against my spine. Jonah leans in close to my face. Drops of spit spray from his mouth when he says, "If you go to the cops, I'll hurt you."

I try to keep my voice steady when I say, "I'm not going to tell my dad anything."

"I'm doing this for Miles."

A greasy strand springs free of his hair, glinting in the sun. He smells like dirty laundry and stale smoke. Smelling him makes my stomachache worse. I don't understand how girls like him so much. He lets me go and takes a couple of steps back, running a hand over his jaw.

"I just want to find my brother."

"Nothing my friend knows is going to help you find your brother," Jonah says. "This is all so pointless."

"I guess we'll see."

"This better go well."

I don't understand. He looks almost scared. Before I can think of anything else to say, he takes a cigarette out of his pocket and clenches it between his teeth until the butt goes out of shape. He glares at me for a second before shaking his head and skulking away. Even though I got what I wanted, something about the casual way he walks, like he's annoyed that he's had to do this and not like two kids are missing and in danger, makes me hate him even more.

"Smoking is bad for you!" I shout. It's such a dumb thing to say, but for some reason, it's the only insult I can think of.

Jonah gives me the finger over his shoulder.

Idiot. I should go thank Miles for convincing Jonah. Judging by the way Jonah reacted, it couldn't have been a super fun conversation.

Hooking my thumbs around the straps of my backpack, I walk back into the school and through the hall toward the newsroom.

I push through the door. "Miles?" I say. A girl in tortoiseshell glasses looks up at me, a scowl forming on her face as she raises her finger to her lips. I glance around at each computer but don't see Miles. That can't be right. He's always here. I lower my voice and whisper, "Miles?"

"He isn't here," says the tortoiseshell nerd.

Maybe he went home. I leave the newsroom, trying to ignore the way my heart sinks as I push through the back doors and walk onto the soft grass. The sun beats down on my bare arms and neck, pricking the pores on my skin and making them sweat. If Miles went home, I might as well go to work now. Be a little early. I'm almost at the front of the school when I glimpse Miles's messenger bag on the asphalt over by the dumpster.

Oh, crap.

"Miles?" I run over to his bag. "Miles!"

I whip around the dumpsters and stumble to a stop. The soles of my sneakers catch on the pavement.

Richie Russo turns his thick head to look at me. Behind him stands his henchman Davey, and another boy named Skip or Scotty or something. They're pinning Miles against the dumpster.

Keeping an eye on me, Davey leans over to Richie. "We can't do nothing to her, Rich. Her brother's missing."

Richie curls his lip. "Get out of here," he tells me.

"Let Miles go."

"Get the hell gone," Skip says.

I cross my arms. When I don't budge, Richie shrugs.

"Suit yourself, sheriff's kid."

He grabs my hair and throws me over next to Miles. A smile flattens his puckered lips and exposes his yellow teeth. His face is disproportionate. His lips are too big, his nose is too small, and his eyes are beady. He crosses his big arms over the motorcycle graphic on his tank top that's pulled tight over his stomach. Dark hair tumbles out the back of his snapback. His pants hang so low that I'll bet if he turns around, his ass crack will show.

There's an expression of dull stupidity on his face. "I was just telling this faggot—" Richie cocks his head at Miles "—that I read his poem in the paper."

"You learned to read?" I smile as if to say I'm unafraid. "Say hey for small miracles, Richie."

"Have you read this?" says Richie.

I glance at Miles. In all the commotion with Jonah this morning, I forgot to read Miles's weekly poem.

Richie puts on a lisping, feminine voice. "'You can never get over the smell of nature. It stirs something inside you.'"

Davey hoots behind him. "It's so goddamn gay."

Miles's face is red. Sweat runs down his temples. I can't even tell if he's breathing.

"I think your poem is beautiful," I say.

Richie's face falls. "He put you up to this?" He jabs his thumb at Miles. "You put her up to this?"

Miles shakes his head. Richie steps forward. Something catches the light in Davey's hand, and I freeze.

Miles makes a noise resembling a rubber chicken. "Is that a knife?"

A snicker escapes Richie's mouth. "You're so dead."

Before Richie can do anything, I swing my backpack around so it hits Skip or Scotty or whatever his name is in the face. He yowls. I grab Miles's arm, pulling him after me as I run past Richie and Davey.

My arm tugs backward. I spin around to see Richie pinning

Miles's arms behind his back.

Davey raises the pocket knife. I scream at them to stop as he pulls Miles's sweater up, exposing his bare stomach and sunken hipbones. Davey rests the tip of the knife against Miles's skin. I throw myself at them, but Skip-or-Scotty holds me back. Blood stains his teeth, and it makes me feel good.

"Get your hands off him," I scream. "I will kill you, Richie!"

Before Davey can break skin, a voice behind us says, "Please, Richie. Stop it."

Richie freezes. I crane my neck to see Francesca standing behind us. She doesn't run. She doesn't even seem to move. One minute, she's calling him from a few yards away, and the next, she's stepping between Miles and Davey, looking Davey straight in the eye. The fight goes out of him.

"Please, you must leave them alone," Francesca says. Richie shoots an uneasy look over at Davey.

Francesca doesn't move. Richie's lips flatten into a line as he considers his options, and then he shakes his head and lets Miles go. Miles stumbles forward. Skip-or-Scotty pushes me so hard I fall over. Davey raises his pocketknife to Miles's face and closes it inches from his eyes.

Miles leans against the dumpster. I walk up to him and take his hand before turning to Francesca, who is rubbing her arm and standing awkwardly a few feet away from us.

"Thank you," I say.

Pink flames on her cheeks. She gives me a shaky nod and scurries back around the dumpsters and out of sight.

As soon as she's gone, I touch Miles's face. "Are you okay?"

Miles pushes his glasses back up the bridge of his nose and pulls up his sweater where Davey had pressed the knife. A small smudge of blood has bubbled up on his skin. I guess Davey did get him with the knife, after all. Miles smears the blood across his stomach with his thumb.

I pick up the newspaper that dropped on the ground. "Your poem was beautiful."

"I didn't know Richie knew how to read." The way Miles

says it is so matter-of-fact that I can't help but laugh.

———

I see them before I reach my house. The reporters. They see me, too, and spring off their van with newfound energy, grabbing their microphones and waking up their colleagues.

"Can you tell us what Max said to you that morning?" a woman with neat brown hair says as soon as I'm in earshot.

The van carries the name of a news station I vaguely recognize. I drop my head and walk faster.

A man points his big camera in my face. Out of the corner of my eye, it looks like a shiny black bug. "Please, we'd just like to ask you some questions—"

I slam the front door behind me, cutting the man off mid-sentence. Mom glances up from where she's standing over the kitchen table and pushes her glasses up through her thin hair. She must notice my wild-eyed look because she asks, "Isn't it terrible?"

"How long have they been out there?"

"Since this morning," she says, lowering her glasses back onto her face and rearranging a few slips of paper on the table. "The Citizen called the house. They want an interview."

I don't remember there being such a media circus when Poppy Rooney went missing. "Why?"

"Because of your father," she says. Of course it is. "He wants as many people looking as possible."

I drop my school bag on the stool and walk over to see what she's working on. Strewn all across the table are photos of Max. His school photos. Our Christmas card photos. Random shots that Mom must have randomly snapped on the playground. There are probably more on her phone. I have some on my iPod, too.

"What's all this for?"

"The poster," she explains, and I notice the red rimming her eyes, betraying her silent tears.

10

FRANCESCA

I do not drop my gaze from Reverend Guessford's eyes. "I will not leave."

Reverend Guessford clutches the cross sitting atop his breast. It is gigantic. I am sure that when he was alive, it was made of gold. "It's too late for you to be here, young lady. You need your rest."

I know he is right. It is past midnight, and I have never stayed at the cemetery so late in my life, but will sleep here every night until the man comes back, if that is what it takes to find him.

"I have a bad feeling about all this." A shudder passes through him. "I strongly urge you not to follow this character."

I stretch my legs out in front of me. I've been sitting against this tree for hours, and my body is starting to feel the effects. My muscles are stiff. I should stand up and walk around, but my eyelids are drooping, and I must save my energy to stay awake.

"Once again, he did nothing to signal he is dangerous."

"Henry's arm was—"

"—an accident," I finish, despite knowing that was not how the reverend intended to complete his sentence.

Mrs. Lewis appears beside Reverend Guessford with her lips pursed. "Francesca, honey, you were not there. I promise you, this man was up to no good."

"You do not know that." I am surprised at the sudden volume of my voice. I do not usually raise my voice to anyone, especially not to Mrs. Lewis. "You do not understand."

The glow from the streetlamps glints off the flashlight I stole from Richie and reflects through Mrs. Lewis and Reverend Guessford. Mrs. Lewis twists her lips to the side, and if I am not mistaken, I catch a glimpse of disappointment in her eyes.

"I'm only worried because I care," she says. "It would kill me if anything happened to you."

I think about telling Mrs. Lewis that she is dead already, but I believe it would be hurtful. I do not care if anything happens to me. Nobody who cares about me is alive. "I am staying here."

Both of them look at me as if I am something to be pitied. I push myself to my feet and trudge through the gravestones to the back of the cemetery, hoisting myself onto the crumbling rock wall to watch the woods.

I kick my heel against the wall in the hope that it will help keep me awake. I had counted on staying up all night, but I had not expected the exhaustion to pull down on my eyelids so hard it is making them ache.

I still cannot believe I spoke to Shiloh Oleson today. I knew I should not have gotten in Richie's way. If they had been tormenting anyone other than Shiloh, I would not have spoken up, but Shiloh has always struck me as somebody whose soul is close to mine. Lonely. Like me. I suppose she is not as lonely now that she is in a relationship with Miles Barot-Renaud. In another life, perhaps, she might have been someone I could have called a friend.

Goosebumps rise on my arms. It is cold. Colder than I anticipated. I should have worn a heavier jacket.

I should probably resume my post under the tree. Reverend

Guessford and Mrs. Lewis are not waiting for me anymore, so I will hopefully not be subjected to more lectures.

As soon as I swing my legs over the rock wall, I catch a glimmer of movement in the trees.

I squint through the shadows, trying to make out what the light could be. I am sure it was a small animal. Perhaps a squirrel scuffing up the leaves.

A wisp of bright smoke wraps up and around a tree. Except it is not smoke.

It is a soul.

The smoke gathers into an undeniably human shape. I squint against the sudden brightness. This soul is brighter than any other soul in the cemetery. I notice the polish on his loafers, the neat folds of his dress pants, and the texture of tweed on his suit. He glances over his shoulder and readjusts his glasses over the bridge of his nose.

Oh my goodness. I recognize him. He looks different from the last time I saw him. Less disturbed, and not on fire, but it is unmistakably him.

"Mr. Haggarty?"

If George hears me, he pays me no mind. I do not understand. It is not possible. Not long after the burning, when I still had not seen George at the cemetery, I asked Reverend Guessford what ever became of him. The reverend told me George had faded away after only a few days.

Nobody comes back after they fade away. It is impossible.

I slide off the wall and follow George into the trees, walking on a carpet of soggy leaves.

"George Haggarty," I call, stumbling closer to him. "Is that you?"

George glances back at me. When he meets my eyes, it is as if someone pours a bucket of cold water over the top of my head. I shudder. George snakes away from me.

Why is he going away? "George, wait!"

He does not wait. I run after him. I try to move quickly, but my shoes are too big. They snag every root and rock, threatening to send me to the ground with a single misplaced step.

"Why are you here?" I ask. "George, please."

I reach for him. Before I can touch his figure, a root catches my toe and I fly forward onto the ground. Pain shoots through my knees. I roll onto my side and grab hold of my shin.

I glance up at where George Haggarty had just been, but he is gone.

————

The sun is rising when I reach the trailer. I drag myself up the stairs like each leg weighs a hundred pounds and rest my shoulder against the door as I twist the doorknob. It does not budge.

"Richie." I press my ear against the door to listen for movement. I cannot hear any, so if he is in there, he is probably fast asleep. I check my pockets for my keys, but they are not there.

Please, Richie, be home. He likes to sneak out at night to meet Ashley, but he is usually home by morning. He is only human, after all, and must sleep before going to school. "Richie? Please, open the door."

I am so tired I want to yell, but I do not want to wake up the neighbors. Lights are off in the surrounding trailers, except for one across the road, where a woman with purple hair tied up off her neck is bouncing a silent baby on her knee. She meets my gaze and scratches her scalp.

School starts in only a few hours. I bang my palm against the door and raise my voice. "Please, Richie. Please—"

The door flies open. I topple forward into our trailer, past Richie, who has his face twisted into a scowl. He slams the door behind me.

"Where have you been?" he asks. I push myself to my feet and tip over onto the couch, resting my cheek against the rough fabric. Because he is the oldest, Richie claimed the trailer's one bed long ago, but I am not sour about it. The fabric on the couch is rough, but the cushions are comfortable enough. I begin to melt into them when Richie asks again, "Huh?"

"I was at the cemetery."

Richie scoffs. He walks back over to the bed and the mattress sinks under his weight. "Don't wake me up again."

"I really am sorry." He makes another noise like he does not believe me and turns over to go back to sleep. I notice the food lying out on the counter. A bowl of mac and cheese lies half-eaten beside my foot. Sharp perfume stings my nose. Ashley must have been in here. My fist curls around the couch cushion. "You were mean to Shiloh Oleson at school yesterday."

"We gave her an out."

"She would not abandon Miles."

"Those people don't care about you. You get that, right?"

His words sting. If I am being honest, I hope they do care. I know Mrs. Lewis cares about me and so does Reverend Guessford, but a small part of me yearns for someone who is alive and can touch me to care about me. When I was small, my mother would stop walking to curl her fingers around every flower she found beautiful. I asked her why, and she told me it was important to notice things that were beautiful because if you do not, the ugly things can overwhelm you.

My voice is barely a whisper. "I hope they do."

"Just shut up, will you?" Richie pulls the blanket over his head. "I'm going back to sleep."

I curl up on the couch. I wonder if that actually was George R. Haggarty I saw in the cemetery, or if tiredness was making me see things. I wonder how much I still do not know about the dead.

If souls can come back after they fade away, why has my mother not come back to see me?

11

SHILOH

A reporter's voice floats down the hallway as I walk into the kitchen, grabbing an apple before I head to school. Dad's sitting on the couch. Mom is on the carpet, crouched in front of the TV, watching the same shiny-haired brunette who'd parked in front of our house yesterday addressing the camera. It takes me a second to realize the house behind her is ours.

I put the apple back in the fruit bowl and walk over to the couch, wrapping my fingers around the soft cushions behind Dad's head. Mom doesn't look up. Dad cranes his neck but doesn't say anything.

On the screen, the video cuts to a clip of us standing on the front porch of our house last night. Dad forced me to do it. I stand between my parents, looking pale and sickly as tears streak down Mom's face and Dad begs, "Please, if you have Max, let him come home."

The clip changes to Earl from down the street. The sun speckles his graying face through the tree above him. "As time passes, the likelihood of finding him alive becomes less," he says.

It changes to one of the teachers at the elementary school, whose name I don't remember. "Having your child disappear has to be the worst thing you can imagine happening to somebody."

Now it's our neighbor, Mrs. Peterson. "I just hope he's with somebody who will take care of him."

What's that supposed to mean? Before I have time to react, the reporter is back.

"Multiple parents picking up their children from tee-ball practice that afternoon reported seeing a man acting suspiciously, hanging around the field." A sketch fills the left side of the screen, showing a man with tight-cropped curls and eyes wide open. He looks almost comically surprised. The reporter keeps talking, but I tap Dad on the shoulder.

"Do you have a suspect?"

Dad stands up with a groan and walks over to the mantel to splash some Scotch into his tumbler. "It's garbage. Cynthia Christensen said he was blond and wore an army jacket. Mary gave him that black hair. No one knows what they saw. It's all just … garbage."

"Really, Ernest?" Mom says. "Starting already?"

Dad shoots her a stern glare. I take this as my cue to start my walk to school.

Even though Dad said the sketch was garbage, I can't get those eyes out of my head. I wonder if those were really the eyes Max decided to trust that day at tee-ball. I wish I could have reached through the screen and torn them right out of the guy's face.

All day, I count down the hours until the final bell rings. As soon as it does, I race to the Upside-Down Tree and find Jonah and Miles already waiting there for me. Jonah has a nasty scowl etched onto his face.

"Where are we meeting your friend?" I ask him.

"Don't ask me questions," Jonah says. "I'm doing this for Miles, not you."

I shut up. It doesn't matter if he's being an asshole. He

doesn't have to be happy about it. All that matters is he's helping.

Jonah's mood lightens up once we're on the bus and moving. I sit by the window and Miles sits next to me, close to Jonah, who's holding onto the loop and leaning over us.

"I'm telling you, Miles. I'm never going back." Jonah grins. "She was beautiful. She was sophisticated." He elaborates every syllable, like it's the most hilarious joke.

Miles raises his eyebrows. "Exactly how old was she?"

"Old enough. Told me she had a daughter in school."

"So around forty."

"Still had everything in its place, though." He knocks elbows with Miles, whose cheeks flush pink as he side-eyes me.

God, Jonah is such a pig. But I don't want him to change his mind about helping us, so I bite my tongue.

"Where did you even find her?" Miles asks. I can't believe Miles is playing into this whole sexist bragging.

"Duncan's," Jonah says, like it really should be obvious. To me, he adds: "They don't card me there because I do Paulie's driveway when it snows."

"Owen Kershner's, too," Miles adds.

There's no way Jonah picked up a forty-year-old at Duncan's. Well, actually, now that I think about it, I guess Jonah is greasy enough to look older than he is. In the dark. In the back of a car. If you'd had too much to drink.

We get off the bus in front of Chipotle. In the parking lot behind it is a Goodwill and some kind of after-school club for kids called Giggle Butts.

A truck whizzes by on the main road. I tuck my hair behind my ears as I ask Jonah, "Where to?"

"Walmart." Jonah jerks his chin down the street. "He told me to meet him after his shift, and we'll walk him home."

"How do you know this guy?" Miles asks as we walk up the hill to the supercenter. By the time we reach the top, my lungs are burning and I hate myself for it.

"We've got the same probation officer," Jonah says.

So the rumor mill was right. "What did you do?" I ask. Jonah doesn't reply. "Steal some top-shelf magazines of old women?" Miles snorts in laughter, which gives me an inkling of satisfaction. "What did your friend do?"

Jonah shoots me a sidelong glance as if to say, Can it. I wonder if being on probation is part of the reason Jonah's friend doesn't want to take what he knows to the police.

We walk inside. I glance at the pale, distorted version of myself on the security camera as Jonah looks around with a pinched brow. He moves a beaded bracelet out from under his long-sleeved shirt. It has beads of every color in the rainbow, with black string tying them together.

I point at it. "Cool bracelet."

"It heals my chakras."

"Is that what you say to all the girls?"

"Yeah, Shiloh. Exactly that." He holds up his hand. "Wait here. I'll be right back."

Jonah disappears down the household appliances aisle. I wonder who this friend is going to be. Jonah told me nothing, so I don't know what to expect.

Someone taps on my shoulder. I glance over to find Miles holding up a T-shirt. Printed on it is a photograph of beets with the caption My heart beets for you.

Miles smiles. "Should I buy it?"

"No."

"But Shiloh, my heart beets for you."

Warmth rises to my cheeks. Even in the artificial lighting, he looks so happy that it makes me momentarily forget about anything but him.

"The shirt's ptero-ble," I say.

Miles's smile widens.

I catch a glimpse of Jonah walking toward us and look up. Next to him is probably one of the biggest human beings I've ever seen. His legs are small, but his upper body spills out of his vest. He must be well over six feet tall because he towers over me, Miles, and even Jonah. Peach fuzz clings to his face. A small pair of glasses with smeared lenses are perched on his acne-covered nose. I read his name tag: Zach.

Jonah gestures at Miles and me. "This is my friend Miles and his girlfriend."

"It's nice to meet you," Miles says, extending his hand for Zach to shake. Zach doesn't take it. Sweat soaks through his armpits. When he looks at me, I can feel in my bones what he's feeling. It's a fear I'm familiar with.

"I'm Shiloh," I say. "Thank you so much for talking to us."

"I don't want to talk here," Zach says in a deep voice.

"Okay," Jonah says. "Let's walk."

Zach doesn't say anything until we reach the bottom of the hill. He spins around to face Miles and me.

"You're not with the cops," he says.

It takes me a couple of seconds to understand he means it as a question. "Uh, no," I say. "We aren't with the cops."

Jonah gives Zach a reassuring nod. Zach starts walking, rubbing his palms together and pushing his glasses up his nose. Only after we've crossed the street does he talk again.

"I met Poppy last summer," he says, "when she came into the store. She was staring at the … you know, the tampons and shit like she had no clue what to do with them. I guess I was staring at her because she saw me looking, and she got all pissed. 'What're you looking at, lard-ass?' That's what she said. I didn't mean anything by it, but she was walking away before I could apologize. I guess she was embarrassed." Zach gives me a look like he's expecting me to understand better than Miles or Jonah. I do, so I give him an encouraging smile.

"I forgot about it, swear to God," he continues, "but she came back a couple days later and said sorry for calling me lard-ass. She came in almost every day after that and followed me around the store, talking about her mom, stuff she was going through in school, things in her life."

Zach stops. Jonah asks, "You good?"

Beads of sweat have formed on Zach's forehead. "I don't know, man. She made me swear not to tell anyone this stuff."

"Poppy needs your help," I say. Max needs your help, I want to add, but he wouldn't care about that.

Zach winces like the words are physically painful to say. "Her mom worked at the laundromat down by that genetics lab —Cropland, I think it's called. Stuff for farms, you know. They lived right there. Sometime in the summer, her mom started seeing a guy named Neil. Poppy didn't know where Neil worked. Before he met her mom, he was living in a tent city behind the laundromat, and he did junk."

I wrinkle my brow. "Junk?"

"Heroin," Zach says. "It's what Poppy called it. That's what her mom and dad must have called it whenever they were kids. Seventies or eighties or whatever. Poppy said Neil did so much junk he couldn't afford a house anymore. She hated Neil. Around the time she went back to school, she started talking about how he scared her. That's the thing about this whole thing that pisses me off. Everyone's been talking about her like they all loved her, but she had no friends. Why else would she hang out with me, you know? Soon after that, she told me she thought she had a stalker. I thought maybe it was someone at school who liked her, or that maybe she was exaggerating. She exaggerated a lot of things to get attention. She had this dream once about Neil, where he sawed off her hands and feet and chained her up by the neck in some basement."

A shiver runs up my spine. It sounds like the sort of dream I'd have.

"Poppy didn't come in the next day. Or the day after. I worried when she didn't come on Friday, but she was back on Monday, her face all twisted like she was going to throw up. She told me it was Neil. He was stalking her. She was sure of it. I told her I'd take her for ice cream the next day. She told me where to pick her up and I met her there after she got off the school bus. I didn't know what to do. I couldn't go to the cops. My record, you know. And then there's my grandmother. I live with her, and she's not in this country legally. I know nothing about restraining orders, but no one would listen to this girl if she said she had a stalker but couldn't prove it. We ate ice cream, but then I got a call from my sister." Zach sniffs the snot back into his nose. "My grandmother collapsed. I didn't know what to do. I left Poppy there. She said she'd be fine. She was going to go to the arcade and then go home."

"That was the day she went missing?" I ask.

Zach nods. "My guess is something happened at the arcade."

I wonder if Neil could be our guy. Maybe he's some kind of child molester. I'm about to ask Zach about him when I remember Poppy's case file. Poppy's family members all had alibis. Is Neil the stepfather who was at a gas station in Utica?

Zach is so broken up. A sharp ache twists my heart. "I'm sorry about your grandmother," I say.

"She was okay," Zach manages, and wipes his eyes with the base of his palm.

We reach the end of Zach's street. He says he has to go.

"Thank you, Zach," I say. "Really, what you did means a lot."

Jonah says bye to him, and Miles offers a little wave. As Jonah follows Zach away from us, I realize something.

Zach said Poppy went to the arcade. I know that arcade. Dad took me there once, when I was twelve or thirteen, and I swore I'd never go back. Not after what he did to me there.

But something could have happened to Poppy at that arcade. I need to go back, and I need to go back today.

12

SHILOH

Jonah runs after Zach. He catches up with him and lays a hand on Zach's arm. Zach's giant shoulders begin to shake.

I'm struck by a twinge of guilt. Turns out Jonah did have a reason for hiding what he knew about Zach. He just wanted to protect his friend.

I glance over at Miles, who's wringing his hands together. "We need to go to the arcade."

Miles frowns. "Right now?"

I grab hold of the neckline of my T-shirt and nod. It's getting dark. I catch a hint of pink over the roofs behind Zach and Jonah. The sky has turned a deeper, more royal blue than before. I told Mom I was going to Miles's house after school so I could probably stay out until after dinner without her worrying. "Do you think Jonah knows how to get there from here?"

"Jonah knows how to get everywhere," he says. "But it's getting pretty dark, and I t-told my m-mom I'd be home for dinner. Could we go to the arcade tomorrow?"

"I'm going now."

"I really don't want to leave you here alone. It's not safe, especially since you're going to a place where a serial killer or child molester could have kidnapped Poppy."

"I can go by myself. I don't care."

Miles presses his lips into a thin line. He releases a heavy sigh, closes his eyes for a second, and touches my hand. "Shiloh. Are you okay?"

I pull my hand away and say, "I'm fine."

"I'm worried about you. It's really scary not knowing where Max is, and I just wish you'd talk to me about it." I don't say anything. He tries again. "You look upset."

"The only thing I'm upset about is that we're not on our way to the arcade," I snap, and Miles doesn't say anything until Jonah comes back.

"Is the arcade close to here?" I ask Jonah, who stares at me for a second before giving me a nod.

"Not far. You want to go now?"

"Yes."

Jonah turns to Miles. "Is that cool with you?" Miles nods. "You should probably call your mom."

"I will," Miles says while still looking at me.

"Cool. Let's go." Jonah starts walking. He glances over his shoulder. "Come on, Scooby."

"Don't call me that," I snap before following him.

Jonah leads the way. I follow him and Miles with my lips sealed, listening to Miles's phone conversation with his mother and then Jonah's boring questions about what Miles's mom is making for dinner tomorrow night. I knew Jonah was Miles's friend, but I've never noticed how the tightly coiled knots in Miles's brain seem to loosen when he's around Jonah. Miles swings his arms at his side more casually than usual and laughs big laughs that I have never heard before. He's comfortable around Jonah. I guess that's what happens when you've been friends with someone for so long. You trust that person with who you are because nothing you ever did could make them pull away from you.

I'm almost jealous. But even the thought of letting someone

get that close to me turns my stomach.

I try to focus on what Zach said, parsing his story like I'm trying to find something in a field of long grass. Why did Poppy want to go to the arcade? In my memory, it's really pretty gross. Definitely not a place I'd go to have fun or blow off steam.

I just need to get this over with. Steel myself up and just be in and out.

By the time we reach the arcade, the sky has turned an inky blue. The streetlamps are on above our heads, bathing everything in an unhealthy sodium glow. I walk past the closing storefronts of the strip mall, up to the double glass doors of the arcade. I push through them.

Barely any people are in the arcade. The air smells of smoke and pretzels—one for the adults, and one for the kids. Its name, The Fun Palace, makes it clear that the owners wanted this to be a place for kids, not a strip club. This arcade doesn't look like a good place to leave a kid alone in. There are even some adults whom I wouldn't want to leave here alone. As far as I can see, only one or two kids are here.

It's better lit than I remember. Less gray. I didn't remember the place as a whole. In my memory, there are just fragments. I remember the narrow lanes between the games and the air hockey tables pushed against the wall. I didn't remember the bar, and I definitely didn't remember so many adults sitting with their elbows on the bar. A scruffy old guy in an orange hunting beanie peers at us through bulging, bug-like eyes before returning his attention to the beer in front of him.

A quiet carnival song plays over the speakers. Why the hell did Poppy want to come here?

Miles rubs the back of his neck. "This place is creeping me out. What are we looking for, exactly?"

I'm not sure. I guess we'll know it when we see it. I pass the token booth, manned by a tattooed woman chewing gum as she flips through a magazine, and move on through the rows of games. I try to put myself in Poppy's shoes. Poppy was upset.

Why? Because she was scared somebody was stalking her. Did she come in here to hide from him?

I stop walking and stare at the face of a joker pressed against the wall. It's big and boxed-in by the arcade game around it. When I was twelve, I thought it was a clown, but now I can see it's definitely a joker with a pale face and jet black hair cascading down its head. The eyes are rimmed in black paint, matching the color of its lips, which are spread wide, revealing a gaping mouth with a protruding red tongue. The purpose of the game is to throw as many balls into the joker's mouth as possible. I played it last time I was here.

Breaking off from Miles and Jonah, I walk up to the game and stand in front of it, looking into its eyes. If I didn't know better, I'd swear they were staring back.

A hand falls onto my shoulder. Miles. "Do you think we should talk to any of the people here?"

"No. Just look around for things that seem weird."

"That clown face looks pretty weird to me."

"Be serious."

"Sorry. I didn't mean—"

I peel away from Miles before he can finish speaking and walk around to the row of games against the wall. I grip the Pac-Man console. Now that I'm here, it's like I've shrunk two feet and I'm back in my pink running shoes, holding Dad's hand as we came through the door. He picked me up from school that day for the first time since Uncle Jim's funeral. It was only a few weeks later. He bought me a giant stack of tokens that were heavy in my hands. I wandered into the rows of games to find something to play. None of the games looked fun to me. I just wanted to go home.

A boy screamed next to me after losing a game. I backed away from him and straight into the legs of an older woman, who glared down at me. Where was Dad? He told me not to bother him until my tokens ran out. I walked over to the ball pit and sat inside it, covering my eyes with my hands.

Back in the present, I glance over at the ball pit in the corner.

Every multicolored plastic sphere sits idle but tense. Like they could burst into movement at any second. I stretch my palm over them, feeling the crackle of static.

After using all my tokens, I found Dad sitting at the bar, throwing back his head in laughter and slapping the table. "Dad?"

His laugh flattened as he reached down and grabbed me under my arms. He hoisted me onto his lap and I sat, stiff as a board.

"Having fun?" he asked, rubbing his pointer finger in circles at the base of my skull.

I re-adjusted my training bra. He was touching me a lot. He didn't usually touch me this much. "Can we go home?"

He fished out his wallet. "Here." Taking out five dollars, he handed them to me. "Go buy yourself some more tokens."

I slid off his lap. "Can we go home afterwards?"

He had already refocused on the television. "I'll come find you."

Slam. I whip my head up. What was that noise? Out of the door marked EMPLOYEES ONLY walks a gangly man with a collared shirt tucked under his overalls. He walks with a limp, like his legs are different lengths. A green army jacket hangs around his shoulders.

He goes down one of the aisles. The top of his head sticks out over the game consoles, bobbing up and down as he limps.

Careful not to draw attention to myself, I follow him. The man looks like a farmer. Rugged, with large buttons on his overalls and mud staining the rough fabric. He glances down the aisles like he's looking for something. Or someone. He reaches the end of the row and turns into the next one. What's he doing? I'm close to him. I'm about to reach out and tap him on the shoulder when he opens the door to the men's room and the door swings closed behind him.

Glancing over my shoulder to check that nobody is watching me, I push through the door to find Jonah drying his hands on his pants.

111

He stares at me. "Wrong bathroom."

I look down the row of stalls, but every door is open. There's nobody in here besides Jonah and me. "Did someone just come in here?"

"You."

"Not me, Jonah. I just followed a guy in here. He couldn't have just disappeared."

I glance into each of the empty stalls. When I reach the handicapped stall in the corner, the air leaves my lungs. I can hear Dad's voice rumbling in my ear like an approaching train.

"It's okay," he said, the stubble on his jaw scratching my cheek as he moved, sliding the stall's latch closed behind him. "Don't tell your mother. This is just between us."

I press one hand onto the door and grip my throat with the other. There's no air in here. I can't breathe.

I push past Jonah to get out of the bathroom.

He follows me. "What's going on with you?" He runs out in front of me and gets in front of my face. "You look sick."

"I need to get out of here," I say. "I want to go home."

"Okay." Jonah takes hold of my elbow. I draw in a deep breath through my teeth. "Come on, let's get you outside, then I'll go find Miles."

Jonah walks beside me through the red EXIT door. Cool air fills my lungs and I gasp for more, pressing my back into the brick wall and closing my eyes. It's freezing out here. I hope Max is warm. I hope Poppy is warm. I hope everybody in the whole wide world is warm because I'm not. Jonah tells me he's going to get Miles. I sink to the sidewalk, pressing my head between my knees and wishing that the invisible hand that's clenched around my throat would loosen and fall away. In the neon light behind The Fun Palace, it's all I can do not to cry.

13

FRANCESCA

I lean against a peeling tree. Jeremy lies beside me with his hands tucked behind his head, staring up at the starless sky.

"His hair was red," Jeremy says, even though I am not paying much attention to him. I am watching the empty road with my thumb resting against the ON button of my flashlight, ready to turn it on at the smallest sign of movement. Jeremy does not seem to mind that I am not responding to him. He lost the need for somebody to talk to a couple of hours ago. "Kind of like lava, but darker. Sometimes, it was white when he bleached it, but in my opinion, it was most beautiful when it was red."

I imagine it is getting close to three in the morning. I do not have a clock, but I do know it is quite late because my body feels heavy. This is only my second night staying awake through the night, and already I can feel myself fading as if I am dead as well.

Jeremy heaves a longing sigh. "Jon wrote poetry on the backs of grocery store receipts."

"Is it possible to return after a soul has faded away?" I ask, picturing George Haggarty and how brightly he'd shone in the shadows last night.

"Can you stop asking dumb questions?"

"Please, Jeremy. Have you ever heard of anybody coming back?"

Jeremy explodes with laughter. His teeth jut out as spit sprays from his mouth. "Nobody comes back, Kika."

I shift my weight on the grass. Jeremy has said many insensitive things to me, but he has also never lied. I suppose he is right. Coming back is impossible. I must have simply been seeing things.

Apart from crickets and frogs, there are no sounds in the cemetery. The dead do not sleep, so nights here are filled with soft conversations and souls lounging against gravestones, in trees, or against the rock wall on the right-hand border. They do not feel the discomfort or the cold, but shedding human habits can be difficult. Mrs. Lewis sits with her arms around Mr. Lewis, who looks closer to fading away than he ever has before. Perhaps Mrs. Lewis realizes her husband will be gone soon. She pulls his overgrown hair out of his face as he closes his eyes. The gesture is so fond and intimate that my heart cannot help but ache a tiny bit.

Gus and Charlie are full of energy, chasing each other around their mother, Esther, and her seven-day-old daughter. Esther catches me looking at them and shrugs as if to say, *What can you do?*

Natalie Dorado takes the infant out of Esther's arms and bounces the baby until Esther takes her back.

Somewhere down the road, a car engine groans. I cannot tell if it is coming toward us or driving on the main road until headlights bounce over the gravestones.

"So, anyway," Jeremy says. "Jon's poem ended with '*my love, my light, my sparrow, endless yearns for endless—*'"

"Jeremy, hush." Behind the gate, a pickup truck slows to a stop with a frightening creak. The driver turns off the lights. I stay absolutely still as somebody climbs out. The figure's shoulders are broad. He is undeniably male, and quite tall. He opens the latch on the wrought iron gate and enters the cemetery, leaving the gate swinging open behind him.

His strides are long, as if he is not in a hurry and knows where he is going. My eyes have long ago adjusted to the darkness, but not enough to make out the color of his coat until he emerges from under the trees.

It is green. Emerald green, like fresh clovers.

My mouth goes dry.

"Stop being so rude," Jeremy says, entirely unaware of what is happening. This must be the man. I cannot imagine who else it would be. Nerves prickle in my stomach as I attempt to recall what I'd planned to say to him, but all the words have flown right out of my mind.

A cool wind billows his green coat behind him like a cape. He whistles as he walks. I do not recognize the melody.

The other souls have all noticed him now. Their conversations have fizzled out to a few anxious words that fall like drizzle against a tin roof.

As the man gets closer, I realize he is not whistling. He is singing. I only start to understand the words when he gets closer.

"Hickory dickory dock." He swings a burlap sack around. "The mouse went up the clock."

Reverend Guessford steps into the man's path. "What is your business here?"

For a moment, the man appears lost. Like he has actually forgotten why he came here in the first place. "I'm, uh, looking for a little girl." His voice is deep, and his accent has an unfamiliar twang to it.

Reverend Guessford rubs his chin. "Who?"

"One little girl," he says again, holding up his index finger to communicate the number one. "Goes by the name of Natalie."

Ice shoots through my veins. I can see Natalie standing over by the wall. Her mouth opens in an *O*.

Reverend Guessford is very still. When seconds go by

without an answer, darkness falls over the man's features. "I said, where's the Natalie girl?"

Natalie does not move. The man scans the faces shining through the shadows until he spots her. He does not smile.

"Come on, Natalie." He beckons for her to come over. "Time to go."

Natalie crosses her arms. "Get out of here, bitch."

To my surprise, the man hangs his shoulders as if in defeat. There is something not quite right about him. Something that causes the hairs on the back of my neck to stand tall. I am not sure that I want to speak to him anymore. "You listen to what I'm sayin', girl. It's time to go. You need to come."

"I'd rather die again, you whore."

The side of the man's mouth twists up, then falls flat. He drops his gaze to the ground. I hear him murmur something. I lean forward to try to make out what it is saying when he explodes into motion and runs toward Natalie.

He runs like an uncoordinated puppet, his arms flinging out haphazardly from his sides. Natalie begins to run away from him. He grabs her arm and holds her up like a caught fish. Natalie kicks the man's chest. Her leg dissolves on impact.

"It's time to go," the man repeats, dragging Natalie toward the gate. My heart surges. *No.* Natalie kicks at the turf and screams at the man to let her go, but his hand does not budge from her wrist. The other ghosts throw themselves at him. They bounce right off.

A hand waves in front of my face. I glance over at Jeremy.

"Do something," he says, his eyes wide. It is the first time I have ever seen him afraid. "Go help her."

He is right. I must do something. Jumping up to my feet, I charge at the man from behind and throw my entire weight into the arm holding Natalie. My arms close around her and we tumble to the ground. Sharp cold shoots through my chest and makes me cry out. My head crashes into the grass. Dull pain shoots through my shoulder. I release Natalie, and she soars out of my arms.

Did I actually just touch her? I do not have time to ruminate on it because the man is standing before me, staring, with his arms hanging at his sides. Moonlight glints off something fixed to the lapel of his trench coat. It takes me a moment to make out the most extraordinary brooch in the shape of a crocodile pinned to the fabric. Crystals line the crocodile's back and head, which is tilted up like it is trying to look me in the eye. It is the most beautiful piece of jewelry I have ever seen.

"You're alive," says the man. "You ain't like them."

He looks innocent, rather like an overgrown child with his big ears and thin hair that's been tossed in haphazard directions. He steps toward me. I step backward.

"W-why do you run?" he stutters.

I do not see any emotion on his face. I no longer want to talk to him.

He reaches for me. I scramble away, but not fast enough. His long fingers curl around my wrist.

He drags me toward the gate. I kick at him.

"Where are you taking me?" I ask. He ignores me. I do not want him to take me away. I do not trust him. In a house across the road, a light comes on.

I scream. The man stops and grabs me by the shoulders, shaking me so hard my neck flies back.

"Quit screamin'!" he says. I scream again. "You stop that."

When I continue to scream, the man cups a calloused hand over my mouth and drags me over to the oak tree. He buries his fist into my hair, pulls me back, and smashes my forehead against the bark.

My vision flashes white. I crumple to the ground. Seeing that the man is going to lift me up again gives my muscles the energy I need to stand and run away from him as fast as I possibly can.

"Why do you run?" he shouts after me.

The world sways from side to side. I keep running. I hear heavy footsteps behind me as I push myself through the gate and run down the lane, not allowing myself to stop until I have reached the main street and I am sure he's not following me anymore. Gasping for air, I tumble into an alleyway behind the Pizza Palace and climb into the dumpster to hide. Pulses of pain course through my head. I press a greasy napkin on my forehead to stop the blood, but I do not think there is any blood.

Is he going to open the dumpster? I dig through the garbage bags and pull them over me to hide myself from view. My eyes water from the smell. Something moves underneath me. I wipe my tears with the napkin and try to pay attention to my breathing.

Outside, an engine starts. I sink deeper into the bags and feel the world pull away from me. The man's empty eyes stay with me until morning.

14

SHILOH

I turn over, pulling my pillow over my head and pressing it against my ear. In my dream, Max is covered in dirt, crawling across the floor. He lifts one hand in front of his face. The hand falls sideways from the wrist—severed. Blood spurts from the stump and runs down his forearm. He buckles over as his other hand disappears, too, followed by both of his feet, sending blood pouring out onto the carpet.

"Help me, Shiloh," he says. "Hurry!"

I open my eyes to my empty room. I slowly pull the covers back over my head. At least Max is the only one in my dreams now. When I first tried to go to sleep, all that showed up was Dad's face in the handicapped stall. His breath was hot on my ear, raising the hairs on my neck.

Being back at the arcade stirred something deep inside me. The memory of that day stays with me like a muscle ache, but actually being back in that bathroom was a sharper pain.

Jonah was helpful yesterday. He didn't have to come to the arcade, but he did anyway.

He might not be as bad as I thought.

I pull myself out of bed before my alarm clock rings. I need to make a list of the people who work at the arcade so that I can figure out who could have been there on the day Poppy went missing. I'm pretty sure one of our neighbor's sons works there. Once, when he was over at our house, he found a dead bird in our yard and brought it inside, pulling out its feathers and throwing them into the garbage can one by one. He was creepy as hell.

I emerge into the kitchen where Mom is already awake, perched in front of the television like a meerkat on watch.

"Hey, Mom."

She doesn't reply. I unwrap the foil from a Pop-Tart and glance back at her. She still hasn't moved.

"Mom?" Under the blanket, Mom's shoulders are shaking. I put the Pop-Tart down and walk over to rest a hand on her shoulder. "You okay?"

Mom looks up at me with swollen eyes. Pointing to the television, she says, "They found her."

I glance at the TV. On the screen is a male news anchor with solemn brown eyes. "Found who?"

"The missing girl."

"What?"

"That little girl. Poppy."

Oh my God. Hoping more than anything Mom is wrong, I walk around the side and sink into the couch beside her. The newscaster disappears. A girl's school photo fills the screen.

No.

The newscaster talks over the picture. "We are learning disturbing new details about the couple who kidnapped twelve-year-old Poppy Rooney and kept her captive in their home."

A clip plays. Poppy looks skinnier and more disheveled than she did in her school photo. Connie, in her uniform, carries Poppy down the front steps of a one-story brick house, kicking and screaming at the top of her lungs.

The anchor continues. "Norton Dorado and his wife, Agnes,

kept the girl in the bedroom of their deceased daughter, Natalie."

Dad is on screen, standing behind a podium and pulling his lips back into a smile. "I'm thrilled to be in front of you under these circumstances. As of today, the 11th of September 2019, the Mount Keenan Police Department has found twelve-year-old Poppy Rooney alive and has reunited her with her mother and stepfather at Mount Keenan Children's Hospital."

The newscaster comes back. "The joy of finding her alive has been obliterated by what investigators have learned about the circumstances under which she was detained. Not only did the Dorados hold Poppy captive, but they brainwashed her into believing that she was their eleven-year-old daughter, Natalie, who died last year."

A new clip of Poppy. On video, she pushes herself from Connie's arms and runs to the reporters, screaming into the cameras.

"I'm Natalie Dorado. Those are my parents. Please, don't take me away from them."

"It's not fair," Mom says. She lets out a muffled wail, and my stomach drops.

They found Poppy. Alone. Which means I was wrong.

Her disappearance wasn't connected to Max's at all.

When I leave for school, a reporter is standing in the driveway like a vulture. I don't want to hear her ask me how I feel about Poppy. Or if I have a message for everyone out there looking for Max. So I ask Mom if she could drive me.

The school hallways could be glue traps for how hard it is to walk. I get to my homeroom and slump in my desk, resting my head against my arms.

Miles rushes over to me after first period. He takes my hand and tells me it's going to be okay. I don't want to hear it.

Later, Jonah meets my gaze from his locker and frowns. I don't frown back. If my face mirrors the intense misery I feel, I don't need to frown to convey that to him.

In biology lab, I have a hideous thought that cuts its way through my brain like the knife Davey cut Miles with.

I wish Max was dead so that this could be over and I could just grieve for him.

I know I shouldn't think like that. But as hard as I try to push it away, the thought is back by the end of class.

15

FRANCESCA

Gray morning light shines through the lid of the dumpster. There is a small gap where the dumpster lid does not fit right, and it is getting more defined as the sun rises higher in the sky. I slept the entire night under the trash bags. Somehow, I managed to not fall asleep but also not be awake at the same time, my pounding head submerging me into a half-conscious state that felt like sinking into a bath of table syrup.

With heavy limbs, I push off the spongy garbage bags so that I can rise to a sitting position, rubbing my eyes in the hope it will make me feel more awake. I cannot believe that I was so wrong about the man. I had been certain he would speak to me, or at least understand me. Why would anybody try to hurt somebody they understand?

Some emotion had been burning behind his eyes. I cannot put my finger on what it was.

Pain runs up through my ankles as my feet find the bottom of the dumpster. I push up the lid, climb up the unsteady bags, and tumble onto the pavement.

The sun has only barely risen, so it must be early. I wander out onto the sidewalk. Only two cars are parked in front of the stores. I use my hand to shield my eyes and peer into the bakery window. A clock on the wall tells me it is nearly six. The bakery is closed, but I hear muted conversation from inside. I can smell bread baking, overlaid with something sweeter. I do not feel well, but I do not have the strength to make it to the trailer without eating something first, so I sit on a bench across the street to wait for the bakery to open.

At six thirty, a lady with curls tumbling out the back of her red bandana locks her station wagon and opens the florist across the street. She flips through her key ring and pulls up her loose-fitting jeans before finding the right key and going inside.

Ten minutes later, the door opens. The woman carries out a bin filled with sunflowers. They are rich yellow with ebony centers, and they have the biggest faces I have ever seen. Close to the size of stop signs. The woman retreats inside and returns with a box of swollen poppies. Each head of crimson petals squashes against the other. There are too many to fit in the box.

As it gets closer to seven, more people begin unlocking the stores. Lights turn on. People flip their signs to OPEN.

The bakery opens right at seven. Digging two crinkled dollar bills out of my pocket, I stand up from the bench and enter the bakery, filling my lungs with the sticky smell of fresh muffins and warm cookies. I wrap my arms around my stomach, close my eyes, and breathe in deep. I want the smell to consume me. To cling to me. I want it to hold me like my mother did, with all the love in the world.

Someone gasps. "Oh, honey, what in heaven's name did you do to your face?"

I open my eyes. Behind the counter stands a tiny woman gaping at me open-mouthed. She is wearing thin-rimmed spectacles and a pair of clean, white overalls with the name of the bakery written in cursive across the front.

I touch my forehead and feel a tender stab of pain. In my most contained voice, I ask, "May I please use your restroom?"

The woman ushers me through a door around the back. I lock

it behind me and walk up to the mirror. It is my turn to gasp. An enormous welt grows from my forehead, and my bottom lip is split open. I run my tongue over the swollen skin and grip both sides of the sink as my vision swims.

Oh my goodness. *The cemetery.* I must ensure the souls are not feeling too frightened. The man gave everyone quite a scare.

I do my best to wash the blood from my skin and walk outside to where the bespectacled woman is handing somebody a coffee. I offer her my two dollar bills. "May I buy one sugar cookie, please?"

The woman's eyes linger on the cash. "Is there somebody I can call for you?"

"I am all right," I say, although just as I say it, the room pulls out from under my feet. I press my hand against the glass counter to steady myself and the woman rushes to get a stool. I lean my pulsing head against the wall as the woman picks a sugar cookie out of the display case. The soft dough folds over my fingers.

I hold the greasy parchment in my hands and nibble on the corner with all the resolve of a mouse testing a cardboard box. I turn my attention to the news story playing without sound on the television in the corner. On the screen is a picture of a girl who apparently went missing some time ago. She has been found. Her family must be so relieved. I wonder if the police are going to find Shiloh Oleson's brother. I hope they do soon.

I take a bigger bite of the cookie. A photo of a man and woman appears. Underneath the picture are their names— Norton and Agnes Dorado.

I sit up from the wall and wave to attract the kind woman's attention. "Could you please raise the volume of the television?"

The woman searches for the remote. I do my best to piece together what is being said from the captions on the screen.

"This is the one," exclaims the woman, brandishing a remote and using it to raise the volume to a discernible level. The sound comes on in time for the reporter to mention the couple losing their eleven-year-old daughter Natalie last year.

"Thank heavens for Sheriff Oleson," says the bakery woman, smiling up at the screen. "That girl's parents must be so happy."

The Dorados must be Natalie's parents. From what Natalie has told me about them, they seem like good people. I did not think they would be capable of something like this.

The reporter starts talking about how the couple brainwashed Poppy into believing that she was Natalie. In the video, Poppy begs the police not to take her away. "Get your hands off me, bitch!" she shouts at the officer leading her out of the house.

She even sounds like Natalie.

Natalie.

I must go see if she is all right after last night.

I stand up. The woman balances me with a careful hand on my shoulder.

"Whoa, there," she says. "Where are you off to?"

"Thank you so much for your kindness." I stumble out from behind the counter, putting my two dollars on the counter. "I really must be going."

"You don't look like you're in any condition to go—"

I weave through the early-morning patrons and out of the bakery. Which way is the cemetery? I cannot think properly. It is as if my brain is full of fog. I hurry down Main Street, quickening my pace to a run.

When I arrive, all the ghosts are huddled near the gate. I spot the flowers on Mrs. Lewis's cardigan in the crowd and rush over to her.

"Is everything all right?" I ask. "Did something bad happen?"

Mrs. Lewis glances at me. She does not seem to notice my face. "You'll need to see it to believe it."

Believe what? I walk through the ghosts into the middle of the circle. I do not know what I am looking for until I see it, and all the blood rushes from my face.

Sitting on a tree stump beside Reverend Guessford is the soul of Poppy Rooney.

Poppy looks exactly like she did on television. Hollowed out face, big knots in her hair, and dirt caked underneath her fingernails. Dark circles hang underneath her eyes, and a bruise mars one of her sunken-in cheeks. She blinks up at me with wild eyes drained of all color.

"I do not understand," I say, doing my best to catch my breath. "I saw you on television this morning. You were alive."

Saliva drips from Poppy's quivering lip. "Leonard. He k-killed me."

I cast a questioning glance at Reverend Guessford, whose heavy hand is resting on Poppy's shoulder as if to guard her from any past or future harm. I keep my eyes on him when I ask, "Who is Leonard?"

"A man."

"Tell her what you told me," Reverend Guessford prompts, keeping his hand on Poppy's shoulder.

Poppy swallows. "He kidnapped me thirty-two days ago." Poppy says each word like it is an effort, as if every word requires the careful pronunciation of each letter. "I went to play some games, and he was hiding in the ball pit. I saw a ball move and looked at it, but he jumped out and grabbed me." Clear snot drips from her nose. She wipes it away, and it dissolves into the fog surrounding her. "He said he was rescuing me. Told me that where I was going was safer than where I came from."

Poppy coughs into her elbow. The sound is thick and phlegmy. She lowers her arm and another cough rips through her. A small feather shoots through her lips, and it dissolves, too.

"Do you remember anything about where you were?" I ask.

"The cage smelled like barn animals."

I try to remember the television in the bakery. Poppy had shouted with such conviction when telling the police that the Dorados were her parents.

A shiver thrills up my arms. I turn to Reverend Guessford. "Where is Natalie?"

He hangs his head. "That vile man stole her away."

"Was anybody else with you?" I ask Poppy. "In the cage. Were there any other children with you?"

Poppy gulps. "Just Max."

The corners of my vision spot. I tell Mrs. Lewis I need to go and run out of the cemetery. It is not possible. It cannot be. But if the man could touch ghosts, who is to say he could not do something like this?

The closer I get to school, the more I know deep in my heart that I am correct.

I must find Shiloh Oleson.

16

SHILOH

I walk out of biology. My lab partner tells me something about homework, but I'm not paying attention. I keep walking until he gets the memo that I don't want to talk and goes away. I'm almost at my next class when a hand lands on my shoulder.

I spin around. Francesca Russo bounces on the balls of her feet, glancing over her shoulder.

"You good?" I ask. I don't know what else to say. It's not like we're friends.

"I do not wish to alarm you," she says, her voice breathy and thin, "but I may know where Max is."

It takes a second for her words to sink in. "What did you just say?"

"I cannot tell you here." Francesca glances over her shoulder. "You never know who could be listening." Her lip is split, and a dark welt is forming in the middle of her forehead. I've seen enough of those to understand what it takes to make one that looks like that. I hope she's okay. "Follow me."

She starts walking down the hallway, and I follow her. What does she mean? Does she know where Max is? How would she know that? Francesca exits through the side door and hurries across the lawn into the woods. I cinch my hood over my head to protect it from the rain. Francesca has pushed her sleeves up to her elbows. Goosebumps speckle her hairy forearms.

Once we're hidden from view of the school, she spins to face me. "I may know where Max is."

"You said that already. I swear, if this is some joke or crazy thing you dreamed or something—"

"I was watching the news in the bakery this morning and I could feel that something was not right. Do you ever have feelings like that? Where you know something is not right, but you are incapable of explaining how?"

"Where is Max?"

"Have you ever heard of a girl called Poppy Rooney?"

The sound of Poppy's name reignites the disappointment in my chest. "Max wasn't with Poppy."

"On the television this morning, Poppy was saying a lot of bad words. Do you know who Natalie Dorado is?" I nod. "Natalie is their daughter, and she enjoys saying foul words."

I try to figure out where she's going with this. "Okay."

"Natalie is a soul in the cemetery on Church Valley Rd."

Oh my God. I should've known this would have something to do with ghosts. Francesca knows nothing about Max. She's just as crazy as they say. If she wants to play games, I'm going to lose it.

"I don't have time for this." I begin to head back toward school.

She grabs my arm. "Wait." I'm not expecting the touch and I freeze, looking down at where Francesca's fingers wrap around my wrist and then up into her eyes. She takes the hint and lets go. "I visited the cemetery this morning, and Poppy was there. She was dead."

"I don't understand."

"Poppy told me that a man named Leonard kidnapped her, and he also kidnapped Natalie. He killed Poppy and brought Natalie back to life inside of Poppy's body."

I blink at her. "What?"

"The girl who the police found this morning is not Poppy—it is *Natalie*."

What Francesca is trying to say suddenly hits me. A naïve part of me hoped she would actually know, but of course she doesn't. She's just trying to get attention, and she's using Max to do it.

I back away from her. "Get away from me, you crazy bitch."

"I am telling the truth." She follows me. "I spoke to Poppy this morning. She told me Leonard was keeping her in a cage and that Max was with her. If we can get Poppy's help to retrace her steps, we could save Max before Leonard kills him, too."

Francesca saying the word *kill* makes me seriously consider it for a second. But then I remember what she said about talking to dead people, and I want to smash her already broken face in.

I quicken my pace. "Don't talk to me."

"Please, you have to believe me."

"Leave me alone."

"Shiloh, Max is going to die."

I ignore her. I knew Francesca was a creep, but I never thought she'd try to pull something this messed up. I can't believe I ever felt sorry for her.

"Poppy can lead us there." Francesca tries to step in front of me, but I go around her. "She is quite traumatized at the moment, but I could talk to her, or Reverend Guessford could talk to her, or—"

I grab her by the shoulders. She smells of something sour and old, like yesterday's garbage. "Do you think this is funny?"

"I am telling the truth."

I push her away from me. She stumbles backward and catches her balance against a pine.

"Never talk to me about Max ever again," I say. "I mean it, you hear me?"

Francesca's lip quivers. She really believes this, like she's deluded or something. "Max will die."

I run back to school. I can hear her begging me to stop, but I don't care. I hate her for talking about Max. I hate her for thinking I would listen to her crap. Max isn't going to die because I'm going to find him, and I don't need any help from Psycho Russo.

————

By the time I arrive in my history class, the lecture has already started.

"Thank you so much for gracing us with your presence, Miss Oleson," says Mrs. Carpenter, my batty old teacher, who talks about as slowly as her class seems to move.

"Sorry." I sink into my seat and cross my arms over my stomach, squeezing to try to press the feeling down.

Class goes on. I dig the point of my pencil into my notebook and watch the graphite flake. Poppy Rooney is alive. Francesca Russo is insane. Ghosts aren't real. Francesca doesn't talk to dead people. She talks to herself, and she needs serious psychiatric help. I press the pencil down harder until the tip snaps. I need to break something. Do something.

I go looking for Jonah as soon as history ends, and find him leaning against a locker, talking to some blonde with hair that comes down to her waist. I stop behind the girl and wait for Jonah to see me.

He does. The girl glances over her shoulder. A frown forms on her face.

"Can I talk to you for a second?" I ask him. Honestly, he looks just as surprised to see me there as the girl does, but he tells her he'll find her later and she leaves.

He cocks his head to the side. "Everything okay, Scooby?"

No. Everything is not okay. But if I talk to Miles about this, he'll give me some well-thought-out logical reasons why I shouldn't be so mean to Francesca. I don't want well-thought-out reasons right now. I just want someone who will agree with me.

"I want to smoke," I say.

"I can roll you a joint," Jonah says. I shoot him a look. He lowers his voice and hisses, "You mean *meth*? Jesus, Scooby. I don't do hard shit, but I know a guy who can hook you up."

"Cigarettes," I say. "Obviously, cigarettes."

"You know, smoking is bad for you."

I remember saying the same thing to him a day or so ago, but I'm not in the mood to smile. "I know you have cigarettes, so how about you get them and we go smoke them behind the school?"

Jonah studies my face like he's trying to figure out if I'm serious before he reopens his locker and pulls a pack out of his bag. "Let's get this over with," he says, gesturing for me to lead the way.

I've never smoked before. I always thought cigarettes were gross because the smell makes me think of Dad and the way the smoke clings to his clothes and the inside of his car, and how it billows backward into his face and out the window while he's driving. I swore I'd never be a smoker. There are lots of ways I don't want to turn out like Dad.

I just want to do something stupid. I head for the Upside-Down Tree because I've seen kids smoke under there in the fall when there are still enough leaves to hide them from teachers. Now, some of the leaves have turned orange, but most are still green and all of them are still on their branches. I push through them to get inside.

Jonah follows me. "You know people can still see us in here, right?"

I reach out my hand, palm facing up. "Hit me."

Jonah flips open the pack, takes out a cigarette, and places it in my hand. He replaces the pack in his pocket without taking one for himself.

"Aren't you joining me?" I ask.

"I quit."

"Since when?"

"Since a week ago." He hands me a lighter and jumps up to

grab a tree branch. I can see the definition of his back through his T-shirt.

I didn't know he'd quit. It's going to be weird if he just stands there and watches me smoke. "Why do you have these if you quit?"

"I just do." He hangs from the branch. "Need some help lighting that?"

"No."

I've watched Dad smoke enough times that I know what to do. I hold the cigarette between my teeth and press the lighter's safety down. It takes me a few tries before the flame jumps out. I hold it to the end of the cigarette until smoke fills my mouth. I inhale. It takes a real effort to exhale without coughing.

I start to inhale again, but this time my lungs burn like I dropped the lighter down my throat. My eyes shoot open.

"Why's it burning?"

Jonah shrugs. "It does that."

Coughing into my elbow, I crush the ember into the tree and throw the cigarette on the ground. It lies still, a little white tube covered in dirt.

Jonah bursts out laughing. "You choked so hard."

"Don't tell Miles."

"What, that I got you hooked on cigs?"

Miles would be mad if he found out I'd smoked. His grandfather died of lung cancer, and he's told me many times never to give in to peer pressure. "Miles is too good for me."

"Miles is too good for anyone." Jonah muscles himself up onto the branch. "The best we can do is enjoy him until he realizes that and leaves us poor bastards behind."

I dig my toe into the dirty cigarette. I can feel Jonah's eyes on me before he asks, "What's going on, Scooby?"

I look up to where he's sitting in the tree. His torn-up combat boots are swinging beneath him. Shadows of the branches and leaves streak his face. If I were self-destructive and hated myself just a little more, I could see why girls like him so much. He's got a bit of a James Dean thing going on. Like *Rebel Without a Cause*, only scruffier.

He's going to get a kick out of this. "You know Francesca Russo?"

"Cranky Frankie?"

I nod. "She told me this morning she knows where Max is."

Jonah looks surprised, like he just learned that chocolate milk is made by chocolate cows. "You're kidding."

"Said a ghost told her."

"Seriously?"

"Poppy Rooney was killed this morning by a necromancer who used her body to bring that couple's daughter back to life."

Jonah falls silent. His silence feels loud, so I keep talking.

"I told her she's deranged," I say. "She's an asshole for making up stories like that." I pause. "Isn't she?" Jonah doesn't respond. "I mean, ghosts aren't real."

Jonah brushes dirt off the peace sign on his shirt. "How do you know that?"

Of all the things he could say, I wasn't expecting that. "You can't be serious."

He kicks his legs into the tree. Sunlight glints off the multicolored beads of his chakra bracelet. "I mean, how do you know ghosts aren't real? Crazier things have happened."

"Name one."

"My tarot card readings have always been eerily accurate."

"Do they say you will become rich and famous?"

"Yeah," he says. "Because I will."

"Francesca sounded so convinced. It's like those guys who say they see Jesus standing at the end of their bed, or in the shower or whatever. I mean, you know they're crazy, but what if they aren't?"

Jonah jumps down from the tree. He takes his hands out of his pockets and looks at me without a trace of humor on his face. "I don't know, Scooby. I'm pretty sure my sister's house was haunted. Doors closed by themselves, and she heard voices and stuff. Once, when my mom visited her, she burned a sage wand

and did some other random things, and Catherine's never had a problem since."

I can't believe he's taking this seriously. "Are you saying you believe in ghosts?"

"After what happened to my sister, yeah, I do. There's something out there, some energy we don't understand."

"There are lots of things we don't understand, but that doesn't mean ghosts are real."

"My mom said something else that made sense. She said that magic is just science that hasn't been discovered yet. But if you don't want to believe that, look at it logically. You can't keep looking for Poppy and hoping she'll lead you to Max, because the police already found her. Nobody at the arcade kidnapped her because if the police are right, that crazy couple took her, and if Psycho Russo is right, that weird dude would have taken her, and he doesn't work at the arcade." He pauses. "Do you lose anything by believing Cranky Frankie?"

I think for a second. "My dignity."

Jonah glances down at the discarded cigarette butt. "What dignity?"

"I guess it's possible that there could be some truth in what Francesca's saying that doesn't rely on ghosts being real," I say. "Max could be in the woods."

"Talk to Miles."

"Do you think he'll believe this?"

"No, but he'd listen."

Music plays as if from far away. I look around and realize it's coming from Jonah's headphones, which are still hanging around his neck.

"What are you listening to?"

Jonah takes off his headphones and hands them to me. I hold one up to my ear. "Is that classical?"

Jonah takes them back and nods. "I like it."

I don't think I've ever heard him listen to anything but heavy metal. Classical music is the last thing I expected him to be into. "Do you like musicals?"

"I'm not exactly a jazz hands person."

"You should listen to *Les Mis*," I say, hooking my thumbs into my pockets. "It's not a jazz hands musical. It's filled with suffering."

Jonah gives a half-shrug. "Sounds like a great time."

Something rustles behind us. I whip my head around in time to see Call-Me-Bill Medina, our vice principal, push through the branches. He braces his hands on his hips and frowns.

"I thought I saw you two come in here." He waves his index finger like he's disappointed in a child. "What are you crazy cats doing?"

Bill is an overweight, round-faced man with a crop of thinning brown hair and an ever-present smile on his face. He's shorter than both Jonah and me and wears his ID card around his neck like a first-time sleep-away camper. I almost expect his card to read HI, I'M VICE PRINCIPAL BILL. HOW MAY I HELP YOU TODAY? But it just has his name on it.

I glance at the cigarette on the ground, then back up at Call-Me-Bill. "Sorry?"

"Someone's doing something naughty," Bill says. "I expected this from Jonah here, but not from you."

Guilt turns my stomach. Jonah rolls his eyes. "Sorry, Vice Principal Medina," he says.

"Please." A wide smile stretches across his face. "Call me Bill." Jonah snorts in laughter. Call-Me-Bill stops smiling. "Shiloh, have I told you just how sorry I am for what happened to your brother? It breaks my heart. I've been joining as many search parties as I can."

"Thank you."

"I'm going to close my eyes for ten seconds, and when I open them again, I will pretend I saw nothing because there won't be anything or anyone to see. Sound good?" With theatrical flair, he closes his eyes. "One." Jonah walks out to the branches. "Two." Jonah beckons for me to follow him. I don't want to leave the cigarette on the ground, so I pick it up. "Three." We're out of earshot by the time Call-Me-Bill reaches four.

"What a nerd," Jonah says as we walk through the back doors into the school. I have a free period now, so I don't need to make another walk of shame into a classroom.

"What are you talking about?" I say. "I think he's super hip and cool."

We both laugh, and Jonah bangs his shoulder into mine.

I push some pasta onto my fork. Dad chews loudly at the head of the table.

He swallows his food. "This is good."

Mom murmurs something. I'm not sure who brought over the lasagna. So many people have been bringing us food, but whoever made this did a good job.

Dad finishes another bite. "I miss Max."

I glare at him. Mom keeps her eyes on her plate and says, "I miss him, too."

"I'm doing everything I can, Heidi," Dad says. "I'm killing myself."

Mom nods. Chair legs shriek against the wood as Dad pushes up from the table with an "Excuse me," before closing the door to the basement. His footsteps are heavy on the stairs, and my eyes linger on his empty chair. Mom whimpers. I grip my fork.

Mom goes to bed right after dinner. Dad follows an hour later. I lie in bed until I'm sure they're asleep, then open my bedroom door with a tiny click.

I pull up a chair to the desktop in the living room, wiggling the mouse to wake up the monitor. It hums to life and engulfs me in its glow. Opening a tab, I type "Real ghost sightings" into the search bar.

I click through a few photos claiming to have captured ghosts, but they look staged. I ask the internet whether ghosts are real, but I get mixed results. One article I read interviewed a psychic investigator who said ghosts appeared after a major trauma, causing disruptions in the energy field. Another post suggests that when people die, there's a transfer of energy, and that energy transfer can create a ghost. I can't find any record of people who say they can see ghosts like Francesca can.

Was Jonah right? Do I have any other options?

Back in my room, I can't sleep. Every creak in the floorboards makes me clutch my blanket tighter.

———

Just after eight in the morning, I find Francesca walking into the girl's bathroom and follow her inside.

"I want to talk to Poppy," I say.

Francesca spins around. She's changed out of the black clothes she was wearing yesterday and is dressed in a long denim skirt. Two thin braids frame her face.

She smiles. "Really?"

"Not the ghost in the cemetery, or whatever," I quickly clarify. "The girl the police found."

"That is Natalie."

I try hard not to roll my eyes. "I want to talk to that girl. I need to know if you're making it up."

I walk away before she can say anything that would make me change my mind. Francesca calls after me, "You will not be sorry!"

17

SHILOH

Francesca is already waiting for me when I get to the Upside-Down Tree. When she sees me, she stands up on her tiptoes and waves. I can't believe I'm doing this.

"Poppy told me that her mother works at a laundromat in Mount Keenan," Francesca tells me as we walk to the bus. "She said she used to go there after getting home from school to do her homework, so I would assume Natalie will be there."

"You think her mom would be back at work?" I ask. "I mean, she only just got her kid back."

"Poppy does not speak very highly about her mother. Unfortunately, I do not believe it will make a difference."

I remember what Zach said about Poppy's mom and Neil. In his description, Poppy didn't have a great mom either.

Francesca and I wait for the bus in silence. I sit on the bench, bouncing my knee, and watch Francesca, who's standing, facing me. She's pale. Almost sick-looking. It's probably an Ohio thing. We don't get a lot of sun.

"Did you have a good sleep last night?" Francesca asks.

"We don't have to talk."

"Oh." She's quiet for a couple of seconds. "Silence is often the best way to relieve tension."

God, she's so weird. She doesn't say anything the whole ride there. We're the only ones on the bus except for one old woman who smells like chestnuts and a young man with dirt on his face. He grins at me as I walk past him, displaying a row of front teeth that stick out at weird angles.

Francesca uses a printed map to lead us to the laundromat. I don't know when she had time to get a map. Maybe she was planning to go even if I didn't believe her, which I guess is a good thing because it would mean she's not lying to get attention. I recognize this road. It's the same one Miles and I took to Edward Metty's house.

Oh, crap. *Miles*.

He called me last night. I forgot to call him back. I haven't told him about Francesca or this whole ghost thing. I guess Jonah will probably tell him. Miles is going to think I'm insane.

I can't worry about that now. As we walk, Francesca tells me everything Poppy's ghost supposedly told her in the cemetery. I'll give it to her. If she's making this up, she's committed.

"According to Poppy, Leonard believes he is doing a good thing," Francesca says, rotating the map as she walks. "From what Reverend Guessford told me, Poppy has had a difficult life. Leonard said that death would protect her. He said he could send her someplace safer than where she was living." Francesca pauses. "I am led to believe that Leonard is targeting children with difficult lives. Did Max have a difficult life?"

I'm not about to tell her any of that. "Max was fine. He had me."

"I believe you."

Francesca's logic doesn't make sense. In the eyes of everyone in town, Max doesn't have a hard life. Nobody suspects anything. At least, I don't think they do. There are days when Mom doesn't show up for PTA meetings. Our neighbors would be dumb not to consider the possibility, but people are dumb.

I've always found that when you expect the worst from people, the worst is exactly what you get.

"Be prepared that Natalie says the b-word a lot," Francesca interrupts my thoughts with the tone of someone telling me something awful. "It can be rather shocking."

I'm pretty sure she means bitch, but I don't care enough to ask.

We arrive at the laundromat and stare at the door. The awning above the entrance is teal. Someone once told me that teal is a color that goes with everything. Even dirty laundry, I guess. A neon OPEN sign hangs in the window, flashing so fast it hurts my eyes. The shop is small, tucked all the way at the end of this road. I doubt it gets much traffic. A cool wind blows my hair into my face, and I tie it off my neck.

"Do you think it would be odd to go inside without anything to wash?" Francesca asks.

I honestly don't think it matters, but I guess it doesn't hurt. I notice the old white paint clinging to the denim of Francesca's jacket and use the collar to tug it off her shoulders. "Use this."

"All right," she says with a smile. "First, I must empty the pockets."

She hands me a handful of coins, some multicolored hair ties, and a thimble. No needle or thread. She stuffs the knickknacks into the pockets of her skirt, and I notice for the first time that she's not wearing a backpack. I wonder how she carries her books to school.

A bell jingles as I open the door. The dryers make horrible banging sounds as they tumble, and there are three machines running. Two people sit in front of them like they're hypnotized by the rotating drums of clothes. Behind the desk is a skinny woman scrolling through her phone. She rips off a piece of Hubba Bubba bubblegum tape and pops it in her mouth, chewing with her mouth open and making the bubblegum rotate in there like the clothes in the machines.

Seeing Francesca and me floating by the door, the woman

drops the bubblegum package onto the desk and pulls her flannel over her Coyote Ugly tank top.

"Help you?" she yells.

"Good afternoon." Francesca holds up her jacket to display the paint. "May I please wash my jacket?"

The woman blinks at her and shrugs, pointing to her left and saying, "Change machine is by the front. Prices are on the wall."

"Thank you so much," Francesca replies. "Have a lovely day."

I walk over to the change machine. I only have enough change on me for the bus ride home, not enough to wash the jacket. But this is a good place to talk. The laundromat is laid out in an L-shape, with a waiting area occupied by a few plastic chairs and a chipped coffee table with year-old magazines on it at the front. Thanks to the banging of the washers, I doubt anyone would hear us.

We turn the corner. My breath catches in my throat.

Sitting on a bench next to the window is Poppy Rooney.

I've spent so much time looking at her photo that it feels like I'm finding someone famous, but in a weird, seeing-the-victim-of-a-famous-serial-killer-I-recognize-from-a-documentary   way. Poppy has the same corn-colored hair and layer of freckles splattered across her face as she had in her picture, but her skin is as sunken in as it had been on TV. A red bandana keeps her hair from falling into her eyes as she slouches over a Mad Libs book.

Poppy glances up at us. Her face blooms in recognition. Francesca gets even more pale.

"Oh my God." Poppy jumps up from the bench and throws herself into Francesca's arms. Francesca catches Poppy and staggers backward into Poppy's mother's line of sight. I glance back at the woman to see if she noticed. She's still looking at her phone.

Poppy, still holding Francesca, mutters, "Took you long enough."

Francesca lets Poppy go. "Natalie?"

"Who else?" Poppy snaps. "I watched that bitch kill her."

"Do you mean the man from the cemetery?" Francesca asks.

"He killed her and did something to me, and next thing I know, I wake up like this." Poppy glances up at the woman behind the counter and lowers her voice. "Poppy's parents are keeping me prisoner. They never let me leave this place, or the house. They're watching me always, those bitches." Poppy seems to notice me for the first time. She crosses her arms over her chest. "Who are you?"

"This is Shiloh," Francesca says. "She goes to school with me."

Poppy narrows her eyes. "You don't believe me, do you?" I don't say anything, and she huffs. "Of course you don't. You're just like all of them." Poppy grabs Francesca's hand. "You have to get me out of here."

"I cannot."

"I don't know where my parents are."

Probably in jail. I don't think saying that would be all that helpful.

Francesca tucks Poppy's blond baby hairs back into her bandana. "What do you remember about the man?"

Poppy swats Francesca's hands away. "He kept me in a bag."

"A bag you could not pass through?"

"Yes."

"How did he bring you to your family?"

"Bitch dropped me off at the end of my driveway and I ran down into the house. I was scared, but when I opened the door, my parents told me we were leaving. They were acting all weird. It's like my mom couldn't even look at me, probably because I looked stupid. I didn't know I looked like someone else. I hadn't seen my reflection. And everything hurt so bad, like my whole body was burning." She breaks off for a while, and I notice tears pooling in her eyelids. "I thought ... I thought I maybe dreamed the whole thing. I was in the hospital and felt like I was floating, and then I woke up again and followed my parents home, then to the cemetery. But you know. I thought maybe I dreamed it, because I was alive again, and my parents could see me." Tears spill onto her cheeks. The tip of her nose gets red. "Then I went to the supermarket with my mom, and somebody must have recognized whoever Poppy Rooney was because the police came to the house and took me away. And now I'm Poppy." Poppy pinches the skin on her forearm and pulls. "This body hurts. Every time I walk, it's like I'm getting stabbed by needles."

"I am so sorry," Francesca says.

Poppy sinks back onto the bench. Her eyes fall on the book of Mad Libs and she swipes it onto the floor. It lands with its pages splayed out under its spine. "I hate Mad Libs. I can't even think like I used to."

I can see the conviction in her eyes. As insane as this is, I don't think she's lying. I try to think of something only Poppy would know. Something that Natalie Dorado would answer wrong.

"Can I ask you a question?" I ask.

Poppy kicks the book and the pages bend beneath her shoe. "Whatever."

"Was there a boy in the trailer with you?"

"I don't remember much. That bitch took me out of the bag, and then I was all woozy when I woke up."

Another idea pops into my head. A better one. "Have you seen Zach since you came back?"

"Who's Zach?" Poppy looks up at me, and my feet root me in place. "I have no idea who you're talking about at all."

———

The bell bangs against the door as I burst out of the laundromat.

"Wait!" Francesca calls behind me. "Shiloh!"

I grasp the telephone pole. Staples dig into my palms, but they don't hurt. Poppy knew Zach, but she said she didn't know him. I guess she could be lying, but I don't know why she'd lie about something like that.

A hand rests on my shoulder. I shrug it off.

"I know this sounds a bit unusual," she says.

"How can any of this be true?"

"It just is."

"How are you not crazy?"

"Most crazy people are not crazy, you know. They simply see the world differently than you do."

"Shut up. Just shut up."

If Francesca is telling the truth, it means that Max is going to be killed, too, and there's going to be another kid walking around in his body, pulling at his arms because they don't belong to him. The kid would smile, but not the way Max smiles because the kid wouldn't know how to move his mouth the way Max does. My stomach churns.

I barely make it to the garbage can before I start throwing up into it, gripping the gum clinging to the bottom of the rim like an anchor and staring down at the banana peels and empty soda pop cans. I run my tongue over my teeth and think of *Les Mis*. Those barricade boys rose up because they believed that the rest of Paris would rise with them. They sacrificed themselves in the name of blind faith. The people of Paris did not rise, but what if they had?

"Can we talk to Poppy?" I ask, wiping the sour taste from my lips with the back of my hand.

Francesca glances over her shoulder, back at the laundromat. "Again?"

"No, I mean the other Poppy. The dead one."

Francesca's face lights up. "You believe me."

I clench my fists. She looks like she's just won a goldfish at the county fair, and I can't look at her anymore. I curl my fingers around the trash can and cough up bile into an empty cup.

Find Max Oleson
Community

Heidi Oleson
September 12 at 1:38 AM
Please don't give up on us. Call me at 740-267-8896 with ANY information about the whereabouts of Maxwell Oleson, last seen FIVE DAYS AGO at Merwin Park wearing a red baseball uniform.

Melissa Orr: Prayers that someone comes forward soon and gives you the answers you deserve. Hugs for comfort!

Paul Hufnagle: Is a search party still going out tomorrow? Where can I find information about that?

Barbara Jerels: Please if you have ANY information. Even if it seems to be insignificant, contact Ernest Oleson at the Sheriff's Department.
[Load more]

18

SHILOH

Miles sways on his stool. I get ready to rush forward and catch him in case he falls off. "Do you hear yourself right now?"

A girl stops behind the checkout counter. I scan her bottles of nail polish and ring her up.

"Have a nice day," I say, handing her a bag. The girl nods and hurries away.

Miles clears his throat like he's reminding me that he's here. "Do you realize how insane you sound?"

I turn to face him and lower my voice. "This girl had no idea who Zach was."

"Shiloh," he hisses as Brian passes by, winking at me as he straightens his vest. I wrinkle my nose in disgust. "There's a really big problem with your logic here. I can't believe I'm the one who's telling you this, but ghosts aren't real."

Another man walks up to the counter. I flash him a smile and pull his shopping basket closer. "Francesca proved they are," I tell Miles.

"How could she possibly prove a thing like that?" he says.

"Exactly which experiment did she conduct to prove that ghosts are real?"

I plaster a big grin on my face as I hand the man a plastic bag with his items. "Have a nice day."

The man curls his lip as he takes his bags and leaves. Now that there are no more customers, I spin to face Miles.

"She took me to see Poppy, and Poppy hugged Francesca. Poppy had no idea who Zach was."

"Did you consider that Francesca could be lying to get attention?" Miles pushes his glasses back up the bridge of his nose. "Or to make friends?"

"I have nothing to lose. Francesca is helping Jonah and me talk to Poppy tomorrow, but you don't have to come."

Miles pauses. "Jonah's coming?"

I nod. "We're meeting Francesca at the cemetery tomorrow morning at six."

"You told Jonah about this before you told me?"

"I did," I say. Miles mutters something under his breath. "Because I knew he wouldn't be such a judgmental asshole about it."

Miles closes his eyes. His shoulders curl before he stands up from the stool and picks up his messenger bag. "I'm going home."

"Fine," I say, and he trudges out of Rite Aid like he's going to face a firing squad. I watch him through the windows until he walks past the last one and out of my sight. I probably shouldn't have said that. I was mean when I didn't have to be. Even though I didn't say it, I want him to come tomorrow. I don't want to do this without him. I should probably go apologize.

I'm about to go after him when another customer comes up to the counter. Exhaling a long sigh, I slap on a smile and greet them.

———

After my parents go to sleep, I sneak back to the desktop computer to search for cases of people who have gone missing and been found thinking they were somebody else. I find one in Colorado from five years ago, and one in Nebraska in 2000. Both of them were kids.

In my dream, I go to the cemetery. Standing in the fog between the gravestones is Max in his zipped-up raincoat.

"Shiloh." His cheeks and nose are red. Black circles are eating at his eyes, and blood drips from his temple and clings to his blond hair, making it stick up on one side. "Can you hear me?"

I push through the fog to get to him. Before I reach him, a masked man appears behind him and pulls a knife out of his jacket. He presses it to Max's neck. "*No!*"

The man drags the knife across Max's throat. Blood showers out, spilling down the front of his coat and onto the grass.

I dive onto Max's feet and hold his ankles as he collapses. The metallic smell of blood pricks my nose as I grip Max's head in both of my hands.

"Please, Max," I say. "Don't leave me."

Blood splatters onto my arms and legs. Max's legs begin to twitch. I look up to see the masked man tuck the knife back into his jacket and run into the forest.

Max gurgles like he's trying to form a word before he falls still. The color drains from his face. I scream.

I sit up in my bed, my body slick with sweat as I scramble to turn on my lamp. My alarm clock says it's four in the morning. I try to fall back asleep with the light on, but it doesn't work. Not that it matters. I need to leave for the cemetery in an hour and a half anyway, so I might as well get up. I pull myself to my feet, peel the pajamas off my body, and lie back down on the blankets to dry off before it's time to go.

By the time I reach the cemetery, the sun is rising. It's humid. Sticky. One of those headache days when thunder isn't far away, and the sky presses down on you like an unfulfilled threat. The air smells like rainwater and electricity.

I stand by the gate for a few minutes before Francesca walks up to me from behind the gate. Jonah arrives soon after. I keep my eyes on the road, but there's no sign of anyone else.

Jonah follows my gaze and elbows me in the ribs. He's wearing his peace sign shirt again today. I'm starting to think he only owns three shirts and wears them in a rotation. "Waiting for someone, Scooby?"

"Did Miles say he was coming?" I ask.

The smile disappears from Jonah's face. "No idea. He's not talking to me, maybe because of this." He waves a general hand at the cemetery.

Francesca pays no attention to us as she unlatches the gate. "There is not much time before we all have to walk to the school, so I will speak to Poppy now. You are welcome to come and watch."

That's the reason we're here. Pursing my lips, I follow Francesca through the gate and into the humid mist that reminds me of my dream from last night.

Because I'm a normal person, I have only been to the cemetery once before, for the memorial of one of Dad's childhood buddies. There's nothing special about it. There are gravestones. A few have flowers on them. The grass is mowed. A large oak tree sits next to the gate, pressed up against the rock wall that's bordering the plot.

Francesca stands beneath the oak tree, her face cloaked in shadow. I don't want to crowd her, so I hang back. Jonah does, too. Francesca begins speaking to the tree. Not to the tree. To the people around it.

She waves her hands as she speaks. I thought coming here with her was going to make me believe she was telling the truth but watching her just makes me think she's even crazier than before.

"Is it just me, or does she look like she's talking to the tree?" Jonah whispers, and I smile.

I'm so caught up in watching Francesca that I don't notice the hand on my shoulder until it's been there for a couple of seconds.

I glare at Jonah. "Stop messing with me," I say, but both of his hands are in his pockets. I whip my head around to the other side of me to find Miles standing there with his untidy hair sticking up straight and his glasses fogged up from the humidity.

I could jump up and down right here and now for how happy I am to see him. "You came."

Miles's entire body is coiled like a slinky sitting at the top of a flight of stairs. One wrong move and it would tumble all the way down.

"If ghosts are real to you, they're real to me," he says. In any normal circumstance, I'd wrinkle my nose at a cheesy comment like that, but warmth radiates through me instead. What am I feeling? I don't know. I want to wrap my arms around Miles and squeeze him.

"Do you think she's talking to someone?" Jonah interrupts.

Miles pulls the neck of his sweater off his chest. "If she isn't talking to someone, she sure is convincing."

"She'd make a good mime if we had a club at school," Jonah says.

"You should start one," I say.

"I'd make a shit mime," Jonah says. "If I was going to fake my death, I'd need someone to stab me."

"People would line up to do that," Miles laughs. I lean my head onto his shoulder, and Jonah averts his eyes.

Once Francesca is done speaking to Poppy, she fills us in on everything Poppy said.

"Leonard kept her prisoner in a trailer and brought her sandwiches twice a day," Francesca tells us, her eyes glassy and darting between things in the air in front of us that only she can see. Or people, I guess. "He lived in the trailer, and it smelled horrible. Before he killed her, he kept telling her how much happier she was going to be where she was going compared to where she had been."

"Jesus," Jonah says.

Francesca smiles a little, as if happy to have just been acknowledged. "Poppy believes Leonard is choosing to kill children with difficult lives so as to reduce the amount of pain he causes when he brings others back." Francesca scratches a booger out of her nostril. I notice Miles's lip curl, and I shoot him a look. I'm not going to let him be mean to her. Even though Francesca is quirky, she is helping us and clearly cares. "Although this logic of his seems rather backward to me. Killing is still killing."

"Did she remember anything else about where the man was?" I ask, desperate to turn the subject away from Max's hard life.

"She believes the trailer was in the woods, because she could hear a stream gurgle at night when Leonard was quiet." Francesca flicks the booger into the grass. "She remembered running through a campground on her way back to Bethany. Oh, and there was a name of a circus printed on the trailer's exterior."

Seems like Poppy remembered a lot, all things considered. "What was it?" I ask.

"The Durand Brothers," she says. "Poppy said there were posters of performers on the walls, and she believes the trailer was used to keep the animals because of the iron cage." Imagining Max in a cage makes me grit my teeth. "Poppy said she looked around for one day to find Bethany, so I guess Leonard should be someplace within a day's walk for a child."

"So he's close."

Francesca shrugs. "It would appear so."

"Is it the Coshocton River?" I ask. "That's big enough to be loud."

"The Coshocton River is fifty-seven miles long," Miles says, in the same tone he uses when answering questions in class. "It would take too long to walk alongside it and look for a random trailer."

"I don't understand how the guy got a trailer into the woods," I say. "Did he drag it in there?"

Jonah shoots me a dark look. "No adult can drag a trailer on foot."

"Maybe he used magic?" Miles offers.

"Do not be silly," Francesca says. "Magic only exists in stories."

———

I buy a map of Bethany on our way to school. Miles says he'll look up a map of the river online to see if there are any details about falls or rapids that might sound loud, but I want a physical copy I can write on. What Poppy told Francesca about the trailer's location isn't a lot, but it's someplace to start. This man would have to be hiding someplace tucked away, where hikers or joggers couldn't easily find him. He probably wouldn't stay close to the road in case somebody heard a scream and went to investigate. Poppy mentioned a campground. There are some campgrounds on the map. There's one on the map near the river, but it would be a long way for Poppy to walk.

As my English teacher drones on about some book I should have read, I flatten the map on my desk and circle pieces of the woods big enough to hide a trailer. It's hard to know how far a ghost could walk. She didn't have to carry any weight, but she was just a kid and also traumatized, so she probably wouldn't have come here directly. I draw a ten-mile radius of the cemetery. The closest campground falls outside it.

I'm still staring at the map by the time school ends. I'm in the newsroom, waiting for Miles to finish working on an article.

I rest the tip of my ballpoint pen on the campground. "Do you think Poppy could have made it from here to the cemetery?"

Miles finishes scribbling something down and looks at where I'm pointing on the map. "I don't know. It seems kind of far." His voice strains with the effort to be quiet.

"He could be in Mount Keenan," Jonah offers from where he's sitting on the other side of me, balancing a pencil between his teeth. On the table in front of him sit two messy paper airplanes. From the looks of it, he's making a third. "Because that's where he found the girl."

I lean my head onto my cheek and catch a glimpse of the headline on Miles's computer monitor. *Second two-headed sheep born to Davis Family Farm.*

"Second one this year," Miles says, like he's proud. "Of course it was back in May, in the lambing season, so it's not exactly *news*. This piece is a feature on the farm and why they think the mutation keeps happening." I ask him to scroll down to the photo. The inner eyeball of each lamb's head overlaps the other. They look like a double-yolk egg.

A shrill voice breaks the silence. "Miles!" I glance over to see Beatrice Kang, an overzealous freshman, and the paper's photographer. She looks like a bug with her reflective glasses and shiny, exoskeleton hair. "Come over here for a sec."

Miles kisses my temple and says, "I'll be right back," before pushing his chair away from his desk and leaving.

I narrow my eyes at Jonah, who's folding back the corners of a piece of lined paper.

"Stop staring at me," he says.

"You aren't very good at making those."

"You aren't very good at minding your business."

I wonder why he's annoyed. "Do you think Poppy could have made it here from past the campground?"

Jonah rubs his temples as if to ward off a headache. The sky outside hasn't let up and there's been no storm yet, so I guess the whole world has a headache today. My eyes are gritty from lack of sleep.

He gets up from his chair and walks over to where I'm sitting. A few seconds go by as he looks over my shoulder. The gold chain on his belt loops clinks. Why is he wearing that? It looks dumb.

Jonah taps the open map. I flinch at the sudden movement.

"Here's where Poppy lives." He presses the tip of his index finger into the table so hard it turns white. I knew that already. I'd circled Poppy's house earlier in black pen. "This guy had to notice her somehow, right? Out of all the kids in the neighborhood, I mean."

I guess that makes sense. "Why do you think he noticed Max?"

Jonah shrugs. "All I'm saying is this is all we have to go on. Places close to where you live and places close to ..." He slides his finger up to a large patch of green right between the laundromat and the river. "This."

I suddenly remember something Zach said. "Is that the tent city?"

"What?"

"The place Zach talked about. You know, the place where Poppy's mom's boyfriend came from, where people live in tents?"

Jonah rubs the back of his neck. "Yeah, that's it."

"Do you think Leonard would hide where a bunch of coked-out maniacs are running around?"

"They're people, Shiloh."

"I'm just saying."

Exhaling sharply, Jonah stands up and tucks the paper airplane into his back pocket. Did I say something to make him mad? I didn't mean to.

"Where are you going?"

"To smoke."

I don't know why, but his words create pressure in my chest. "I thought you quit."

"Guess I didn't." He walks out of the newsroom.

I scoff. Whatever. I return my attention to the map.

Jonah might be onto something. The tent city is close to Poppy's house, and it's near the river, too. I don't understand the connection to Max, but it's a place to start.

19

SHILOH

"I think we need a name," Miles says as the four of us walk to the bus stop from the Upside-Down Tree the next afternoon. I wanted to go to the tent city yesterday, but Francesca had already gone home, and none of us knew where she lived, and she had to come. She was the only one who could talk to Poppy directly. Besides, none of this would be possible without her.

I give Miles a funny glance. "A name?"

"You know," Miles says, like I should know. "A name. For our group." Francesca shoots him a meaningful glance. It's probably the first time she's been included in anything like this. Or anything at all.

"Why?"

"Because it would be funny. We're a mystery-solving team, and all teams need a name." He pauses to think and readjusts his glasses. "What about the Ghostbusters?"

"It's been done," I say.

"The Ghost Hunters?" Miles suggests. I catch Jonah's eye roll in the corner of my eye.

It's Francesca's turn to frown. "I am not sure I like that one because we do not hunt ghosts. The dead are our friends." After a moment, she offers, "How about the Ghost Helpers?"

If we need a name at all—which we don't—I guess the Ghost Helpers would be fine.

Jonah looks disgusted. "I hate you all." His comment prompts Francesca to smile unexpectedly.

Miles sits next to me on the bus. I look out at the cornfields. If I were to stand out in the middle of one and scream, the sound would carry forever, rolling over the plain to the hills, winding through the trees, and raising hairs on the backs of people's necks as they went about their days. I know it doesn't work like that. Max could be screaming his throat raw right now and I hear nothing.

I pull my jacket tighter around my shoulders. How long has it been since Max disappeared? I have to count the days on my fingers because for the first time, I can't remember. Six.

I try to picture him in my head. I try to remember what it felt like to fold my fingers around his entire fist, what it felt like to get splashed by water spraying up from the puddles he jumped into. I try to hear his laugh. Not the small one he does when he's thinking about something else. The huge one he laughs when I throw him over my shoulder or wrestle him to the ground. My fingers curl around the armrest. I remember him laughing, but I don't hear him anymore. It has been six days and I'm already forgetting him.

Miles nudges my knee. "Hey, what are you thinking about?"

I sigh. "Nothing."

"You look upset." His voice drops to a whisper. "Are you thinking about Max?"

Something about the way he says it, like it's pitiful to be thinking about Max and feeling the way that I am, makes me pull away from him.

He notices and looks hurt. "You know you can talk to me about your feelings, right? I'm here for you. I won't judge you, no matter what you're feeling."

I can see from his face how much he wants me to talk to him, but putting my thoughts into words will make my feelings real, and then I would have to face them. No part of me wants to face the possibility of never finding Max, so I focus on the rolling miles of corn that extend to the horizon and say, "I'm fine." Miles sighs, but he doesn't ask again.

When the four of us reach the entrance to the tent city, we pause to stare at it.

"Are you sure that people actually live here?" I ask, glancing at Jonah for confirmation.

"They do," Jonah says, staring right ahead.

"Will they be mad that we're going in there?" I ask. "What happens if they try to attack us?"

"They won't attack you," Jonah says. "Just stick to the path and don't go into their camps." Something in Jonah's tone sounds weirdly sad. If I didn't know better, I'd say he looked scared.

I'm not the only one who picks up on it. "I get scared, too, sometimes," Francesca says. "Just because you are afraid of something does not mean you cannot do it."

"I'm not scared," Jonah snaps. "Chances are this dude's not even here, but it's close to where Poppy lives, so it's worth checking out, anyway."

"You sure you're okay?" Miles asks him. Jonah starts walking into the woods without waiting for us. I exchange a glance with Miles and follow him.

I step over some rusted metal poles I assume used to be part of a gate and walk into the woods. Spindly branches cast dark shadows onto the ground. Clouds, combined with the thickness of the surrounding trees, block the light. My foot sinks through a rotten log. Rocks and roots stick out of the dead leaves like claws, ready to hook onto pant legs, shoelaces, or anything that might send its wearer tumbling to the ground.

I can hear the river. It gargles, like someone gargling saliva while getting ready to gobble you up.

Francesca walks beside me with her hands in the deep pockets of her denim jacket. Miles and Jonah are walking in front of us—just out of earshot for me to hear what they're saying.

A plastic bottle sits just off the trail. Not far away, a toothbrush is sticking out of the dirt. I guess people really do live here. I stop walking, crouching down to pull the toothbrush out of the ground. An empty can sits near it, sunken into the leaves a few feet off the trail. I step off the trail to pick that up, too.

"Don't go in there," Jonah warns. I don't listen and take another step forward. A branch snaps under my sneaker.

"Stop walking, Shiloh," Jonah says. "I mean it."

I follow Jonah's gaze to the blue canvas poking out from behind an evergreen. I inch forward to see better and Jonah glares at me, holding his finger up to his lips.

"This is someone's home," Jonah whispers. "Leave them alone."

He's right. This isn't a trailer. It's not what we're looking for.

I glimpse the river through the trees and walk over to the bank. It's wide, but shallow enough to wade through. Closer to Bethany, the water moves slower, but here it races over rocks. Dad never let me swim in it. He used to tell me the river looks calm on the surface, but there are strong currents under it, ready to pull you onto the boulders where the weeds will wrap around your ankles and hold you there until your last breath bubbles to the surface. According to him, strong white water is less scary than a sluggish river, where there is the illusion of calm. For once, I can see what he means.

I look both ways at the trees that overhang the river and block the view from the other side. On the map, the woods stretch off in both directions. I don't know which way to go.

"We need to split up," I say. "Two of us go left, and two of us go right."

"Are you s-sure that s-splitting up is a good idea?" Miles asks.

I don't know why he needs to disagree with me all the time. He might be a nerd, but it doesn't mean he has to talk to me like I'm stupid.

"We're trying to find Leonard, not attack him," I say. "If we split up, we can look in both directions and don't have to choose."

"I'm down," Jonah says. "As long as you stay quiet. If you find the guy, don't say a word."

"I won't."

"He can't know we know he's here," Jonah says.

"*If* he's here," Miles says.

"Yeah, *if* he's here," Jonah echoes.

"I'll go with you," Miles says.

"Go with Francesca," I say, because he's annoying me so much right now that I can't look at him. I just know that as soon as I'm alone with him, he's going to start asking me more questions about how I'm feeling, and I don't have the energy to deal with that right now.

"Be quiet," Jonah says to Francesca and Miles, who nod. "Don't be a pain in the ass, and don't disturb anyone."

"Meet back at the gate in an hour," I say.

With that, we all split up.

20

FRANCESCA

Something stirs behind me. I turn around, but there's nothing there. There is something quite peculiar about this place, but I cannot identify what it is. I can feel something in the air. Something palpable that makes the air around me thick and sour in my lungs.

Something dark.

Miles has not said a word since we abandoned the others. His hands are hidden in his pockets as if he does not want them to get cold even though it is warm outside today.

"Is everything going on with you all right?" I ask.

I do not know how Miles will react to this. I know that Shiloh would be frustrated with me for asking that question. She often acts frustrated at things she can't control, which makes me sad for her. There is a lot of anger boiling underneath her skin, but I do not sense the same kind of anger from Miles.

Miles runs his fingers through his warm brown hair. "I'm just a little frustrated. I'm sorry. It has nothing to do with you."

"What are you frustrated about?"

"Just ..." His voice trails off as he notices a garbage bag

caught on a root off the trail. He walks over to pick it up and adds it to the collection of trash in his arms he has collected since we started walking. "Shiloh won't talk to me about how she's feeling, and it makes me sad. I don't know what to say to make her open up to me."

"Shiloh is going through unimaginable pain."

"I know," he says, "but, I mean, I'm trying to be there for her, and she won't let me in." He picks up another scrap of plastic. "I want to make things better for her."

"You cannot make this better for her."

"I know. I just wish I could."

His eyebrows pinch together like he is in pain, physical pain, for Shiloh. From what I have heard, that is part of being in love. The pain your love experiences pulls you in with them.

I shift my attention back to the woods. Immediately, a chill seeps into my bones. I hope for Shiloh's sake that what I am feeling is the presence of Leonard, but I am not so sure.

There is a strange feeling tugging at me, like we are doing something wrong. I could never tell Shiloh, but I believe I can understand why Leonard thinks that he is doing a good thing. Poppy's mother does not appear to pay attention to her even after she has been found, and at the cemetery, Gus and Charlie never leave her side. Natalie was in pain during her last weeks on Earth, but in the cemetery, there was none. If it were not for the way Natalie spoke at the laundromat, like she was a prisoner trapped inside a body that was not her own, or for the way Poppy's hands had still not stopped shaking since her arrival, I might even agree with Leonard's actions. But I do not believe he sees the consequences of what he does, or even thinks about them very much.

At least Poppy's mother does not know it is not her daughter behind Poppy's eyes. If it happened to Max, Shiloh would know. Even imagining the pain it would cause her makes me walk faster.

"I believe it would be a good idea to speak to somebody who lives here," I tell Miles. I would not like to bother anybody in their home, but this is important. "If Leonard is here, somebody must have heard something out of the ordinary that could lead us to him."

"Jonah didn't think that was such a good idea."

I am about to insist when I hear what sounds like a sob from very far away.

I stop walking. "Did you hear that?"

Miles stops, too. "Hear what?"

There is another sob. The sound is unmistakably female and filled with grief.

Which direction is the sound coming from? I rush forward in one direction, but the sound comes from behind me, so I turn the opposite way.

"Hello?" I call out at the top of my voice. "Where are you?"

"Francesca." Miles grabs my arm. "Jonah said to stay quiet."

"I can hear somebody crying," I say. "I believe someone is hurt." I have never heard a sound imbued with such misery. Not even George Haggarty sounded so sad. "I think it is coming from over there."

I run toward the sound. I can hear Miles's shoes crunch behind me, and know he is running after me.

I see the tarp before I reach the campsite. The sound is loud. I run up to the tent, and after a few seconds, I notice a woman bundled in fleece coats and lying on her back in the leaves. Her inky hair is splayed out over the ground behind her, and her head is hanging to one side. She is dead. Recently dead, because her soul is only half-raised from her body and sitting up inside her torso. Her head is buried in her hands as she sobs.

Miles catches up to me. When he sees the woman, he gasps. "Jesus, is she dead?"

I get down on my knees and reach out my hand to the woman. "Are you all right?" The woman lifts her head, her wild hair falling to frame both sides of her face. "I heard you crying."

"It happened so fast." Her chin jerks down at the needle that has fallen out of her body's left hand. The tip is brushed with dirt. I am not sure why she has a needle. Is she ill? "I didn't mean for it to happen."

I press my fingers to her corpse's neck and find that it is still warm. "How long ago did this happen?"

"I just woke up." She pauses. "This means I'm dead, doesn't it?"

I give her a solemn nod. The woman reaches her hands out in front of her to look at them. Both of them are trembling. I must comfort her.

I reach to take the woman's hands. Instead of passing through them, my fingers curl around hers.

Liquid ice shoots up my arms and up to my temples. I cry out in pain and release her, staring down at my red palms. The woman continues crying. I must do something to help her. Gathering my strength, I reach back out to take her hands in mine. I can feel her squeezing them. The increased pressure makes it hurt even more, but I force myself not to let go.

Slowly, I push the woman down toward her body. Her eyes shoot open. "What are you doing?"

"Trust me." My voice and body are surer of myself than I feel. I lower the woman until she is lying inside her corpse, where she shines like a shadow made of sunlight. I hold her there as the cold intensifies before being replaced by something hot. Burning.

I must not let go. I must hold her still.

I grit my teeth, feeling the heat burn through my organs as the woman dissolves into the fleece of her coat. Once she disappears completely, I let go of her and fall over onto the leaves.

"Oh my God," Miles says above me. "We n-need to call the police. What do you do when you find a dead body?"

I lean forward and press my fingers to the woman's neck, feeling a slight pulse.

"*Francesca.*"

"She is not dead," I say. Because of me. I may have brought

her back to life. A violent shiver travels through me, replaced by a deep exhaustion that I feel in my bones.

"Okay. So we need to get her to the hospital."

I glance around the camp. There is nobody else here. I stand up and immediately stumble into a tree as blood rushes from my head and pulls the world away from me.

"Help me pick her up," Miles says.

The two of us manage to get the woman into a sitting position. All strength has left my body. My arms and legs are no stronger than pieces of overcooked spaghetti.

"This is not going to work," Miles says. "We need to get Jonah. You stay here. I'll go find him."

I nod and grip the woman's hand as Miles disappears into the woods.

21

SHILOH

"Help!"

The sound cuts through the silence. My blood runs cold. I know that voice. I'd know that voice anywhere.

Because it belongs to Max.

"Max!" I scream. "Max, is that you?"

He calls again. It's him. It's definitely him. I leap off the trail and run toward the sound.

"Shiloh, wait."

Jonah is behind me, but I don't stop running. I'm lucky it rained earlier today so the leaves are wet enough not to skid out from under me.

"Help!" says the voice. My lungs are on fire. It feels like they've melted in my chest cavity, dripping like molten metal through the gaps in my rib cage. I run through a gap in the trees and see him. My hand crashes into the tree beside me as I stop.

He's standing in the trees, his feet hidden behind a tall, fallen log. A long-sleeve shirt hangs over his bony shoulders. There's a tear in the shoulder. I can see his skin through it.

A choked sob bursts from my throat. It's him. It's really him. And he's alive.

I made it in time.

"Max," I cry, stumbling toward him. He glances up, stares at me for a second, and then runs away.

Where's he going? "Max, wait!" I run after him. Max is small, but he's fast. He jumps over logs and around trees, but my legs are long. I keep up with him. "Stop running, Max, it's me."

I've almost caught up to him when something slams into me from behind, pulling me to the ground. I jab my elbow into my attacker's ribs. There's a yelp, and I scramble to my feet. Where did Max go?

"Ow," Jonah says, holding onto his stomach where I hit him.

"What are you doing?" I look past him to where Max was just a few seconds ago. "I found Max."

"That's not Max," Jonah says.

Yes, it is. It has to be. The boy stares at us from behind a tree. He focuses before my eyes and my heart sinks. Jonah's right. This boy has brown, tangled hair, and he's tall. Taller than Max.

"Why would Max run away from you?" Jonah asks me. I don't know. I hadn't thought of that. "You need to shut up because you're making a scene and if the real Max is here, the man could have heard you."

The boy blinks at us with terrified eyes. I back away, gripping a tree to keep my balance.

Jonah drops to his knees in front of the boy. "You okay?"

The boy's voice is barely a squeak. "I want my mom."

"What's wrong with your mom?"

"She's hurt."

Jonah's face widens in a way I've never seen before, and he springs up to his feet. "Where is she?"

The boy gestures for him to follow. Jonah glances back at me, as if to tell me to follow, too. I force my aching legs to move.

We run after the boy, ducking under branches and darting around trees until we reach a campsite and stop.

A body leans against a tree. Standing over it is Francesca.

"She is alive," Francesca says. "Miles went to look for you."

Jonah shoulders Francesca out of the way and presses his fingers to the woman's neck. "We need to get her to a hospital." Jonah lifts the woman into his arms, shifting to catch her limp limbs as they threaten to pull her back down. With a grunt, he hoists the woman over his shoulder. I reach for the boy's hand. He doesn't pull it away.

"Go find Miles," Jonah barks at Francesca, "and meet us at the hospital."

Francesca scampers out of the way as Jonah carries the woman out of the campsite. Grabbing a quilt from the ground and wrapping it around the boy's shoulders, I lead him after his mom.

22

SHILOH

Jonah raps his knuckles on the waiting room chair. He's white as a sheet and looks like he's about to throw up.

It's just the two of us, now. The boy, Liam, sat with us until the social workers arrived. I gripped his hand. More for my sake than his, but I couldn't let him go. There were two social workers. Both of the women were dressed almost the same, with cardigans buttoned over their chests and a few hairs falling out of their tidy pins. Cardigans are a good choice for social workers. They make people seem warm. The taller of the pair crouched down in front of Liam. I stared at the heel of her shoe. It was the width of my thumb. If I wore shoes like that, I wouldn't make it out of the house without splitting a bone in my ankle.

"Hi, Liam." The woman's voice was warm like a towel fresh out of the dryer. "How about you let go of this nice girl's hand and come with me?"

Liam's hand slipped out of mine, and he marched after the social workers on stiff legs.

I wrap my arms around my stomach and try to meet Jonah's

eyes. "Do you think they're going to take Liam away from his mom?"

Jonah doesn't look up. "They do that."

"I guess that's a good thing." I remember the canvas tent and sleeping bags inside it. In a few weeks, it's going to get cold. "Living like that is not good for a kid."

Jonah digs the toe of his boot into the linoleum. "Foster care's not a lot better."

"Some people just aren't good parents."

An unreadable expression crosses Jonah's face. The white light above our heads casts an antiseptic film over him, draining his face of color and making his black hair look even darker. It falls over his forehead and into his eyes. I remember the way he looked at the edge of the trees before we walked into the tent city. He was scared, like he knew what was waiting for us behind those trees. "Was today your first time in the tent city?" I ask.

"Yep."

I'm not exactly good at dealing with feelings. I don't get feelings the way Francesca seems to, but I can tell there's something wrong.

"Jonah," I say. He finally looks up with his clear, blue eyes. Something sharp aches in my chest. He's sitting across from me, his feet kicked out in front of him. If I moved my sneaker an inch or so to the left, it would touch his boot. "Why were you scared?"

Jonah's eyes soften. He doesn't look angry at me anymore. Just kind of sad, like Liam did.

I reach my hand out to him, but he jumps to his feet, shoves his hands in his pockets, and says, "I'm going to call Miles and make sure he's coming."

Oh. I sit back in the chair, hide my hands under my thighs, and try to play it off. "Good, yeah. Sounds good."

He leaves through the sliding doors.

I slouch down in my chair and shake out my hands to try to

rid myself of the sticky feeling that has come over them. I can't believe I just did that. What was I going to do? Hold his hand?

I should ask the nurse if I could borrow a phone and call Miles, too. Or maybe not. Calling him while he's on the phone with Jonah would be pointless.

Jonah still hasn't come back inside when I hear a vaguely familiar voice. I twist around to see Connie speaking to the nurse behind the table, and relief crashes over me. Her curls are impossibly red in the bright hospital light.

I race over to her, tapping her on the shoulder. Connie pauses her conversation with the nurse and turns around. Warmth pours out of her smile like honey from a jar. "Hey, sweetheart. What are you doing here?"

Detective Finnegan's standing a few feet away. He glares at me and reaches down to adjust his badge. He's strutting. Puffed up with his own sense of self-importance as he side-eyes the nurses.

I don't want to answer Connie's question in front of him. Anything I say in front of Finnegan will go straight back to Dad.

"Can I talk to you for a second?" I ask her. "Alone?"

Connie glances at Finnegan. "Is there something wrong?"

"I need to tell you something."

"All right."

Connie leads me away with a hand on my back, out of earshot from Finnegan. We stop over by the doors. She opens her mouth to say something, but I beat her to it.

"I think I know what happened to Max," I say, "and I might know where he is."

Getting some help in our search would help us comb through the woods faster. Connie is a detective. She could tell Dad that Max could be in the tent city, and he wouldn't have to know I was the one who found that out.

Connie's eyes widen. "You *what?*"

"I don't know where he is exactly, but I'm pretty sure a man is keeping him in a trailer in the woods close to the Coshocton, probably near the tent city in Mount Keenan."

Connie takes a few seconds to digest this. "Who do you think would do something like this?"

I know this is going to sound dumb before I even say it. "A guy named Leonard."

"How do you know about Leonard?"

What am I supposed to tell her? *Oh, some ghosts told me. Well, not me exactly, Francesca Russo. Yeah, that Francesca Russo. No, she's not crazy, but she's been talking to ghosts.* Connie will think I'm insane. "I know it sounds weird, but I know I'm onto something. I can only cover so much ground alone, and I think if you could get involved or send search parties through there, we could find out if Max is there."

Connie gives me a too-quick smile, before dropping her gaze and shifting on her feet. "I hate to break it to you, hon, but I can't send people marching into the woods without a reason."

"I just gave you a reason."

"I'm sorry, but I can't help you."

I narrow my eyes at her. She's looking at me with skin crinkling at the corner of her eyes, the kind of look you give someone you feel sorry for. I can't believe she's dismissing me so fast. I thought they'd be looking for all the help they can get. Unless, I realize, there's a reason she wouldn't want to look in the woods. "Is there something you're not telling me?"

Connie shakes her head. I can see it, behind her eyes. That thing she isn't telling me. "I'm sorry, hon. I need to go. Some poor woman just overdosed, and Scott and I need to talk to the kids who found her."

Just as Connie says that, the doors slide open and Jonah walks through them. I gulp, and say to Connie, "That would be us."

Connie's eyebrows shoot up. She beckons Finnegan, who seems to be examining a scattering of dead flies trapped in the panels of light above his head, to come over.

"Did you get Miles?" I whisper to Jonah.

"Yeah, he's on his way."

"Good."

Connie and Finnegan take us to a room down the hallway. They sit on one side of the table while Jonah and I sit on the other. My chair swivels. I bounce up and down. The springs creak under me.

Finnegan flips open a spiral notebook. "Am I to understand you found this woman?" he asks Jonah.

Jonah leans back on the chair like he isn't bothered by the whole situation at all and could be talking to a reporter from the school paper for how little respect he has for Finnegan and the uniform he's wearing. It's annoying Finnegan. I can tell.

"What were you doing in the woods with Sheriff Oleson's daughter in the first place, *Mr.* Weatherby?" Finnegan sneers with a note of familiarity, like the two of them go way back.

"Shiloh, what were you doing in the woods?" Connie asks me.

She already knows the answer to that question. With a sinking feeling in my stomach, I open my mouth to reply when Jonah cuts me off.

"We were on a hike," he says. "With our friends, who will be here soon and back me up, *Detective* Finnegan."

Connie doesn't buy it. "A hike?"

Finnegan rubs his bald head. "Sure you were. Do you often hike so far away from home?"

"I used to live over by there," Jonah says, not rising to Finnegan's unspoken accusations. "I know the area."

I knew it. Jonah did lie to me. But the way he says it sounds like he doesn't want to say it, like they've cornered him, and he has to give it up. Maybe that's why he looked scared going in there.

I hope this whole thing doesn't get back to Dad. Even if he doesn't figure out I'm searching for Max, he isn't going to like me running around with boys he hasn't met.

The interview ends. Connie sends me a troubled glance, but she and Finnegan leave and Jonah and I head back to the waiting room.

Jonah's watching the television when I kick his leg. "You can't lie to the police like that."

"I didn't lie."

"You said we were on a hike."

"A hike is a walk in the woods."

"Why did you lie about living by the tent city?"

"It's none of your business."

From behind me, someone says, "Oh my God, Shiloh."

I swing my head around to find Miles rushing over through the double doors with Francesca trailing behind him. He barrels up to me and pulls me from the chair, wrapping his arms around my shoulders like I just came back from the dead.

"Are you okay?" he asks, his voice muffled in my hair.

I nod against his shoulder, and he lets me go. Two stray curls have fallen out of his gel hold and they bounce as he talks.

"About time you made it," Jonah says. "You get lost?"

"Just a little disoriented."

"Like how you need a GPS to find your way to school?" Jonah asks, grinning like it's easy and he didn't just look sick two minutes earlier.

Miles glances over at me, heat flooding his cheeks. "He's lying. I don't actually—"

"Don't be embarrassed," Jonah laughs. "It's better than following a homing pigeon or dropping pebbles like a tween from a fairytale."

Miles rolls his eyes. I drop my eyes to the floor. I can feel the energy draining through the bottom of my feet, replaced by the ache of worn-off adrenaline. "I want to go home."

"I'll go with you," Miles says.

I'm not really in the mood for company, but I'm too tired to fight, so I pick up my jacket, wrap it around my shoulders, and leave Francesca and Jonah in the waiting room with Miles trotting after me.

On the walk to the bus, Miles asks me if I'm okay and I say I'm fine. He keeps asking me questions, but I stop answering them, and by the time we board the bus, he gets the hint that I don't want to talk. I wonder why Connie wouldn't help me look for Max. She was acting kind of weird, and there has to be a reason for it. Dad hasn't mentioned knowing anything. The drinking's still starting in the morning, and I don't think it would be if he didn't feel so utterly powerless.

Maybe he doesn't. I don't know how his brain works. Either way, Connie has nothing to lose from listening to me. With every day that passes, Max is in more danger.

"Can I ask you a question?" Miles asks. His voice sounds far away, like I'm underwater and he's standing on the edge of the pool.

I rub my eyes. "Sure."

"Did I do something to make you mad?"

"No." Annoyed, yes, but that's not his fault, so there's no reason to bring it up with him. "When did Jonah live near that tent city?"

Miles averts his eyes. "He lived *in* the tent city."

I wasn't expecting that at all. "In it?"

"Yeah. Or at least he did until his mom OD'd and moved to Florida. That's why he's in foster care." Oh. I didn't know he was in foster care. That must have been why he looked so sick at the hospital, and why he didn't want to go into the woods.

I can't believe he didn't say anything. I would have never asked him to come if I'd known something like that.

"When did she OD?"

"I don't know, a while back. Elementary school. Before Jonah and I met. She went to the hospital, too, and got separated from Jonah. She sold a ring she wore and took the first Greyhound out."

God, I can't even imagine.

That must be how they became friends. I don't remember knowing Jonah in middle school, but if he looked anything like Liam, I understand why Miles would want to be his friend.

"I hope he's doing okay," Miles says. "What happened with that woman ... that would have been tough for him."

I'm an idiot. All that stuff I said about foster care being better. I had no idea.

I chew on my nails. A toddler screams in the back of the bus. An old man with a long, gray beard sits in front of me. He turns at the sound of the baby crying and glares at me. I can't tell if he's looking at me like he wants to kill me or kill himself, but then I realize he's not looking at me. He's looking at the crying kid without an ounce of compassion.

Liam looked so lifeless, trailing after those women. When things with Dad first started getting bad, I used to have a recurring dream of being rescued by social workers. When Dad smashed my grandmother's handmade vase or I caught him slamming Mom's head onto the corner of the porcelain bathroom sink, I would calm myself down by closing my eyes and imagining knocks on my front door. Mom would answer to one man and one woman standing on the welcome mat. Dad would be on the La-Z-Boy. The officers would walk calmly into the house to where Max and I were playing with plastic dinosaurs on his bedroom floor. The woman would take my hand. The man would pick Max up in his arms and carry him out. Dad would scream outrage. Mom would cry, but I would only smile as Max held his plastic T-Rex by the tail. In my dream, we always stayed together.

But even back then, I knew it wouldn't happen. I couldn't take the chance of them splitting us up. Besides, Dad is too charming and too well-liked. And he's the sheriff. He'd smile and say, "Kids, am I right? Heidi just fell in the bathroom, didn't you, honey?" Mom would nod because he has such a tight clasp on her throat that she's forgotten how to breathe without his hand there. Every time I've begged her to leave him, she has simply cried and gotten a bag of frozen peas from the fridge to put on my face.

If it's true and Leonard really is kidnapping kids with hard lives, I wonder how he could have known about Max.

Or who he could have gotten the information from.

"Can I talk to you about something?" Miles's voice jars me out of my daze.

I drive my knuckles into the back of the seat until they leave white marks on my skin. "Okay."

"I feel like you're being a bit mean to me, and I don't exactly understand why."

He doesn't say anything else, and it takes me a second to realize he's waiting for me to say something back. I didn't realize he felt this way. Honestly, I've been so focused on Max that I haven't been thinking much about Miles's feelings. "Sorry."

"You're distant and dismissive of me and I'm trying to be understanding because I know you're going through something, but I need to tell you that it's hurting my feelings."

"Max is missing."

"I understand that."

"I'm trying to find him."

"I want to be there for you," he says, "but you need to let me in."

Need? I bristle. "I don't *need* to do anything."

"Shiloh, come on."

The bus stops. We're only one stop away from downtown. It's a thirty-minute walk to my house from here, but I don't want to sit here and talk to Miles about my feelings.

I stand up. "I'm going home."

"This isn't our stop."

"I'm walking the rest of the way."

I step over his knees and climb off the bus. With a long hiss, the door closes, and the bus leaves me standing alone next to an empty field of corn. I use my hand to shield my eyes from the sun, squinting up at the water tower looming over the trees. Downtown isn't far. I can walk.

So, I start.

I don't want to go home. It's only a matter of time before Finnegan tells Dad I was in Mount Keenan during buddy-talk. Or I-wanna-be-your-buddy talk. *Hey Ernest, I got something to tell you, buddy.*

Guilt begins to settle deep in the pit of my stomach. I shouldn't have said that to Miles. Why do I do this to him all the time? It's like the second I actually consider opening up to him, letting him see the parts of me that I don't like or even scare me, something in my brain shuts down. Like I don't even know how to do that. At the same time, when I look at him looking at me and see the crinkle of his eyes that's so open and honest and giving, I want to lose myself in him. I want to touch my hands to his face and run them over the cupid's bow of his upper lip and into the dimples that form in his cheeks when he smiles. I want to press his skin to mine. To close my eyes and feel it, feel him, and let everything else in my mind slip away. But then he would say something in that sympathetic tone, or ask me to talk about my feelings, and suddenly I wouldn't even want to be in the same room as him.

I'm too tired to figure out whether any of that made sense. I'm so confused.

I don't know how we're ever going to find Leonard by wandering around in the woods. There has to be a better way to narrow down potential places he could be hiding. Could I find the answer by just learning more about him?

Thirty-five minutes later, I'm walking up the steps of the library—an outdated beige building which hasn't been renovated since the '60s that has a flag and brick columns out front.

I pull out the chair in the computer lab, sink onto the rough cushion, and click the mouse a couple of times to wake up the monitor.

Francesca mentioned the name of the circus. I rub the heels of my hands into my eyes as I try to remember. When I do, I type "The Durand Brothers Circus Ohio Leonard" into the search bar.

There are actually a few results. I don't know what I'm looking for, but I open the one at the top of the results, which takes me to a website called thecircusandthesideshow.com.

The website looks amateurish, like a kid cobbled it together for a school project. The background is black. The text is red and written in a curly font which I find hard to read, but it seems to have cut-and-paste entries for a bunch of different sideshows, documenting their histories and showing a collection of photos from their performances.

I find an entry for the Durand Bros. Circus and click to see more. On top of the page, there's a poster of peacocks, cobras, and clowns with white faces. Circuses creep me out, but I didn't have any real reason for being scared of them until now.

I read the description. I don't know who wrote this. Something about the font makes this website seem untrustworthy.

The Durand Brothers Circus is an American circus that toured from 1923 to 1944. The circus was founded by Joseph, Malcom, and Elias Durand, the sons of a French immigrant. Malcom was in the auction business. He followed circuses closely, taking advantage of the crowds they attracted to sell to.

While following the Kellogg and Clark Circus, Malcom was captivated by "The Big-Footed Girl," Mavis Mills, who performed in the circus freak show. He told his brothers about Mavis, captivating them and inspiring them to start a circus of their own. Joseph, Malcom, and Elias pulled together $5,000 to buy animals and equipment. Joined by Big-Footed Mavis Mills, a bearded lady, and the Human Frog, they opened in Cincinnati, Ohio, in 1923.

Joseph Durand managed the show. Malcom was the treasurer, and Elias acted as a general agent. After a successful first season, the brothers pooled their life savings to expand, bringing on more freaks —including the famous Lobster Boy, Landry Hilton, and a pair of conjoined twins, Audrey and Aubrey Miller. In 1925, the brothers had enough money to purchase their first elephant.

By the 1930s, the Durand Brothers Circus became one of the most successful in the country.

Who wrote this, a twelve-year-old? On the left side of the screen, there's a picture of Mavis Mills. Each of her legs is as wide as her torso. Each foot is as big as three of her heads. The caption on the photo spells Malcolm's name right.

In 1938, Malcom added an act to the freak show. The act featured an 11-year-old boy, "The Necromancer," who could bring animals back from the dead. Crowds amassed to watch the boy strangle small animals—usually chicken, squirrels, or rabbits—with his bare hands, and then bring them back to life. As the boy grew older, he killed larger animals. He reanimated goats, before moving onto cats and dogs.

After Joseph Durand's death in 1941, Malcom and Elias loaded a ship with the circus in San Francisco and set sail for Australia. The Australian tour took a turn for disaster when an infectious disease (glanders) spread throughout their animals. The Australian government quarantined the animals that did not die, causing the Durand Brothers to lose their entire menagerie. Upon their return to the States in 1942, they had to purchase new animals and needed financial assistance.

Malcom proposed selling the circus to Barnum & Bailey. Elias did not want that to happen and proposed another plan to attract more attention from the audience. In 1944, Elias volunteered his youngest daughter, Evangeline, to the Necromancer's act. In a tragic turn of events, the 17-year-old Necromancer fatally strangled her during the show. The Necromancer, Leonard Gailis, was found dead in a stable car later that night.

Malcom, alongside a grieving Elias, sold all interest of the Durand family to Barnum & Bailey later that year.

I scroll down to the bottom of the page to find a photograph of Leonard "The Necromancer" Gailis. The poster shows a teenager kneeling over a dead goat, holding a circular ball of light in both hands. Each of his hands has only three fingers.

I run another search for Leonard Gailis and find a photo of him standing in a group of other sideshow performers. Francesca has seen Leonard before at the cemetery. I print the photograph out to show her.

This has to be the Leonard who kidnapped Max. But how can that be true if Leonard died seventy-five years ago?

I search for "Evangeline Durand death," which pulls up an article from the *Cincinnati Enquirer* in 1944. A black-and-white photo shows a young girl who looks no more than fifteen, with her arm around a balding man who must be her father. Blond ringlets frame her fair, symmetrical features. An enormous bow sits on top of her head.

After getting the photo from the printer, I know I can't put off going home much longer. The image of Leonard's three-fingered hands is glued to the front of my mind. I can't stop thinking about them.

I wonder if he was born like that, and that's why he ended up in the freak show. I hate freak shows. Maybe I have a weak stomach, and maybe this makes me a terrible person, but body mutilations make my skin crawl. In school, I remember learning about a guy from London called the Elephant Man. I saw a picture of him once and couldn't stop thinking about it for days. I'm the same with videos of surgery. I have to watch them through my fingers.

I walk down the library steps. Cold wind licks at the warm spots beneath my chin and the base of my neck. Just as I turn the corner onto Main Street, I catch a flash of green on the opposite side of the road.

I stop. Across the street, walking past Stratford Guns, is a man wearing a long, green trench coat. Emerald green. It's not army green. Vibrant, like grass in a crayon drawing. He walks with long strides, his arms swinging at his sides. I glance down at his hands. One, two, three—five. He has five fingers.

He turns the corner. I consider following him when the

whoop of a police siren sounds right next to me, and my heart lodges in my throat.

I clutch the straps of my backpack as Dad rolls down the squad car's window. "Get in the car."

The flashing red and blue strobes hurt my eyes. Dad's elbow hangs out the driver's side window. He pulls his sunglasses down off his eyes to look at me. He doesn't look happy. Finnegan must have already told him I was at the hospital. "But—"

"Get in the goddamn car. Right now."

I do as I'm told. He takes a long drag at his cigarette and flicks it onto the pavement, pulling away from the curb with an unnecessary screech of rubber. He's bigger than I am. So much bigger. My shoulders shrink away from him, but I force my spine to stay straight.

We stop at a red light. He peers over at me from under his wide-brim hat.

"When we get home," he says, and goosebumps rise on the back of my neck, "I want you to take your clothes off."

23

JONAH

On the walk back, it starts to rain.

As if this day could get any worse. I pull my hat lower on my head, but Psycho Russo turns her face up to the sky and sticks her tongue out. She tries to eat raindrops for a second before bending over in laughter.

"Rain is the best," she says. "Do you agree?"

This girl's on something strong, but I don't know what. I actually believe her and her whole ghost thing. So I manage, "Sure."

"May I ask you a question?" she asks, skipping beside me.

"Go for it."

"Do you actually believe in the dead, or are you only pretending to so you can impress Shiloh Oleson?"

I glare at her. She blinks back at me with huge eyes, like she isn't expecting anything but is still interested in what I'm going to say. I want to say I'm not trying to impress Shiloh, but I think Psycho would know I'm lying. All that time getting left out of stuff has made her good at noticing things, I guess. "I believe you."

"I was unable to tell," she says. "You can be quite difficult to read."

I guess that's a good thing. I tilt my face back a little, so it points up into the rain, and drops run down my face like cold tears. Psycho's onto something. This feels kind of good.

"I believe we are a tiny bit alike, you and me," Psycho says. I want to tell her I don't see it, but I stop myself. I don't want to be a dick to her. What she did for Shiloh took courage.

I stop walking because it's time for me to turn. "This is me."

She salutes me with two fingers. "See you later, alligator."

For some godforsaken reason, I find myself replying, "In the light of the moon, raccoon."

Psycho giggles. "That is not the response."

"It's mine."

Technically, my sister came up with it, but Psycho doesn't need to know that. She waves goodbye. I wave back before walking away.

Psycho's weird, but she's growing on me. I guess I shouldn't call her Psycho anymore. Habit, I guess. The rain starts coming down harder, making the pavement slick and wet and making the surrounding air smell like steamy asphalt. I hang my head.

I shouldn't have gone back to the camp. It was dumb. I knew it was dumb before I did it, but I did it anyway. "Can't fix stupid," Aunt Moe, my foster mom, would say. In this case, she'd be right.

Seeing that woman overdose didn't help. And her son … man, if I keep thinking about it, I'm going to end up at Duncan's instead of Moe's, which would make Moe take my head off at the shoulders. I didn't tell her I'd be back from school so late. I also told her I'd clean the yard this afternoon, and that didn't happen. Can't seem to do anything right.

Why did Shiloh ask me so many questions? If I stayed in the waiting room for a minute longer, I would have told her about my mother. Shiloh just doesn't let up. She knows what she wants, and I just can't say no to her.

By the time I get to Moe's street, the rain's soaked through my jacket and hat. I brush the ends of my hair out of my eyes. It's getting long. Moe keeps telling me I have to cut it.

A burner phone buzzes in my pocket, and I give it a quick glance as I'm walking, just to see that it's Rachael.

U around?

No. I tuck it back into my pocket. Rachael's hot. It's not like there's anything wrong with her, but after this afternoon, I don't want to see her. I don't want to see anyone.

Down the street, a dog's barking. As I get closer to Moe's house, I realize it's her pit bull, Bessie, standing as rigid as a board in the front yard. Bessie sticks her fat nose through the fence when she sees me, her tag clinking against the silver chain around her neck.

"What's up, Bess?" I scratch her head through the chain-link wrapped around the front yard, still covered in Kaylee's plastic slides and toys. I only live a twenty-minute walk from Shiloh, but she lives where the folks with money do, in the houses with the pools. Moe's house is on the edge of town, and the kind of shithole you don't have to go inside to know it needs some work. It's small and ugly with white paint chipping off the sides and a yard of yellow grass speckled with small mounds of dog shit. Moe used to have me pick it up once a week or so, but she hasn't asked me in a while, and I don't care enough to remind her.

Bessie's cloudy eyes dart around. She smells something, then barks again. Rainwater runs down her fur.

I twist around to see what Bessie's barking at, but there's no one there. Bessie's nose is pointed at the house across the street. "What are you looking at, huh?"

In the house's upstairs window, a light turns on. I stare at the window for a second. I'm about to look away when a girl appears, staring down at me. My eyes squint through the heavy rain to see her better, but she disappears, and the light turns off.

Okay. So that was weird. I wasn't lying when I told Shiloh I believe in ghosts. I believe in them because my mom does, which is ironic because I don't believe much of what she says anymore.

I'm supposed to go to Florida for Thanksgiving this year. Jury's still out on whether that will happen. Doubt it. Last time I saw my mother was three years ago, when she took me to McDonalds, let me buy all the food I could eat, and told me she was clean. She'd gotten a place in Florida, near the good schools where you could walk to the beach. Told me I could learn to surf. Like I'd want to. Catherine, my sister, was twenty-one at the time and glued to her boyfriend in Columbus, so she was a lost cause, but I could go live with Mom. That night, Moe and my mother got into a shouting match so bad the ceiling shook. Mom ran up to me and grabbed me by the shoulders and promised she'd come back, steal me away in the night and bust me out of here. Moe drove her out of the house, but I waited at my window for her to pull up until morning. She never showed.

She sends me a postcard a few times a year, telling me she's visiting, or I should make plans to come down. But every time I've hoped to actually go, she's called to change her mind.

It makes me feel like kind of an asshole, you know, dealing when my mom's a junkie. But I stayed away from hard stuff and I'm done with all that now. I don't want to mess with my probation, and the way I see it, there are some things in life that just aren't worth it.

Deadbeat mom or not, Catherine's house was definitely haunted. She was hearing voices. Floorboards creaking. All the classic poltergeist shit. I can tell Miles doesn't believe in any of this. I'm surprised he's putting up with it at all. I didn't realize how serious he was about this thing with Shiloh.

Shiloh.

I grip the fence links until my knuckles turn white. What am I doing? Miles's the one friend I've got, and he's the one who shows up for me. But no girl's asked me questions like that before.

I turn toward the house across the street. I haven't looked at it close up. It's just a house. Tall and narrow, with a covered porch and a rocking chair.

It's probably nothing. I've been spending too much time with

Psycho Russo … Francesca … Frankie—that's what it is. Even so, I glance both ways and cross the street.

I climb the house's porch steps. Something twinkles to my left. I look over. Hanging from the top of the porch are a bunch of wind chimes. It takes me a second to realize why they look weird—some are made of beads, others are pieces of glass. Some of the chimes are forks, spoons, and even seashells, which is weird because we're pretty far from any beach. I step closer. One of the chimes is made of keys hanging from pieces of twine.

I touch one of the keys. When I take my finger off, it clinks against another, ringing like a tiny bell. All at once, the keys stop moving.

Behind me, the front door opens with a creak. I turn around to see an old lady standing in the doorway.

The woman is small and bony, with black hair that's almost all gray. She hangs onto the side of the door like it's the handle of a cane as she peers out at me through a large monocle. It magnifies the eye it's over and makes it look bigger than the other one.

I lift my finger. "How did you—"

"Know you were out here?" Her voice sounds thin, like parchment paper. "It's not every day that I find kids lingering outside my house." She shuffles onto the porch and tightens the cinch on her bathrobe. I can't tell if the robe is purple or brown, but it looks like a bat's wing. "Do you like my chimes?"

That's one word for it. "Sure."

Slowly, the woman moves over to the chimes. When she gets there, she reaches out her wrinkled hand to touch the keys. Even before her fingers reach them, they start to move again.

I point. "How'd you do that?"

"There are things you can't see," she says, adjusting her monocle and looking at me through it. The lens is thick—thicker than Miles's glasses, and Miles is pretty much blind. It looks like a camera lens, twisting back and forth as if to get me in focus. Her giant brown eye darts around, looking at me, looking over my head, and looking to each side. "All around us."

Wait. I lower my voice. "Are you talking about ghosts?"

"Things are not all they seem."

I remember that girl I saw in the window. "Do you live alone?"

"It can get lonely in this old house." Her eye settles on something next to my head and she smiles, exposing nasty yellow teeth. There's a long pause before her smile disappears and she says, "I need to go."

She must be talking about ghosts. That silhouette in the window … it has to be. "What are you talking about?"

The woman goes back inside. I try to follow her, but she slams the door in my face, just inches from my nose.

Damn it. I'm pounding my fist against the door when Aunt Moe's guttural voice yells my name.

"*Jonah Alexander.*" I turn around to see Moe standing on the porch, balancing her one-year-old daughter Kaylee on her hip. "Have you lost your damn mind?"

Knowing I have no choice, I walk back across the street. "Sorry."

"Get inside."

I do as I'm told. She shuts the door behind me, a frown etched deep into her face. Aunt Moe is not my aunt. I only call her Aunt Moe because that's what she told me to call her when we first met. It's what everyone calls her. She knows everyone because she never stops talking, and everyone calls her Aunt Moe.

She's stocky and no more than forty. Her ponytail's so tight that it pulls back the skin on her scalp like a facelift. Dark eye makeup clings to her lids and a blend of perfume and cigarette smoke sticks to her black, zip-up sweatshirt, covering her tattoo sleeves and holding in the gut that would otherwise spill over the front of her jeans.

"What am I gonna do with you?" she says, bouncing Kaylee, whose face is red from screaming. I'm used to this from her. I don't take out the trash. *What am I gonna do with you?* I don't take Bessie outside and she goes on the carpet. *What am I gonna do with you?* Kershner at Duncan's needs to bring me home because I'm drunk and professing my love to strangers in the bar? Okay, I guess I deserved that one. "I mean, seriously. What are you doing going and bothering poor Ms. Ruggles like that?" I shrug. Moe jabs a finger at me. "Don't you shrug at me that way." She moves the finger closer to me. I step backward. The couch trips me behind the knees, and I sit down. "Don't do it. I mean it. I'm up to here with your shrugging."

Moe's always been tough, but ever since I got put on probation last summer, she's been busting my ass for even the smallest things. I'm not complaining, really. As far as state care goes, I could have gotten a lot worse than Moe. "Sorry."

"Did you show your counselor your Career Center application today?" I rub my face. I was supposed to do that after school, but we went to the camp instead. Moe narrows her eyes. "You promised you'd do that today."

"I forgot."

"You can get a damn good job coming out of there." I know this. What Moe doesn't know, and what I can't seem to get through her thick head, is that they aren't going to let me in. It's not like the application committee is going to smile when they see my record. Or my grades. "Have you talked to Officer Groves about it?"

Talking to my probation officer is not going to help. "No."

"Do that tomorrow."

Shit, I forgot she's coming over tomorrow afternoon. Nothing seems important compared with all this stuff going on with Shiloh. "Sure, Moe."

"Don't you 'sure-Moe' me. You're a smart kid. You could do well if you just applied yourself." Moe nuzzles her nose into Kaylee's, ignoring the baby's screams. "Jonah is being a big idiot boy," she tells her. Kaylee continues screaming. "Yes, he is."

"You want me to clean the yard today, right?"

"It's raining cats and dogs out there. Do your homework first." I'm not going to do homework now. I'm on my way to the backyard when Moe calls, "You know I bug you because I care."

I slip on my shoes and walk out the door. As I pick up Kaylee's plastic bucket and shovel, I take one final look at the house across the street. In the upstairs window, the same girl as before stares down at me through the pouring rain.

24

SHILOH

Dad throws the car in park. I drag my feet up the front steps as he says hello to our neighbor, Mrs. Peterson, who's opening her umbrella as she prepares to walk her scruffy dog. She makes an offhand comment about the weather, and I go inside.

I close the door, cutting Dad off mid-laughter. Natural light seeps through the window, casting a shadow over the countertops, the dinner table, and Mom, who's sitting on the couch with a knitted quilt pulled around her shoulders.

"Mom," I say, but she doesn't move. With every passing day, she seems to get more and more lifeless. She was barely alive when Max was here, and I think his absence is killing her. She walks for miles with the search parties, and every time she comes back from the woods, it's like she's left more of herself inside of it.

I wish I could scream at her. Shake her shoulders and force her to wake up from this daze by telling her that I know where Max is and that I'm going to get him back. I can't.

The door clicks open. Dad walks into the house. He slides off his boots and leaves them by the door before pointing at my feet.

"No shoes in the house," he says, brushing past me to take a seat in the La-Z-Boy, groaning and stretching his arms over his head like a bear settling in for hibernation. "Go on. You know what to do."

Mom glances from Dad to me. The sadness in her eyes tells me that she knows what's going to happen, and she can't do anything to stop it. Or that she isn't going to do anything to stop it, which is definitely worse.

I pull off my sneakers, line them up beside Dad's, and walk down the hallway in my socks, pushing open the door to the master bedroom. The room is colder than the rest of the house, which is already cold because that's how Dad likes it. I unbutton my pants, slipping my icy thumbs through the belt loops and sliding them down my hips. I pull my sweatshirt over my head, then my T-shirt, until I'm in just my socks and cotton underwear.

I force my joints to bend as I sit on the edge of the bed. I catch a glimpse of Dad's belts hanging from hooks on his closet door. The buckles glint, even in the dim light.

Heavy footsteps sound from down the hall. I turn onto my stomach. The door opens, and he huffs, "Good girl."

I stay still as he walks behind me. Belt buckles clink against each other.

"Scott told me about your hike." I knit my hands into the comforter. Of course Finnegan told him. I knew he would. "Why were you in Mount Keenan?"

"My friends and I wanted to go."

"You're lying." The footsteps get closer. I don't dare look back at him because I know he doesn't like that. I hear him breathing. I can feel him standing over me. "You're a liar."

"I'm not—"

He brings the belt onto my back. Pain cuts through my skin. I clench my teeth and stick my face into the down.

"You can never lie to me." He hits me again. "Scott said you were with a boy," he says. "Jonah Weatherby, of all people. I know that kid on a professional basis, Shiloh. And you know I don't like you running around with boys."

I know why he doesn't like me hanging around with boys. It's because somewhere down at the bottom of it all, I'm still his little girl, and boys like Jonah and Miles threaten that. The belt brushes against my back like a caress. It's all I can do not to shiver in revulsion and fear.

He hisses in a breath. Lifts the belt.

"You're trying to find your brother, aren't you?" I don't respond, and his voice twists into a horrible, thin version of itself. "You are. I know you are. You promised me you were going to stay out of it. Keep yourself safe."

Even though I know he doesn't like it, I crane my head around to look at him. "I'm not a kid anymore. I know what I'm doing, and if you would just listen to me—"

"I have it under control."

Now he's the liar. The cops have no idea where Max is, and they're never going to find him. *Dad, ghosts are real.* I can just picture Dad's face. The contempt in his eyes. He'd laugh me right out of the room. "You're useless," I mutter.

"What did you just say?"

When I was little, I looked up to Dad. Right now, Max needs him. He has built his reputation protecting this town, but he does a piss-poor job of protecting his family, and I want him to know that. I want him to know how pathetic he is in my eyes.

I flip onto my back and stare at him. Knowing what he could do to me, I should be scared of him. But suddenly, I'm not afraid of him anymore. It's just me and Max against the world, and now Max is gone, so there's just me, and I have nothing left to lose. Except for my fear of the person standing over me. The top buttons of Dad's dress shirt are unbuttoned. His eyes travel down my body, lingering on every pucker in my stomach and tracing the curve between my hip bones.

"I said, you're useless."

Dad's jaw bulges. He shoots out his arm to flip me back over, but I kick him before he can. His soft gut squishes under my toes. He steps backward. I push off the bed and lunge for the door.

He grabs my ankle. I crash onto my knees and kick out as hard as I can. "Let go of me."

His grip is like iron. He bends down to grab my other leg. I drive my foot into his groin.

He howls and lets me go. I kick him in the face as hard as I can, so hard it hurts my foot, and now he doesn't know which part of himself to hold. He's got one hand over his balls and the other over his eye and he's hopping to keep his balance. I claw myself to my feet and run down the hall.

"Shiloh Oleson, get your ass back here."

I make it to the kitchen. I glance around for something to protect myself with. I can't run out of the house because I'm still naked, although I guess if I screamed loud enough, Mr. Peterson might call the cops. Who would call Dad. So that would be pointless.

"Shiloh, honey, don't make your father upset," Mom whines. "You know how he gets when he's mad."

Dad hobbles down the hallway with one hand over his eye, his nostrils flaring like a Jurassic Park dinosaur. He glares at me through the angry slit of his other eye, and all I can see is the picture of the Minotaur in Max's mythology book. Dad transforms before my eyes. He's no longer Ernest Oleson. He's a beast. Half bull, half child-eater. He swings his belt like an axe and digs his feet into the wood like he's preparing to charge. My blood runs cold. When he smiles, his incisors are long and pointed.

He runs a hand over his cropped hair. "I'm going to count to three, and I want you back on that bed." I dig my feet into the ground and root myself in place. "One." I don't move. "Two." I glance at Mom, who's looking at me from the couch. The light goes out behind Dad's eyes. "Three."

"Ernest, don't hurt her," Mom says. It's as close to support as she's ever going to give.

Dad rushes at me. I run over to the kitchen counter and pull a knife from the block, holding it out in front of me with both hands.

"Don't come any closer." My voice is loud. Dad stops. I can taste salt in my mouth, and I guess I'm probably crying. Dad inches forward. I shake the knife. "I will put this in you."

"Shiloh," Dad says, lowering the belt and reaching out his hand. He's smiling, but it's not his usual confident grin. I wonder if he's even a little scared. "Scooter, what are you doing? Put the knife down."

I shake the knife. Harder this time. "Don't come any closer to me."

"This is crazy." Dad laughs, looking over at Mom, who is still staring at us. Overwhelming hatred for her burns in my chest. How can she just sit there? "Heidi, come on. Tell your daughter she's crazy."

Mom stays silent. I point the knife at her. "What is wrong with you?" My voice breaks on the words and I know I'm definitely crying now. "Why are you just sitting there? You know what he does to me, and to Max, and you just sit there." Dad steps forward. I point the knife back at him. "Stay back."

"Put the knife down," Dad says. I guess he may have confronted criminals like this before, although he'd probably turn tail and run. Sheriff Oleson prefers his victims weak.

"You know what he does to me," I yell at Mom, who stands up from the couch, "and you let him. You might as well be doing it, too, and you still won't leave him. God, I hate you so much."

Dad comes closer. I'm gripping the knife so hard my knuckles turn white. He reaches for the knife. "It's okay," he says. "Come on Shiloh, hand it over." He touches my hand.

Something inside me snaps.

I drag the knife across his forearm.

Dad stands still. Oh my God, what did I just do? The knife sliced through his sleeve, and the fabric peels back to reveal a gash in his skin. Blood starts to seep into the shirt and drip to the kitchen floor. It drops onto the wood like raindrops on a plastic roof.

Dad clamps his hand over the wound, his face twisting in pain. I loosen my grip on the knife handle.

"Dad? Are you okay?"

Before I have time to register what's happening, Dad slaps the knife out of my hand and grabs me by the shoulder. His face swims before me as he pulls his fist back and smashes it into my nose. I scream in pain. He punches me again. Once more in the stomach. He throws me to the ground.

"You are nothing," Dad spits, gripping his arm where I cut him. "You will always be nothing."

"I'm not nothing."

Dad grabs me by the arm and pulls his hand back to clock me again, but before he can, there's a deep thud. Dad stiffens against me. He stumbles to the side to reveal Mom holding a frying pan by the handle.

She stares down at me, her eyes wide and wild like she can't believe what she just did. Dad clutches his ear. He looks up at her slowly.

"How dare you!" he says.

She stutters as she tries to find an answer. Dad yanks the pan from her hands and brings it down on her. She raises her arms to defend herself. He's stronger than she is. He hits her once. Twice. Then he pushes her buckled-in body to the floor like she's a doll he doesn't want anymore.

Dad turns to me. "Go to your room."

"Go fuck yourself."

I want to smash his head in. I want to cut him deeper. Mustering all the strength I have, I push myself into a sitting position and pull myself to my feet. The room sways. I grip the counter and walk over to where Mom is curled up on the floor. "Mom?"

"Go to your room," Dad says again. I ignore him.

Mom's eyes burn with an intensity I haven't seen before. I help her to her feet and pull her arm over my shoulders to keep her standing. I start walking with her toward my room.

Dad calls from behind us, "If I catch you involving yourself in this investigation further, I'm going to make you sorry, Shiloh. I mean it."

I glance back at him. He's still holding his arm. In the dim light of the kitchen, he doesn't look so scary anymore.

"Believe me, Dad, you couldn't make me sorrier than I already am."

I close my bedroom door. Dad doesn't follow us.

My arm falls away from Mom as she climbs onto my mattress, pulling my fleece blanket over herself. I lie down next to her. Pain reverberates through my skull, pulsing like rocks are being dropped rhythmically into my brain. I'm bleeding. I hope my nose isn't broken.

"Next time," I whisper to Mom. "Next time he touches us, I'm going to make him pay."

Mom sobs harder. She grabs hold of my hand and squeezes, shutting her eyes against the pillowcase.

Fifteen minutes go by. I listen to the television in the living room as I stare out the window at the setting sun. Mom's breathing is shallow but steady.

"I'm sorry," she whispers, finally, like it's a secret she and I share. "I'm sorry, Shiloh. I'm so sorry."

I don't reply, because it's not okay, but Dad's the one who should be sorry.

Thirty minutes go by. I pull my comforter over my naked body and touch my nose. It feels swollen, but I think the bleeding has stopped and I can't feel any breaks in my skin. I don't think it's broken.

The television turns off. I wonder if Dad's going to try to come in. He pauses outside my door on his way to his bedroom, but after a few seconds, his feet shuffle off again. He's not a dinosaur anymore. Or a bull. More like a wounded bear.

After he's been gone for a while, Mom climbs out of bed and leaves my room, creeping back a few minutes later to bring me a glass of water.

She touches my hair, kisses the side of my head, and then leaves.

Nobody in the house stirs. Air trapped in the heating pipes rattles as the radiators battle the autumn chill outside.

I hope Max is warm.

The glass of water feels good going down my throat. By some miracle, I manage to fall asleep around nine, but just after one in the morning, the ache in my body pulls me awake. I want to be held, but not by anyone here. Pulling on my pajamas and tucking my hair into my hood, I creep out of my bedroom, slip on my sneakers, and sneak out the front door.

25

SHILOH

Miles's house is tall and gray, with ivy climbing up the chimney and shutters on the windows that don't actually close. It's the kind of house I dream of buying for Max one day, a house that feels like home with a white picket fence wrapped around the front.

Both of Miles's parents are college professors. His dad teaches French because he is French, the kind of French who has a thick accent and reminds me of a detective in an animated movie who strokes his mustache with a baguette when he's thinking. His mom teaches something to do with brains. I like them. Even though Halloween is not for another month, they've already decorated for it. Spiderwebs cling to their bushes and fake ghosts hang from trees. In a way, I hate Miles for having a family who decorates, and a dad who doesn't snap his twelve-year-old's wrist for forgetting to put the dishes away or touch him where he's not supposed to in a public arcade bathroom.

I trudge through the wet grass to the backyard. I keep my shoulder against the side of the house to avoid triggering the cameras or motion sensors. Miles's bedroom is on the ground floor. His curtains aren't closed all the way. I lean close to the glass and peer inside to see Miles stretched out on top of his blankets with his arms up over his head.

He looks so innocent when he's sleeping. Who am I kidding? He looks innocent all the time.

I check my reflection in the window. I'll probably have some bruises tomorrow, but for now I look fine—at least fine enough that Miles won't notice anything is wrong as long as he keeps the lights off.

I tap on the glass. He rolls over and I tap again—louder this time.

Miles sits upright. Seeing me in the window, he widens his eyes. He gets out of bed and turns on his lamp, but instead of coming to the window, he walks down the hall.

I'm trying to figure out my next move when he comes back and opens his bedroom window. "Sorry, I just had to turn off the alarm," he says. "What are you doing here?"

Oh. He might still be angry at me for this afternoon. Yesterday afternoon, I guess, since it's after midnight. I'd completely forgotten about our fight on the bus.

"Can I come in?" I whisper.

Miles hesitates. After a second, he pops out the fly screen for me to pull myself through the window. Walking over to his bed, I collapse onto my side and pull the sheets over my legs.

Miles sits on the edge. He isn't wearing his glasses, and he looks younger because of it. A white T-shirt clings to the bones of his shoulders and ribs. Underwear with red and white stripes hugs his legs, making them look like candy canes. He's so much skinnier than me. Sometimes, I forget how skinny he is because he's so tall.

"What are you doing here?" Miles sits on the edge of the bed. Maybe lying down with me would be too much to expect, given what I said to him earlier. "It's two o'clock in the morning."

I pat the bed. Miles slowly lowers himself beside me. I roll onto my side to look at him. He's cute. Really cute, in an angular sort of way.

"Are your parents asleep?" I ask.

He looks at me, curled up in his bed like I've been here much longer. "I hope so. They went to bed hours ago because, like I said, it's two o'clock in the morning."

I focus on his eyes. His ears. The way his collarbone juts out of his T-shirt. I touch his smooth, clean-shaven face. His jaw sits in my hand. Holding his face feels like I'm holding something made of glass, like if I move too fast in one direction, something will shift and break.

The wrinkle disappears from Miles's brow. His voice is a whisper when he asks, "What are you doing?"

Keeping my hand on the sharp bones of his face, I shift closer to him, look him in the eyes, and kiss him.

Our lips barely touch. I don't remember the last time I kissed him. Before Max went missing, probably. Or maybe at the labyrinth. I can feel his lips against mine, warm and soft like small pillows. I try to gauge whether he's pulling away, and when I'm sure he isn't, I kiss him harder. His long fingers curl around my head, guiding him to me like he wants me. I need to catch my breath. I pull away from him and gasp.

Miles's eyes open. "Shiloh? W-what is happening right now?"

"Just kiss me," I mumble, pulling him back over to me. His lips crush mine, closing all the space between us. All the sadness and pain melt away every time he touches me. I melt away myself, like soap in hot water or butter on the stove.

He rolls on top of me. I hold his face with both hands to keep it right where it is, with me, bringing my body back to life. His hipbones dig into my thighs as he slides his hands down my sides. His finger passes over where the belt hit me. A whimper snags in my throat. He pulls away. "Are you okay?"

My cheeks are burning hot. "Yes."

His breath brushes against my skin. "Are we going to talk about what happened?"

I don't want to talk. I want to touch him. I want him to touch me. I want to destroy the memory of what Dad did earlier, and wash away the grime beneath my fingernails. Dad is not here, and he can't stop or control me. I am my own person. Mine. I slide my hands under Miles's shirt, running them down his back before hooking my thumbs through his waistband. He flinches.

"Is everything okay?" I ask.

Miles glances down at my hands. "I … I have never done this before."

"We don't have to."

"No, I want to. I just, I'm not—I don't look like Jonah does."

Gently, I pull his T-shirt over his head and toss it over the edge of the bed, onto the ground. The air catches in the back of my throat. I knew Miles was skinny, but I've never seen him without his shirt on. His hip bones protrude. I can see every one of his ribs under his skin.

Miles looks at me looking at him and grimaces self-consciously. "I know, I'm sorry."

His cupid's bow is flat, and I touch it with my thumb. "Miles, you're perfect."

A wide smile spreads across his lips. He starts pulling up my shirt. I remember the welts on my back, and I hold it down. "Can I keep it on?"

Miles stops immediately. "Oh, yeah. Of course."

He kisses me again. Every part of my body feels alive. For the first time since Max went missing—hell, maybe even for the first time in my life—I am filled with honest and undeniable desire. I want more. More of Miles. More of this feeling. Deep down, I've always been afraid of anyone touching me. I was worried that even when I felt ready, I wouldn't be able to stomach anyone touching me because my only experience of someone touching me there had eaten a hole right through me. All I want right now is for Miles to touch me more. I pull at his candy cane underwear.

Miles quirks up his eyebrow. "Are you absolutely sure you want to do this?"

Heart pounding in my ears, I nod. "Do you have any … you know?"

Miles stands up, walks over to his closet, and retrieves a small box with such purposeful excitement that I can't help but smile.

"Somebody's prepared," I say.

"Yeah, the eternal Boy Scout. What can I say?" He flops back down on the bed with a cheeky grin. "I like to be prepared."

I laugh and cup my hand over my mouth to stop the sound. Miles lowers himself onto me, and I wrap my arms around him.

———

Miles falls off me and onto the mattress. I lie still, listening to his fast breathing as he wipes sweat off his forehead and props himself up on his elbow to look at me, his curls falling into his eyes.

"Was that okay?" he asks.

I utter a choked, "Yes," but I don't want to move. What we just did dawns on me. The adrenaline fades away, and the places where Dad hit me fill with blood, start to ache, and fuse my skin to the sheets. I run my tongue over my teeth. There's a bad taste in my mouth. I wonder if Miles can smell it.

"Can I get you a tissue or anything?" Miles reaches down to grab his shirt and uses it to mop the sweat from his brow. He lowers his voice. "Did you, you know. Is there any blood or … anything?"

"There's no blood."

He drapes his arm over me. I breathe heavily into the pillow. I can feel him bury his nose into my hair and I squeeze my eyes shut, focusing on his arm and his skin touching me and not on the dawning realization that now that the adrenaline is wearing off, I don't remember why I came here in the first place.

"Your hair smells good." Miles curls a dirty strand around his finger. "You smell good. Everything about you is perfect. You're, like, the perfect girl."

I feel disconnected from my body, like I'm floating up and I can look down and see myself lying under Miles's plaid comforter. I should be happy. Miles is holding me and nothing bad is happening, but something heavy sits in my stomach, eating away at its lining like battery acid.

My voice is barely there when I say, "Sometimes, I don't know how to be a person."

Miles pulls his arm away. I turn around so I'm looking at him. His cheek presses against the pillowcase so heavily that I can almost see the fabric wrinkling his skin. Our faces are inches apart.

"What do you mean?" he asks.

"I don't know. Just … things seem easier for other people." I know Miles wants me to open up to him—he's been trying to get me to talk since Max went missing. But I don't know if I'm saying this right. I've never talked about this before. "Like, some people just know how to do things, or to handle themselves, but I don't." I drop my eyes to the ribbed neckline of his T-shirt. "I don't know who I am."

"I know who you are," Miles says. He must see the disbelief cross my face because he says, "I do, okay? You're the most obdurate person I know." My eyebrows wrinkle together. I have no idea what obdurate means, but I don't feel like asking. "You would do anything for Max. Even though you don't like to show it, you care about things so much and you do such a good job protecting him. I've never met someone who's brave like you. You're walking out the back of the wardrobe straight into Narnia believing Francesca even though she hasn't proved anything to you, and you're just putting yourself at the heart of it and trying to find the person you love. You're an incredible person, Shiloh. I'm just … amazed by you."

I know what he's saying is nice, but it's just making me feel sticky. How can Miles say I protected Max when I so clearly didn't?

Miles touches his fingers to my lips and nose, like he's making sure they are still there. "You're so guarded with me," he says. "I don't know what it is you're hiding, but whatever it is, I want to know. I want to know everything about you."

I pull the blanket up to my chin. In the darkness, Miles's Darth Vader nightlight cuts into his hips and the indentations of his ribs and collarbones. "I wish I were stronger than I am."

"You're so strong already."

That's not what I meant. I'm talking about the kind of strength that can catch Dad's arm before it touches me and throw it back.

Suddenly, Miles laughs. The gesture takes me by surprise and my stomach leaps to my throat.

"I'm sorry," he says, still smiling. "It's just that when you're with me, I get physically happier. Like I can feel it in my body." He presses his nose to my nose. It's all I can do not to flinch or let the pain of the contact show. "I don't know what's happening to me. You walk into a room and even if you're stressed or angry about something, I don't want to be around anybody else. Even afternoon. I knew you wanted to be alone, but I still wanted to be with you. I deserved what you said. I was being annoying, but I want to be with you even in the bad parts. I've never felt like this before." His arm is uncomfortable to lie on. I adjust my head so that it doesn't hurt as much. "Do you know what I mean?"

I don't think I feel the same way. Sometimes, when I walk into a room and Miles looks at me with those eager eyes, I want to be somewhere else.

"Shiloh." A disbelieving look crosses his face. "I think I love you."

I laugh. The words are so ridiculous that he has to be kidding. He's kidding, right? He's not smiling.

I pull away from him and sit up on his bed. Oh my God. He's serious. "No, you don't."

"I do." He sits up and takes my face in his hands. His eyes are beautiful. So big, so open. "I love you."

"But …" I fight for words. "You don't even know me."

He drops his hands. "What do you mean?"

"You wouldn't love me if you knew me."

"I want to know you. That's what I've been saying, all the stuff we've been talking about."

"We've only been dating for a couple of weeks."

If he's never felt this way about anyone, how does he know it's love? He doesn't.

"What made you panic when we went to the Fun Palace?" he asks. "How are you holding up with Max being gone?"

"I don't want to talk about this."

"I do." Miles takes my hands in his under the covers. I take in a shallow breath, and Miles lowers his voice. "I know there are things that hurt you. You can tell me about them. Staying silent about the things that silence you gives them power."

Miles's eyelashes flutter as he waits for a response. *I love you.* The words echo. I need to get out of this bed. Miles has no idea what he's talking about. Love is a stupid promise, and just another demand. To love him back. To be this person he thinks he loves.

Where the hell are my pants? I bend down to pick them up and hear Miles gasp.

"What's on your back?" he asks.

My hand shoots out to pull my shirt down. The fabric presses down into the welts. "Nothing."

"Nothing?" Miles's voice is so high it almost breaks. "Are you seriously telling me those are nothing?"

"Help me find my pants." I stand up to walk over to the other side of the bed, and he follows me with his eyes. His mouth is wide open in an expression of unmasked horror.

"Who did that to you?"

I find my pants under the bed, put them on, and pull the drawstring tight. Miles grabs my wrist. He curls his long fingers around it. I can feel how much he wants me to stop moving, to tell him I love him, and start to cry as I explain that Dad is a monster and I'm stuck in a labyrinth with him, running, always running away from him and I don't know how to wield a sword well enough to stop him. I can't tell Miles any of this. The thought of doing so makes me want to run until I end up in a cornfield somewhere on my back in the middle of nowhere, looking up at the empty sky until dawn breaks. I don't know what's wrong with me. He *loves* me. I should be happy. He's looking at me like he's waiting for me to unravel in front of him like a flower blooming in slow motion, revealing every piece of my soul for him to examine like some rare species. Or dissect like a worm in biology lab.

There's a ringing in my ear. As I listen to it, I realize it's not ringing. It's a voice. Telling me that if I unravel in front of Miles, if I let him see the person I really am, the person who wishes I could have plunged that knife into Dad's chest and twisted it with all my strength, Miles wouldn't still love me.

"You need to talk to me," Miles says, leaning off the bed to take my hand. I look down at where he's holding my fingers. "Please."

"Don't touch me." I yank my hand away. "I don't love you, and I don't need to do anything."

"You don't love me?"

"I don't love you and I don't need you. I don't need anyone."

I'm about to climb out of the window when he says, in a voice so small and defeated that I can barely hear him, "I love you, but I don't know how if you won't let me."

I glance back. He's sitting on the edge of the bed, still naked. Hot tears press against the back of my eyes. "Then don't."

My feet crash onto the hard turf outside his bedroom window. I run through the front gate and make it to the end of the street before tears spill down my cheeks. What just happened? I didn't mean for this to happen. I didn't think he would tell me he loved me. How was I supposed to respond to love? I don't know what that feeling is.

I grip the pole of the stop sign at the end of Miles's street and cry so hard it's almost a scream.

26

SHILOH

I wake up the next morning in so much pain.

I don't want to get out of bed. As long as I stay where I am, I don't have to think about Max. Or Miles. I can pretend Max is in his bed across the hall.

Mom cracks open my door at six thirty. "Honey, are you awake?"

Her voice quivers when she asks the question. I want to tell her no, but I don't want to lie, so I just don't move.

"Your father made breakfast," Mom says. "Can you please come eat with us?"

She can't be serious. I prop myself on my elbow and glare at her. Pink silk pajamas hang on her bones like they're hanging off hooks. "Why do you stay with him?"

Mom flinches. Something behind her eyes darkens, and she lowers her voice when she snaps, "Everyone has baggage, Shiloh. Now come to the table."

I remember what she looked like last night, curled up across from me, damaged and discarded on top of my bed. At what point does it become enough? Is she ever going to say that it's

209

enough, or is she going to keep taking it until one day Dad kills her?

Out of nowhere, I remember something Miles said last night. *Staying silent about the things that silence you gives them power.*

I'm done giving Dad any power over me.

I sit up in my bed. I can hear Dad humming along to the radio in the kitchen, so I lower my voice. "Two weeks after Uncle Jim died," I tell Mom, "Dad took me to an arcade in Mount Keenan and made me touch him." My throat narrows around the words, but I swallow hard and force myself to be specific in my description. I don't want to leave anything up to her imagination. "He put my hand in his pants and asked me to touch him, and I did it because he said it would make him happy. He made me promise not to tell you."

Mom digests this. Her fingers wrap around the doorframe as she raises her other hand to cover her mouth. I don't want to look away or back down. I want her to hear me. I want her to look at me. "What's it going to take, Mom?"

She opens her mouth to say something, but with a trembling lip, she shakes her head and walks down the hallway back into the kitchen.

A breath rattles out of my lips. I fold over my knees, gripping them until Dad calls, "Shiloh! Breakfast!" from the kitchen.

I slide into a chair in the kitchen. Did I make a mistake telling Mom? I can't read the expression on her face as she sits across from me. She drums her fingers on the table like she's playing a repetitive song on the piano, and she has pulled her bottom lip between her teeth.

It's bright this morning. Early sunlight slices through the windows at a low angle, filling the room with warmth. Last night, the shadows were sharp, and the night closed in around us, but today, an outsider would never guess anything like that could have happened here. I look for the knife I used on Dad. I can tell it's been through the dishwasher because the wooden block on the countertop is full of handles with no gaps.

Dad is at the stove, an apron tied around his waist. He moves his hips in time with the gentle hymns rising from the radio, using tongs to transfer bacon onto a plate beside him. He sees me and holds up the plate. "I made bacon."

Because you're a pig.

He's made more than just bacon. A plate of eggs sits in front of Mom, next to a plate of French toast and a jug of maple syrup. The smell of cinnamon and melting butter hits my nose and I start to salivate. Dad makes good French toast. But it doesn't change what he did.

Dad puts the bacon down in front of me, and I notice a strip of gauze poking out from under his shirt sleeve.

"I'm sorry for last night," Dad says, reaching his arm around me and hugging me from behind. "I lost control of my temper." I train my eyes on the bacon. Drops of grease cling to the top of each piece, and the fat glistens.

Dad squeezes me. "Can you say you did too?"

Lose control of my temper? I didn't. I'm tired of living in fear of him. I know he blames himself for Jim's death, even though I don't know why, but Jim's death definitely wasn't Mom's fault. Or mine. Or Max's.

When Dad realizes I'm not going to reply, he drops my shoulders with a sigh. His chair screeches the wood as he pulls it back and sits down. Mom pours coffee into my mug. The stream shakes as her hand trembles.

"I just can't do anything right," Dad mutters. "Is it too much to ask to have a nice meal with my family?"

Mom looks at me. The skin on her forehead has split where Dad hit her with the pan and a purple bruise is growing there. I imagine my face looks just as bad, but I haven't looked in the mirror yet. Dad glances between us and then lowers his head into his hands before letting out a hard breath. He looks up and plasters a big old smile onto his face.

"Dig in, everyone." Dad forks a piece of bacon onto my plate. "Shiloh, come on. Eat some bacon."

I raise a piece of bacon to my lips and let the grease cover them like a balm. Dad moves three pieces of French toast onto his plate. "Heidi, can I have a glass of water?"

Mom gets up to get him one. On her way back to the table, the glass slips from her hands and shatters all over the floor.

Dad tells Mom to clean it up. I take advantage of the commotion to sneak off to the bathroom and sink onto the toilet. I wrap a strip of toilet paper around my hand and slowly touch myself with it, chomping down on my lip as I do so. It stings. I raise the tissue out of the toilet. Blood covers the top. I've heard that some girls bleed after their first time, but I didn't expect it to hurt this much. My skin feels like it's been ripped apart.

Folding the toilet paper, I shove it in my underwear and stand up, wash my hands, and finally work up the courage to look at myself in the mirror. My hands curl around the edges of the sink.

There's a small break in the skin on my nose, but my right eye is where the real problem is. Underneath my bottom lid, it's purple. Dad's not going to let me go to school like this.

I open the drawer and rummage through it, hoping to find Mom's concealer. Dad usually doesn't hit me in the face. He's careful like that. I check under the sink but don't see any makeup. Mom must have some in her own bathroom. God knows she uses it.

Before I can open the door to check, I stop myself.

No. Screw this. I shouldn't have to cover it up. If Dad is ashamed, so be it. I'm done making myself smaller for him.

I press my hand against the door. I can still feel Miles's hands on me in the dark, sliding over my ribcage. Part of me wishes it had felt weird when he touched me, and that I wouldn't want him to do it again, but it felt so good. His touch was kind. Safe. I want him to touch me again. I want to lose myself in him and forget myself while I'm doing so.

Miles loves me. I don't know what love means. I know I love Max, but the way I feel about Miles is different, and Max will always be more important to me than Miles.

I press myself harder against the door. I don't want to go to school today.

I don't have much of a choice in the matter because Mom still drives me there at seven o'clock. I thought Dad would stop her, after seeing my face and all, but he didn't. He did tell us to go make ourselves presentable. Mom did. But I refused, and I guess Mom didn't have the heart to make me.

Every couple of minutes, she turns her head to look at me and I think she's going to ask me a question about what I told her, but she doesn't, and turns her attention back to the road. The hum of the engine fills the silence. I don't know what I expected when I told her, but I expected her to say something. It's weird that she's so silent.

She pulls up to the curb. I unbuckle my seatbelt. I'm getting out of the car when Mom says, "Are you sure you want to go in like that?"

I know immediately she's referring to my eye. "I have nothing to be ashamed of."

Mom pauses and nods. I might be wrong, but I think there's a hint of pride in her eyes. "I will be here to pick you up at two forty-five."

"Okay." I close the door and walk up to the school. A flurry of leaves fall down from the trees. If I were Francesca, I'd probably want to catch them, but I'm not.

Hanging above the entrance is a flashy banner announcing this weekend's homecoming dance. I pause to look up at it. With everything going on, I'd forgotten all about it.

The banner is purple with gold, squiggly letters spelling out WE BELONG TOGETHER, which must be the theme of the dance. School dances are dumb, especially ones with such corny themes. My parents met in high school. I imagine they went to the homecoming dance together and swayed to the same romantic music with their hands on each other, and look how that turned out.

Miles probably likes these kinds of cheesy things, but I doubt he's going to ask me to go after last night.

As I turn the corner to get to the homeroom, Jonah falls into stride beside me.

"You got a second?" he asks. His blue eyes are bright against his black coat. A frown curves the side of his mouth. "Who did that to you?"

He asked *who* did that. Not what happened. I can't say I walked into a pole, or something stupid like that, because he'd see right through it, and even though I'm not going to cover it up, I'm not ready to talk about it. So I ignore his question. "What's up?"

"I'm pretty sure my neighbor can see ghosts."

Of all the things he could have said, this is not what I was expecting. "How do you know?"

"I don't think she sees ghosts like Frankie does." Jonah makes a circle between his thumb and pointer finger before holding it up to his eye. "She wears this monocle, right? And I'm pretty sure she can see ghosts through it."

I try to picture a monocle in my head. "Those one-eyed glasses things?"

Jonah gives a quick nod. "It was a rich person thing that was big two hundred years ago, so I don't know why she had it. But the thing is, she wasn't looking at me. She was looking at things around me while she was talking to me."

"So you're telling me you've found a monocle that lets people see ghosts through it because your neighbor couldn't focus on you while she was talking to you?"

"Exactly."

"Couldn't the reason she didn't focus on you be that you are … how do I put this nicely—" I pause for emphasis "—boring?"

Jonah looks so flustered I almost want to laugh. "It wasn't that."

"Keep telling yourself that, buddy."

"We should go talk to the lady."

This is a dumb idea, but I appreciate his enthusiasm. I underestimated Jonah when I first met him. He's actually turning into a decent friend.

"I want to find Max," I say, "not more people who can see ghosts. I'm perfectly happy with the Francesca we have, Jonah, and I have to go."

With that, I enter my classroom and leave Jonah standing out in the hallway.

———

I'm walking to my next class when I get approached again. This time, by someone I wasn't expecting.

"Shiloh Oleson," says Call-Me-Bill, walking toward me. *Crap, what's this about?* "Principal Orr wants to have a little chat."

My mind immediately goes to Max. "Have the police found something?"

"Oh, it's not about your brother. I'm sorry." His face is so round. Like a tennis racket. He jerks his thumb over his shoulder. "Walk with me?"

Call-Me-Bill is smiling at me in a way that makes me think I don't have a choice, so I follow him down the hall.

"Are you going to the homecoming dance?" he asks, swinging his arms as we walk.

"No."

Bill's face falls. "Why not?"

I'm about to tell him I think dances are stupid, but then I realize it's not even my honest answer. As dumb as I think school dances are, if Miles asked me to homecoming, I'd go.

"Because I don't think my boyfriend is going to ask me."

Bill looks almost disappointed. "Why do you say that?"

I focus on the tiles beneath me. It's not like Call-Me-Bill is going to tell Miles my answers to these questions. He just wants to be everybody's friend, so I might as well just tell him the truth. "My boyfriend told me he loved me, and I said I didn't love him back."

"Hm." Bill pauses for a second. "Did you mean it?"

"I don't know."

I glance over at Bill and see he's already looking back at me with a hopeful look on his face.

"Sometimes, I lash out when I get uncomfortable," he says, "but usually it's a sign I'm about to grow."

Before I'm done digesting the idea that somewhere, in some parallel universe or maybe inside of the Death Star, Call-Me-Bill would actually get mad about something, we reach Principal Orr's office door. Bill hooks his fingers through his lanyard. "Ready?"

"I guess."

He opens the door for me to walk inside, and I do to find Principal Orr lowering herself into her chair.

"Miss Oleson," she says, in a high-pitched, raspy voice. Her voice is classically feminine, but domineering. "Please, take a seat." She nods her thanks to Bill, who leaves.

Principal Orr is a tall woman with black hair pulled into a bun. She has stern, pointy features that look like they've been trained to spot misbehavior. She has no patience for children acting out of line and doesn't hesitate to send students to detention if they speak out of turn. Her sharp attitude has always scared me, but in the way you're scared of people you respect. You don't want to disappoint them.

Principal Orr has never called me to her office before. I've always kept a low profile in school. I don't get in trouble.

I lower myself onto the chair. Principal Orr folds her hands on the surface of her desk before leaning forward and pressing her lips into a thin line.

"I don't know how to phrase this," she begins, "but I'm coming from a place of concern. I'm aware of the personal issues you have been facing in the past two weeks, and I'm sorry about that. Nobody should have to go through what you are going through."

I try to figure out what this is about. I haven't been paying attention in class because I have been preoccupied thinking about Max. Could she be mad about that?

My heart quickens with every second of silence. Principal Orr clears her throat and asks, "How are you holding up?"

"Oh, you know …" I gesture at nothing, and don't know what else to say. "I'm sorry. Did I do something wrong?"

"One of your classmates approached me this morning, concerned you might have gotten into some kind of trouble."

She's talking about my eye. She has to be. I try hard not to touch it, and fight to keep my voice steady as I ask, "Trouble?"

"Are you comfortable telling me how you hurt your eye?"

I should have used the concealer. I knew it. I also know this is my opportunity to tell her, to accuse Dad of what he did, but my mouth can't form the words. What's she going to do, call the cops? Even though I didn't cover the black eye, Dad is still charming, and people still won't believe me. Even if Principal Orr does believe me —even if every person in this town believes me—there's still a part of me, as much as I hate to admit it, that doesn't want to put Dad through the humiliation. And if Dad finds out I told someone— God, I don't even want to think about what he would do to me then.

"I fell," I say.

Principal Orr raises her eyebrows. "I'm not coming to you as your principal. I'm coming to you as a resource." She leans back in her chair. "If you're in some kind of trouble, I can get you help."

I don't know what kind of help that would be. Regret pricks my chest. I was wrong to draw attention to myself like this. "I don't need your help."

"I understand why you're hesitating," she says. "It's all right. I'm in no rush. I'm happy just to sit here for a while until you feel comfortable talking to me."

I don't really want to sit here, but I guess sitting in here is more comfortable than sitting in class with everyone staring at me, so I sink back in my chair.

It's been about five minutes when I realize—oh, crap. *Miles.* Maybe whoever reported me thinks that quiet, smart, poetry-writing Miles Barot-Renaud finally lost his mind. If Call-Me-Bill hints to Principal Orr that Miles and I got into a fight because he wouldn't invite me to the dance, Miles would be the next one in here.

"It has nothing to do with Miles, if that's what you're thinking," I say. "I swear on my life."

Principal Orr looks at me for a few seconds before she reaches forward and crosses something out with her pen.

The silence stretches out. This chair is actually pretty comfortable. Principal Orr pushes her spectacles up her nose with her thumb and wakes up her computer, transferring her attention to the monitor on my left. She doesn't have a big office. It looks like a lot of the other office rooms in our school, with maroon fabric chairs, a dark oak desk, and a bookcase stretching up to the ceiling. In the bookcase are a lot of folders, stacks of papers, and a pair of gold theatrical masks. One mask is twisted into a painful smile. Another into a grimace. They're pretty creepy. She didn't strike me as the kind of person to be into theatre stuff. I wonder if she used to be a theatre kid.

I point up at the masks. "What are those?"

Principal Orr lowers her spectacles and twists her head around over her shoulder to check them out. "Those are the masks of comedy and tragedy, representing the Greek muses Melpomene and Thalia."

She was definitely a theatre kid. She looks way too excited about them. "Why do you have them?"

"I used to teach drama," she says, and I smile in satisfaction. "I picked those up on a trip to Italy. Actors in classical times used to wear them so the audience would know whether to expect good emotions or bad. Gives a new meaning to the term 'two-faced,' don't you think?"

Interesting. I fall silent, and Principal Orr returns her attention to her computer. Behind her head, in the bookcase, I notice a framed photograph of her looking a little younger, standing with a young, toothy boy and grinning into the camera.

Another picture of this boy hangs on the wall. This one is just of him, not of Principal Orr, and it looks like it was taken in the park. The boy's hair is combed neatly, and he is wearing a collared shirt with the top button undone. He looks kind of like Max, just a couple of years older and with neater hair. No matter how much I brush Max's hair, his cowlick never flattens like that. I could keep it in place for a while with gel, but it always springs back.

"Is that your son?" I ask.

Instead of smiling the way she had with the masks, her face falls like a pale imitation of her tragedy mask. She takes off her spectacles again, and they hang from a chain around her neck. "That's Louis."

"Louis?"

"My grandson." Principal Orr turns back to her desk. I notice that the tip of her nose has been brushed with pink. "He went missing three years ago."

Even though I never knew him, I can feel my heart shrink. Louis's smile looks even more like Max's than I remember.

I don't want to be insensitive, but I really want to know. "What happened to him?"

Principal Orr stares at me for a drawn-out moment. She must take pity on me because of my eye, or feel some kind of camaraderie because Max is missing and I would understand her pain, because she says, "He drowned. My son took him swimming in the Coshocton. He ..." She pushes her glasses back up to dab the moisture collecting under her eyes. She looks like Mom has ever since Max went missing, only Louis has been missing for three years. I can't imagine holding onto this for three years. If I can't find Max, I don't know what I'll do.

An unexpected pang of appreciation for Dad warms my chest. It was Dad who told me never to go swimming in the Coshocton. He was looking out for me. It also makes me understand, in a way, the families that Leonard reunites. Losing Max would bring so much pain and, as much as I want to believe I wouldn't, I'd do anything to bring him back, too. No matter the cost.

"He was only ten," she says. "We never found him."

"I'm sorry," I say, meaning it. "Was he your only grandkid?"

"Just my Louis." Principal Orr exhales sharply and wipes her eyes. "I'm getting emotional. I'm sorry. This is inappropriate, especially given your circumstances."

"It's okay."

"I miss him every day," says Principal Orr. "And every day, all I look forward to is the day I get to hold him again."

The words bounce off the walls of my skull. *Hold him again.* I immediately think of Leonard and get a chilling thought.

Could Louis be the kid Leonard is trying to bring back?

If he's been missing for three years, I doubt he's alive. They must have just not found his body. I glance back up at Louis's picture. He looks like Max. They have the same dimpled smile.

I search Principal Orr's eyes for a glimmer of darkness. Some hint that she might know more than she's letting on. Principal Orr must see the change on my face because her eyebrow quirks up. "Are you all right, Miss Oleson?"

When I swallow, my throat is dry. "How do you deal with it?"

"I'm afraid I don't understand."

"Louis being gone," I say. "It must be so hard."

"I think about him every day."

"In what way?"

"I think about the day he will be with me again."

My heart is pounding against my breastbone. I'm probably making it up. I want to find Max so badly that everyone looks suspicious to me. "Principal Orr, can I ask you a question?"

"Of course."

"Do you believe in ghosts?"

Something shifts behind her eyes. Something that raises the hairs on the back of my neck. But then the look is gone, and she's smiling again. "You would be amazed at what's possible when you are certain that the people you love will come back to you."

27

SHILOH

I'm standing at the curb outside of school when Mom pulls up in her minivan at two forty-five.

I climb into the passenger seat as she flexes her fingers on the steering wheel, pulling her bottom lip through her teeth. "Mom?"

"I'm taking you somewhere," she says. She's still wearing her silk pajama shirt, but with her nice coat over the top. If I was wearing an outfit like that, she'd make me change before I set foot out of the house.

"Where?"

"You're not to speak a word, you hear me?" Mom's knuckles are white. There are splotches of red on her cheeks and a simple ponytail keeps her hair out of her face. "Not a word."

I don't know who I'd speak a word to, but I nod anyway. She pulls out of the school parking lot with a sense of urgency.

I try to figure out where we're going from the roads we turn down, then how long we stay on Route 13. We're headed in the direction of Mount Keenan, heading the same way we usually go to the grocery store, but she's acting weird, so I doubt we're going shopping.

Fifteen minutes later, she turns down a narrow road I don't recognize into what looks like a business park full of identical beige buildings. She turns into one of the driveways. I try to read the sign, but she's driving so fast it disappears before I can. One sign across the street is for a chiropractor's office, and another is for a place called Tender Foot Care.

Oh my God. Maybe she found out I had sex with Miles and she's taking me to a doctor. I don't know how she could have found out. Not to be dramatic or anything, but if that's what we're doing here, I'd die of embarrassment.

She swings into a parking spot. "Leave your things," she says, gesturing at my school bag. She's starting to scare me. I'm about to ask where we are when she slams the door shut, leaving me with no option but to hurry after her.

She punches in a code into a keypad and lets herself into the building. The smell of disinfectant and something weird— chlorine, maybe—hits my nose as we wait for the elevator. This feels like a doctor's office. Or a hotel, but I notice mailboxes along the wall, which would be unnecessary if it were a hotel. On the third floor, we pass numbered doors until we reach the end of the hallway and Mom plugs a key into the knob, opening it with a click. She holds the door open for me and I take the cue to walk inside.

It's just an empty room with wall-to-wall shag carpet the same beige as the outside of the building. I can see dimples in the carpet that suggest there was once furniture there, but there's no furniture now.

I turn around to see Mom with her back pressed against the closed door, the same crazy guilt still darting around in her eyes. "What is this?" I ask her.

"Don't say a word," she says, and then it hits me. This is not a hotel or a low-budget golf course motel.

This is an apartment.

"Whose apartment is this?" I don't want to jump to conclusions, but above all, I don't want to be wrong.

"You can't say a word," she says, and I can't help it. A sharp, broken laugh flies out of me.

"When did you do this?" It's her apartment. It's true, it's happening, it's real. I walk deeper into the room, tracing the outlines of the furniture with my eyes. There was a couch here once. There's a wall mount in the corner for a flatscreen TV. "How did you pull together the money?"

"I put down the deposit today." She's not smiling, but it doesn't matter. She keeps talking—about the two bedrooms, the tennis court, the pool. I wouldn't have to change schools, and if we find Max—

"When we find him," I correct her.

"Then you will have to share a bedroom," she says.

I race down the apartment's internal hallway into the smaller of the two bedrooms. I press my palms against the floor-to-ceiling window that opens onto a balcony looking out over a pool, framed by concrete and a halo of lounge chairs. "When are you going to do it?"

"Not yet," she says. "I want to know about Max first. You can't say a word, Shiloh. I mean it."

"I won't." I almost want to hug her. I don't even care if this place gets any furniture at all. It's safe, and it's out of Bethany. It's somewhere else. It's away. "I won't say a word."

———

Mom has to stop at the grocery store on our way home, and I can't stop smiling all the way there. Mom got us an apartment. She's finally had enough. When Max comes home, he will have a place to go that's safe, away from Dad.

Away from everything.

I'm practically skipping as I push the cart through the sliding doors. The grocery store is big, and it's in Mount Keenan, which is where we go to get groceries because Bethany is too small to have a chain supermarket. We get meat from the butcher, and we get eggs and milk from a farm near the school, but we get most things here.

Mom squeezes tomatoes, checks the expiration date on some spinach, and chooses the right can of beans from the selection on the shelf. She wants to make chili for dinner. Chili is Max's favorite. Most times Mom announced she was making chili, Max would wriggle his arms in a sort of happy dance, and later when we were eating, he would pile on so much Mexican cheese that there was more cheese than chili in his bowl.

I notice the bruised skin on Mom's wrists when her sleeves ride up as she reaches to take things off a high shelf. My stomach churns. I wish we could just go now, but I understand why she has to wait.

"I'm putting maple syrup in the chili because it's how Max likes it," Mom says, putting a large container of syrup into the cart. "He's so cute, the way he loves maple syrup on everything. Remember those candies he made when he put the syrup out in the snow?"

I do remember those. I love Max, but they were gross. "Don't we have syrup at the house?"

"It's not enough." She loads two more containers, then another one into the cart, clearing the entire supply on the shelf. "I'm going to put it in the chili." She moves on. "This way."

Mom must be going out of her mind with worry. I know none of her search parties have turned up anything, and it's been nine days now. At least I know something. I can't imagine how hard it would be to have all your actions feel random and pointless.

Mom puts a bag of onions into the cart and wipes her eyes with her palms. "Have you decided to go to the homecoming dance?"

I blink at her. With everything going on, talking about the homecoming dance feels so stupid.

I honestly wish I could stop thinking about the dance. I managed to avoid Miles until gym class, the one afternoon class that we have together, and made embarrassing eye contact with him as I emerged from the locker room. I wrapped my arms around myself, trying to hide in the shorts that I realized were hugging me in all the wrong places, but he just looked away. He's mad at me. Of course he is. I know what I said really hurt him, but I don't know how to make it better.

I'm not ready to love him, but that doesn't mean I'm ready to lose him.

"Probably not," I say.

"Hm." Mom taps her fist into her palm, as if she's trying to remember what else she needs. She remembers, and scurries toward the spice aisle.

"I had a wonderful time at my homecoming dance when I was your age," she says as I follow her with the cart.

"Didn't you go with Dad?"

"No, actually. It was before I met him. I went with a boy who I knew had the biggest crush on me at the time, and it was actually quite lovely."

She chuckles, and I raise my eyebrows at her. It's easy to forget that Mom had a life before Dad because they met so young. Imagining her dancing with another boy is hard. Based on the look on her face, it must have been nice. "That's awesome."

"You should try to get Miles to ask you." Mom looks almost cheeky. "It would be nice for you to have a little fun."

I don't have it in me to tell her what I told Call-Me-Bill earlier, that I don't think Miles will want to go. So I lie, and say, "I will."

Mom looks pleased with this. Farther down the aisle, she runs into Mrs. McNabb, who is full of questions about how we're doing and when the search parties are going out this week. I can tell Mom is not in the right headspace for this because her gaze keeps flitting around the room as if she's looking for a way out. I train my eyes on the row of salad dressings on the shelf across from me. If I don't focus on them and squint a little, the labels swim together, making all the bottles look like one super long bottle.

I glance up from the dressing over Mom's shoulder, and I spot Principal Orr carrying a shopping basket past the dairy section. Her hair is down, cascading over her back in long, dark waves. A floral skirt that I hadn't realized she was wearing earlier in school molds to her ankles.

What is she doing here? I lean over so I can see her around Mom. Duh, she's getting groceries. Even principals have to eat. Principal Orr disappears down another aisle, and I step after her.

"Where are you going?" Mom asks me.

"I'll be right back," I tell her. "Just one second."

I slip around the aisle after Principal Orr. She's made it to the freezer section. I hang back so she doesn't see me. I don't think I've seen Principal Orr outside of school, and never with her hair down. She balances her basket in the crook of her arm as she opens the fridge and peers inside, reaching out to grab a packet of dinosaur chicken nuggets.

She was weird in school earlier. Talking about Louis and how she wants to hold him again. Giving me that weird, cryptic answer to the question of whether ghosts are real. She keeps walking until she stops in front of a row of snacks, reaching up to get a box of Gushers to put in her basket. Why is she getting Gushers? I thought she said Louis was her only grandkid. She does not strike me as someone who would buy dinosaur nuggets and Gushers for herself. I've never seen an adult eat Gushers in my life.

I'm turning the corner toward the self-checkouts when my elbow catches a display of tortilla chips and knocks it to the floor. Principal Orr glances backward and notices me. "Shiloh?"

I don't think I've ever heard her use my first name before. I hurry to straighten the display stand and Principal Orr joins me, picking up a bag of chips and rearranging it on the cardboard stand. Once it's done, I glance at her awkwardly, and take a few steps back. "Hi, Principal Orr."

"I didn't see you there."

I try to come up with an excuse to have been following her. "I was shopping with my mom and I saw you. I was just coming to say hi."

"Hello." She gives me a little wave. I hope Mom doesn't show up so Principal Orr won't see our matching bruises, although Mom's are better covered up than mine.

I glance down at her basket. It's only the box of Gushers, sitting next to the chicken nuggets. "Are those your groceries for the week?"

Principal Orr pulls the basket closer to her chest. "Those aren't for me."

"Who are they for?"

Her eyes dart behind my head. "I'm sorry, Shiloh, but I'm in a bit of a rush. It was good seeing you."

Principal Orr hurries to the self-checkout. I stare at her. She looked almost guilty, like she was doing something I knew she wasn't supposed to do. I think about parents who don't go into their kids' rooms after they've died, leaving everything the same as it always was, like some kind of shrine. Never being found is almost worse than being dead. I wonder if Principal Orr's freezer is a shrine to Louis, full of nuggets and burgers and ice cream. She scans the nuggets and candy before hurrying out of the store with her bag.

Something occurs to me, something I haven't thought of before. I've been trying to find Max by tracking down Leonard, but maybe that isn't the only way to do it. Leonard wants to use Max to bring back another kid, and that kid must be someone with a family who misses him and wants him back. A kid exactly like Louis.

28

SHILOH

It makes sense. Principal Orr knows who Max is. And she obviously knows—or at least suspects—what our situation at home is like. Leonard must have found out about our home life somehow. I don't think he snuck into our house to watch. No, he had to have heard about it from somebody.

Who better than the school principal?

She was torn up after I mentioned Louis in her office. She's obviously in pain, and pain makes people do crazy things.

Mom and I eat bowls of chili in front of the TV for dinner, since Dad isn't home to tell us we can't. Mom has to remind me to act upset when Dad gets back. Can't have him suspecting anything.

I need to tell Francesca about Principal Orr. She doesn't react to things as emotionally as I do, so she will be able to tell me whether there's something to this or not.

As soon as I get to school the next day, I scan the hallway for Francesca and quickly spot the blue ribbon she's woven into her braid. I race up to her.

"Hi," I say, tapping her on the shoulder. "I like your ribbon."

Francesca's cheeks flush red. Her hand flies up to her hair. "I was feeling quite sad about all this going on, so I wanted to do something pretty."

"It is pretty." I lower my voice. "I had a conversation with Principal Orr yesterday, and she acted kind of weird."

Francesca's eyebrows knit together. "What makes you say so?"

I glance over both shoulders before grabbing Francesca's wrist and pulling her around the corner and into the women's bathroom. There's no one in here, so it's as safe a place as any to talk.

"She told me her grandson Louis went missing a few years ago," I say, "and she said some weird things about how she's going to see him soon. But get this. I also saw her at Kroger after school buying snacks for kids."

"I thought children and adults eat the same snacks."

"I'm talking dinosaur chicken nuggets and Gushers. Like, kid snacks."

"Oh."

I scratch my temple. "Do you think Leonard might be trying to bring Louis back?"

Francesca tightens her ribbon. "Nobody named Louis is in the cemetery."

"I'm sure he's dead. Does it matter where he is as long as Leonard can find his ghost?"

"I suppose not."

"I know it's a long shot, but it just made me think—Leonard has to bring back somebody, right? Finding him isn't the only way to find Max. If we can figure out who he's going to bring back, their family might know where Leonard is."

Francesca purses her lips. I lean onto the balls of my feet and watch her consider it, turn it over in her brain and parse through it. I hope she agrees with me. It will make me feel less crazy.

"I suppose you are right, and it is worth inquiring into," she finally says, "but there is something I do not understand. If

Leonard is kidnapping children with difficult lives, why did he choose Max?"

She asks the question like she's just wondering, not like she's accusing me of anything. I pull my bottom lip between my teeth. I remember the nights Dad came home from the bar throwing things. Max would sit immobile and silent until I grabbed his hand and took him to his room to make a tent with the bedcovers where we'd stay quiet and wait for Dad to calm down or sober up. Sometimes, that would take a long time. I didn't want Max to hear too much. I couldn't play music, because Dad would get angry if he heard us playing music, so I did my best to distract him with bad stories about his dinosaurs that I'd make up on the spot. Dad didn't usually come into the room. Once, last month, on the night Miles asked me to be his girlfriend after watching *Star Wars*, I came home to find Mom holding a bag of frozen peas to a welt on Max's arm in the bathroom.

I can live with it when Dad hurts me, but when he hurts Max —I want him to burn. I don't care how drunk he gets or how much he misses Jim. For hurting Max, he deserves to rot in hell. Or someplace worse.

"Principal Orr called me to her office to talk to me about what happened to my face," I say, glancing at my reflection in the mirror. It still looks bruised, but the swelling around my eye is going down.

Not thinking through what I'm doing, I lift up my shirt and turn around to show my back to Francesca. She sucks in a tight breath before I drop my shirt and turn back around to face her. Her eyes stay wide for a moment before they return to normal size.

"My dad hits us," I say. "Nobody else knows." Red hot shame burns my face. I can't believe I just said that to another person. I've never told anyone about Dad before. "Please don't tell anybody."

Francesca raises her finger to her lips. "I will not tell a soul. I promise you." A couple of seconds of silence pass. "People remind me an awful lot of metal, sometimes. They often treat their struggles like rust, but I like to think they are more like tarnish."

I have no idea what she means, but she sounds like she's trying to comfort me, and I appreciate that.

During my next class, I try to pay attention to the lecture, but I just can't stop fidgeting. I drum my fingers against my desk. My foot taps on the floor. I can't believe I finally told someone. It's such a relief that I smile, and that makes me feel like a crazy person, grinning like an idiot as Mr. Mueller drones on about mitosis. All the time I've spent thinking about how I should maybe tell Miles, and I can't believe I told Francesca. I just said it like it was no big deal. *My dad hits us.* A statement of fact. *My dad is an alcoholic and hits us because he can't control his surroundings but wants to control us.* Saying it feels good. I thought it would be harder. Putting things into words makes them real, but this is already real. It's not like Dad would stop hitting us if I kept my mouth shut.

I need to find Miles. This is what he wanted from me, to open up to him and talk to him about what I'm going through, wasn't it?

Miles has a free period now. When the bell rings, I race to the library to catch him before he leaves for class. It only takes me a second to spot him, sliding a notebook into his messenger bag at the table by the window. He's wearing a gray sweater that I know is scratchy because he wore it once when we watched a movie together and my face broke out in a rash from where I rested my head on his shoulder. I might be allergic to wool. Whatever.

My heart tenses at the sight of him. He looks almost angelic, with the light shining from behind his head and forming a kind of halo.

I run to him and tap him on the shoulder. He looks up at me, and his face twists like he's just sucked on a lemon. Seeing him look unhappy to see me, my chest deflates a little.

"Hi," I whisper. I glance over at the librarian, who is glaring at me. I shoot her an apologetic smile before returning my gaze to Miles. "Miles, my dad hits us."

Miles stares at me for a long second. "What?"

"My dad hits me," I repeat, relief washing over me as the words leave my mouth. I hope nobody else can hear me. The girl sitting over by the window doesn't look over, so I guess that's a good sign. "He hits my mom, too, and Max. He gets drunk and angry."

Miles's eyes are locked on me. He doesn't say anything. As the silence stretches on, the smile on my face sinks on both sides.

"He hit me two nights ago because he was mad that I was trying to find Max after he told me not to," I continue. "He hit me with a belt, and when I fought back, he punched me. That happened before I came to see you."

Miles's brow furrows. Why is he mad? I thought he wanted me to open up to him. I touch his shoulder and remember what it looks like under his shirt, how I could see its sharp definition against his sheets in the lamplight. I curl my fingers around it. I think he wants me to keep going.

"I don't like talking about bad things that happen to me," I say. "I'm not used to it. I'm bad at talking about my feelings, but I know you said it was important to you, so I'm trying."

Miles pulls away from me. He zips up his bag and slings it over his shoulder. "I need to go to class."

"I thought—"

"I'm sorry that happened to you," he says, "but I have to go to class."

He walks away. All the excitement drains out of my body like water running out of a bathtub. I don't understand. I thought that's what he wanted.

Maybe he was just in a rush. A part of me doesn't believe that. I sit down behind one of the computers, letting my backpack fall beside my chair. Numbness creeps into my chest.

I can find him again during lunch, but until then I'll distract myself. I angle the monitor slightly toward the wall before typing "Child drowns Bethany Ohio 2016."

An article recounting the drowning appears in the *Bethany Citizen*. I click on it and read.

Search called off for 10-year-old boy presumed drowned in Coshocton River

Published: 9:12 AM EST August 26, 2016

No further searches are planned after Bethany Police & Fire spent a fourth day combing the Coshocton River for a missing 10-year-old boy from Youngstown who is presumed to have drowned, authorities said.

Louis Orr, 10, was reported missing at 1:44 p.m. Thursday from the river where it runs through Bethany. The boy had just finished 5th grade at St. Parish Elementary in Youngstown, was last seen swimming in the river with two of his cousins and an adult.

The stretch of river where the boy was last seen contains a large tree hanging over the water and there are also underwater rock formations, crevices, and dangerous currents that pose potential hazards for swimmers, according to a release from the York County Sheriff's Office. Over the past four days, first responders used boats, sonar, divers, and K9 units in the effort to locate the victim.

"Crews are disappointed they have not been able to bring closure to the victim's family," said Sheriff Ernest Oleson in a press release.

One comment under the article reads that there's a bad undercurrent in the river and it's not safe to swim there. My fingers curl around the mouse. I can so easily picture Louis's father turning his back for one second while his child slipped under the surface, never to return. If it were Max, I would never be able to forgive myself. And if I found a way to get him back, I'd do anything to make it happen. No matter what it took.

———

I find Francesca sitting alone in the cafeteria, peeling back the skin from a browning banana. I slide onto the bench across from her and lean forward onto my elbows.

"I want to look through Principal Orr's office," I say, taking my sandwich out of the paper bag. "Watching your grandson drown can mess with your head, so I want to see if there's anything suspicious on her computer that could lead us to Leonard."

"I suppose it wouldn't hurt," Francesca says. I'm happy with that response. Miles would respond to the idea of breaking into Principal Orr's office and searching her hard drive with all sorts of doubts and protests, but not Francesca.

A crinkled paper bag sits in front of her. I tip it over to peek at what's inside and find that it's empty. "Is that banana all you packed for lunch?"

Francesca crumples the bag in her hand. "Richie has not gone to get groceries for this week yet."

She's going to be hungry. I take my peanut butter sandwich out of the Ziploc bag and give her half. "Take this."

The white bread dimples between her fingers. "I cannot take your food."

"Just take it, dummy." I flash her a smile. Francesca's been a good friend to me. I feel a sort of protective urge toward her, like it's my job to make sure she doesn't starve. "One banana isn't enough."

She takes a huge bite of the sandwich. Peanut butter sticks to her teeth as she smiles back.

At the table behind Francesca, some girls are passing around magazine cutouts of dresses. They're probably talking about what they're wearing to homecoming. I catch a glimpse of leopard print on one of the photos and roll my eyes back into my head. Judging by the gold lettering on the banner and the "WE BELONG TOGETHER" theme, I'm guessing whoever's in charge of the props is going to go with the smoke machines, a disco ball, and pastel purple party favors to make everyone feel like they're in a bad music video, or some kind of luxury shampoo commercial.

I'm just being a downer. Going to the dance would probably be pretty fun. If I went with Miles, he would tell me how pretty I looked in my dress, and we would dance to dumb music while he talked about how impressive the yearbook committee's decorations were. He would enjoy it enough for me to enjoy it.

I hope we can still go. I know he's mad at me now, but I really hope he doesn't stay mad at me forever.

Suddenly, I remember something. I rummage through my backpack to find the crumpled-up photo of Leonard I printed out at the library two days ago. I flatten it against the table and slide it to Francesca. "I've been meaning to ask you—is this guy the same guy you saw come to the cemetery?"

Francesca holds the photo up to the light and frowns. "This is not him."

My stomach sinks. "Really?"

"This man only has three fingers on each hand, see?" Francesca points to each of Leonard Gailis's hands, and I nod because I knew that already. "The man I saw come to the cemetery had all his fingers."

Weird. In every photo of Leonard on that website, he only has three fingers. I wonder how this can be possible when a tray clatters down onto the aluminum table beside me, and I jump.

"You were rude to me yesterday," Jonah says. "Rude."

I try to remember what he said to me yesterday. So much has happened that it feels like a long time ago. "Oh, right. About your magical monocle."

Francesca looks at me strangely. "There is no such thing as magic."

"It isn't magical," Jonah says, sliding onto the bench next to me. "But I think my neighbor can see ghosts through it."

"Somebody else can see ghosts?" Francesca asks.

Jonah's black hair tumbles out over his forehead as he nods. "With the monocle, she can."

Francesca looks suspicious. "Are you sure about this?"

"He's not," I say quickly, shooting a glare at Jonah. I don't want him to give her false hope that someone else can see ghosts when it might not even be true. "Don't listen to him."

Jonah glares at me. "And don't listen to Scooby. She wasn't even there."

"I told you yesterday and I'll tell you again," I say, "we don't need anyone else who sees ghosts because we have Francesca." I smile at Francesca, and she smiles back at me. Jonah looks annoyed, but honestly, I don't really care. "Glad that's settled." Jonah usually eats lunch with Miles. I glance past him, over at the rest of the cafeteria, but don't see Miles anywhere. "Where's Miles?"

"Avoiding you." Jonah wipes tomato sauce from the corner of his mouth before taking another big bite of cafeteria pizza. "You were mean to him, too, I guess."

I search his eyes to try to figure out how much he knows. "What did Miles tell you?"

"He didn't have to say much, but he had the look on his face like he did the day after he finished all the Lego Star Wars sets, so I know it was bad. What did you do to him?"

"Why do you assume I'm the one who did something?"

"Just a feeling," he says.

Hoping he doesn't see the guilt I feel, I take another bite out of my sandwich. "I need to go find him."

"He is walking over right now," Francesca gestures behind me, and I twist around to see that she's right. Oh my God, Jonah didn't lie. Miles looks miserable.

He sits down next to Francesca. With jerky motions, he takes his food out of his lunchbox.

Francesca shifts toward him. "Hello, Miles."

Miles arranges his Tupperware containers in a neat line in front of him. "Hi."

"Shiloh was just telling me she believes Principal Orr may know a thing about Max and Leonard," Francesca explains.

Miles glares at me, and I'm suddenly cold. "Why does she think that?"

"I just think we should look through her office," I mumble.

Miles lets out a pained sigh and opens his Tupperware with a small pop. I notice the thin bread folded against the side, and I pull my bottom lip between my teeth. I had that last time I ate dinner at his house. His mom's cooking is legendary. I want to ask for a bite, but I'm scared he'll say no.

"So you're saying you want to break into the school principal's office?" Miles asks. "Go on a top-secret mission like we belong in *Scooby-Doo*?"

"Yeah," Jonah says. "We're going to unmask the evil principal for the villain she is. Then, Velma and Daphne are going to go to the dance while Shaggy sparks up and Scooby gets the munchies."

I laugh. Jonah is better at teasing than I am.

"If we're going to look through Principal Orr's office," I say, "we need to do it when she's not there."

"Because you're so good at being sneaky," Miles says.

There is a moment of silence. Jonah's remark was funny. The one Miles made was just mean.

"Do you think Leonard's running a business?" Jonah says to nobody in particular.

"You mean like advertising on the black market?" I ask. "Give me ten grand and I'll bring your kid back from the dead?" I scoff at the idea. "I doubt it. I bet he approaches the families himself."

"The dance," Miles whispers absentmindedly.

I glance at him. "The homecoming dance?"

He nods. "School administrators have to chaperone during functions, so it's unlikely Principal Orr would be in her office at the time. If we go to the dance, we can search her computer while she is distracted."

That might actually work. "You're a genius," I tell him.

"I can get her password from someone at the paper," he continues. "He knows all the administrator passwords and uses them to access student files and things. She probably wouldn't keep anything incriminating on her school computer, but her Chrome search history would sync between devices, so we can look through it if we find a way to go to the dance."

"Gee, and here we are, two boys and two girls. How the hell are we going to do that?" Jonah asks.

"I have never been to a school dance before." Francesca bounces on her seat and glances over at me. "Do you think it is a good idea, Shiloh?"

I wonder if Dad would let me go. He has barely spoken to me since breakfast yesterday. As much as I don't want to ask him, he does have the power to stop me from going. "If I can convince my dad, I'm in."

"We can do it without you," Miles mutters.

Something burns inside of me at the idea of being left out. "Nobody's doing anything without me. It's my brother who's missing, remember?"

"Do whatever you want." Miles stands up from the table. "I'm going to sit outside until next period."

"You okay, buddy?" Jonah asks. "Want company?"

"I'm fine."

Miles is definitely angry with me, but this is my chance to talk to him, so I grab my lunch. "I'll come."

Miles holds up his palm. "Please don't."

He walks away from the table. I plop back down onto the bench in defeat. Miles has never spoken to me like that before. I glance at Jonah helplessly.

"Go," Jonah urges, dropping his attention back down to his pizza. I glance back at Miles. He's already almost out of the cafeteria, carrying his messenger bag like a suitcase. Jonah waves his arm. "Go after him, Scooby, or I will."

I grab my sandwich and hurry after Miles.

———

Miles is sitting on a bench in front of the school. I stop walking, mostly because I want to put off having to face him for as long as possible. The doors close behind me with a soft thud, but Miles doesn't hear them and instead opens a book on his lap. I can't tell what the book is. I focus on the rise and fall of his shoulders, the stiffness of his posture, and the way his hair swoops into his face as he angles his head into the pages.

I walk toward him. He notices me, averting his eyes but closing the book over his finger. I catch a glimpse of the cover. It's poetry. Something called *Lyrical Ballads*.

"Can I sit with you?" I ask.

He slides over. I sit down next to him and fold my hands on my lap as he looks down at the two old guys on the book's cover. I don't exactly know what I'm supposed to say. I just know I feel guilty about telling him I don't love him, even though it's the truth. Just because I don't love him doesn't mean I don't want to be with him. I need him to be patient with me.

I consider asking him what the book is about, but the bell is going to ring soon, so I should cut to the chase.

"My dad hits us," I tell him for the second time. Miles doesn't say anything. All he does is nod. He probably wants me to keep going. "And I feel ..." How do I feel? "Bad about that, and about Max. He hits him, too."

Miles still doesn't react. I pivot on the bench so I'm facing him. "Come on, Miles. I'm trying."

Miles hangs his head and sits forward on his knees. "I don't know if I can do this."

My heart double-thumps. "What are you talking about?"

With careful and capable fingers, Miles opens the book to where the receipt he's using as a bookmark is poking out of the pages. I realize it's a receipt from Rite Aid he must have kept from this summer. Even small things matter to him. Maybe that's what love is.

"Read this poem," he says, touching a title reading "We Are Seven" by William Wordsworth.

I look at him funny. "Seriously?"

"Please read it."

"Class is starting soon, and I want to talk."

"It's short. There's time."

Partly because I'm curious and mostly because I know I won't be able to avoid it, I sigh and pull the book onto my lap. Miles is right. The poem is short.

I start to read.

The poem tells the story of a girl who, when asked how many siblings she has, says that they are seven. When she's asked where her siblings are, the girl says that two of them are buried in the churchyard. If two of them are buried, that means there's only five, but even though two of them are dead and up in heaven, the girl is adamant that they are still seven.

It's cute. Poetic. I hand Miles back the book. "Why did I just read that?"

"Because that's how I feel."

I try very hard to figure out what he means. "You have six siblings?"

Miles sighs. I'm being deliberately dumb. He's an only child, I know that. "I feel like the girl." His eyes are filled with real emotion, like they are windows to his pained and bleeding heart. "With all the problems. You don't love me. You don't open up to me—"

"I did open up to you."

"Because you felt you had to, not because you wanted to." He pounds his fist into his palm. "You don't love me, but I still love you. I hold on to that and ignore the very real reasons I shouldn't, like the girl in the poem does." He pauses to think. "Why did you come to my house that night?"

"Because you make me feel safe," I say. "I was upset, and I wanted to feel good."

"What I'm hearing is that I love you, and you used me."

"You don't understand," I say. "You don't have a family life like mine."

"Definitely don't try to explain it to me, because I'd be too dumb to understand."

I sigh. "Opening up is hard for me. I don't like being vulnerable …" *because it makes me feel weak.*

"What we did was a big deal to me," he says. I'm struck by the overwhelming urge to kiss him and make it better, but that's probably not the right thing to do. "I've never done that … you know … with anyone before."

"Me neither."

"Really?" He sounds genuinely surprised. I don't know if I'm supposed to be offended by that or not. Miles buries his head in his hands for a couple of seconds before looking back up at me. "I don't know, Shiloh. I don't think this is what falling in love is supposed to be like. This is too hard."

My heart drops into my stomach. I sit on my hands and look out into the parking lot. Wind rustles through the tops of the trees. Over by the school field, I can see through the Upside-Down Tree now. It's dropping its leaves like secrets, letting them float away with the breeze. Max used to say that trees look like skeletons without their leaves. I agree with him. Swaying in the wind, they look like they're dancing.

I've never broken up with someone, but this sounds like he's breaking up with me. I don't understand how he can go from loving me to not wanting me so quickly. But he looks like he's already made up his mind.

I take a ragged breath and stand up from the bench. "Okay."

Miles sits up straight. "I'm still going to help look for Max."

"I can do it myself."

"I don't want to break up with you and stop helping look for your brother."

"Okay. Thanks, I guess."

He looks at me with flat, brown eyes. My chest tightens. I walk back into school just as the bell rings and go straight to biology, where my lab partner and I have to dissect an earthworm.

Chris pins the worm in place like it said to do in the textbook. "It says to make a single incision from here," he says, pointing at the pin at the top of the worm, "down to here." He looks up from the book. Cloudy safety goggles cover his eyes. "Do you want to do it, or should I?"

I take the scalpel and press down on the worm where Chris told me to, drawing the blade down the worm's skin. I press down too hard. Both halves of the worm spring away from each other and tiny clusters of intestines fall onto the dissection board.

29

SHILOH

I'm finishing up with a customer when two women enter Rite Aid. I vaguely recognize one of them, but I don't know where I recognize her from. Her spine is straight as she disappears down one of the aisles, then reappears soon after holding a tube of Pringles. She walks up and sets them down at the counter with a soft *clink*.

I scan the barcode, and the scanner beeps. "Will that be all?"

"Yes, thank you." Her eyes stick to me as I bag the Pringles, and when I go to hand them back to her, her eyes are glued to my face.

"Shiloh Oleson," she says, with an edge of warmth in her voice. A clip holds her shiny hair low on her neck. "My name is Phoebe Huang. I'm with the FBI." She flashes the badge. "I'd like to ask you a few questions if you have somewhere we could talk in private."

Oh, right. That's where I recognized her from. Walking out from Dad's office in Mount Keenan. I glance back at Sandy, my manager, for permission, and he gives me a brief nod.

"We can use the break room," I say.

I walk around the counter on stiff legs, past Brian, whose eyebrows are raised in an "I knew it" way, as if he'd known this whole time it was me who kidnapped Max. I want to slap that expression right off his face.

I lead Agent Huang back to the break room. Her partner joins us without introducing herself. My body folds into an aluminum chair across from them, my foot drumming against the floor.

"What is this about?" I ask Agent Huang. I don't want to talk to her partner, whose bob is cut at an angle as sharp as the one on her nose, turning it upward. For some reason, I just have a bad feeling about her.

Agent Huang leans forward, clasping her hands out in front of her on the table. "You aren't in any trouble, Shiloh. Do you mind if I call you Shiloh?"

"Sure, I guess."

"Okay, Shiloh. As you know, we've been looking for your brother, Max, and there are some things that just don't line up." Her voice is made of silk, like she's leading a meditation. Even though there is no one else in the room except the three of us, the slight echo of her voice from the walls makes me feel very exposed. "I'm going to be very frank with you, Shiloh, and I want you to be honest with me. Has your father ever raised his voice to you, your mother, or Max?"

I pull my vest tighter over my chest. "Why, do you suspect him of something?"

"Please, Shiloh, just answer the question."

I read somewhere that people can gain a psychological advantage and establish trust by using your name a lot. It's probably the first thing these guys learn during training.

I run through the day Max went missing in my head. Dad was the one who went to pick Max up. I had to remind him to go because he was late, and he had been drinking. Coach Boeshart said Max disappeared at pickup time, and Dad arrived late, so Max was taken before Dad got there. Duncan's is close to the park. In their eyes, what would have stopped him from picking

Max up on time, losing his temper, and going back to Duncan's to drink off the guilt of what he did, only return to the park to avoid suspicion after I called him reminding him of Max's pickup time?

That's not what happened. But the women sitting across from me don't know what happened. Without Francesca, how could they trace it back to Leonard, who supposedly died in 1944? It wouldn't take Agent Huang long to stop Shiloh-ing me if I ran the whole ghost thing past her.

I wring my hands together in my lap. Agent Huang is not asking me if Dad is guilty. She's asking me if Dad has ever raised his voice at me. Don't all dads raise their voices at their kids every once in a while? I know just by looking at her that's not what she means.

Is this where I'm supposed to admit it? With the backing of the FBI and a black eye that the whole town has probably seen by now? Would the town believe it?

Mom has already gotten the apartment. They can't take me away from Max because he's not here right now.

I drop my eyes to the table. Guilt wraps a spindly hand around my throat as I whisper a soft, "Yes."

Agent Huang exchanges a glance with her bob-haired partner before saying, "I understand he's a drinker. Has he ever lost his temper, or done anything to hurt you?"

I'm doing something wrong. I can't do this to Dad when I know he wasn't the one who hurt Max. Before I can fully comprehend what I'm doing, I reach into my pocket and take out my iPod.

Agent Huang scrolls through them, one after the other. Of all the ways I pictured this moment going down, this is not one of the scenarios I played out. I always imagined the audible gasps in the court as I whipped the photos out as evidence. I imagined my attorney turning them into a slideshow like a giant gotcha finger pointed at Dad.

But Agent Huang doesn't look that impressed. I guess she's seen worse. Upside-down, I see the broken glass on the carpet, my almost-naked torso, a lip Dad said I busted playing catch. She asks my permission to copy the photos. I've come this far. I can't back down now.

After she's done, she slides the iPod back over to me. "I'm so sorry," she says, as I tuck it back into my pocket. She's stopped using my name now.

The partner with the bob pipes up. "Did he hurt Max that same way?" she asks. "Does he hit your mom?"

Keeping my eyes on Agent Huang, I nod. Seconds pass.

I don't know how I feel. If Dad didn't want it to get out, then he never should have done it in the first place. Still, the guilt is still there.

"I'll let you get back to work," says Agent Huang, and her partner stands up.

"What are you going to do to him?" I ask.

Agent Huang takes a card from her wallet and gives it to me. I hold it by the edges in the fingers of both hands, like it's about to self-destruct. "If you remember anything else," she says, "please contact me. Anytime."

I stand up and follow her back out to the counter because I don't want anyone to think there's something wrong.

———

Did that really just happen? I force myself to keep my head up until my shift is over, as my brain races to try to figure out whether I did the right thing. Sandy and Brian keep side-eyeing me. Dad might not have killed Max, but if he'd smashed his head a little harder into the wall that time, he could have.

I'm starting to wonder if right and wrong matter as much as people say they do. Everything's too complicated for that.

I'm going to need to ask Dad for permission to go to the dance tonight. I'll have to get him in a good mood so he'll let me go.

I'm still rehearsing the way I'm going to ask him when I turn down my street and see the squad car lights flashing, soundless, by our house. In front of our house. I quicken my pace to a run. I hear Dad's voice before I reach the mouth of our driveway, where I stop in my tracks and watch Connie and Finnegan walk him out of the house with his hands behind his back. Agent Huang and her partner stand on the grass, watching.

Dad's eyes lock on me. "Shiloh, tell them. They're making a mistake."

I hurry around him to where Mom is standing in the doorway, watching him go with her hand over her mouth.

"What's going on?" I ask.

"They're arresting him," she says, in a far-away voice. "For killing your brother."

What? "They didn't find a body."

"It doesn't matter, apparently," she says.

Finnegan pushes Dad's head down as he gets into the back of the car. I look at Agent Huang and she looks right back. I can see the weight behind her eyes. It's like she's waiting for me to breathe a sigh of relief, cry, or react in some way. As they take Dad away, I don't know how to give her what she wants.

———

It won't last forever. When I find Max, they'll let him go. But the beloved sheriff's fall from grace is all over the news. Ernest Oleson hits his kids. Ernest Oleson beats his wife. They don't know the worst of it, and I hope they never will, but they have most of it.

Mom makes me turn it off. I know how it must make her feel, but I can't tell whether she believes he did it.

She hasn't asked me how they found out. I wonder if the reason she hasn't asked is because she said something to them herself. Maybe we reached our breaking points at the same time.

Going to the dance tomorrow will be hell. With everyone staring at me, I wonder if I'll be able to get away long enough to get to Principal Orr's office.

Mom gives me permission to go. She says she'll drive me.

Once she's had time to process what's happened, she'll turn to me and start demanding answers, but hopefully, it won't get to that point. Tomorrow, something in Principal Orr's office will lead me to Max, and I will have him home before Mom has time to believe he's dead.

30

SHILOH

At seven o'clock, half an hour before I have to leave for the dance, Mom knocks on my bedroom door.

She holds up a comb. "I thought you might need some help getting ready."

I wasn't planning on dressing up. I want to blend in, but I also want to wear something I can move in. I already censored my black eye with concealer, but I guess I could let Mom do my hair. "Thanks."

I keep my hands folded in my lap as Mom takes out my hair tie, sending my sandy hair cascading over my shoulders. She runs her fingers through the freshly washed strands, combing it so it's out of my face.

"My beautiful, strong girl." Mom's hands rest on my shoulders. Her fingers feel like they're made of twigs, like I could break them if I moved too fast. "I'm so sorry for what I did to you."

"What did you do to me?"

"If I had left earlier, your father wouldn't have taken him from us." Her words are empty, like they don't have any real meaning yet. Like she doesn't truly believe they're real. Because they're not.

I twist around to look her in the eye. "I'm going to bring him home."

"Shiloh …"

"I will," I say, gripping the back of the chair. "He's not dead yet, and I will save him. I promise you that."

Mom looks like she's about to cry as she tells me to sit back down. Once she's done straightening my hair, she leaves the room and returns with a yellow dress hanging over her arm. The dress is long. I don't know if I'll be able to run in it.

"This was the dress I wore to my homecoming," she says like a puppet, moving through the motions without any life.

She turns her back. I wriggle out of my jeans. I pull the dress on before tapping on Mom's shoulder for help zipping it up.

She gasps when she sees me. She zips me up, and I walk over to the mirror hanging over my door. The air catches in my throat. Oh my God. The dress is beautiful. It hugs my ribcage and flares out at my hips. A fabric rose attaches to the middle of the chest. The dress smells musty and dusty, like it's been sitting in the back of a closet for years. In high school, Mom was shorter than me, so the dress stops just above my ankles. I twist around, and the material flares out around my legs.

Mom smiles behind me. "I have matching shoes. Let me get them for you."

"I'll just wear sneakers." I can hike up the dress to run, but if I wear nice shoes, I know I'll trip.

Mom touches my hair again. "Let me put a braid in your hair."

She ushers me back into the seat and braids the front of my hair back so it's out of my face. She cups my cheek. "You look beautiful."

"Thanks, Mom."

"Do you want to take that bracelet off?"

I cup my hand over the rubber bracelet Max gave me. "No, it stays on."

"Are you sure you want to do this tonight?" she asks. I know how it looks. To her, I'm going to a dance, having fun after the news of my father's arrest for my brother's murder. She doesn't know that tonight, I'm going to war.

"Yes."

"All right."

She leaves the room. A shuddering breath slips through my lips. I have to do it now. This is my chance. Pressing my ear to the door to make sure Mom is in the kitchen, I step into the hallway. I turn the corner and find that Mom and Dad's bedroom door is already open.

I slip inside. The lights are off. A stale smell lingers in the air as I walk around to Dad's nightstand and pull the top drawer open. It's empty. He keeps a gun by his bed, that much I know, but I thought it would be in the nightstand. I glance around the room. My eyes settle on his closet door.

Belt loops clink against the door, but I silence them with my hand. The television turns off in the living room. I freeze, waiting to hear if Mom is coming toward me, but she's not.

I push Dad's dress shirts to the side and crouch down to rummage through the piles of papers and trays of random items on the floor. Nothing is here. I lean up onto my toes to take a frayed shoebox from the top shelf and pull back the lid.

A pistol, two magazines, and a bag of ammo roll around in the box. I know it's semiautomatic because I've asked Dad about it before, and after Mom went to bed last night, I watched a bunch of YouTube videos to learn how it works. I've never shot a gun before. I'm not planning to shoot it tonight, but if we find something in Principal Orr's office that leads us to Max, I don't want to confront Leonard unless I'm prepared.

I pick up the pistol and carefully release the magazine the way the video showed me. I pull back the slide. It's not loaded.

"Shiloh?" Mom calls from down the hall. I grab a loaded magazine and hide the gun under the fabric of my dress. "Ready to go?"

"Coming."

I rush out of their room and around the corner to see Mom standing in the mouth of the hallway. I brush my hair out of my face and hope I don't look guilty. She wouldn't be mad about me going in her room, but I don't think knowing I'm bringing a gun to the dance will make her all that thrilled. "Sorry, I was in the bathroom."

"I'll wait for you in the car."

I close my bedroom door and use a scarf to wrap the gun and magazine before tucking the bundle into my purse and leaving to join Mom.

———

My bag sits heavily on my lap. I fold both of my hands over it.

Mom drums her fingers against the steering wheel. I can feel the gun through the fabric. This is okay. I'm only going to use it if I really have to. I'm going to be glad I have it if I find Max tonight. Leonard probably has a gun. What's the point in finding Max if I can't get past Leonard?

We're getting close. I can feel it in my stomach.

Mom pulls up right in front of the school. Parents stop talking and crane their necks to peer into the car and look at us. I jerk my chin up. I need to do what I came here for. I will not let them get to me.

Mom grips the steering wheel hard. "Call me using the school's phone, or borrow someone's phone if you need to be picked up."

"I will."

She drives away. I turn to face the doors.

Here goes nothing.

I keep my head high as I walk through the doors. Am I going to look heartless? Will they see me differently? One mom looks like she's undressing me, wondering what kind of bruises or scars could be lurking beneath the fabric of my long dress. I knew people would know, but every head turns, and every eye is glued to me. One foot in front of the other. I don't know why I think it'll be better when I get to the gymnasium.

I stop in front of the ticket booth and clear my throat. The girl blinks up at me from under long, fake eyelashes that press up against the inside of her glasses. A small gasp slips through her lips.

I pull the ticket from my purse and hand it to her. She's still staring at me. I can't deal with this right now. I leave the ticket on the table and push through the red streamers hanging over the door to the gym.

"Happy homecoming, Shiloh," the girl calls after me, but she sounds far away as I stop to take in the gym.

Whoa.

The place has been transformed. Red, black, and purple balloons arch over the doors. Streamers and lanterns hang from the ceiling, lighting up the black-clothed tables and bowls of snacks on the side of the room. Someone dressed in an eagle costume is standing in the corner. Sad fabric feathers sag under his arms. I can't help but laugh a little. Poor guy. I hope the school is paying him well.

The most striking decoration in the gym is the large fake tree in the middle of the dance floor. Red lights circle the trunk. Nobody's dancing yet, so I walk closer to it and find that its branches are covered in leaves cut from construction paper. Glitter glue clings to the edges, making them look as if they're rimmed with frost.

I do a quick sweep for Jonah, Francesca, and Miles, but by the looks of it none of them are here yet. I can hear the whispers as I cross the room to take three chocolate chip cookies from the snack tray and sit alone at an unoccupied table to wait for them.

A bouncy pop song starts playing. It's still early into the night, so for the most part, people are eating or wandering around like I just was talking about how cool the tree looks. There are so many sequins on some of the girls' dresses. If the dresses aren't sequined, they're metallic, making most of the girls look like different breeds of the same teenage alien. I'm glad my dress is comfortable. I catch glimpses of smudged red paint on some of the people's faces and hands. I totally forgot—there was a football game today. A lot of people go to those, but I've never been interested.

By the time Jonah arrives, I've just finished my third cookie. He walks through the streamers wearing a crinkled gray shirt tucked into khakis. A brunette in fluorescent green hangs off his arm.

A frown tugs at my mouth. Why did he bring a date? I thought we were all coming alone so that we could focus on the mission. Come to think of it, I didn't tell him that's what I expected.

Jonah waves at me, and I run over to him. "Cool dress," he says.

I flatten the front of the skirt. "Nice shirt."

"I didn't iron it."

"I can tell." I smile at his date, who is not paying attention to me and is pushing her bangs out of her face. I don't recognize her—either because I don't know her or because of the amount of makeup she's wearing. "I'm Shiloh, by the way."

She smiles like she doesn't care. "Rachael."

"I thought you were going with Miles," I say to Jonah.

Jonah shrugs. "Turns out I'm not his type."

Without warning, Rachael shrieks in excitement and exclaims, "Cindy!" in a high-pitched voice. She drops Jonah's arm and stumbles on her high heels toward another girl standing by the snacks.

I shoot Jonah a mocking smile. "She seems nice."

Jonah quirks up his brow. "Is it true?"

He asks straight-up, not like he's gossiping, and not like there's weight attached to it. Jonah seems like he's had a tough life. He gets it. So I say, "Yeah."

He echoes my nod and purses his lips. He looks like he's trying to come up with something to say, but there isn't anything to be said about it, so before he can get anything else out, I ask, "Are Francesca and Miles here?"

"Miles is never late," Jonah says. "He'll be somewhere in here."

As if on cue, I spot Miles walking through the streamers with Francesca on his heels. Francesca's face opens when she sees the decorations. She steps into the light, and I notice she isn't wearing a dress. She's wearing a T-shirt with a chain of bandanas tied around the middle. I totally spaced. I know Francesca likes to feel pretty. I should have given her one of my dresses to wear. Miles's shirt is ironed under his pea coat, and the coat's rows of buttons glint in the red light.

Francesca sees us first and waves before bounding up to us. "This is so wonderful!"

She meets my eyes. Even though she already knew about Dad, I can tell she's feeling sad for me but isn't going to say anything. Francesca always knows the right thing to say. In this case, it's nothing.

Miles knew already, too, but he isn't good at hiding the shock on his face. "Shiloh, I didn't know—"

Yes, you did. I literally told you. "I don't want to talk about it."

Two red-lipped mothers are standing by the door. They look close enough to hear what we're saying. I don't want anyone to hear, so I beckon for everyone to step away from the wall, closer to the middle of the room. Francesca reaches up to touch one of the tree leaves while I go over the plan. Principal Orr isn't here yet, so there's nothing for us to do but wait.

Miles wanders off with Francesca to talk to some kids from the paper. Jonah goes to get food. Not wanting to stand on the dance floor alone, I sit down at a table.

There are four doors leading in and out of the gymnasium. Two are blocked off, and both are guarded by chaperones. Standing against the wall is Call-Me-Bill, who catches me staring at him and looks almost disappointed. I probably look pathetic, sitting alone. I hope he's not going to come over here. Call-Me-Bill takes a step forward.

Jonah drops his paper plate onto the table and lowers himself into a folding chair, saving me from whatever that conversation would have been like. "How's it going, Scooby?"

I appreciate his attempt at normalcy. I say the first normal thing that pops into my head. "Where's your date?"

"Rachael? She's not my date."

I remember the way she hung from Jonah's arm. "Well, she sure looked comfortable with you."

"She's friends with my sister," Jonah says. "Or actually, her sister is friends with my sister."

"You're not going to try to find her?" Jonah shakes his head. I can't help but smirk at him. "She's that boring?"

"She's drunk."

"You're kind of a jerk to abandon her."

"She abandoned me, remember? You were there. And besides, it would be just as rude to abandon you, sitting over here looking all sorry for yourself."

I'd never admit it, but I'm glad he's here. I raise my eyes over Jonah's shoulder to where Miles is standing next to Francesca. He seems to be introducing her to the other kids from the paper. Francesca shakes the hand of the girl with the bug-eyed glasses. She looks happy, which makes me happy, at least until Miles puts his hand on Francesca's shoulder and my stomach drops.

"What are you staring at?" Jonah asks and follows my gaze over to Miles. "Oh."

"Do you think they're going to date?"

I can't believe how stupid the question sounds coming out of my mouth. Jonah's reaction is immediate.

"Those two?" He laughs, kicking back in his chair. "No way."

"You didn't see the way Miles looked at me."

"When?"

When I told him I didn't love him. I can't say that to Jonah. He's Miles's best friend, and he will always take Miles's side. So I tell a joke instead. "When he learned I had a lover."

Jonah mocks surprise. "He learned about Tiny Tim?"

Imagining the *Christmas Carol* character in a romantic context brings a smile to my face. "There's just something about him. What can I say?"

Jonah fits an entire chip into his mouth. "It's the crutch."

I laugh. Jonah's eyes glint in playful amusement. He looks like he's about to say something else when I catch a glimpse of the turquoise rock sitting on Principal Orr's chest as she walks through the door in a conservative black dress. The smile disappears from my face. If she's in here, then she's not in her office.

It's time.

"Come on, let's move," I say.

Jonah gives me a burner phone and says he'll give the other to Francesca. If he's done what he said he would, he already saved his and Miles's numbers on both phones so Francesca can reach us if she sees anything while she's on the lookout. Jonah goes to tell Miles and Francesca that we're starting.

As soon as he reaches them, I tell the chaperones at the main door that I have to go to the bathroom and walk out the door. We need to leave one at a time, so nobody suspects us. Francesca and Jonah will leave through the side door. Miles will leave through the far door because it's the closest to Principal Orr's office, and he needs to meet me there in case his friend's password is wrong. Before I meet him, I need to get the key from the janitor's office.

I walk straight to the women's bathroom. I stop in front of the door, and when I'm sure nobody is looking, I slip around the corner and run toward the janitor's closet.

The door is closed. I try the handle to find that it's unlocked. With one last glance over my shoulder, I open the door and step inside.

My hand claps over my mouth, but it's too late. The sound has already escaped.

Sitting on a stool against the back wall is the janitor. I forget his name, even though I know Miles has told me. He's a mean, crotchety old man with a scowl etched across his face. He doesn't talk much, and I've always been a little scared of him. He looks like the kind of person who collects bugs, who enjoys catching them alive and sticking needles through their abdomens and pinning them to a display board until they stop twitching and die.

He frowns. I didn't think the janitor would be working during school dances.

I glance up at the master key. There it is, as Miles promised, hanging on a hook behind the janitor's head.

The janitor blinks at me. "Students aren't permitted to leave the gym during dances."

"I got lost." It sounds lame even as I say it.

The door opens behind me. I glance back to see Francesca walk in. What is she doing here?

"I saw the door open," Francesca explains, as if reading my mind. "Oh, hello, Alfred."

Alfred. That's his name. Alfred's brow pinches together. "What are you doing here, huh?"

"We need to borrow the master key," Francesca says, and I glare at her. Why would she just say that?

"Get back to the gym," Alfred says. "Or I'm going to call Bill."

Bill would love that. Call-Me-Bill has this security earpiece he wears sometimes because I guess he thinks it makes him look like he's guarding the president.

Francesca frowns. "I am sorry, Alfred, but I am afraid we cannot leave without that key."

"What are you gonna do, huh?" Alfred stands up. I can't get around him. He's too big. "Set me on fire like you did that poor guy?"

Pain flashes across Francesca's eyes. Oh, that's it. Before Alfred can say anything else, I reach across Francesca, grab the mop leaning against the wall, and drive the end into Alfred's side. He yells in surprise. I race around him, slip the key off its hook, take Francesca's wrist, and pull her after me into the hallway.

I run around the corner as fast as I can and slip into one of the classrooms, locking the door behind me. Francesca and I crouch under the window.

"What on earth did you do that for?" Francesca whispers. "Alfred is a good man."

"He was going to call Bill," I say.

"He is certainly going to call him now," she hisses. "You did not need to hurt him with a mop."

"Should I have unzipped my dress instead?"

Alfred's heavy footsteps drum against the hallway floor. I know I shouldn't have done it, but the way he was talking to Francesca sent me over the edge. Hopefully, we were fast enough for him not to see us come in here.

"We should not stab good people with mops," Francesca says. "We should not hurt people and then act as if it means nothing."

I'm surprised Francesca is so upset. Death doesn't seem to bother her, but I guess there's a difference between death and pain. Not that Alfred is in much pain right now. I didn't hit him that hard.

"Okay," I assure her. "Not again."

Alfred is speaking on the phone. Must be to Call-Me-Bill. Hitting Alfred means that Bill will probably go and find Principal Orr.

I peer through the window. Sure enough, there's Bill, running toward Alfred with Principal Orr walking on his heels. They go around the corner, probably in the direction Alfred thought he saw us go.

"Stay here to keep watch," I say to Francesca. "You've got the burner phone?"

She does. "I will call Miles if Alfred returns."

"Good. Thanks." I slip out the door and run in the direction of Principal Orr's office. My heart is pounding, but my head is clear. If I can get into Principal Orr's office and keep the lights off, we might have a little time. I don't think they're going to open every door to check for Francesca. Do they have a second master key?

I hope Alfred isn't hurt. I didn't mean to hurt him. I just wanted to surprise him enough to get out of the way. Something's wrong with me. I don't get violent with people, and I know this is going to mean more than a suspension, but I can't worry about that right now.

Miles is waiting in front of the door when I get there. "Where's Jonah?" I ask.

"By the library, where you said he should be."

"Good." I hold up the key. "Let's do this."

My hands are steady as I push the key into the office lock and twist the handle with a *click*. Principal Orr's office is quiet. Everything looks the same as it did when I was here last, except there are more shadows. The masks look like demons. Their eyes and mouths are hollow and bottomless.

I walk around to her chair and sit down, bracing my forearms on the leather armrests. Miles looks over my shoulder. He rubs his hands together like he does when he's anxious about something.

I memorized the password Miles provided, but I pull the piece of paper out from under the gun so that I don't make a mistake as I type it in. *Please work.* I hit Enter.

The desktop fills the screen. Relief washes over me as I open Chrome. "Go look through her drawers," I hiss at Miles.

"For what?"

"Anything weird. Anything that could link her to Leonard, or suggest she might be thinking about ghosts."

"Pay attention to her search history," Miles says. "She wouldn't leave anything incriminating on a computer she doesn't properly password-protect, but her search history syncs between all her devices."

"Okay."

Miles uses his phone flashlight to look through Principal Orr's desk so we don't have to put the office light on. He pulls a stack of papers out of her drawer, and I open her search history. My hand curls around the mouse as I scroll through it. Max went missing two weeks ago. If Leonard approached Principal Orr with a promise he could bring Louis back three weeks ago, I bet Principal Orr would have wanted to check whether he's legitimate. If she's a logical person, which she seems to be, she would have gone through the same period of questioning that I did. She would have had to consider whether ghosts were real. Who Leonard was. Whether he could do what he said.

This means she would have found the circus profile. Articles reporting Evangeline Durand's death. Googled reasonable questions like *Are ghosts real?*

I scroll back to four weeks ago and move forward to the day Max went missing.

"What are you looking for?" Miles asks.

"Something weird, I guess." There's an online shopping website. A Romance Writers of America forum. Searches for words like "adjacent" she probably looked up how to spell correctly. Nothing weird.

"Do you think Principal Orr could do something like this?" Miles asks.

"I don't know."

I wonder if there's something on her home computer. An email or something. Miles may be right. If Leonard uses email, she would not email him from work, she would email him from home. What's the first thing cops do when they have a suspect? Search their computers. Principal Orr might be many things, but she's not an idiot.

Is all this for nothing?

"She's so normal." Miles puts the papers back into the drawer. "I'm sorry, but I just don't buy any of this."

"So why are you helping me?"

"Because I love you."

I sigh sharply. I didn't expect him to say it so easily, like it's an easy thing to just say. "Stop."

I've just returned my focus to the monitor when Miles's phone starts to vibrate. I feel a sudden pang of warmth for him. The eternal Boy Scout has set his phone to vibrate rather than ring. *I'm a planner*, I remember him saying, before, in his room.

Miles glances at the screen. "It's Jonah."

Jonah's only supposed to call if he sees someone coming. Miles picks up the phone. I can hear Jonah's voice through the line.

Bill, the janitor, and Orr passed the library. They didn't see me, but they're headed your way.

Come on. Think. What else can I search for?

"Shiloh, we've got to get out of here," Miles says.

I tighten my grip on the mouse. I know we've got to go, but there has to be something I haven't thought of yet.

Miles goes to the window. "Oh God. They're just down the hall. They're going to see us if we leave. Oh my God, Shiloh, what do we do?"

I close out of the browser and put Principal Orr's computer to sleep. "We need to hide."

There isn't enough space under her desk for both of us. The front of the desk is open, so they'd see us, anyway.

Miles presses his back against the wall behind the door. I drop behind the chair and pull the material of my dress close to me. I keep my breathing shallow.

The door clicks open. I don't dare look to see if they see Miles pressed up behind the wood. I bite down on my tongue.

Principal Orr clears her throat. "Did your mother not teach you it's rude to hide from your superiors, Miss Oleson?"

Blood drains from my face. Slowly, I stand up to find Principal Orr standing in the doorway in front of Call-Me-Bill and Alfred. The janitor is holding his side and wincing theatrically. Even Bill is frowning at me.

Anything I say as an excuse is going to sound weak, so I settle for, "I'm sorry."

"Am I to understand that you assaulted Alfred with a mop?" The calmness of her tone makes me shift in my shoes.

Dropping my eyes to the floor, I say, "Yes, ma'am."

"I cannot begin to tell you the severity of such an action, as well as the severity of the consequences you will face," Principal Orr says, "but right now is not the time for such things."

Huh? I look back up and watch a smile slowly stretch across her face. What's going on? Why is she smiling?

"I have good news for you," she says.

"Good news?" I ask. "What do you mean, good news?"

"I was going to make an announcement over the loudspeaker to ask you to come to my office, but you appear to be one step ahead of me." Her smile gets wider. "The police have found your brother. Your mother has been here, but we couldn't find you and she couldn't wait. She has left for Akron to confirm it's him."

The news sinks in. "They found Max? In Akron?"

Principal Orr nods. "They found Max, Shiloh. He's alive."

31

SHILOH

I shove past Principal Orr and Call-Me-Bill. Someone shouts my name, but I keep running down the hallway and out the doors. They couldn't have found Max. If they found Max, it means I'm too late.

The Max they found isn't Max at all.

My sneaker snags on the edge of my dress. I stumble forward and grip the fence in front of the school, pressing my forehead into the chain links.

Jonah appears beside me. I don't know where he came from. His face swims in my field of vision. "Stop running, Scooby. I'm not in good enough shape for this."

"I failed," I say.

"You don't know that."

"Leonard wouldn't let him go. If someone found him, it means he's dead, and someone else is walking around in his body."

"You don't know that either," Jonah says. "You don't even know it's him."

Miles catches up to us with Francesca on his heels. He must

have told her that she didn't need to be on lookout duty anymore. His face is red. He holds Francesca's shoulder to steady himself.

Miles sucks in a deep breath. "Where are you going?"

"To the cemetery," I say. "I have to see if Max is there."

Francesca scratches her temple. "It took Poppy nearly a day to walk to the cemetery after Leonard killed her. I am not sure Max would have arrived there already."

"I'll wait."

Another thing dawns on me.

I grab her shoulders, and she yelps in surprise. "Did Leonard come back to the cemetery?"

"No," Francesca stammers. "I promise, none of the souls said anything about it."

"I swear to God, if you're lying—"

"I would never lie to you."

Jonah pulls me off Francesca. I don't realize how hard I was gripping her shoulders until my hands are hanging at my sides.

"I am not lying," Francesca repeats. "I promise, Leonard did not come back."

"She's not lying, Shiloh," Miles says, and I want to punch him in the face. First, he's touching Francesca's shoulder, and now he's defending her.

I know he's probably right. I grip my knees and force myself to focus. "I'm going to the cemetery. I need to see if Max is there."

Jonah says he's coming, too. So are Miles and Francesca, but I've already started walking.

I run at the beginning, slow down to breathe, then run again. Jonah keeps up with me. He's in surprisingly good shape for a stoner. Miles gets tired, so Francesca hangs back with him. My hands won't stop shaking.

Is Max going to be there? Am I too late? I can picture his small, ghostly face—a face I know I'll never be able to see, looking at me with his arms crossed like I've failed him. I'm supposed to protect him, and I didn't make it in time. Twice. I run faster. Only Francesca will see him, but will she tell me the truth? Why is she hanging back with Miles when she should be up here with me? She knows how important this is. She knows how much I need her.

I push through the creaky gate. Jonah is by my side. There are crescents of sweat at the armpits of his wrinkled dress shirt.

Miles and Francesca arrive five minutes later. When I see Francesca, I stand up straight.

"Is he here?" Desperation saws at my words. Francesca glances around.

Do not cry. Do not do it.

"Everything is all right," Francesca says with a gentle wave of her hand. My head snaps up, but I realize she's not speaking to us. She's answering a question from a ghost. She asks if anybody has seen a boy, around waist high.

"Dead," I add.

"They understand," Francesca says. After a moment, she says, "Nobody has seen a boy."

"They haven't seen him?"

"He is not here."

I sink back against an oak tree, feeling a moment's relief. "Are you sure?" I ask, and she nods. "You said it took Poppy a day to get here?"

"I believe so, yes."

Just because he isn't here yet doesn't mean he's not dead. "I'm going to wait for him."

"Do you really think that's smart?" Miles asks, a wrinkle appearing between his eyebrows. "I mean, shouldn't you call your mom? That boy in Akron might not be Max."

I realize Mom won't have my number on this burner phone, so I call her and reach her voicemail. Probably because she's driving. So I leave her a message and tell her it's me, and to call me on this number as soon as she has news.

I turn the ringer on. "If Max comes here, I'll be waiting for him. If Mom calls and it's Max, I'll go back to the school."

I stretch my legs out in front of me. The grass is damp, and my dress is going to be ruined, but I'm sitting close enough to the road for the glow of the streetlamps to reach me. I can see if anyone is coming. Anyone alive, anyway. "Please, Francesca. Tell me if he gets here."

Francesca nods. "I will."

I lean my head back against the bark. Jonah sinks to the ground across from me, and after a moment's hesitation, Miles does the same. Slowly, the moisture from the grass absorbs into the fabric of my dress and presses against my bare skin. Francesca sits down, too. She runs her hands through the grass like it's the locks of somebody's hair.

I hope Max doesn't get lost in the woods. All the safety rules I drilled into his head relied on memorizing phone numbers and asking restaurant workers to use their phones—things he couldn't do if he were dead.

Stop thinking he's dead. Besides, I don't think those safety rules stuck. I also told him not to talk to strangers and look how that turned out.

I wrap my arms around my stomach and try to push the nervous feeling down. Half an hour of silence goes by, and I notice Miles's head begin to droop. His curls fall and cover his face, and my heart can't help but ache.

After an hour, Francesca stands up without a word and wanders into the shadows. I watch her wander among the gravestones. She starts to talk, but I'm too far away to hear what she's saying. I wish I could see ghosts like she can.

I glance back at Jonah. He meets my gaze. His blue eyes shine even in the dark, reflecting the glow from the streetlamps.

"Thinking about Max?" he asks, and I nod. "What about him?"

"I guess I'm trying to figure out what I'm going to do if he comes," I say.

Jonah thinks for a second. "How to see him?"

"How to move forward." This whole time, I haven't allowed myself to confront the possibility of Max being dead. Not really. Living in a world without him would destroy me to the point that I don't even know how I could exist as a person without him. He is my entire world, so I had to save him. I didn't have the option to fail.

If the boy in Akron really is Max, Mom will bring Max home, but he won't be Max. We would have an alien living inside our house. A completely different kid who wouldn't want me as a sister. I wonder if I'd ever get used to it. I wonder if Mom would think Max acted differently because he had PTSD. I could come to the cemetery with Francesca and talk to the real Max, but I could never see him, and Francesca would have to help me talk to him even though he's *my* Max. I'd rather he was just plain dead and never became a ghost. I force myself to take deep breaths so I don't start to hyperventilate or cry.

"If it's Max, then you find Leonard," Jonah says. "You stop him from doing this to another kid."

"But it will be too late for Max," I say.

"You have to dig deep, and you have to stop Leonard because it's the right thing to do."

He's right. I know he's right. Even just thinking about it, my body fills with tension that I've never felt before. I'm going to kill Leonard. Whether he killed Max or not, I'm going to make sure he pays.

I reach into my purse and pull out the scarf, unwrapping it from around the pistol. Jonah sees it and shoots upright.

"Jesus, Shiloh. Where did you get that from?"

"It's my dad's." I turn it over in my hands. Jonah is pressed up against the gravestone, his face twisted in fear. "Don't worry, it's not loaded."

"You can't bring a gun to school. You know how seriously they take that stuff."

"I wasn't going to use it at school. It's for Leonard. I'm not going to fight him without a way to defend myself."

Jonah pauses. For a second, I think he's going to say something else about the gun, but instead, like his mind is somewhere else, he says, "Hold on. You said you want to see ghosts."

I blink at him. "I mean, sure, yeah. Seeing ghosts would be cool, but it's not like I can hit my head against a wall and *bam*, you know?"

A smile creeps onto his face. "What if you could?"

"I'm not following."

"Remember that old woman I told you about who lives across the street from me?"

Oh no. This again? "The one with the magical monocle?"

"What if we go take it?"

What he's suggesting sinks in, and my heart begins to pound. "You mean steal it?"

"Borrow it," he says, "so you can see Max." Jonah nudges Miles with his leg. "Wake up."

Miles sputters to life like an old car. "Huh—?"

"Get up," he says. "We're going on an adventure."

"To …?"

"To get the magical monocle." Jonah looks back at me. "We need to go to her house and nab it from her. If we have the monocle, then we can see ghosts like Francesca."

"And I could see Max," I say.

"And she could see Max," Jonah says.

I guess it's better than waiting. Anything is better than waiting. "What if you're wrong and it's just a normal monocle?"

"Then I'm wrong and we give it back."

"Or we get arrested for breaking into this woman's house?" Miles interrupts, catching on to our plan. "We break the law, assault a senior citizen, and I lose all hope of getting into college?"

"Quit the drama," Jonah says, grinning. "We aren't breaking into anyone's house or assaulting any old women. She knows me. I'm just going to knock on the door and ask her."

———

Jonah explains his plan. I have to admit it sounds insane, but so does just about everything we've done this week, so I go along with it.

"We should ask if Francesca wants to come," Miles says. "I don't want her to feel left out."

I glance back at Francesca. I know it's not fair, but when I look at her, I remember Miles's hand on her back and I'm struck by a sense of betrayal I have no right to feel because she didn't do anything wrong.

"Why don't you go ask her," I say.

Miles gives me a funny look, then goes off to ask her. I guess she wants to come because she hops up and runs over to join us.

Jonah assures us the woman knows who he is. He's had a conversation with her before. I suggest sneaking into the house through a ground-floor window, but he wants to knock on her door. We'll need an excuse to do that.

"We could ask if we could borrow something from her," Francesca suggests on the way there. "Perhaps sugar, for baking cookies?"

"It's the middle of the night," I say, and then pause. "Maybe we can fake an injury?"

A puff of air leaves Miles's nose. "You don't need a first-aid kit to fix a sprained ankle."

Without warning, Francesca drops to the ground. I spin around to see her on her knees, her face twisted in pain. She pushes herself to her feet, and the air catches in the back of my throat. Skin peels back from her left knee. Dirt and pieces of pavement speckle the wound, along with pricks of blood.

Miles's jaw drops. Francesca kicks out her legs like a puppet taking its first steps. "You see, now we do not need to lie," she says.

Miles looks like his brain is being held together by fraying rubber bands. Any second they could snap, and pieces of his brain will fly in all directions, splattering over our clothes.

"Is it just me," he says, "or has everybody lost their *freaking* minds?"

Jonah places a hand on Miles's shoulder. "Deep breaths, buddy."

"I can't do this." Miles bends over with his hands braced against his knees. "This is insane. Everything is insane. It's too much. I was trying to hold it together, but I can't do this anymore."

I put a hand on his shoulder. "Miles—"

"Shut up." He shrugs me off, and my chest tightens. "Not you. Don't touch me."

I take Francesca's arm instead and walk out of earshot of what Jonah and Miles are saying. Francesca picks at her cuticles like she's bored. A line of blood runs down her left knee.

I can't imagine it hurts that badly, but she doesn't seem to be feeling any pain at all. She dropped without thinking. "Why did you do that?" I ask.

Francesca shrugs like it was no big deal. "No one else would have," she says airily.

A few minutes later, Jonah rejoins us. Miles trails behind him with his lips pulled into a scowl. I raise my eyebrows at Jonah to ask whether we're good, and he waves his arms and says, "Come on, let's keep going."

Jonah leads us down his street and stops on the sidewalk in front of an old, purple house with white shutters and a rickety porch with wind chimes hanging off the front. The wind chimes are ringing, but there's no wind. In the silence of the street, it makes the hairs rise on the back of my neck.

"Those wind chimes sound like stars," Francesca remarks, "if stars could make sound."

Hearing a deep, muffled bark, I spin around to see a massive white dog press its face into a window. "Jonah, is that your dog?"

"Kind of."

"Kind of? How can you kind of have a dog?"

"She's my foster mom's," he says, and I feel stupid. "Bessie's going to wake up Moe, though, so we've got to get off the street."

271

Francesca loops an arm around both Miles's and my necks. As soon as her arms touch my skin, the strength leaves Francesca's body and I stagger to hold her up. I can't believe I ever underestimated Francesca. She's kind of badass.

Jonah raises his arm to knock on the door, but then he pauses as if he just remembered something. He walks over to one of the wind chimes twinkling on the porch, unties it from the rung, and hands it to me. I turn it over in my hand and realize it's made of keys.

"Just in case you need to unlock something," he says. "It's a hunch. Keep that in your bag."

What a weird and random thing to make a wind chime out of. Some of the keys are new, but some are old and long, with clover-shaped loops on the end. I'm not exactly a home security expert, but I feel like hanging up the keys to pretty much everything you own in front of your house for anyone to grab doesn't sound like a great move. It's a convenient move for us, though, so I unzip my purse and nestle the chime in there on top of the gun.

Jonah knocks on the door three times. There's no movement in the house. The woman could be sleeping. It was close to ten o'clock when we left the cemetery, so it's even later now.

Jonah knocks again. A light turns on. I hold on to Francesca as the door opens with a creak and a small woman peers out at us.

"Please." Jonah steps aside to reveal Francesca's torn-up knees. "My friend just fell and hurt herself, and I'm locked out of my house. Do you have a first-aid kit we could use?"

The woman looks up at Francesca's face, then down at her knee. The woman is way shorter than me, with frizzy hair, a hunched back, and warm skin etched with wrinkles. She's wearing a pair of matching purple pajamas, but she's not wearing a monocle. Her eye twitches. I'm bracing myself for her to say no when she steps out of the way to let us inside.

Before I can get through the door, the smell of old carpet and incense hits me. I'm usually not squeamish around smells, unless it's like a dirty toilet or something, but there's something weird about this smell. Only when I spot the cage do I realize what I was smelling. A bird cage stretches up from the floor to the ceiling and has newspaper on the bottom. A thick layer of runny black and white crap covers the headlines. I stare the bird in the eyes. It's huge. Easily the size of a jack-o'-lantern. It's one of those red and white parrots people have in movies, the ones who know how to talk. Talons the size of fingers wrap around wooden dowels and fake tree branches. Its beak looks sharp enough to take an eye out.

"Intruders," the parrot cries, and I jump. "Intruders, Winnie! Intruders."

"Don't mind Malcolm," says the woman, walking past the cage and dismissing the bird with a wave of her hand. "We don't get many guests."

We walk into the adjoining room. A red carpet with short-cropped pile and gold trim stretches beneath our feet.

Miles and I carry Francesca into a room that looks like a display room in an antique store. Long oil paintings of wrinkled men with unique hairstyles hang on the wall. Flowerpots decorate the windowsill. A bowl of pinecones sits on the coffee table, and an iron chandelier hangs above our heads. One of the bulbs is flickering, casting long shadows across the room.

Miles helps Francesca onto a couch. Francesca hisses in a breath. The woman pays her no attention and wanders into her kitchen.

The hair on the back of my neck stands up. There's something weird about this place. Something is weird about the fact that the woman seems unfazed.

I whisper to Jonah. "Are you sure your dog wasn't barking at that parrot?"

"I swear."

"That parrot's big enough to pass as a dog." Just as the words come out of my mouth, I catch a glimpse of one of those creepy hairless cats posed on one of the armchairs. There are too many weird animals in this house. It gives me the creeps. "I'm going to follow her."

I find the woman in the kitchen, elbow-deep in a cabinet. I don't know what to say, so I muster, "Thank you so much for helping us."

A pile of dirty dishes sits in the sink. Food sits open on the counters, and mold clings to the soggy peaches clumped together in a fruit bowl. I hope this woman is okay. I imagine it would be hard to cook and clean by yourself in a house this big.

I glance over my shoulder back at the portraits of men hanging on the living room wall. "Do you live here alone?"

"I live here with my sister." The woman pulls out a roll of yellowed gauze from the cabinet. "She is sleeping."

"Oh."

The woman shuffles back into the living room. "The phone is over there, if you're needing to use it."

I need to go look for the monocle. "Can I use your bathroom?"

The woman stops and peers back at me. She's slow, almost mechanical in her movements, like every joint needs to be greased.

"Down the hall and up the stairs," she says.

"Thank you."

Walking down the long hallway, I get the illusion that the walls are creeping closer to me the farther I go. Once I reach the bottom of the stairs, goosebumps rise on the back of my neck and I rub my hand over them to make them go away.

Every rickety stair groans under my weight. I glance between photographs along the wall until my gaze settles on one. It's a photo of two girls, in their teens, smiling and sitting on a bale of hay in long dresses with puffs on their shoulders. This must be the woman and her sister.

I hurry inside the bathroom, close the door, and flip on the lights. It's a pretty standard bathroom. Maybe a little outdated. The toilet seat looks like it was once white but has turned a pale shade of yellow. Probably because it has had decades of butts sitting on it.

I open every drawer and cabinet to try to find a monocle, but all I find are towels, toiletries, and orange prescription bottles. I flush the toilet to make it sound like I used it, then turn off the light and open the door. I can hear Miles's voice downstairs, blabbering nervously about how much he loves scarlet macaws. His voice is super high-pitched. Probably because he's lying. He definitely doesn't love birds. At least, I don't think he does, because he flinched really hard when I showed him that dead bird's foot at the labyrinth.

I glance down the hallway. There are three doors. Each of them is closed. The woman's voice echoes in my head.

I live here with my sister, but she's sleeping.

The sister must be sleeping in one of those rooms.

If I open the wrong door, I'm going to get caught snooping around. One door sits at the end of the hallway. The other two frame it. In my house, the master bedroom is at the end of the hallway. When you live with your sister, do you share a master bedroom? Probably not. My guess is that the woman downstairs sleeps in the master bedroom—unless this is their childhood home, in which case my guess is that neither of them would want the master bedroom because their parents would have used it.

I turn the glass doorknob with a soft click and poke my head inside.

It's hard to see anything through the shadows. There's a bed, but the sheets are pulled tight. No sister, which is a relief. I slip through the door and close it behind me. Slowly, my eyes adjust. It's definitely a bedroom, but it's neat. I remember the dishes piled in the kitchen sink. Something tells me this is not the woman's bedroom. I'm pretty uncomfortable being in someone else's private space, but I have to push through it. I walk up to the bedside table. There's nothing on it. I open the drawer and crouch to look inside it. No monocle.

I honestly don't even know what I'm looking for. On the

walk here, Jonah described the monocle as being thick, made of glass, and weirdly mechanical, but no matter how hard I try, I can't picture it in my head. I open the closet and push a bunch of musty clothes to the side. Could the monocle be on the ground? I don't find anything, so I close the door and reenter the hallway.

Miles is still babbling about parrots. Good. He's still talking, which means the woman is still distracted. I don't hear any footsteps on the stairs, but I need to move fast in order not to be noticed as having left the bathroom.

There are two rooms left. I press my ear to one of the doors. Maybe the sister snores? Hearing nothing, I close my fist around the knob.

I open the door and peer into the room. There's also a bed in this room, but the covers are pulled tight like the last one. I pause. It looks kind of like a kid's room, with pink sheets and a teddy bear sitting between the pillows.

This can't be the woman's room. Can it? I guess it's possible, so I check the nightstand, drawers, and closet and still don't find anything that could be confused for a monocle.

On my way out the door, I collide with something hard and I stumble backward.

"*Jonah*," I hiss. Jonah presses a finger to his lips. "What are you doing up here?"

"Coming to get you," he says. "You've been up here so long that Miles has started telling the old broad about his stamp collection."

"I didn't find the monocle," I say. "Her sister is sleeping in that room, so I can't look there."

"The monocle isn't up here."

"How do you know?"

"She's wearing it."

My eyes widen.

"She has it," he says. "It was in her pocket the whole time. She took it out, and she's using it right now. This place is so haunted. I wasn't making it up, I swear to God."

"How are we going to get the monocle if she's using it?"

Jonah grabs my arm. I glance down at the place his fingers are digging into the fleshy part of my forearm. "Just come downstairs."

Downstairs, the woman is using a cotton ball to help Miles dab Betadine onto Francesca's knees. When she turns around to see us, I see the monocle. Clear as day, hanging around her neck.

"Your friend here is just about ready to leave," says the woman, screwing the cap back on the bottle before walking into the kitchen to put it away.

I spin on Jonah and whisper, "What are we supposed to do?"

"I don't know."

I glance down at my purse. Once Jonah realizes what I'm suggesting, his eyes bulge out of his head. "Don't."

"But we need the monocle."

"You can't draw a gun on an old woman."

We're still bickering when a voice behind us asks, slowly and sweetly and without a hint of antagonism, "Am I seeing things, or are you kids trying to steal my monocle?"

32

SHILOH

Should we run? The woman doesn't look capable of attacking us. Jonah could take her. So I say, "Yes?"

"*Shiloh,*" Jonah snaps.

"What am I supposed to say?"

The woman takes the monocle from her neck, holds it in her hand, and gestures to the couch. "You kids, take a seat."

With nervous steps, I sit next to Miles. Jonah sits on my other side. My mouth goes dry as the old woman lowers herself into an armchair. The bald cat stalks around the corner, flicking its tail before curling around the woman's legs and continuing into the kitchen.

Resting the cane beside her, the woman leans forward and slides the monocle across the coffee table toward us. I blink at it. Multiple lenses cross over one another and move like they are made of clockwork, but there are no gears.

The woman's eyes settle on Francesca. "I see that you can see her."

I realize Francesca isn't looking at the woman. Instead, her eyes are focused just to the side of the woman's head.

"What are you seeing?" I whisper to her.

Miles makes a noise. "Is there a ghost in here?"

"I see a girl," Francesca whispers, as if transfixed. "Of no more than thirteen."

"Fourteen," the woman corrects. "Yes. You kids, meet Winifred."

"I told you this place was haunted as shit," Jonah says. When the woman glares at him, he hangs his head. "It's true."

The woman makes a swooping gesture at the monocle resting on the table. "You may take a look for yourself, if you'd like."

Everyone looks at me. I stare at the monocle like it's challenging me. My heart thumps inside my chest. Part of me wants nothing to do with that thing, whatever it is, but Francesca looks so scared that I have to see what she's looking at.

Careful not to drop it, I pick up the monocle and raise it to my eye. It's heavier than I expected, and slick from the oils the woman was rubbing into Francesca's knee. I move my eye around the room. Every couch and painting looks the same as it did without the lens. I scan the space beside the woman, where Francesca seems to be looking, but I see nothing. "It's not working."

"Look harder," urges the woman.

This is dumb. I'm about to put the monocle back on the table when a face appears in my field of vision only inches from my nose.

I scream and drop the monocle in my lap.

"What did you see?" Francesca asks. I can't breathe. What the hell was that? Did I really see that face? I pick up the monocle and slowly raise it back to my eye.

I see it again. A girl's face. Right in front of mine. The girl is breathing fast. Her face doesn't really have a shape at first, but it becomes more human as it comes into focus in the fog. I can see a hooked nose, pinched eyebrows, and a down-turned mouth, open enough for me to see that she's baring her teeth at me.

Francesca was right. She's young. Looks around thirteen, with sunken-in eyes and uneven strands of hair springing from her skull. The girl's eyes burn with a frigid intensity that makes me want to wrap my arms around myself. She runs her tongue over her teeth. I tighten my grip on the monocle. "What is that thing?"

"Did it work?" Jonah asks. I pass him the monocle in response and watch the blood drain from his face as he sees the girl, too.

It's Miles's turn. He takes the monocle and leaps back against the couch. He spits out a slew of expletives, more than I've ever heard him use.

I lock eyes with the old woman in the chair. She looks like she's having a great time, watching us squirm so much. I narrow my eyes into slits. "What's your name?"

"My name is Ella Ruggles."

"When did you die?" Francesca asks in a kind voice, and it takes me a second to realize that she's talking to the ghost.

"She won't talk to you," Ms. Ruggles says.

"Why not?" Francesca asks.

"She never talked to anybody, not even when she was on this planet."

"How long ago did she die?" Francesca asks.

"When she was fourteen years old. Could be sixty, seventy years ago. In all my years, I have lost count of time."

A crease appears between Francesca's eyebrows. "I do not understand. How can she have been dead for sixty years? The longest I have ever seen a soul stay before fading away is twenty."

A finger drags across the top of my left shoulder. I turn around, but there's nobody standing behind me. "Did that ghost just touch me?"

"Souls cannot touch us. It is not possible." Francesca glances at Ms. Ruggles. "Is it?"

Instead of replying, Ms. Ruggles pulls a cable-knit quilt over her legs and says, "You'd be surprised at what is and what's not possible, my dear."

Ms. Ruggles goes on to tell us that her sister, Winifred, was born different.

"Winnie was not the same as you and me," she says. "Never was. They say my Ma made Winnie slow, holding her head in so long, but I guess that's something we'll never know. She never cried. Only moaned and groaned 'til somebody came to help her."

Behind me, a book topples over and lands with a flat *slap*. I sit up at the noise.

Ms. Ruggles tells us Winnie grew up without speaking. As soon as she could walk, she followed Ella around the house, and Ella woke up in the middle of the night to find Winnie standing over her bed, touching her cheeks, her lips, her throat. The whole thing is so creepy that I wrap my arms around my torso and try not to think about this girl wandering around us. I wish I were wearing more than this stupid yellow prom dress. Something warmer and more practical.

Ms. Ruggles tells us that when Winnie turned eight, their mother sent her to an institution that promised to fix her, but it made her come back different. The first night Winnie spent back home, Ella woke up to see Winnie standing over her bed with a letter opener in her hand.

Crash. I spin around to see another book on the ground, its pages splayed open.

Miles points over his shoulder. "Did the ghost do that?" he says, his voice much squeakier than normal.

When Francesca asks the next question, my blood goes cold. "How exactly did Winnifred die?"

"I never meant for it to happen," Ms. Ruggles says, completely deadpan. "I was awake, and her hands were on my neck, like this. I had always been small, as a girl. See, we got to the landing right there, and—" She gestures up at the landing in front of the bathroom, with a creaky wooden banister hanging onto the side. Ms. Ruggles waves her hand. "I told them she'd gone and fell."

Francesca's face furrows. I don't think I've ever seen her look so angry. "You killed her."

"You kids can't conceive of what it was like. I felt so afraid," Ms. Ruggles sputters. "I wasn't twenty years old when I noticed strange, *strange* things going on in the house. Lights came on without any one of us touching them. My soul nearly left my body when Malcolm began saying her name. *Winifred, Winifred.*" It takes me a second to remember Malcolm is the name of the parrot. "I was haunted, see. My parents, too. My mother, bless her heart, passed after contracting the hiccups, and my father from getting a peanut lodged deep in here." She gestures to her throat. "Winifred was torturing us. I was sure of it. Surer than I've ever been of anything in my life. Why, when I was a girl, I went to the circus show and saw this young man kill a rabbit, stone-dead, then bring it back to life like he was the Lord himself. I couldn't believe it. Not a soul would believe that on television these days, they'd say it was some trick. Mind, I thought it was a trick myself until the day he choked that girl to death."

Shock roots itself in the pit of my stomach. She has to be talking about Leonard. I don't know how many other teenage necromancers were performing in sideshows when she was growing up. "Did you go looking for him?"

"When he killed that girl, he was in such a state that he took himself a shotgun and blowed his own head clean off." I pull my purse closer to myself and feel the gun beneath the fabric. "The circus show was quiet about it all, of course. Said he died of shame. He liked one of the boys looking after the horses. That horse-boy, he wasn't the same after that. Nobody knows what became of him, and I swear I don't know myself where he ran off to. Maybe him and Leonard were sweet on each other. I do believe that's allowed now, but of course it wasn't then."

I'm having trouble feeling sorry for Leonard. I'm about to ask where she found all this out when she continues.

"Off into the winds the performers went, joining this and

that. I paid a visit to the lady who told the show's fortunes, who gave me this monocle, here. She had just about anything you could imagine. Potions that'd make you believe your left foot was your lover. Told me all sorts of stories about that murdering circus boy." Ms. Ruggles reaches over to the table to take the monocle into her hands. She holds it up to her eye, and a smile stretches across her face as she sees what must be Winnie standing behind the couch.

Francesca grips her bleeding knees and leans forward over them. "But Winifred must fade, eventually."

Ms. Ruggles's eyes sparkle with a hint of mischief. "Nobody ever dies, my dear. Every person who dies—they stay."

"No, they fade," Francesca says, "I am sure of it."

"They stay," Ms. Ruggles emphasizes. "See, when they fade, they don't go away. They only go somewhere else."

"How come Winnie has not faded?" Francesca asks. "Why can she touch the material world?"

Ms. Ruggles lowers the monocle. "Because Winifred returns."

"The dead can return?"

"You." Ms. Ruggles gestures at Francesca with a bony finger. "Would you be a dear and retrieve some cling-wrap from the kitchen? I keep it in the drawer to the right of the sink."

Francesca is back moments later with a long carton. She hands it to Ms. Ruggles, who opens it, takes hold of the end, and pulls upward.

"It's not so much a place of their own as a version of this world. A layer that exists side-by-side, atop of ours, resembling this cling-wrap." She rotates the plastic wrap so it lies flat across her lap. "See, the dead live among us, but they cannot touch us. Unless they died long ago, and there is a tear in the barrier." Using her pointer finger, she pokes the plastic wrap. It bends around her forefinger, and she presses harder, puncturing the film and breaking through to the other side.

"Around these parts, the cling-wrap's thin," Ms. Ruggles continues. "No reason why. Just one of those places. Souls can occasionally break free on their own accord and return here. Or, perhaps, one could help them." Ms. Ruggles puts the plastic wrap on the floor and stands up, walking over to the bookcase and pulling out a thin, leather-bound book. Running her finger over the frayed spine, Ms. Ruggles opens it on her lap. "A palmist in Toledo swore this book's incantations could send the dead back to their place crying." She thumbs through the worn pages. "Worked almost a day before Winifred came back."

A hand lands on my shoulder. When I glance back, there's no one there. A fist of terror lodges down my throat. "I thought ghosts couldn't touch things," I say.

"The older they become, the more mana they accumulate."

"What is mana?" Francesca asks.

"It comes from some belief. Polynesian, I believe. The word don't matter so much as the idea. It's spiritual, supernatural energy. Released in death and held onto by souls in what comes after, feeding back to into our world without us so much as noticing and causing odd mutations."

"Like the sheep with two heads," Miles mutters, like he's realizing something.

"Or sunflowers the size of stop signs," Francesca adds. "Did the palmist mention how to tear through the barrier?"

"Oh, dear—the living cannot cross through, nor should they want to." From behind Ms. Ruggles, another book crashes onto the floor. Harder this time. Ms. Ruggles doesn't even flinch. She must be used to this, although how anyone could ever get used to this is crazy to me. She leans forward onto her knee. "My dear. In all my life, I have never met anybody who can see the dead. You are fascinating." A toothless grin spreads over her lips. I'm surprised she hadn't heard about Francesca setting that guy on fire, but something tells me this woman isn't too connected with the outside world. She's looking at Francesca like she belongs in a museum of medical oddities, like Miles's two-headed sheep or a baby in a jar. Francesca seems unaware of how creepy this lady is being, and I want to get her out of here.

"Can you hear the dead as well?" Ms. Ruggles asks.

"I can," Francesca says. "Usually, souls have quite a lot to say, but she has not spoken to me."

I glance at Jonah. He seems to be thinking the same as me because he shoots up from the couch and says, "Come on, Francesca, let's go."

"You see, I never could find out how to communicate with Winifred." Ms. Ruggles pushes herself to her feet, looking at Francesca like the rest of us aren't even here. Her cane wobbles beneath her weight. "Perhaps you'd be able to help an old woman out, hmm?"

Miles holds Francesca's upper arm. "We r-really ap-ppreciate your time, Ms. Ruggles, but we need to go. Now."

Francesca stands up. The woman tries to steady herself on her feet and grabs hold of the wall. "Please, you must tell her to leave me."

Behind us, there's a loud bang. I take Francesca's hand and pull her behind me. She's tugged backward. I see the woman gripping Francesca's arm so hard her knuckles have turned white. "I'm *begging* you."

Something creaks above my head. I glance up to see the chandelier swinging.

I'm done with this. I yank Francesca free and pull her down the hallway and out through the front door. Jonah pushes Miles after us, out from under the swinging chandelier.

"Please!" Ms. Ruggles screams after us as we run down the steps and out into the street. "You must help me. She has ruined my life. I am begging you, please."

I squeeze Francesca's hand and don't slow down until we've turned the corner and are out of sight of Ms. Ruggles. Miles and Jonah catch up. I drop Francesca's hand and wipe my sweaty palm on the front of my dress as Miles wheezes to catch his breath.

"What was she talking about in there, about ghosts fading away and stuff?" I ask Francesca.

Francesca's brow pinches. "I am trying to figure that out for myself."

"Who decides when they disappear?"

"God."

Somehow, I doubt it, but whatever. I don't know how Francesca can be religious when she sees the things she does, but more power to her, I guess. I don't believe in God. Or at least, I don't think I do. I don't know how God could sit by and watch Dad beat the crap out of his kids without doing anything to stop it. If God can, then that's a god I don't want to meet.

But that's not important right now.

It's almost midnight when we get back to the cemetery. I'm worried that I haven't heard anything from Mom. Does she have Max? Is it another kid? Is she losing her mind because Max is saying he's not Max? I pull the phone out of my bag to check if she called me. *No no no.* I click the power button and beg for it to turn on, but it's dead. Maybe if I hold it over a gravestone that deep supernatural ghost energy would bring it back to life. I utter a short, high-pitched laugh at the ridiculousness of this entire situation.

I just saw a dead person.

With a pang, I realize that, in the commotion of trying to get Francesca out of that house, I forgot to steal the monocle.

"Is Max here?" I ask Francesca.

She shakes her head. "I do not see him."

"I'm staying awake," I say, leaning against one of the gravestones. Miles sits next to me this time, opposite Jonah, who's leaning against a grave facing me and away from the road. Francesca sits next to me on the other side, her shoulder pressing against mine. I'm glad she's here. I know Francesca is calm, so her pressure on my shoulder calms me down, too.

I close my eyes. Just for a second. At least, that's what it feels like because when I open them again, Miles has fallen onto his side and is fast asleep.

Jonah's eyes are closed, too. Francesca isn't here anymore. She's leaning against the front fence, looking out onto the road.

My eyes rest on Miles. I remember what it felt like to be tangled in his arms, with my head resting on his chest, feeling his breath against the back of my shoulder blade. He told me he loved me. I never believed anybody would ever say that to me, let alone someone like Miles. Is there a problem with me? Am I incapable of feeling love for anybody except Max?

Careful not to wake anybody up, I push myself to my feet and walk away. I wander through the gravestones. Some are arranged in rows. Others are clustered more randomly in the grass. I scan the people's names but don't recognize any of them.

Until I do. Toward the back of the cemetery, I find a short stone with a cross carved on top.

Natalie Dorado.

"Hey." I glance behind me to see Jonah running a hand down his groggy face. He gestures at the stone. "Paying your respects?"

"I wish we remembered the monocle," I say, returning my gaze to the moss growing from the cracks in the stone. "I was so focused on getting Francesca out of there that I completely forgot about it."

"What, this monocle?" Jonah reaches into his pocket. The moonlight glints off the copper casing and the glass.

I gape at him. "How did you—"

"I took it when the chandelier started swinging," he says, offering it to me. "When she was distracted."

I reach out to take it, but hesitate. Part of me doesn't want to hold it up to my eye because I'm scared of what I'm going to see.

Jonah must understand what I'm thinking because he jerks his chin at the old shed near the trees, and we both sit down with our backs pressed against the splintering, dead wood.

"Remember, they can't touch you," Jonah says, handing me the monocle.

"Somebody did, back in that house." I take it this time. "I don't think the dead have rules."

Pressing my back hard against the shed, I lift the monocle to my eye. I see them immediately. The ghosts look like they're made of fog, hovering around the gravestones like the opposite of shadows. They are shapes of people made of shades of gray, much paler than Winifred Ruggles. I can see right through them.

There's an old, bearded man in a suit with thin hair sticking straight up from his head, wearing a black overcoat and clutching a book to his chest. Over by the wall is a young, blond soldier wearing camo with a bandage strapped across his left eye, barely working to hold back the blood soaking through the gauze. I actually remember him. Sam. He used to work at the deli. I had a crush on him for about a week in middle school. I knew he'd joined the army because the paper put a picture on the front page when they sent him to Afghanistan, but I didn't know he died. I guess this town likes its heroes whole.

Under the tree stands a sad woman wearing an old-fashioned dress with lace around the collar. Pieces of her raven-black hair fall out of her up-do. Another woman holds a shawl tightly around her shoulders. Her arms are stripped of all her skin from what must have been a fire. They look like Mom's hand did that time when too much oil splattered up from a hot pan.

Or maybe Dad threw it on her. I'd never thought of that.

Two ivory-haired boys peer down at Miles, who is lying fast asleep. They have matching bowl cuts and are giggling as they try to mess with Miles's long hair. Their hands go straight through him.

I don't see Max anywhere. My fingers tighten around the monocle before I lower it from my eye and pass it to Jonah.

He keeps it on his lap. "It's nuts that they've been here all this time, and we didn't know."

"Tell me about it."

Jonah reaches into his pocket. I wonder what he's going to pull out when he procures a carrot stick and offers it to me in his palm. "Want one?"

I bet he took those from the dance. I usually wouldn't want to eat something that's been sitting in someone's pocket for a few hours, but tonight's been a weird night and I'm kind of hungry. "Sure."

I bite through the carrot stick and find that it's warm, but for some reason, I don't want to stop eating it.

I look back over to where Miles is sleeping in the grass. I wish I was over there with him. A small sigh tugs on my lungs. "Did Miles ever tell you what happened with us?"

Jonah shakes his head. "He didn't want to talk about it. Why?"

"I made a mistake," I say, "and I don't know if I can fix it."

Jonah glances over at me with a playful glint in his eyes. "You finally told him you don't like *Star Wars*?"

"He told me he loved me." I'm surprised at how easily the words come out.

The glint disappears from Jonah's eyes. "Did you say it back?"

"No." I rub my eyes with the heels of my hands. "Growing up, my dad would tell me that I was nothing and that I was lucky he put up with me at all. I hated him for it. But I think he got to me on some level. Like, deep down, I think I'm nothing, too."

Jonah swallows a bite of his carrot stick and doesn't take another. I've never said that out loud before. I should feel naked, or uncomfortable, or scared. I don't know why I don't.

"It's weird how that works," Jonah says.

"I don't think I can love anyone other than Max." The words are pouring out of me now. "And that scares me because Miles is so good. If I can't love him, I guess I can't love anybody."

Jonah spins the hemp necklace around his neck, and I stretch my legs out in front of me in the dirt.

"I'm probably biased," Jonah says, "but Miles is a good person and worth being good to."

"What I'm saying is that I can't do it, Jonah—"

"You opened up to me just then."

"Yeah, but it's different."

"What's that supposed to mean?"

"I don't know. You're … you." Why is he looking at me so

weirdly? "I don't like you like that, you know? So there's no pressure on anything. You're my friend."

"I'm your friend," Jonah echoes.

"Yes. Friend."

Jonah sighs. He turns the carrot stick over in his hands, flipping it upside down, then right side up, staring at it like it's somehow going to tell him what to say. Finally, he says, "Just because you've gone through stuff doesn't mean you don't deserve love."

"I want to love Miles." As I say it, I realize it's true. I want to be the person he loves. I want to be the person who's capable of loving him.

Jonah smiles over at me, an unreadable glimmer in his eyes. "Even the darkest night will end, and the sun will rise."

A smile tugs at my lips. "You listened to *Les Mis*?"

"I thought it was good," he says. "Still a little too jazz hands for my taste, but good. Depressing as hell."

"Can I ask you a question?" I ask, a weight lifting off my shoulders. He nods. "Did you really steal Melissa Mulvey's underwear, like everyone says?"

Jonah stares at me. For a second, I could swear he looks unhappy, like I just asked about someone who died, but then a cocky smile wipes the sadness from his face. "She left them in the bathroom."

I laugh. "So you just took them?"

"What do you want me to do, hold them up in homeroom and ask if they were hers? I'm a disgusting human being. What can I say?" He says it as a joke, but there's an edge to his voice.

"You're not disgusting." I point over my shoulder. "I'm going to go wake up Miles."

Jonah balances a carrot stick between his teeth like it's a cigarette. "See you later, Scooby."

I grab my bag and walk back to where Miles is sleeping on the grass. I don't want to tell him I love him because it would be a lie. I don't want to make any declarations. I just want him to feel that I care. Careful not to hurt him, I lift up his arm and crawl under it, pressing my back into his chest and resting my head on his bicep.

Miles stirs. "Are you okay?"

"I'm good," I say, pulling his arm tighter around me. A small sigh leaves his lips, but he doesn't push me away. I melt into him, and the world goes away. The last thing I think of is Max.

I won't be able to avoid knowing forever.

33

FRANCESCA

Sitting on the rock wall and facing away from the cemetery, it is easy to forget where I am. The scrapes on my knees have long since stopped burning, but part of me wishes they still were. Pain is good. It makes me feel alive. More connected to my body in a peculiar way.

I wonder how Ella Ruggles would have responded to me if I told her that I could only see ghosts, but I could bring souls back from the dead, like Leonard can. I glance back at Shiloh, curled up in Miles's arms on the grass. How would she react? She no longer looks at me the way she used to, like I had unknowingly wet my pants and was walking around school with a stain on them. Actually, she doesn't seem to mind me anymore, and I have grown fond of having a friend. But if I told her that I had the same abilities as Max's kidnapper, I am afraid she would hate me.

Reverend Guessford would assure me it is not the abilities I have, but the way I use them that defines who I am as a person. Surely Leonard has not always been this way. Do some abilities have the power to warp your mind?

I dig my finger into the wound on my knee, sending a needle of pain up through my thigh. I am considering going for a walk around the cemetery to keep myself awake when I catch a soul glimmering between the trees.

I notice the loafers. The tweed. I slide onto my feet.

"Mr. Haggarty," I whisper. "Please, do not run from me."

George hurries away, but I will not let him get away this time. I run after him. My sudden burst of energy appears to take him by surprise. Before he can get away, I grab hold of his arm. Cold shoots up my wrist as my fingers curl around something firm. I force myself not to let go as George gapes at me.

"Hello, George," I say. "Do you remember me? I am Francesca Russo."

"L-Little Francesca R-Russo?" George stutters, and I nearly smile. He said the same thing to me that day at the funeral parlor. He shines brightly against the night, more brightly than anybody else in the cemetery, although not quite as bright as Winifred did. "Oh my, you've grown up."

I drop his arm. He does not run away. His hands are trembling. Even after all this time, he appears to be just as anxious as he is in my memories.

"How is it you were able to come back from the other side?" I ask. "You already faded away."

He moves his wire-frame glasses up the bridge of his nose. "Through a hole," he says. "A hole in the wall."

I remember how Ella Ruggles poked her finger through the plastic wrap. From her description, it seems like there are small passageways opening and closing all over Bethany, like the spores of a fungus. These must be the holes George speaks of. "Will you take me there?"

"I found one a good half-hour's walk from here," he says. I glance back at the cemetery. I cannot stray far. I must keep watch for Max. "I come back here any time I happen to find a hole. They open, they close. In different places. They never stay open for long."

"Why have you returned?"

He shifts uneasily between his feet. "Oh, Francesca Russo, it is dark over there, and cold. I come to see my granddaughter, my little girl. I cannot see her while I'm in that place, at least not clearly."

An uncomfortable feeling settles into my stomach. Deep down, I have always hoped the afterlife would be a happy place. Somewhere you go to get all the things you want, but perhaps I was wrong about that, too.

"I am very sorry I did not succeed in burning you," I tell him. As I say it, I realize I have been wanting to tell him that for a very long time.

"I should never have asked you to," he says. "Besides, Francesca Russo, I would have ended up in the same place just the same. Oh, it's a terrible place. If people knew where they were going … I'd bet you they wouldn't write so much poetry about death, or half as many hymns."

I am about to ask him for more details when, somewhere down the road, an engine sputters.

34

SHILOH

I wake up to the sound of an engine. Pushing myself onto my forearm, I nudge Miles. "Do you hear that?"

Miles blinks his eyes open. "What?"

The engine cuts out. A car door opens. On the street, there's a truck parked against the curb. Out of it steps a tall figure.

Miles gasps. "Is that—"

"Leonard." I spring to my feet.

Miles pulls me down. "What are you doing?"

"Rescuing Max," I say.

"By doing what? Even if this is Leonard, which it might not be, it's not like he would bring Max with him." The man walks around the front of the car. "Quick, come on. We have to hide."

As much as I don't want to admit it, Miles is right. I follow Miles to the edge of the cemetery and climb over the rock wall. We crouch behind it, and I crane my neck up just enough to see a man walking through the gravestones. He's wearing a long trench coat, but it's too dark to see the color.

Miles clutches my upper arm. I can't breathe. The man swings a piece of cloth around his arm as he surveys the

295

gravestones, mumbling the words of a tune I don't recognize. Under the moon, his coat comes into view.

Emerald green.

I turn to Miles, whose finger is glued to his lips. Leaves crunch to my left and I glance over to see Jonah moving toward us, ducking behind the wall.

"Where are you, Henry?" Leonard spins around. "I'm here for you, boy."

I didn't expect him to have such a thick Southern accent, but Francesca was right—he doesn't look like at all the man in that photo I printed out. I look down at his hands.

Five fingers.

Those hands touched Max. They took him away from me. This man deserves to die. Cold metal burns my palm as I grasp the gun.

Before I can draw it out, Jonah's arm shoots out to grab my wrist. "Stop," he whispers.

"I'm going to kill him," I say.

"Then he can't take us to Max." Jonah glances at the car, and my eyes widen in understanding.

Leonard stops walking. His eyes are glued to the air in front of him. "Well, hi there, Henry." Brandishing the burlap, he lunges forward and grabs hold of something invisible, pushing a shape I can't see into the sack and drawing the string closed. He strolls out of the cemetery holding the sack like a grocery bag. The bag moves around like it's alive.

"He's going to get away," I say. "We need to follow him."

"How?" Miles asks. "We can't exactly climb into the car without being detected, and I'm definitely not fast enough to keep up with a car on foot."

A door slams. I look over to see the headlights turn on as the engine revs to life. I spring to my feet and tear through the gravestones. I don't have a plan, but I can't just sit there and watch him get away. I need to follow him. The truck pulls away from the curb and I run into the street.

I wave my arms over my head. "Hey!" My feet pound against the asphalt. "Wait! Come back!"

Leonard's truck doesn't slow down. My legs burn as I turn the corner, but the truck is already at the end of the road. I keep running. An arm pulls me back.

I spin to face Jonah. "What are you doing?"

"You're not going to outrun a car, Shiloh."

"We need to follow him," I say. Francesca catches up to us, breathing heavily. Where did she come from? "We can …" My voice trails off as I remember what Leonard said. *I'm here for you, Henry.* Hold on a second. "Francesca, who is Henry?"

Francesca itches her eyebrow. "One of the children in the cemetery."

Could it be that Leonard hasn't killed Max yet, and is coming to the cemetery to get the ghost? If that's the case, who is Mom going to see in Akron? Maybe I was wrong about Louis and the whole thing with Principal Orr. Maybe this Henry kid is the one meant for Max's body. Why else would Leonard have come to get him?

Max is not dead yet.

We have more time.

"What's Henry's last name?" I ask.

"I am fairly certain he died in a car accident, but I am not entirely sure. Henry does not speak very much. He has not told me the exact story of how he died, but I believe I remember Mrs. Lewis mentioning his mother had been driving the car when the accident occurred."

"Francesca, what is Henry's last name?" I ask again.

"Vaughn," Francesca says. "Henry Vaughn."

My blood goes cold. Vaughn is Connie's last name. Connie from the Sheriff's Department. Connie who works for Dad. But it can't be her. "I know someone with that last name, but she doesn't have any kids."

"It's a common enough last name," Miles says. "If we go to one of our houses—not mine, because I didn't tell my parents I'd be out all night and when I say my mom's going to be mad, it's a gross understatement—but maybe yours, Jonah, we can search the town directory."

It hits me. Hard and square in the chest.

Connie doesn't have children.

But she has a sister.

Blood rushes from my face. All it would have taken was an ear to the door for Connie to have found out about the abuse. Or for her to see Dad grabbing me by the neck in the supply closet after he found the mess Max and I made making paper airplanes. I picture the framed photograph on her desk of her and her sister looking so alike they could be twins. Connie loves her sister. If her sister was in pain, she would want to help.

I grab Miles's shoulder, and he steadies me. "What's wrong?"

"It's Connie's nephew," I say, and explain everything. The more I talk about it, the more it makes sense. I even remember Dad talking about having to put more time in at work a couple of years ago because Connie was off on some kind of compassionate leave. Connie didn't want me poking around looking for Leonard because she knew I was onto something. I had seen something shift behind her eyes that day I spoke to her. She has always been so nice to me. The betrayal knits my hands into fists and makes me want to tear Connie's eyeballs out of her face.

She must know where Leonard is, or at least know enough to help us find him. I know where she lives. I went to her house with Dad one time he had to drop something off. I stayed in the car, but I remember the house. "She lives in Mount Keenan."

"That's way too far to walk," Miles says.

"So we drive," Jonah says, staring at Miles. "We're close to your place."

Miles goes pale. "Absolutely not."

"You have your permit."

"I've only taken, like, three driving lessons."

"You passed the written test."

"Yes. The *written* test."

"It's practically the same thing."

"It's not the same thing at all. Just because I know how much a sixteen-year-old would have to pay in fines if caught going more than twenty miles over the speed limit, doesn't mean I know how to actually drive."

"I hate to break it to you, but tonight you're going to have to go over the speed limit."

"I'd have to steal my m-mom's car," Miles says. "Not to mention driving with passengers is illegal on a permit."

"The alternative is to steal a car and hotwire it," Jonah says. "But I don't know how to do that, and I'm assuming none of you do either. And you know what else is illegal? Murder. Which is what is going to happen to Max if you don't get that car. So we're doing this."

Miles swallows hard. Jonah steps backward and gestures for us all to follow. "Come on," he says. "This way."

———

Miles goes inside to get the keys as the rest of us wait at the end of his street. I realize we're standing next to the stop sign I was holding onto the other night after Miles told me he loved me. I wrap one arm around my stomach.

Francesca leans against the sign. "Sometimes, bravery is about quieting the fairies in your belly, but other times, it is about turning those fairies into angels and asking them to help you be strong."

I sigh. The truth is, I'm terrified. "I'm not feeling very brave right now."

"Excuse me, Shiloh, but I was not talking to you," Francesca says.

Oh. "Who are you talking to?"

"My friend George Haggarty, who has come with us to help," Francesca says. I use the monocle. Standing beside Francesca is a scruffy-looking man in a tattered suit with burn marks on the front. "He said what you are doing to find your brother is very noble."

"Isn't that the guy you—"

"Yes."

"Cool," I say. I don't have the bandwidth to ask her why he is there, or why he wants to help, but the more help we have, the better, I guess. I wonder if ghosts can ride in cars. I have a sudden mental image of us driving off and leaving George Haggarty in a sitting position, midair, a foot or so above the road, and that makes me feel a little better.

In a couple of minutes, Miles hurries out of the house with the keys and unlocks the car. The taillights flash. He starts it and moves it as quietly as possible from the driveway to the end of the street. He gestures. "Get in, I guess."

I climb into the passenger seat. Jonah sits behind Miles, and Francesca sits in the middle, leaving the seat next to her for George Haggarty. She reaches out as if she's holding on to something—or someone. Maybe that's how you transport a ghost.

"Nice digs, buddy," Jonah says. "Spacious. Comfortable."

Miles pulls away from the curb. "Where are we going?"

"Get on Route 13 to Mount Keenan," I say, buckling my seatbelt.

As Miles turns onto the road, the porch lights come on and the door opens to reveal Miles's mom, clutching her bathrobe around herself. She shields her eyes with her hand and peers at the car. Crap. She's seen us. Her lips form Miles's name.

"Drive!" Jonah urges from the back seat. "What are you doing, man? Let's go!"

Miles's mom hurries down the steps. Without warning, the car lurches forward and shoots down the road.

"Shit." Miles grips the steering wheel. "Shit, shit, shit."

I glance over my shoulder to see his mom standing in the road, waving her arms at an alarming rate.

"Yeah, buddy!" Jonah makes a loud whooping sound. "I've never been more proud."

Miles swallows hard. I can't tell if he's going to puke or pass out.

"She's going to kill me," Miles says. "My mom is going to actually kill me."

I look around for some water and find a crinkled plastic bottle wedged into the passenger-side cupholder. I unscrew the cap and offer it to him. "You're looking pale."

Miles sniffs it. "I'm not drinking that."

I sniff it, too. It reeks of plastic. I don't blame him for not wanting it. "Can you drive faster?"

"I don't even know how to drive slow!" Miles's voice cracks. "If I go any faster, we'll end up in a tree."

"Just hit the gas." Jonah leans over the center console and presses on Miles's leg. The car lurches and speeds up, and Miles screams.

"Everyone shut up!" he asks. "Jonah, get your hands off me."

Once Miles reaches Route 13, he drives faster. Because it's so late at night, there's nobody on the road, which is lucky, because Miles is driving like he's drunk. He gives me his phone and asks me to text his mom, telling her not to worry. Like it's going to make a difference. I do it anyway and then turn the phone off. I don't want Miles checking for a reply while he's trying to drive.

We turn down Connie's road. I try to picture her house. It's tan, with a brick chimney and a bronze star on the front. I can't remember the number.

Both of the first houses are tan—the next is blue. None of these are right, but the road feels familiar.

I spot the bronze star and yell, "Stop!" Miles slams on the brakes and I lurch forward into the seatbelt.

Connie's red sedan is parked on the curb. Realization settles deep in my bones. "This is her house."

Jonah waves his arm. "Park behind the trees so she doesn't see us."

Miles parks, turns off the headlights, and lets out a shaky breath as he leans his forehead against the steering wheel.

"You did a very nice job, Miles," Francesca says. "I felt extremely safe."

None of the lights are on in the house. My sneakers crunch on the gravel of the neighbor's driveway as I creep up Connie's front path. I run my fingers over the house's red railings as I climb the front steps, wincing at every creak I make.

Using my hand to shield my eyes from the glow of the moon, I lean up and look through the window on the door. I squint to see through the shadows. Nothing moves. Maybe Connie is asleep. Maybe she's off duty. Maybe she knows nothing about Max being found. If it is really Max who was found.

I grip the door handle. One glance over my shoulder shows Jonah and Miles behind me, with Francesca on the grass. I can't just knock on the door, like we did to Ella Ruggles. Connie knows I'm onto Leonard. I told her when I saw her at the hospital. If she knows it's me, she might not answer the door. Or she might know we're here and is inside, preparing herself for a fight. If she doesn't care about Max's life, who's to say she'd care any more about mine? I close my eyes and go through the standard cop arsenal. Police issue gun, nightstick, Taser, pepper spray—if four kids break into her house at stupid o'clock in the morning, no one's going to blame her for asking questions later, are they?

My heart is beating so hard I can't hear myself think. I have to be smart. I have to be strong. Leonard might kill Max tonight, and I don't have a lot of time to stop him. I take the gun out of my purse and click a magazine into place. I'm not going to shoot Connie, but I have to be prepared in case she tries to shoot me. I try the door handle, but it doesn't budge. Of course it doesn't. I try to count how many cops would leave their doors unlocked at night, and come up with zero.

Jonah looks down at the gun in my hand, but he doesn't say anything. He must be thinking the same thing I am.

Miles comes up the stairs. I hide the gun back inside my purse before he can see it.

"Are you going to knock?" Miles whispers.

"I need to catch her by surprise." It's everything I can do to keep my voice steady. "We don't have much time and need answers."

Miles doesn't look happy with this, but he doesn't protest. Instead, he says, "Check if there's an alarm. Usually, if there is an alarm, people put a card up to warn burglars, but sometimes people put a card up even when there is no alarm to make burglars think there is an alarm."

That might just be the most I've ever heard the word *alarm* used in a sentence. I'd be surprised if Connie doesn't have an alarm. She knows how terrible people can be. But Jonah checks the windows and says, "No card."

"She has to have a spare key," Miles says, and I agree. Jonah walks around the back of the house and Miles scours the sides. Where would she keep a spare key? I lift the doormat and find nothing but dust. The key isn't in the ceramic pumpkin by the door, nor is it stuck behind the bronze star. The mailbox pops open, but there's no key. With my hands on my hips, I turn around.

Connie isn't tall, so it can't be in the gutter. I bend over to reach my hand up the downspout, feeling for anything stuck to the edge. Jonah comes back and I raise my eyebrows in question, but he shakes his head.

"Come check this out," Miles whispers. He pokes his finger into what looks like a birdhouse. "It's blocked off, see?"

I touch the opening, but my finger catches on wire mesh. My lips curve upward. There's a reason Miles takes AP classes.

He points to a small padlock on the bottom. "Needs a code."

As I try to think of what the code could be, Jonah takes the birdhouse off its hook, carries it to the path, and smashes it with his boot.

"What the hell are you doing?" Miles asks.

Jonah pulls a key out of the splintered wood. "Stopping you from wasting time."

I take the key and walk up to the front door. I remember what Francesca said earlier.

Sometimes, bravery is about quieting the fairies in your belly, but other times, it is about turning those fairies into angels and asking them to help you be strong.

Please, angels, help me be strong.

I glance back at Jonah, who says, "We're right behind you."

I notice Francesca wander around the back of the house. I take the gun out of my purse.

Miles gasps. "Is that a gun? Where did you get a gun? Why do you have a gun? Did you bring that to *school*?"

Balancing my finger on the trigger, I turn the key in the handle and open the door.

Jonah closes the door behind us. I tighten my hold on the gun and try to ignore how fast my heart is beating. Connie must be in the bedroom. If we can wake her up and catch her by surprise, Jonah and Miles could hold her back and we could force her to take us to Max. That's all I have in terms of a plan, but I don't have time to stop and think of a better one.

I reach a hallway that looks like it leads to the bedrooms, but before I can start walking down it, there's a clatter behind me.

I spin around. Miles is frozen, staring at the knitting needles and yarn that just fell onto the floor. He looks up as if to say, *what do I do now?*

In the living room, there's a creak. I look up to see Connie standing in the shadows, facing me and holding a baseball bat.

35

SHILOH

I hold the gun out in front of me. "Don't move."

Connie steps out of the shadows and into the moonlight. Her eyes widen in recognition. "Shiloh, what the hell do you think you're doing?"

"I know what you did." I'm so scared I can't move. "You're going to take me to Max. Right now."

"Shouldn't you be with your mother in Akron?"

"I want you to take me to Max."

Connie grips the bat. She glances at Jonah, whose arms are crossed over his chest, and then at the front door behind us. We've got her cornered. "I don't know where Max is," she says.

"I know about Leonard, and what he can do. I know about your nephew. I know about everything."

"How did you—" She runs her tongue over her lower lip. My stomach twists. She just admitted to it. I was right. "You have to understand." Her voice is thick with resignation. "I didn't mean for it to happen. He came to me. Said he had a way to bring Henry back. I swear, I didn't know he would do this."

"You're going to take me there." I'd trusted Connie—looked

up to her, even. I always thought she was on my side. "Right now."

"I can't." Connie doesn't lower the bat. "He came to me. Gave me no way to contact him. Said he'd find me if he needed something."

"How could you do this to Max?" Behind Connie, there's a flicker of movement as Francesca turns the corner with a branch in her hands. I keep my eyes on Connie so as not to betray Francesca's presence.

"I know it's hard, hon, but Max's life was also hard," she says. "Now Henry has a chance to get his life back, with a family who loves him."

"I love Max."

Connie twists her lips into a sad, pitying smile. "But you aren't enough, are you? Not against your father."

Francesca swings the branch into Connie's side. Before Connie can spin around with the bat, Jonah rushes in and knocks it from her hands, pinning her arms behind her back. Miles grabs the bat and points it at Connie like a sword.

I point the gun at Connie's face. "You're going to take me to Max."

"I told you, I don't know where he is." Connie struggles against Jonah, but he holds her still. I was right. He is strong. "Leonard only ever met me places. He didn't tell me where he's living."

"Take me to where you met Leonard. The exact location, and stay with us until we find him. Miles, she'll have handcuffs somewhere here. Find them and put them on her."

Miles looks startled. It's Francesca who moves over to Connie's uniform jacket, which is hanging on her coat rack in the hall. I see the handcuffs, the baton, and the spray. I put the spray in my pocket and pick up the baseball bat as Francesca clumsily locks Connie's hands behind her back. I don't want to underestimate Connie's strength. She's a cop, and I know from Dad that they get trained in restraining people and escaping from situations exactly like this one. There's a click as Francesca finally locks the cuffs.

A smile flicks across Connie's face. "You're too late to stop him."

I jerk my chin in the direction of the door and tell Jonah, "Get her in the car."

Miles pulls the car up to the curb. Connie sits in the back next to Jonah, and I keep the gun trained on her from where I'm sitting in the passenger seat so that she doesn't see an opportunity to try anything. Connie shoots Francesca a questioning look as Francesca squashes up against her, leaving what looks like an empty seat next to the rear door.

"If you don't take us to the exact location you met him," I tell Connie, trying to keep my voice steady, "I swear to God, I will shoot you dead and go to jail for the rest of my life. I lost my brother and I have nothing left to lose. Got it?"

Connie keeps her eyes on me as Miles pulls away from the curb. She tells Miles to go to the church by Mount Keenan's elementary school, then directs him past the university and down a long, winding road into the parking lot of an unmarked brick building surrounded by trees. Miles's headlights cast long shadows into the tall grass and trees. I realize we're close to the tent city we walked through. We're just approaching it from the opposite side.

I peer out the window at the woods, lit up by the headlights. "Are you sure this is it?"

"I met him in the woods, over there." Connie points across the street. "A little past those trees, but I parked my car here."

"All right." Jonah claps his hands. "Looks like we're going into the woods. Miles, what are the odds you have flashlights in this car?"

"Given my parents are professors, close to zero," Miles replies. I can sense that he's stretched to his breaking point. Francesca and I have each assaulted someone tonight. Miles has stolen a car and driven without his license, and we're all guilty

307

of kidnapping an officer of the law at gunpoint. I don't know how Miles is still breathing.

Miles and Jonah walk around to the trunk and open it while I keep the gun on Connie.

Connie exhales through her nose. "Next time your dad hits Max, remember what you did to enable it."

"Dad isn't going to hit Max again, because Mom is going to dump his ass and take us with her. I'll bet he'll also lose his job." The thought fills me with satisfaction that is inappropriate for the current situation. "It's a pity. If you'd played your cards right, you could have been the new sheriff." I think of Detective Finnegan. "It's not like you have much competition."

Jonah opens the door to announce that Miles found a flashlight. He leads Connie across the street. I'm holding the gun in Connie's vague direction, but I quietly slip the safety back on because my hands are shaking so much that I don't trust myself with it. We cross the street, pass a no trespassing sign nailed to a tree, and walk into the woods.

Jonah keeps hold of Connie's arm. Francesca holds the flashlight and walks out in front of us. Miles walks next to me, beads of sweat running down his face. They drip onto his lips and glue his curls to his forehead, making him look kind of sick.

"Miles," I say, "you don't look so good."

He glances back at me. "That's not a very nice thing to say." But he doesn't look mad.

My shoes crush leaves. There are no streetlamps on this road. The flashlight is the only thing lighting up our path, as the canopy is still thick enough to stop the moonlight from cutting through.

"George Haggarty says he can see something over that way," Francesca remarks, pointing to our right. I forgot George was there, and Miles looks up in surprise.

We walk in the direction Francesca indicated. Connie doesn't say a word. Nothing appears in the flashlight other than trees and rotting logs. I'm beginning to doubt that we're even in the right place when I see a flash of blue and tell Francesca to stop.

Francesca runs the flashlight over a rusted blue pickup truck sitting between the trees, half-covered by a dirty brown tarp. I glance back the way we came, amazed that a truck could get so far into here. There must be another entrance into the woods from the other side. I take the flashlight from Francesca and hand Jonah the gun, and I creep around the tarp and peek into the bed of the truck. There's a coil of rope in there, and a spare wheel. A crowbar rests on the torn leather. Imagining what that could have been used for, I dig my nails into my palms.

"It's the same truck from the cemetery," I say. "It has the same plate."

My eyes rest on the burlap sack and the ratty fleece blankets on the floor. A hand rests against my back. I just manage to stop myself from jumping in surprise. Miles is watching me, sweat beading on his temples.

"Max is close," he assures me. "You're going to find him."

I hope so. I hope we aren't too late. I have this grainy feeling behind my eyes from not sleeping enough. It won't be long until the sun starts to rise. I wonder where Mom is. She's probably wondering where I am. Does she have some strange kid? She's lost her husband, her home, and both of her children. She'll be going out of her mind with worry. I can't think about that now.

I glance at Connie, who is as rigid as a board next to Jonah. If Leonard's truck is here, he can't be far away. I don't want to bring Connie along to fight him. She's a loose cannon, and she'd be on Leonard's side. I can't focus on two of them at once.

I open the unlocked truck door and reach inside to grab the coil of rope.

Jonah keeps Connie at gunpoint as I pin her against a tree and tie her to the trunk with Leonard's rope. I imagine Connie telling Leonard about Dad, and Leonard luring Max into his car with an ugly smile, yanking the rope tight around his wrists. Something worse occurs to me. Maybe Connie took him herself.

Come on, Max, I hear her voice say, *your Dad's at home watching the game, he asked me to come get you.*

Max knew not to talk to strangers, but he would have gone

with Connie. I run my hands down the sides of Connie's pajama pants to check for any weapons she might have hidden before I use a rock to tear a strip of fabric from Mom's old dress. It's ruined now anyway, that's for sure. Max would have gone with Connie more easily than Leonard. She's not a stranger. I think of Connie leaning over in the squad car to open the passenger door. I think of Max's trusting smile as he hops in and runs his hands over the siren switches, and I want to smash the rock into Connie's teeth until there's nothing left but a gaping hole. Instead, I shove the cloth into Connie's mouth. I can't have her screaming or giving us away. Connie's eyes grow wide. Rage boils inside me as I shove the fabric down harder.

"Let's go," Miles says, taking my hand. I grip his fingers as he leads me away from Connie, who stands secured against the tree with her hands cuffed behind her. God only knows where the keys are, and right now, if I had them, I'd throw them into the brambles.

I turn off the flashlight. We walk deeper into the woods, past the truck. My heart quickens with every step we take. Is Max around this tree? Or the next one? It takes every ounce of self-control I have not to run forward and scream for him. If I betray our position, we might lose our chance to rescue him.

Francesca waves her hand and whispers at us to stop. She holds her finger up to her lips as she creeps forward to run her hand along a sheet of camouflage netting that obscures the path, which has been secured to the trees with zip ties.

Jonah makes a face at it. Francesca peeks around the netting before darting behind it, her eyes wide.

I creep up to the net and peer through it. My breath catches in the back of my throat.

Sitting in the woods, framed by mostly leafless trees and half-covered by dusty netting, is a small trailer. It's the kind of trailer you'd attach to your car while moving, not a trailer you'd live inside. There are no windows, and it's long. I can tell it had once been painted, but years of wear have rusted the metal and reduced the paint to pale outlines of its original designs. There are stars. Flames. An enormous elephant, uncovered by the unevenly applied netting.

The circus. The freak show. The tragic accident.

"We need to get in there," I say.

Jonah points at the heavy chain pulled between the trailer doors. "Doesn't look like we can."

"I wonder where Leonard takes baths," Francesca says. "He must be extremely smelly."

"Interesting point, Frankie, but not important right now," Jonah says. He's the only one who calls her Frankie, but she doesn't seem to care. "Miles and I can lure him out. When he's distracted, Shiloh and Frankie, you get in that trailer, grab Max, and make a run for it."

"I will get Max," I echo.

Jonah nods and pats the gun, which he's still holding. "And I'll keep Leonard away from you."

"Okay," Miles says. I hand him the flashlight.

With a brief glance around the netting, Jonah slips out of hiding to get closer to the trailer and Miles follows him. As Miles is walking away, I realize I forgot to wish him luck.

"Come on." I grab Francesca's hand and pull her after me as I run out from behind the netting and press my body against the side of the trailer. We need to be close to the door so we can slip in as soon as Miles and Jonah lure Leonard out. But we're too out in the open here. He's going to see us the second he steps out. And if Jonah has a gun, Leonard might, too.

Getting an idea, I drop to the ground and squeeze underneath the trailer on my stomach. Francesca follows me as I inch close to the edge, staying under the rim so that Leonard won't see me. Pressing my shoulder against a tire, I watch Jonah and Miles approach. Jonah points the gun at the trailer. Without warning, Miles steps forward and pulls the chain from the double doors. I guess it wasn't locked after all. The chain slides through the buckles with a loud clang and tumbles onto the dirt. One of the ends falls onto the ground inches from my fingers, and I pull my hand away in a reflex action.

Miles slams his palms on the door. Jonah calls, "Open up, Leonard. It's over."

I don't know what's over. Nothing is over. But he says it with such confidence that I'm almost convinced.

No sounds come from inside the trailer. Jonah cocks his head at the doors. Quickly, Miles grabs onto both door handles and yanks them open. They crash onto the sides of the trailer. I listen for something. A voice. A laugh. A whimper from Max, even. Miles shines the flashlight up into the trailer's bed. I'm trying to read Miles's and Jonah's faces to figure out what they're looking at when I hear a low voice above me saying: "I, uh, didn't expect no visitors."

It's the same as the voice of the man in the cemetery. Hearing it sends chills up my spine.

Jonah holds the gun in both hands. "Step down from the trailer, asshole, or I'll shoot."

"Why would you do a thing like that?"

Footsteps creak above my head. I press my body closer to the ground.

"Step down from the trailer," Jonah repeats, enunciating each word like he's talking to a child, "or I will shoot you."

"I don't mean you kids no harm." Leonard's boots land on the ground with a thump. In the light of the flashlight, I see the bottom of his coat brush against his calves.

"Step away from the trailer," Jonah says, and Leonard takes a step forward.

Miles holds up his cell phone like a weapon. "I'm c-calling the sheriff," he says. "He's g-going to want to know we found his son."

My throat closes. Can they see Max? Is he up there? I pull on the rubber bracelet on my wrist, and it's all I can do not to burst into tears.

Leonard laughs. It's not a nice sound, and there's not a drop of humor in it.

"That sheriff don't care 'bout that boy," Leonard says. "He

beat the livin' hell out of him. Still, ain't nothin' compared to what he did to his little girl."

Miles says nothing, but I can hear him breathing from here. I bury my head in the carpet of leaves, shame crawling all over me like an army of invisible spiders. Jonah takes the phone from Miles. He taps the screen, making it glow against the night.

"Finding Max would make him a hero," Jonah says. "He wants to be a hero."

I sense Leonard's bravado slipping. "Who'n the hell are you?"

"It doesn't matter who we are," Miles says. I hear a tremor in his voice. Leonard must hear it too, because he chuckles.

"I didn't think no one would find me way out here," Leonard says. His voice is a soft mumble. It's lulling me. I shake my head and lean forward to hear him. "It's one of those things that, you know … no one ever did."

"It's about time someone found you, because what you're doing is wrong," Miles says. "You're playing God."

"Only God plays God." There's an edge of anger in Leonard's voice. "And no one ever dies, if truth be told. People just move, ain't nobody that's ever gone."

"Death makes people gone," Miles says. "That's literally what death is."

Leonard takes a long breath and eventually sighs. "Know that little girl, Poppy? Her stepfather had the carnal knowledge of her, and her mother watched 'em sometimes." His voice is such a low mumble. I have to concentrate hard to hear him. "Reckon I'm doing good, doing this. You must always do good."

"Another step away from the trailer, man," Jonah says. I notice the design etched in the leather of Leonard's shoes. Francesca is staring at Leonard with her mouth wide open. Leonard takes another step forward. If I were to jump onto the trailer now, he would be close enough to grab me before I even made it on the bed. I need a better distraction. I want to kill him. I wish I had the gun now because I swear I would shoot him stone-cold dead.

I press my mouth against Francesca's ear and whisper as softly as I can, "You need to get out there."

"Me?"

"You can see ghosts, too," I say. "He's going to want to meet you, and you're a better distraction."

"All right."

Francesca crawls out onto the leaves and walks around from the side of the trailer, appearing in Leonard's periphery. As soon as Leonard sees her, he gasps. "You." His back and shoulders stiffen. "From the graveyard."

"Hello."

A sharp laugh prickles out of Leonard. "Gee, we're the same, girl, you and me. You're like me, and that means you should understand what I'm doin' is good."

"I am nothing like you," Francesca says.

Leonard scoffs. "You know, there's somethin' about this place," he continues. "It's one of them places where, uh, the wall is thin. I can get through it here, you know. I can find her again."

"Her?" Francesca asks quietly.

Leonard inches closer to Francesca. Seizing my opportunity, I push myself out from under the trailer and hoist myself onto the bed. My nose prickles at the smell. It's rancid—mold and feces and rotting animal flesh. Dirt cakes the floor. The mangled maroon carpet is stained brown and even black in some places. To my left is a couch and, across from it, there are three wooden chests with cast-iron latches pressed against the wall. They're all closed.

Sitting on the coffee table is a lantern with some kind of candle inside, sending weak golden light flickering across the rest of the trailer. Chained to the wall is a single handcuff. An old banner stretches from the floor to the ceiling announcing that the Durand Brothers Traveling Circus presents The Amazing Necromancer. A cartoonish illustration shows a young boy holding a spot of light over a dead chicken and staring forward. It's the same picture as the one I saw online.

All the way at the back of the trailer is a wall of iron bars.

They're thick. Probably big enough to hold a lion or tiger. Hay sprinkles the floor. Behind the bars is a small body lying on the floor, curled inward, facing the wall. The red uniform. It's a size too big. *He'll grow into it,* Dad had said. It's wrinkled because I forgot to tell Mom it needed to be washed before practice. His usually clean white pants are caked with grime.

Max.

I creep toward him, past the candle and deeper into the shadows. Leonard is speaking behind me, but he's talking to Francesca. I can't make out what he's saying, but it covers any noise I make, so I don't care.

I grip the bars. The cage is unlocked, and the door is sitting slightly ajar. It makes a soft creak when I push it open, and I glance backward to see if Leonard noticed. He is too busy with Francesca to notice.

I rush inside the cage, crushing damp hay under my knees as I pull Max onto my lap. His head falls back, turning his face to the ceiling. His eyes are closed. Grease has glued his hair together, but his cowlick has not been flattened. Oh my God. He's so cold.

I press my forehead into his hair. He smells like the rest of the trailer, and the smell makes me want to gag, but I'm never letting him go again. I move my fingers and check his pulse. It's faint, but still there.

"Max," I say, relief crashing over me as I hold him in my arms. He isn't waking up. Why isn't he waking up?

I need to get him to a hospital. Jonah told me to grab him and run, but I need to make it out of the trailer first.

I hoist Max into my arms and stand up. He feels lighter than he did before. I carefully place one foot in front of the other as I walk down the filthy carpet. Max's head bobs against my shoulder. I steady it with my hand. I step over a crinkled towel lying on the ground. I can hear Francesca's voice now. I'm almost at the mouth of the trailer. I'm in full view of the candle. I can't be more than ten feet from Leonard. Just a few more steps and I'll be on the ground.

Something falls on the floor of the trailer. I look down to see the burner phone on the dirty carpet. It must have fallen out of my purse.

Leonard turns around. His eyes fall on me for a second before they darken in recognition. Or with the realization of what I'm doing.

"Stop walking," he says. I step forward. "Do not keep walking!"

Jonah hurries around into Leonard's field of vision with the gun. Leonard's eyes are fixed on me. He has a lazy eye, I realize, that looks off to the side. It makes him look like he can watch two things at once.

"I'll shoot you," Jonah repeats. I realize he has to repeat it because he doesn't want to do it.

"The boy is mine." Leonard's eyes bore into me. "Give him to me."

I hold Max to me and jump off the end of the trailer. As soon as my feet hit the ground, Leonard screams. I look up to see him barreling toward me.

I run as fast as I can for the netting. Leonard yanks me back. He knocks his hand into my head. I writhe away from him.

"No!" I scream, pulling Max out of his reach.

Bam. A gunshot sounds from behind Leonard. He falls still. His grip loosens on my arm. I pull away from him. Leonard arches his back. When he crashes onto his knees, Jonah comes into view behind him. Jonah lowers the gun, his mouth opening and closing.

Leonard's eyes narrow. He's so big. A single gunshot won't hold him for long. He grips the dirt in front of him as he twists around to look at Jonah, a deep growl gurgling from his throat.

"Run, Shiloh!" Jonah shouts. "Go!"

I run from Leonard. Holding Max's head to my shoulder, I brush past the tarp. I need to get to the road.

I'm in sight of Leonard's truck when Francesca screams behind me, "*Shiloh!*"

I glance back. In the moonlight, Leonard is holding Miles

from behind. One of Leonard's hands holds Miles's torso, while the other holds a gun against Miles's temple. Jonah's hands are empty. Where's Dad's gun? The air is knocked out of my lungs when I realize Leonard has it.

My heart hammers like a fist inside my chest.

"Stop running!" Leonard's voice breaks over the words. Miles's eyes dart around, not focusing on anything. "Bring me the boy," Leonard says, "or I'm gonna kill your friend."

"Please," Miles stammers. "I'm just sixteen. I do well in school. My parents will miss me."

Leonard bristles, as if he's annoyed that Miles is speaking. "I'm warning you," he tells me. I grip Max tighter. Leonard presses the gun harder into Miles's skull. "Give me the boy. I don't wanna hurt you."

Leonard is tall and broad. He's easily double Miles's size. Jonah is shouting at Leonard to let Miles go, but he can't do anything, or Leonard will hurt Miles. I glance over my shoulder at the woods stretching behind me. If I run right now, I might be able to make it to the road.

"One." Leonard begins to count. "Two." What do I do? I can't give Max to him. Leonard stomps his foot on the ground. "I will shoot him. I swear to God almighty I'll blow his brains all over the goddamn place."

Jonah grabs a rock by his feet and pelts it at Leonard's head. It whizzes past Leonard's ear. Slowly, Leonard turns to face Jonah. He buries the gun into Miles's hip. His features twist into something unrecognizable. "Don't you move, I said, and you moved! This is on you. It's on all of you."

Miles's eyes bulge out of his skull. "*Shiloh!*"

Before I can do anything to stop him, Leonard pulls the trigger and shoots Miles in the side.

317

36

SHILOH

I scream. Miles crashes backward into Leonard's chest before crumpling to his knees. His legs thrash out as he falls onto his side. A cough tears through his body.

I run to Miles and drop to my knees in front of him, resting Max on the dirt next to me. I grab Miles's shoulder as he retches. He gasps for air. There's so much blood. Miles's eyes are bulging from his head.

This can't be happening. This isn't real. I gather my dress, press it against the wound, and shriek, "Jonah, where are you?"

Jonah stares at Miles, his face white with shock.

"Call an ambulance," I say. "We need to get help."

Jonah takes out his phone and his fingers fumble on the buttons. "I can't."

"What do you mean, you can't?"

"No service."

Miles grabs the strap of my dress. His grip is so tight that it registers as being painful, yet I don't feel any pain.

"We need to get him to the road," I say, tapping the side of Miles's face to keep him awake. "Come on, Miles, please."

Miles groans.

Jonah rips off his shirt. I use it to pack the wound before helping sling Miles around Jonah's shoulder.

I knit my fist into the sleeve of Miles's shirt. "Stay awake, okay? We're going to get help. I'm right behind you with Max." I tell Jonah, "*Go.*"

With a crazed look in his eyes, Jonah carries Miles away from the trailer. I reach down to pick up Max, but he isn't there.

No. Oh my God.

Where's Leonard?

A rattling sound comes from the trailer. I look up just in time to see Leonard hunched over, with Max's tiny body slung over his shoulder like a dishrag. Blood stains the hole in Leonard's coat. With a glance back at me that seems to betray sadness as much as anything else, he pulls the doors closed.

"*No!*" I scream. A loud bang sounds as the doors click into place, locked from the inside.

I throw myself against the doors. I smash my shoulder against them once. Then again.

"*Help me!*" I shout back at Francesca, who's standing where Miles was shot, with saliva and snot dropping from her trembling lips. Francesca wipes her mouth on her sleeve and comes to help me push, but the doors do not budge. "Open the door, you son of a bitch!"

I had Max. I *had* him. If I had kept running and not come back for Miles, we would be on the road.

I grab a branch from the ground, wedge it between the doors, and press all my weight into it. Francesca comes behind me and helps. We open the doors enough to see that Leonard has latched them closed with a wooden plank, but then the branch snaps and I stumble backward.

I bend over with my hands on my knees, gasping. There has to be another way. There has to be some way to open the trailer. Something I overlooked. Something I don't see.

Come on. *Think.* I rub my hands over my hips before feeling a bulge in one of my dress pockets. My hand closes around the monocle, and I get an idea. "Can the ghost do it?"

Francesca sniffles, wiping the snot pouring from her nose with the back of her hand. "I do not believe souls can touch things."

"The one at Ella Ruggles's house did. It touched me. Can George whatever-his-name-is get in there and pull out the wood?"

I raise the monocle to my eye and scan the trees for the man in tweed, who's standing behind Francesca and rubbing his arm.

"Please," I beg, the words catching in my throat. "It's my brother. Please, can you try?"

George glances over at Francesca, who nods. He balls his hands into fists and rushes through the trailer door.

I press my ear to the metal. I can't hear anything other than the clunk of Leonard's footsteps inside. *Please, don't notice the ghost.* There's a scratch. Did I imagine it?

A loud clatter comes from inside. The trailer doors open. Before Leonard can reach them, I yank them open and throw myself inside.

Max is lying still on an old, overstuffed couch. Leonard's giant hands are wrapped around his throat, but Leonard drops them when he sees me. Dad's gun is on the floor between us. Leonard moves toward it. I pull Connie's pepper spray out of my pocket and let Leonard have it right in the face.

He cries out, clutching his eyes as he staggers back to the couch next to Max's feet.

I reach for Dad's gun, sitting discarded on the floor, and point it at Leonard. "Get away from my brother."

Leonard takes his hands from his face. His nose and eyes are streaming. He grips the side of the couch with one arm and forces himself to his feet before grabbing the coat rack. All the blood has left his face. Underneath his open coat, blood is soaking his white shirt.

"There's no point in tryin'," Leonard says. "See, Max is already gone from this world."

37

FRANCESCA

Bam. Bam. Bam.

Shiloh shoots Leonard in the chest, shoulder, and head. The gunshots are so loud that I have to cover my ears, and Leonard falls into the back of the trailer as the bullets rip through his flesh. The last one goes in underneath his right eye and appears to take the whole of the back of his head off. I do not realize until the noise has stopped that Shiloh is screaming.

I am about to try to comfort her when I spot a glimmer of light shining out from inside Max's body. I pause.

The light sparkles, then dims. Max sits up from his body, rubbing his eyes. He blinks at the room as if he is trying to get his bearings, glitching and freezing like a picture on a scratched DVD as his greasy cowlick falls across his face. When his eyes land on Shiloh, his entire face blossoms with relief.

"Shiloh!" he exclaims, leaping up from the couch to throw his arms around her leg. Instead of colliding with her, his soul passes right through her and stumbles face-first out of the trailer, landing softly in the grass. He looks down at his hands in confusion.

Shiloh shoots Leonard again. I'm pretty sure he is dead at this point. His final thoughts are sliding down the back wall of his trailer, although I do not see a soul rising from his body. Perhaps he does not have one.

Shiloh sinks to her knees, still screaming. I lean over the end of the trailer and reach out my hand.

"Max?" I ask. The boy looks at me with sad and confused eyes. I am struck by how like Shiloh's they are. "Will you take my hand?"

Max rubs his nose. "Why is my sister crying?"

Shiloh stops screaming and turns around. I open my palm and say, "It is all right, Max, take my hand."

Max hesitates before putting his small hand in mine. I curl my fingers around it, feeling the now familiar sharp chill shoot up my arm as I pull him up to where I am standing. I understand why Shiloh wants to protect him so badly. He is tiny.

"Is that Max?" Shiloh asks, fumbling to get the monocle from her pocket and raising it to her eye.

Max brushes off his translucent pants and points at his body lying on the couch. "That's me, isn't it?"

"Come with me." I lead him back over to his body, pick him up by the crook of his arms, and set him down on the couch.

Max twists around to look at his body. The corpse's eyes are closed, like it is sleeping. Max presses his finger into its cheek. His finger passes through the corpse's clammy skin like a bad special effect in a movie.

"Could you do something for me, Max?" I ask.

Max stares at me. Not like he is afraid. Simply like he is interested in what I am going to say next. "Okay."

"I need you to relax and lean back for me when I tell you to, all right?"

"Okay."

I glance back at Shiloh, who is clutching the monocle to her eye, and then at Leonard, who is lying still and bloodied on the ground. Trying to remember what I did in the tent city, I lock

322

eyes with Max, take both of his hands, and lower him until he is completely aligned with his body. His hands are ice cold, like the woman's were that time, but I do my best to embrace the pain. I tell Max it will be all right as he lies down, stiff as a board.

Slowly, his soul dissolves. A searing cold sensation fills my body, freezing my bones in place. It is a sharp, overwhelming pain. I grasp at my ribcage, writhing backward onto my haunches until the pain withdraws and dissolves and then becomes a searing heat.

A sharp exhale leaves my lips. I lean forward and press two fingers against Max's wrist. He has a pulse.

Shiloh staggers toward me. "What did you do to him?"

I do not answer her. I cannot put it into words. She checks his pulse too, before looking up at me. What I did registers in her swollen red eyes. I wait for her to gasp, push me away, to look at me like all the other girls at school, but instead, she gets up and throws her arms around me. My spine stiffens. I did not expect the gesture. I do not remember the last time I was hugged by anybody. She presses her hands into my shoulder blades, and I release a shaky breath as she whispers, "Thank you, Francesca," and lets me go.

An empty feeling fills the space she had just taken up. She drops back to her knees, pulls Max to her chest, and lifts him off the couch. She jumps off the end of the trailer. "Come on, let's go."

I look back at Leonard on the ground, bullet holes tearing through the front of his shirt. Holding Miles, he had resembled a wild animal, but now, the expression on his face is peaceful. In a way, I feel a bit bad for him.

"Francesca," Shiloh calls again, her voice breaking. "Please."

With one last glance at Leonard, I hop to the ground and follow Shiloh as she runs into the shadows of the trees.

38

SHILOH

Small puffs of air leave my lips. Francesca and I have to be getting close to the road, but the trees all look the same.

"Jonah," I shout, holding Max close to me. It's so quiet I can hear him breathing. Tiny breaths. The burner phone is dead, so I can't call 9-1-1. I need to find Jonah before Miles's ambulance comes.

I stop. Was that—did I just hear a car?

I turn in the direction of the sound and make it two steps before I stop in my tracks. My blood goes cold.

Miles is sitting propped against a tree. His head hangs down. Brown curls fall into his face. I reach down and pinch the matted strands. Crimson coats my fingers.

Keeping Max pressed against me, I tilt Miles's head back. His open, glassy eyes stare up to the sky.

"*Jonah!*" I scream. Blood runs out of the corner of Miles's mouth. I wipe it away with my thumb, smearing it over his lips. "Jonah, where are you?"

Jonah crashes to the ground beside me. "I had to go to the

road." He's out of breath, gasping for air. "He was losing too much blood. I needed to call an ambulance …"

Jonah's voice trails off when he sees Miles. The color drains from his cheeks. I can see the realization settle over his face. Jonah grabs Miles's shoulders and pulls him to his chest, wrapping his arms around him and knitting his fists into Miles's shirt. I sit back on my heels. Out of Jonah's throat comes a scream so raw that it seems to strip the skin from his windpipe on its way out. He screams until his lungs run out of air, sucks in a breath and screams again until those screams turn into sobs. He pounds his fist on Miles's chest.

This can't be happening. Miles's face swims before my eyes. I remember the way he looked in Leonard's grip, mouth open, screaming my name.

Leonard asked me for Max, and I refused. Leonard used *Dad's* gun. I knit my hands into the dirt as tears spill over my cheeks.

Miles had screamed for help, and I wasn't fast enough.

A siren sounds, as if from far away. I gather Max in my arms. "Jonah, come on," I say, but he doesn't move. He's still holding Miles. "We have to go."

Tears shining on his cheeks in the moonlight, Jonah lifts Miles under his arms and carries him through the trees and onto the road. Lights from the ambulance glance around the corner at us. I wave my arms and it slows down. Paramedics rush out. When a woman pulls Max from my arms, my chest deflates. A young man straps Miles to a gurney. I climb into the ambulance after Jonah and pull Francesca in after me.

Jonah shakes as the paramedics rip open Miles's shirt. A woman charges the paddles. Jonah's broken sobs grow louder. I turn his face into my bare shoulder to muffle them.

The woman shocks Miles. His back arches. I watch for his heartbeat on the monitor, but the line stays flat.

Come on, I pray. *Please, Miles, you can't be gone.*

The paramedic shocks Miles again.

On the monitor, there is a single peak. Then another.

A heartbeat.

Miles's heartbeat. I elbow Jonah in the ribs. He looks up. It takes him a second to notice, but when he does, he says, "He's alive?"

I grab Miles's arm and press my forehead into the gurney, rolling my face over to look at Max propped up on the paramedic's lap with an oxygen mask strapped to his face. Even though the world threatens to pull away from me, I don't take my eyes off Max's face until we reach the hospital.

———

I press my nose into Max's dirty hair as I lie next to him on the small hospital bed. Tape holds tubes inside his nostrils. There's another tube in his mouth. The doctor didn't let me on the bed before, but he's gone now so he can't say anything to stop me.

He said that Max looks healthy. Completely fine. All that's left to do for Max is wait for him to wake up.

Hope for him to wake up. Pray for him to wake up.

Mom hasn't stopped praying since she arrived. Her hands are clasped and pressed against her forehead as she rocks back and forth in a chair in the corner. I prayed, too. There are no atheists in emergency rooms, I guess.

I'm not going to let him go. No matter what happens, I'm going to hold him.

I tried to ask Mom what happened in Akron, but she waved me into silence. "Later. We're here. He's here ..." was all she said. My guess is they found the wrong kid. It obviously wasn't Max, because Max is right here.

We sit in silence for a while, listening to the reassuring steady beep of the monitor.

"How are you feeling?" Mom asks eventually, looking up and resting her chin on top of her clasped hands. Mascara runs down her face, but it's dry, like a scar from a long night of crying.

"I killed the guy," I say, surprised by how easily the words come out. "I said I would if he hurt Max. I told him, Mom. I had to." I start to shake.

Mom comes over and holds me. "Shh. There, there, my brave girl."

I don't feel that brave. All I feel is scared.

I don't dare go to sleep. I know that as soon as I close my eyes, Leonard would be flying backward through the air, the back of his head opening like some dark red flower. My hand knits into the comforter. I hate that I did it, that I killed someone, but more than anything, I hate that it felt so good.

I remember Miles's face, the crescent moon reflected in each of his pupils, and his eyes looking through me, blank and unrecognizing.

Miles is alive. He's not dead. Even though I know that, all it takes is a glance down at the front of my dress, covered in Miles's blood, for the sick feeling to come back. He looked pretty dead in the woods, and when the ambulance pulled up, I was sure he was gone. The boy who loved me. The boy I couldn't love back. I broke his heart, and he gave me his life.

He's still sleeping after his surgery. Francesca promised to come get me when there's news. She said she would wait with Jonah, to keep an eye on him, and I'm relieved she is because he didn't look so good in the ambulance. Without Francesca, I'd worry he'd run off and do something dangerous, but with Francesca there, and Miles's parents too, I know he won't do anything.

Shiloh! I replay the last word Miles said over in my head. I pull Max to me tighter as hot tears spill out over my cheeks.

Please, dear God, protect Miles, I pray, just in case someone hears me. *Please have him be okay.*

"You must be dehydrated," Mom says, feeding her arms through the sleeves of her oversized sweater. "How about I go and get you some water? Would you like anything else? Crackers. Saltines, or—"

I stop listening when I see Francesca in the doorway, lifting her hand in a small wave. I prop myself up on the bed.

"Is he—"

"Miles has woken up," Francesca says.

I glance back at Max. Mom seems to read the expression on my face because she says, "Go, honey. It's all right. I'm here with him, and I'm not going anywhere."

I push myself to my feet slowly, gripping the side of the bed to steady myself. Mom's right. I am dehydrated, or something else is wrong. Fatigue and stress from the last few days. Shock from tonight. General lack of sleep from the past two weeks. Francesca steadies me by pulling my arm around her shoulder, and we walk up the stairs to Miles's room together.

"I listened in when the doctor spoke with Miles's mother and father," Francesca says. "I believe the surgery went well, as he is awake now, but he appears to be a bit loopy."

Jonah is down the end of the hallway, standing in a doorway with his arms hanging at his sides. I know it's the perspective of the hallway, but he looks small. Like he's been crying.

He doesn't look over when Francesca and I reach him. I follow his gaze through the window and gasp.

Miles is sitting propped up on the bed with his eyes closed, completely still. The hospital gown is split open to display the wires strapped to his bare chest, but the sheets are bunched up over his stomach.

I brush past Jonah into the room. Miles's mom and dad stand together, huddled beside Miles's bed. His mom has her thumbs hooked into her necklace, pulling the golden pendant up to her chin, while his father pinches the bridge of his nose under his glasses. His hair is sticking up haphazardly, like he had come here straight from bed. Miles's mom sees me first. Her hand flies to her mouth.

I remember my dress. Out in plain sight. Covered in Miles's blood. I look like a prom queen from some Halloween nightmare.

I try to cover myself, but it's too late.

"I'm sorry." My voice is breathy. "I just heard he's awake. I wanted to know how he's doing."

"Is that …?" Miles's mom can't say it. She points to the stains on my dress instead. I notice the redness around her eyes and realize that she isn't just sad—she's angry. It's obvious she wants nothing more than to make me pay for letting such a terrible thing happen to her son.

Miles's dad removes his glasses. "He has a lot of medications. Can you tell us what happened, exactly? A nurse told us he had been in the woods."

"I …" As I try to fit my mouth around the words, I knit my fists into the yellow tulle of the dress. A tight whimper slips through my lips. "I'm so sorry."

I walk up to the foot of the bed. Miles is completely still, like he's sleeping. I thought Francesca said he was awake.

"Miles," I say, touching his foot under the blanket. "I'm so sorry."

Miles's eyes shoot open. An urgent groan escapes his lips as he kicks his foot into my hand. I leap away. He thrashes under the white blanket.

"Miles." I rub my gummy nose with the back of my hand. "I'm sorry."

Miles sounds like he's screaming through clenched teeth. He throws his head from side-to-side. The nurse who had been checking his IV turns to me and says, "Step out of the room, please. He's going to hurt himself."

Miles groans louder. The sound he's making is almost inhuman. Saliva bubbles at the corners of his mouth.

"Get out," Miles's mom hisses. She points at me again, like she's exorcising a demon.

I back out into the doorway, behind Francesca, who's watching Miles through the window with a sad look on her face.

"He must be in immeasurable pain," she says, and I realize Jonah is not here anymore.

"Where did Jonah go?" I ask.

"I believe he could not bear to watch his friend like this, and so he went back downstairs." Francesca twirls a piece of hair between her fingers. "I wish Miles strength. It will be a difficult recovery, but I believe he will be all right. We can come back and visit him again tomorrow. If his parents allow us to."

Watching Miles's thrashing slow down, it takes everything in me to believe her. I let her drag me away from the window.

———

I hear it as soon as Francesca and I exit the stairs. A familiar laugh, sounding weaker than usual.

I stop walking. "Did you hear that?"

Francesca's brow pinches. "Hear what?"

The giggle sounds again. My heart soars. Every shred of guilt or worry flakes off me and drops to the floor.

I run forward. Which room is Max's? I don't remember. They all look the same.

I slide to a clumsy stop in the doorway. Mom is sitting on the foot of Max's bed, a teary smile plastered over her face. Max looks over at me. The ends of his hair hang into his eyes.

"Scooter!" Max exclaims.

I laugh. Before he can say anything else, I run across the room and launch myself onto the bed. I press my face into Max's greasy hair. He coughs a small cough.

Oh my God, I'm probably crushing him. I let him go. "Are you okay?"

"Yes," he says, and I take his face in both hands. He wriggles away from me. "Why is your dress all dirty?"

I pull him into another hug. I wrap my arms all the way around his small body so that I'm holding my own elbows, and I bury my nose in his hospital gown. He smells like the trailer. Of hay and dirt and something sour. But I don't care. I don't care at all.

Max giggles in my arms. "You're squeezing me too tight."

I let him go and rub the smear of dirt on his cheek. "Sorry."

"Why are you crying?" he asks, and I laugh again. I didn't even realize I was crying. I don't feel any tears my face.

"I'm sorry," I say again. Mom rubs my back before pulling both of us closer to her, and the three of us stay there, laughing under the artificial lights, free from Leonard, free from Dad, free from the fear of never seeing Max again, and I have a feeling that this just might be the happiest I've ever felt in my whole entire life.

Sometime later, after Max has fallen asleep again, I open my eyes to see a steady rain falling against the window of his room. I have a sudden realization and look around for Francesca, but she's gone, and there's no sign of Jonah. Did either of them tell the cops about Connie, tied up against a tree out there in her pajamas? I guess I'll tell someone.

Soon. Just not right now.

39

FRANCESCA

On my walk home, my steps are light. Shiloh and Max's laughter plays in my ears like an old favorite song, nearly drowning out the memories of what happened last night and of the things Ms. Ruggles told me that I am still struggling to make sense of.

Souls go to an afterlife after they fade away, and there is a way to get to it from inside Bethany.

There is still so much I do not understand. How do you open a passage into the What Comes After? Is that what Ms. Ruggles called it? Is it really as bleak as George described? If Ms. Ruggles and George are correct, that would mean that there is a way to get there. Not necessarily a way to get back those who are gone, but to see them again. Leonard said he was going to try to break through to the other side, but something tells me he will not be able to do so now.

I cannot wipe the image of him from my mind, collapsed on the floor of the trailer. In his final moments, as he gazed up at Shiloh, he looked nearly sad. As if he had found peace, at least of a sort. I would be lying if I said it did not make me more than a tiny bit sad.

I am too exhausted to dwell on any of it right now and need a long sleep before I think about it more.

My neighborhood is rather active for this time of morning. It is a Sunday, and on Sundays, there are not usually many people milling about, apart from those with children. I dodge a young child barreling down the road on a scooter. I wave at our neighbor sitting out on his lawn chair. I am turning around the end of our trailer to the front door when my sleepy eyes settle on a familiar figure on our front steps. I stop walking. My heart plummets.

Miles stands up so fast that it takes his soul a moment to reassume its shape. His hands and feet are barely visible, wisps of fog spinning around each other.

It cannot be. I was just there, with Shiloh, in his hospital room. He was alive.

The boy standing in front of me is not.

"I remembered where you live from walking you to the dance," he says by way of explanation. "I didn't know where else to go."

I gape at him. He glances down at his transparent figure in the fog.

"Francesca," he says. "I think I might be dead."

———

Will Francesca be able to save Miles's life or will he remain a ghost forever? Grab your copy of *They Whisper*, Book 2 in the They Stay series, using the code below:

A NOTE FROM CLAIRE

Thank you so much for taking the time to read *They Stay* and solve this mystery with Shiloh, Francesca, Miles, and Jonah. I love this story. I hope you enjoyed reading it as much as I enjoyed writing it. If you have a second, I would love it if you told your friends and considered leaving a review to help more readers discover the series. Can we keep in touch? Claim your free copy of *The Day I Lost My Job at the Bookstore*, a short story from Miles's POV, when you sign up for my newsletter:

Resources

Even though *They Stay* is a work of fiction and to my knowledge nobody knows whether ghosts are real, the characters in this book deal with many challenges that teens and their families deal with in real life. If you or someone you care about needs information, resources, or someone to talk to, here is a short list of resources that could help.

The National Domestic Violence Hotline
A free, confidential hotline available 24/7 for anybody who is experiencing domestic violence or questioning aspects of their relationships.
1-800-799-SAFE (7233)
https://www.thehotline.org/

SAMHSA's National Helpline
A free, confidential, 24/7, 365-day-a-year treatment referral and information service for individuals and families facing mental and/or substance use disorders.
1-800-662-HELP (4357)

https://www.samhsa.gov/find-help/national-helpline

PACER Center's Teens Against Bullying
A website run by PACER's National Bullying Prevention Center created to help teens learn about bullying, how to respond to it, and how to stop it.
https://pacerteensagainstbullying.org/

National Suicide Prevention Lifeline
The Lifeline provides 24/7, free, and confidential emotional support to people in suicidal crisis or distress.
1-800-273-TALK (8255)
https://suicidepreventionlifeline.org/

RAINN National Sexual Assault Hotline
A 24/7 hotline that connects individuals who have experienced sexual assault, or who know someone who has, with a trained staff member in their area.
1-800-656-HOPE (4673)
https://www.rainn.org/about-national-sexual-assault-telephone-hotline

Acknowledgements

This book would have stayed just as an idea in my head if it weren't for so many amazing people. Firstly, to Jay Cantor, who believed in the nervous college sophomore who came to his office hours after our first day of fiction writing class to ask some questions about a book idea I had. I'm so grateful for your mentorship. When you suggested I stop trying to make the ghosts in this book scary and instead make them a source of comfort, Francesca's world began to take shape.

To Eve Porinchak for helping me find the beating heart of this story. I'm so grateful for your sharp insight in the early stages of this project, and it helped me bring this world to life.

To my editor extraordinaire, Perry Iles. I extend the biggest thanks to you. Thank you for immediately seeing exactly what I was trying to do with this book, for helping me bring it to life with all of your ideas and additions, for the long conversations we had about every element of this book and how it should best work, and for your endless energy and enthusiasm. Thank you so much for believing in this book and also in me, and for helping me turn this into something that I'm proud of. You have been the best editor and guide anyone could ask for.

To Stuart Bache, Natasha, and the Books Covered team for such an incredible cover design. It's perfect, I love it, and I'm so glad it's the first thing readers will see when picking up this book.

To my wonderful beta readers. Amanda, you provided such amazing, spot-on feedback that motivated an entire rewrite of this book. Valorie, you gave me hope that I was on the right track, and for that I'm extremely grateful. Both of you made the story so much better.

But none of this would have been possible without the incredible support system I am lucky enough to have.

To Tristan, who inspired the entire heart of this book. There is nothing I wouldn't do for you, and I am so privileged and proud to be your sister.

To Mum, for showing me what hard work looks like and inspiring me to go after what I want with unwavering determination. You are the person I aspire to be.

To Papa, for believing in me even when I didn't believe in myself. Thank you for reading everything I write, and for listening to me talk about my stories ever since I started writing them.

To Andrew, for being the best cheerleader a girl could ask for. You also have some really great ideas.

Finally, to each and every one of you who reads this book. Thank you for spending time with this story, and for allowing me to share it with you.

Claire Fraise is a bestselling author of critically-acclaimed young adult thrillers. Her books include *They Stay*, Grand Prize winner at the 2023 Writer's Digest Self-Published Book Awards, as well as the rest of the series. She published her debut novel *Imperfect* when she was still in high school. When Claire is not writing, you can find her spending time with her dogs or baking gluten-free desserts. Even though it goes against every introverted bone in her body, she is on social media. Connect with her on YouTube at Write with Claire Fraise, Instagram at @clairefraiseauthor, or visit her website at clairefraise.com.

Made in United States
North Haven, CT
01 July 2024

54292139R00211